WESTERNS OF THE 40's

Novels

A for Anything
Beyond the Barrier
Hell's Pavement

The Other Foot
The Rithian Terror

Story Collections

The Best of Damon Knight
Far Out
In Deep
Off Center

Turning On
Three Novels
World Without Children
   and The Earth Quarter

Anthologies

Best Stories from Orbit,
   Volumes 1–10
Beyond Tomorrow
A Century of Great Short
   Science Fiction Novels
A Century of Science Fiction
Cities of Wonder
The Dark Side
Dimension X
First Contact
The Golden Road
Happy Endings
100 Years of Science Fiction
The Metal Smile

Nebula Award Stories One
Now Begins Tomorrow
Orbit, Volumes 1–20
Perchance to Dream
A Pocketful of Stars
A Science Fiction Argosy
Science Fiction Inventions
Science Fiction of the 30's
The Shape of Things
A Shocking Thing
Tomorrow × 4
Tomorrow and Tomorrow
Toward Infinity
Turning Points
Worlds to Come

Translations

Ashes, Ashes by René Barjavel

13 French Science Fiction Stories

Biography and Criticism

Charles Fort, Prophet of
   the Unexplained

The Futurians
In Search of Wonder

WESTERNS

Of The 40's

Classics From the Great Pulps

Edited by

DAMON KNIGHT

THE BOBBS-MERRILL COMPANY, INC.
Indianapolis/New York

Designed by Paula Wiener
Manufactured in the United States of America

First printing

Library of Congress Cataloging in Publication Data
Main entry under title:

Westerns of the forties.

    1. Western stories.   I. Knight, Damon Francis, 1922–
PZ1.W55   [PS648.W4]   813′.0874   77-76880
ISBN 0-672-52036-2

ACKNOWLEDGMENTS

GUN-DEVIL OF RED GOD DESERT by Tom Roan, copyright 1943 by Popular Publications, Inc.

BOSS OF BUCKSKIN EMPIRE by Cliff Farrell, copyright 1943 by Popular Publications, Inc.; reprinted by permission of the author.

GOOD-BY, MIMBRES KID by Frank Bonham, copyright 1944, 1972 by Popular Publications, Inc.; reprinted by permission of Harold Matson Co., Inc.

BEARHIDE'S MOONSHINE WAR by Roy M. O'Mara, copyright 1944 by Fictioneers, Inc.

TEETOTAL AND THE SIX-GUN SPIRITS by Murray Leinster, copyright 1947 by Fictioneers, Inc.; reprinted by permission of the author and the author's agents, Scott Meredith Literary Agency, Inc.

FLATWHEEL DRAWS THE LINE by Tom W. Blackburn, copyright 1944 by Fictioneers, Inc.; reprinted by permission of the author.

THE LINE CAMP TERROR by Walt Coburn, copyright 1943 by Popular Publications, Inc.; reprinted by permission of Mrs. Walt Coburn.

HELL TRAIL PILGRIM by Murray Leinster, copyright 1947 by Fictioneers, Inc.; reprinted by permission of the author and the author's agents, Scott Meredith Literary Agency, Inc.

THE PARSON OF OWLHOOT JUNCTION by Charles W. Tyler, copyright 1943 by Popular Publications, Inc.

TRAIL CITY'S HOT-LEAD CRUSADERS by Clifford D. Simak, copyright 1944 by Fictioneers, Inc.; reprinted by permission of the author.

CRAZY SPRINGS' WRITE-IN VOTE by Roy M. O'Mara, copyright 1944 by Fictioneers, Inc.

COL. COLT BUYS A BORDER HERD by Bennett Foster, copyright 1947 by Fictioneers, Inc.

THE CORPSE RIDES AT DAWN by John D. MacDonald, copyright 1948 by Popular Publications, Inc., renewal copyright by John D. MacDonald; reprinted by permission of the author.

THE LONG ARM OF THE LAW by James Shaffer, copyright 1946 by Fictioneers, Inc.

BY THE GUNS FORGOT by Murray Leinster, copyright 1947 by Fictioneers, Inc.; reprinted by permission of the author and the author's agents, Scott Meredith Literary Agency, Inc.

DEADMAN'S DERRINGERS by Tom W. Blackburn, copyright 1947 by Popular Publications, Inc.; reprinted by permission of the author.

Contents

WESTERNS OF THE 40's

By Tom Roan

GUN-DEVIL OF RED GOD DESERT

Last of his feuding clan, young
Fate Jackson dared the oven-hot
hell of Red God Desert, to prove
that a hill-country Jackson was

With one wild jump, he was up and running....

just too damn' tough for the most
treacherous killers that Walker
White could gather in all Gun
River!

CHAPTER ONE
Return of the Red Gun-Prodigal

Jets of volcanic ash were funneling little red clouds behind the heels of the lone rider's long-legged black horse heading southward across the desolate valley, with the man keeping his head lowered against the hot midday wind. Eighty miles of this same dry and red desolation lay behind him, and forty miles more of this same burning worthlessness lay ahead until Fate Jackson hit the next mountain chain, already looming in the haze ahead.

The red dust covered everything. Even the sweat the horse dripped was like blood. Jackson had been garbed in black when he came over those tall mountains behind him at midnight. Now everything about him had become a dull, rusty red, from the toes of his new boots to his face and hands.

He lifted his head at last, his face grim and far too old for a man who was still a couple of years on the sunny side of thirty.

Returning by hell's own back door to the country he had not seen for four years was typical of the Jackson breed, he reckoned. A man could not have picked a worse entry, and yet it was the one way that would take him back among the clans where the Jacksons had fought so long—and ease him down to his old surroundings before his enemies found him out.

Only a fool, or some hard-pressed outlaw desperately on the go, dared Red God Desert in the middle of summer. Not even a buzzard lent its lazy shadow against that blazing ball of sun, for life of any sort avoided this hell-hole of heat. Yet, within five seconds after Fate Jackson looked up and swore, the sound of a shot came to him, punctuated by a scream that filled the valley with a crescendo of echoes.

The sounds, as startling as the unexpected striking of a snake, had come from ahead and to his right beyond another one of those clusters of red volcanic shapes. Half-consciously he slid his long Colt forward, his gray eyes narrowing in the dusty-red face.

Rounding the rocks and pulling rein, he looked down at the sight of water in a bowl-shaped depression eighty yards below. But the rest of the scene was not a good one.

A two-wheeled oxcart drawn by two shaggy gray horses and covered with an ungainly hood of ragged canvas stood under a low cluster of droopy willows.

2

At the edge of the water, looking as if he had just wheeled to face the cart an instant before death struck him down, sprawled an Indian youth lying flat on his face with his arms flung straight ahead of him. Redder than the sand rimming the pool was the slow-pumping stream of blood coming from his back.

Backed against the horses harnessed to the heavy cart was a little, gray-bearded man and a tall, light-haired girl of somewhere around twenty. They stood rigidly, horror in their faces and their hands above their heads, their widened eyes staring at two big gunmen lolled forward in their saddles, their horses half hidden in the low brush on the side of the water hole nearest to Jackson.

Each horseman held a six-shooter in his hand, and each wore an evil grin. One of the gunmen was a tall redhead, in the saddle of a big bay just to the left of the dark half-breed on a handsome pinto. Each man seemed to be taking his own brand of enjoyment out of the look of terror in the faces of the helpless couple in front of them.

The dark one spoke, his voice lazy and muted with Spanish:

"And that ees how we do theengs, eh, no, Miss Hamlin? Little Eagle was the senseless red fool. How did we know he did not turn back to the cart for a rifle or a six-shooter? He turned, and so"—he shrugged—"I shot heem—and he ees dead, eh, no?"

"You—you knew very well we had no weapons!" gasped the girl. "The Gun River sheriff and the miserable, murdering crowd he is backing saw to that!"

The dark man laughed. "But that was yesterday that the sheriff searched your log cabin, señorita. You had all the night to travel, and who knows where one may find a gun? Also, the youth was not weeth you when you left the cabin on Horsethief Creek under the cloud of darkness—"

"Oh, damn that!" interrupted the redhead impatiently. "She knows she an' her ol' granpa didn't sign no relinquishment to that claim at the head of the crick. An' yuh know, Bill Day," he leered straight at the old man now, "that Walker White ain't a man yuh can sneak out on. Yuh mighta figured, too, that some of us would find out that Little Eagle'd try to lead yuh crost Red God Desert, Day, an' that some of the Walker White bunch would be waitin' somewhere ahead. We got here just about an hour ago—"

"We oughta knowed a lot of things, Bates McGinty!" Old man Day was finding his voice at last in a quavering falsetto. "Yuh an'

Ricardo Costa are a pair of wolves the devil wouldn't have—"

"An' all yuh have to do now"—the redhead ignored the sudden outburst—"is to put both yore John Hancocks to the papers we got all made out. If yuh don't come across, well, when a fella dies out here, the wind blows an' the red dust covers his bones. Gimme that ink, Ricardo."

Each man holstered his six-shooter. Ricardo Costa handed over the bottle of ink. Bates McGinty swung his bay to ride on around the water hole, but he was snatching to a halt before his horse had gone six paces.

"What yuh starin' at, Bill Day?" he snarled, turning his head quickly. "Look, Ricardo, we've got company!"

"*Madre de Dios!*" Costa had also looked around with a jerk, alarmed by Bill Day's wide-mouthed interest. "A devil weeth a gon, Señor McGinty!"

Yet Fate Jackson had advanced two-thirds of the way to the rim of the mean-looking little pool before his horse had snorted. The dust and red sand covering the ground had made a perfect cushion to deaden the sounds of his black's hoofs, and now he pulled up, the long barrel of a cocked Colt lifted.

"It seems that we have met before," he said calmly.

"Jackson!" hissed McGinty, his eyes round buttons in his face. "Comin' in through hell's back door!"

A little splatter of mocking laughter came from Jackson. "You might call it payday. I promised you and a lot of others I'd someday be back. You'd better start going for your fighting tools, both of you. Take a look." The big Colt went back in its holster. "It's two to one. Reach for your guns, damn you!"

"Ho, no, amigo!" Costa was suddenly lifting his hands. "I am not yet such a fool! Once before I refused to fight the Señor Bloody Fate. But you are one who cannot shoot me with my hands— *Por Dios!*"

Bates McGinty's right hand had dropped to the butt of his six-shooter. As something moving faster than the eye could follow it, the Colt had come back into Jackson's right hand. A flash of red lightning, the roar of two shots spread in the quivering dance of the swirling heat waves.

With a hoarse bawl of terror and pain, McGinty's arms dangled uselessly, roaring with the pain of two bullet-shattered elbows. His horse snorted and lunged at that moment, reeling him out of the saddle. Hat flying off, he stumbled to his knees, his horse kicking at him as it lunged on to one side.

"*Madre de Dios!*" groaned Costa.

He was sitting there with his hands still up, popping eyes staring at that thing of a man on his knees only a few yards away. His face changed, a foolish smile trying to take root in the splotched coloring of his features.

"Señor," he whimpered, "as you see, I am helpless. The thing on the ground, now, he was never any good, a loud-mouthed monkey who would always rather shoot a man in the back than eat. We have met before, you and I, of course, but you have known me as—"

He stopped as if fascinated by the merciless smile on Jackson's face. Jackson's voice was remindful of a death bell tolling:

"You won't sugar-talk yourself out of this one, Costa." With no danger now from the pop-eyed McGinty, he had slipped his six-shooter back into his holster for a second time. "That boy there in the sand is not the only one you have killed—"

"These two devils killed yore brother, Jim Jackson," suddenly put in old man Day. "They laid in wait for him in the dark, just four weeks ago. Me an' Lane went to the funeral, an'—"

"Damn you, señor!" hissed Costa. "I will kill—" Desperately he had suddenly flung to his left, trying to throw himself down on the other side of his horse and away from Jackson. His six-shooter was half out of his holster when a ball from a Colt that seemed to spin into Jackson's hand tore through his arm.

Costa's horse lunged, black-and-white-spotted fury suddenly in action. Snarling like a stricken wolf, Costa smashed to the ground. With one wild jump, he was up and running, his left hand sawing for a six-shooter.

It was cold-blooded hell after that. A second Colt had flung into Jackson's left hand. Reins in his teeth, he spurred forward, firing at the running thing on the ground.

A yell came from Bates McGinty. In a buck-jump start he was up, and Jackson let him run for almost eighty yards; then the rolling thunder of the .45's cut him down.

"Now lie there!" Jackson barked. "Lie here and wait for the buzzards, and curse them when you see their shadows. You've done that to other men out here, and now it's your turn to see how it feels."

Reloading his weapons, he wheeled his horse and came riding

back toward the old man and the girl. The girl stood and stared at him as if something had nailed her to the ground. Then she was wheeling and running away from him—a scurrying, wild-eyed screaming thing.

"Run, Granpa, run!" she was crying.

Jackson slammed spurs to his horse and plunged after her. He caught her just before she would have been gone like a rabbit into a tall clump of rocks. Janet Hamlin was like a fluttering, dying bird when he swung her up and across his lap. At once she was limp in his arms, her face as white as death as he swung back to the water. To his surprise Day was down on his knees, hands raised, face uplifted and eyes closed.

"Don't let 'im kill us, Lord!" he was praying. "Even at Shiloh, I never saw nothin' as awful as this! He's wild, Lord, he's plumb wild an' don't know what he is doin'! There ain't no wonder now why they call 'im Bloody Fate in this country."

Costa's voice was lifting, louder and fiercer than ever before, a lament broken with sobs and curses. "The dark angel of death is upon me!"

McGinty was the strong one, lying where he had dropped, with a leg shot to pieces under him. "If I could get my gun out I'd finish this. Anyhow, Jackson, I killed yore kid brother, busted 'im square in the back!"

"The dark angel has come!" wailed on Costa, concerned only with himself.

"Get up from there, Mr. Day!" Jackson was coming on around the pool with the limp girl in his arms. "I may have a hell of a reputation in this country, but I have yet to make war on helpless folks."

CHAPTER TWO
Telescope Hank Sits In

Fate Jackson had just washed his face, and now he stood there looking at the terrified girl with that cold-slitted stare. "That pair helped to send me to the pen for life. Now you say my kid brother's dead. I thought it was something strange, the governor suddenly pardoning me when I least expected it.

"I was there four years, but I never gave up hope of someday coming back to reckon things. Five years ago in this same Red God Valley I found what was left of Sam Jackson, my father. He had been wrapped in a wet cowhide and left where the sun would hit him best. Wet cowhide, dryin' in the sun, is a bad thing, ma'am. I've seen it break whiskey bottles, and you might guess what happens to a living man wrapped inside one. I didn't know the body of my own daddy except by his clothes, Miss Hamlin. When I kill Walker White, I'm hoping to kill him like that."

"I—I pity you!" She looked at him with tears on her pale cheeks. "Your own brother was afraid of you. He told me that without my asking. He was even—even glad when they sent you away. He thought you might be safe from—from yourself. Why, oh, why did this ever start?!"

"It started, ma'am," he grinned, "'way back yonder in the moonshine-making hills of Virginia many years before I was born, I reckon. The Jacksons seemed to get the worst of it back there. What was left of my particular bunch had to shove West. The others fought it out and died there.

"I was born just seven years before we loaded our wagons in the dark to come out here, but the talk of feuding was something I heard from the cradle up—and then the Whites came out here, and it was all in the family again.

"You see, ma'am, Walker White's a fourth cousin of mine. Before this we always tried to keep it a Jackson-White fight, but Walker dragged in outside help. In the high mountains of Virginia, kinfolks stick to kinfolks, holding their powder and ball for each other—and damn the outsider who sticks his bill into it!"

Neither the girl nor the old man wanted to turn back when they finished burying the body of Little Eagle in the sand and rocks. But now that the boy to guide them was gone, they could never make it across that burning eighty miles. Even Jackson did not know that this deep, cold pool of water existed in Red God Valley. Only the Indians knew how to get through here, and there were very few of those hardy travelers who wanted to dare this desert in midsummer.

It was almost like telling two doomed souls that they could take their choice of going on and slow-dying in the heat or turning back to be murdered. Only the keen eyes of Little Eagle had been able to point out the markings of an old Indian trail this far. Ahead it would be much worse.

Three of the rusty hoops had parted on the old water barrel in the cart on which Day had staked his last bet, and the possibility of replacing the hoops with withes from the nearby willows had to be forgotten when it was discovered that the bottom of the barrel was leaking through the rotted wood. Little Eagle, in spite of his good intention, might have been leading them only to death, after all.

"He just sorter attached himself to us," explained Day, "when we come to these parts from Texas an' took up a claim on Horse-Thief Creek the year after yuh was sent off. He was of a queer turn, an' a mind of his own. He liked peace an' quiet.

"We—we"—his voice cracked—"got to like that boy a heap, Fate. Sometimes he used to wonder out loud why yore brother wasn't a fightin' man like you. When they picked up Jim he had only a little penknife in his pocket. He used to carry a pair of earrings in his watch pocket, but they was gone."

Jackson's lips twitched. "The gold earrings he carried were my mother's. For her sake he swore he would never carry a gun, and he kept his oath. She got my father to quit Virginia between suns—a little disgrace hard to live down. Not that I blame her!"

He stiffened again, the hawkish glint coming back into his eyes. "She died in a saddle out here one night when a blue norther hit the country. She was quite a hill-woman doctor, and she'd been to help a Mexican girl bring a baby into the world when the wind and cold caught her. That was quite a while before the Whites came."

He frowned. "Jim always pictured her dying in the saddle with a smile on her face, thinking she had brought us where our troubles were at an end."

He caught Costa's pinto and McGinty's bay. There were a couple of big canteens and a package of food on each saddle. In addition, each saddle carried a rifle and a belt of cartridges for it. He took all that as he stripped the riding-gear from each horse, leaving it free to return at will to the rich grasslands to southward.

He filled the canteens and the big one on his own saddle and placed them and the weapons in the cart. They heard cursing when he walked away to return with the belts and six-shooters he had stripped from the wounded men to throw them into the cart.

He held out his right palm. In it were two old-fashioned and unusually large earrings shaped like half-moons. "They were Jim's last anchor, I reckon. When things were breaking fast I'd catch him holding them in his hand and sort of looking up at the sky. He had a queer notion that she was watching him all the time.

"Here, ma'am." He thrust his hand out to the girl quickly. "They'll look mighty pretty in your ears."

"But—but you can't do that!" she cried, suddenly taking a backward pace. "They—they're beautiful. I always admired them, but you *can't* give them away! You must keep them, as Jim kept them, as Jim used to hold them—"

"Yes, ma'am," he cut in, "like his rock to cling to. But I'm wanting none of that!" He shook back his shoulders. "Miss Hamlin, I'm back here on the kill."

"You've come back here," she cried, "to this awful part of the country only to die, Fate Jackson."

"Yes, Miss Hamlin"—he nodded—"I'm right down expecting that. What I have cut out is a big job for one man, too much to chew, a lot would say, but I'll be walking the mountain tops when they cut the feet from under me, and that's why, ma'am, I want you to have these. Jim wrote me you were mighty kind to him. Take 'em, ma'am. Damn it, I'll have no anchors holding *me* down!"

A cold blue eye as round as a button watched them for a long time through a six-foot brass telescope on the crest of the mountain to southward when they left the water hole with two loose horses slow-trailing the cart. Mounted on a sturdy tripod, it was the most powerful telescope anywhere within five hundred miles of hard riding. The owner of the instrument—a lean old man in shaggy buckskins with his face clouded by a gray beard—was one of the most colorful characters in the country.

Mr. Henry Bridgewater Butler, better known as Telescope Hank, had been everywhere, had seen everything, and had done everything one could find to do without actually working, and each time he had changed his profession his name had changed with it. His coming to Gun River twenty years before had been heralded by a brass band blared by eleven Negroes in red coats and helped by a patent medicine salesman's platform. He had worn the same buckskins then, along with the same broad-brimmed white hat, and a Buffalo Bill face and curling brown hair. The medicine had failed, and he had become Wind Wagon Hank by trying to sell stock in a scheme to send wagons flying across the prairies under a full head of sails, like ships at sea.

A few had invested in the scheme, and the wagon had failed to run, and Wind Wagon Hank wound up in jail. He had turned to patent churns in a cow country where a cow was never milked; and then it had been lightning rods, then chill tonic where no one ever had a chill. . . . He had landed in jail again, this time with a broken jaw.

Once out, he tried to start a land boom, landed back in jail, and come out with the telescope, something half-honestly won at last in a poker game with a wandering carnival man who had charged ten cents a look at the moon before trying to jump a month's board bill with the Widow Hooligan. By the grace of God, hell or high water and a dime-a-gander, he had managed to mostly stay out of jail for nearly four years.

"Sorter figured that rooster would someday come back like that." He spoke to himself from long habit. "Yep, sorter figured it, so I did."

Lying in one spot for hours was something he could do without having to worry about a senseless waste of energy. He remained there, cat-napping from time to time, and no more excited about what he was seeing than the old white horse grazing behind him. His sky-lookin' eye-piece was off the telescope and in its case on his saddle. The old 'scope was strictly a land-looker instrument now.

Double-barreled tragedy had struck at that water hole in the distance. Buzzards were uncanny devils, able to see or suspect the prospects of a meal countless miles away from it. Telescope Hank was fascinated. Not a continental tinker's damn of a buzzard had been in sight for hours in any direction. But two had appeared, winging up from southward and heading out over Red God Desert within an hour after that oxcart and its shaggy old horses had left the water hole. Others were there now, winging through the blue from apparently nowhere, until a lazy circle was being formed high above the water.

"Ricardo an' Bates are stayin' behind." Telescope Hank got up enough energy for a chuckle. "Nice finish for them! I got two dollars once to keep my mouth shut about seein' 'em come outa Red God a few days before Bloody Fate found the body of his daddy out there. Promised fifty an' never got the rest of it. This time I don't aim to be cheated."

He arose at sundown and carefully dismantled the telescope. He put it in his case and folded his tripod. Lazily, he mounted his old Puddin' Tame, telescope and tripod strapped to his back, and slowly headed for Gun River, seven miles down the slope to southward.

Darkness had pooled around him before he struck the street and pulled up at the hitchrack in front of the porch of the jail.

Two impatient fellas were waiting for him inside, but men like Homer Ledbetter and Sheriff Pike Redfern were a pair not to show it if they could help it. Telescope Hank knew that. Just to keep them waiting, he stopped on the porch and loudly cleared his throat, taking his own time about depositing his chaw on the door. Pike Redfern never did have sense enough to keep a spittoon handy for a chawin' man.

It was the usual picture of two fat porkers together when he stepped inside and eased the load carefully from his back.

The two men sat behind a huge desk at the east end of a long, almost bare room, their bald heads shining in the lamplight. Ledbetter was to Telescope Hank's left, Redfern to his right. Behind them were the dodgers on the wall and a well-filled gun-locker at either side of the flat sheet of steel that covered the doorway to the corridor of the jail.

"And he comes," Ledbetter's shining head bobbed slowly, "like lice falling off a dead dog."

"Howdy, Leadbelly, an' howdy, Hog-Face." Telescope Hank mockingly plucked off his old hat and bowed when he reached them. "Yes, I know!" He held up his hand for silence. "I know a fine prosecutin' lawyer like you don't like the name I call yuh, an' Pike don't like his, but ever'body calls yuh them names behind yore back. Bein' an honest man I say 'em out plain, lettin' the chips fall. Ricardo an' Bates stopped the bullcart at the water hole. Gimme a dollar."

"Finish!" snarled Ledbetter. *"Honest man!"*

"The worst jailbird," nodded the sheriff, "in the country."

"Dollar on today's account first." Telescope Hank stretched out a dirty talon. "Gimme! I know yuh two roosters. Five year ago, Hog-Face was makin' Indian whiskey an' sellin' it in the bushes, an' yuh, Leadbelly, was measurin' ribbon on the counter of ol' Lydia Grey's store down the street. You've come up in the world."

"That's better." He grinned when the sheriff tossed a silver dollar into the waiting palm. "Ricardo an' Bates, I reckon, have sorter decided to stay out there. Another dollar, Hog-Face. Does that lawyer fella have fish-hooks in his pants? In all the time I've knowed 'im I've never seen the color of his money."

"Damn it, go on!" snapped Ledbetter. "Pay the fool, Pike."

"And that's two," growled the sheriff, coming across again.

"Two dollars a day is sixty dollars a month, more than any cowboy gets for riding his brains out—"

"I ain't ridin' my brains out," grinned Telescope Hank. "I'm no ordinary man. I'm the walkin', talkin' socklopeedy of this country. The bullcart's turned back this way. Gimme. Thanks. Never dreamed yuh could part with money so quick. As I said, Ricardo an' Bates seemed to have sorter decided to stay out there. Gimme."

"Damn it"—Ledbetter leaped to his feet, face as red as an overripe tomato—"you've got three dollars—"

"An' I'll have me twenty-five 'fore I'm done!" snapped the old man, his cold blue eyes glittering. "I've rid an' spotted an' rid for yuh two. Yuh owe me money, both of yuh. I've even tried to get Flap McGilley crost the street to try an' collect. The only honor I know among thieves is betwix lawyers. They won't sue each other. I've got information to peddle. Unless yuh know what I know, yuh two squirts are apt to be dead before mornin'.

"Wouldn't yuh look fine, down the street in that back room of ol' Doc Charles Gainsborough's office?" He leaned forward, grinning.

"They'd have to rip down the front an' back ends of the public stables across the street to find doors big enough to stretch yuh out on. Yuh two have got awful damn fat since the voters started feedin' yuh. Of course there's the kick-back a heap of prosecutin' lawyers get from other lawyers for makin' cases—"

"Go on!" snarled Ledbetter. "Cut your damned horse-play, you simple-minded old hellion! Are you threatening us? Are you—"

"Twenty-two dollars more an' yo'll know it all!" snarled back the old man. "If what I say ain't worth it, then, Hog-Face can shut me up in jail for gettin' money under false pretenses, like some 'round here say I used to get it."

He bullied them, turned and stamped up and down the room, and twice started to pick up his telescope and tripod to quit them cold. In the end—as much to his surprise as to theirs, the sheriff grudgingly handed over a twenty and a five-dollar bill, so mesmerized by it he did not think of asking for his change.

Telescope Hank grinned from ear to ear. "Believe I,ll start another land boom. Ricardo an' Bates hit some bad luck at the water hole, I reckon. I saw 'em push outa the brush when the bullcart had been there about five or ten minutes—"

"The old man put up a fight!" Ledbetter's eyes widened. "Why, Pike, I thought you took everything out of the cabin—"

"—that looked like a gun," quickly finished Telescope Hank. "Yeah, he did, I guess. But Bill didn't do the powder burnin'. Bloody Fate Jackson was at that water hole, gents."

"Jackson?" The sheriff's voice was a faraway whisper that came like a wheeze, his eyes fattening in their puffy lids. "My God, Homer, we—well, what in the hell!"

He turned, staring. Ledbetter had dropped back in his chair, a mountain of quivering jelly with a face suddenly as white as a sheet. "Get—get a bucket of cold water, Telescope!" The sheriff's voice was a croak now. "Can't you see Homer's just about fainted?"

"Damn'f he ain't." Telescope Hank turned, heading for the front door. "But I ain't signed up to be water-boy 'round here, Hog-Face. Better get it yoreself."

Without giving the amazed sheriff time to answer him, he picked up his instrument, swung it on his back, and turned to the door. Two big, black-bearded deputies were just coming in.

He stepped to one side. Slick Darby and Rush Cardiff were of the type to be strictly left alone. They looked alike and dressed alike, always in sombre black—the Devil's Twins, men sometimes called them behind their backs.

Telescope Hank gave them plenty of room, then quickly moved on into the darkness outside. He mounted quickly, anxious to get away before Hog-Face remembered that he had three dollars coming.

He despised Homer Ledbetter and Pike Redfern for the cheap crooks they were, and it gave him a lot of satisfaction to know that they were right now sitting on a keg of gunpowder with the fuse already lighted under them.

But a news-selling man could not sit and gloat. The information inside his head was still hot, and he rode quietly on down the street to sell it again. This time he would be paid in hand just what he was promised, right off the reel, by jingo, without having to haggle like a beggar peddlin' pencils!

CHAPTER THREE
Hellfire Hill

Fate Jackson had known they were being watched before they were an hour away from the water hole, with the girl having become as silent as a stone, just to the left of her grandfather on the swaying plank seat. Jackson kept to his saddle beside the old man and did not once try to force the girl to talk. A flash in the distance had suddenly caught his eye.

At first he had not known what it was, but it was the long and shining brass barrel of the old telescope up there being shifted from time to time to follow the slow progress of the cart.

"It's Telescope Hank Butler, I reckon," finally had speculated Bill Day. "He beats me, that fella. He does more work tryin' to keep outa work than any man I ever laid eyes on. Has some cards printed what says on 'em, 'Professor Henry Bridgewater Butler, Master of the Stars, Lessons to Man or Beast.' Nobody pays much attention to 'im. He runs for office of some kind at ever' election, an' always gets the same one vote he casts for 'imself. Last year he run agin Jimblejaw Lige Purdy for judge."

"I know Butler." Jackson had been able to laugh then. "If he started out to sell coffins, everybody would quit dying. I dreamed once in prison"—he laughed again—"that he had actually been elected sheriff of Gun River."

"He'd beat Pike Redfern, at that," had frowned the old man. "There ain't a meaner fella born than Pike-Hawg-Face, they call 'im now. An' they call Homer Ledbetter Leadbelly. Telescope, they say, give 'em to 'em. Wonder they don't have 'im killed one of these days. Still, I reckon, he's harmless enough in his ways—an' not too bad after all, maybe."

Jackson had deliberately kept the pace a slow one, never once allowing Bill Day to hurry his old and worn-out horses. The scene behind him, he knew, was one that would remain with the old man and the girl for the rest of their lives, but the words the two wounded men had hurled at the girl as the old cart was grinding away from the water hole had taken some of the sting out of it.

Ricardo Costa and Bates McGinty were getting exactly what they deserved, and yet it was a certainty that help would be sent to them. Jackson knew that Telescope Hank's report would see to that. And Costa and McGinty were just the kind to set medical science back on its heels by actually pulling through where others would have no chance at all to live.

Slick Darby and Rush Cardiff would be the next ones immediately on the list. It had taken a little one-eyed horsethief in the pen to tell Jackson the straight story of how those men had helped McGinty and Costa wrap old Sam Jackson into that wet cowhide.

And Darby and Cardiff would be tougher than those two at the water hole. Wanted in Texas, that unholy pair had come to Gun River on the run and had gained protection here from the start. No one had ever known them to fight face to face, unless the kill was a sure thing.

Jackson led the way off the faint markings of the old Indian trail when the sun vanished behind the hills. Then he turned back to catch the pinto and the bay trailing them. Horse-stealing was one of the few things, he reckoned, that they had forgotten to charge him with in Gun River. It was the one charge one could not beat in this country, but he was pressing the horses into use within a few miles after they had left the trail.

The lumbering cart simply had to be left behind. Jackson knew this part of the valley well, and in the right place he left the vehicle, certain that it would not be found for a day or two. With the small belongings of the old man and the girl loaded on the grays, they were soon mounted on the extra horses with rope bridles, and the traveling was faster.

Under the moon they were mounting the slopes, miles yet from their goal but getting into country where water and grass could be found. Dog-tired when midnight came, the horses ready to drop under them, Jackson called a halt at a water hole near the head of a narrow gorge where overhanging rocks blotted out the sky.

Bill Day and the girl were philosophically resigned to anything by this time. They flopped down on a blanket spread on a strip of sand, and fatigue had them almost at once. Jackson perched himself up in the rocks above them like a hawk on a roost, on guard while the tired horses rested below and nibbled at the thin grass growing around the little pool. As dawn grayed the east he was up, rousing Day and the girl.

"There's a little grub on my saddle," he told them, "and you have some. We'd better kindle a blaze and cook something to eat before it's light enough for anybody to see the smoke. We're just about in the toughest part of it now, but I think I know a way that we can travel unseen. You have heard of Hellfire Hill, of course?"

"Who ain't heard of that ol' tradin' post!" Bill Day's eyes widened. "More rattlesnakes an' bob-tailed wildcats up there, they say, than yuh could find in all Montana! I've never seen an Indian yuh could get in a mile of it. Little Eagle used to say, 'Spirits get livin' man where ghosts of many, many men lie.' "

"Yes," nodded Jackson, "and a lot of the bones were still there the last time I tackled it with Jim. One Hell Bender and thirty men made their last stand there in the late sixties. In a two-week fight they stood off two thousand Apaches and killed more than three hundred of them before they were wiped out. That's where we're going. Even my Cousin Walker doesn't care for snakes.''

''An' I ain't goin' there!'' Bill Day dragged off his old hat and threw it on the ground. ''I ain't takin' Janet there, no, sir, I shore as hell ain't! Why, Fate, I'd heap yonder be shot to death than be bit in a thousan' places by a swarm of rattlers that crawl up there!''

''And I know they do!'' cried the girl, all the stupor of sleep suddenly going out of her. ''I rode up there once with Jim and a school teacher from Gun River.'' Her eyes grew wide. ''In the morning when the sun isn't too warm, they cover the rocks, hundreds and hundreds of them, twisting and curling! Jim threw a stone and—and I'll never forget that sound. It came up and up, as if a million-tailed dragon had been angered and was starting to fight.''

''Yes, ma'am,'' cut in Jackson, grimly. ''It is kind of bad. My one big hope right now is that it has grown a lot worse. We want to reach there this morning before the rocks get warm.''

''But I've said,'' began Day, shaking his fists, ''that I ain't— ain't,'' he stumbled, ''goin', Fate, an' where I don't go, Janet shore won't. Yuh just can't drive . . .''

Then he turned suddenly and flung his arms around the girl. ''Of course we're goin'—got to go! If I wasn't such a cantankerous ol' fool I'd know it's the only place in the country for us right now. Hush, gal! We've got enough troubles without gettin' this fella mad. . . .''

They refilled the canteens and headed on in the broadening daylight. It was a long climb and a steep one in places. True to the country—hotter than blazes by day and cold at night—it was still cool when they worked their way through a tangle of low piñons and saw the stone and log ruins ahead of them on a rise that gave one a view of the land for miles in all directions.

Many of the old walls and roofs were still intact. If all the wild tales were true, the notorious Hell Bender and his whiskered gang of buckskinned rowdies had enslaved hundreds of Indians to erect his mighty-walled castle here. A renegade offshoot of the California gold rush of '49, he had stopped here to chop every trail where trains of covered wagons rolled, his robber-baron hands stretching far into Mexico, until he made the last mistake of ruthlessly taking an Apache chieftain's daughter, which had brought the whole Apache tribe of warriors howling for his blood.

The first shock came when Jackson rode into one of the old courtyards. A terrific squall filled their ears as if it had been timed for the moment. A wildcat flung out of an old window overgrown with poisonous vines. It slid to one side, spitting and bristling, and sped on away as another head appeared and powerful forepaws clung on the stone sill. It took one look at the riders, snarled, and vanished back into the darkness.

"What a panther!" cried Bill Day. "I'll swear that head looked a yard across!"

"There are big ones here, now and then," nodded Jackson. "But they'll turn and run when they can."

Right after that they were entering the center courtyard, a big square surrounded by stone walls with a long stone balcony to the right and left looming down on it. Jackson had pulled up and was swinging out of his saddle when a mocking voice spoke to him from behind.

"Hold it, kinfolks! A shotgun squad's got everybody covered. One move, and the old man and that right pretty girl will be blown straight to hell with you!"

Grinning gunmen had appeared on both balconies before a man could blink his eye, but the tallest one of the lot held Jackson's cold stare as he slowly lifted his hands.

Walker White stood there grinning, a smooth-faced man of fifty in dull black. He was over six feet, square-shouldered and arrogant, his dark eyes looking down over the twin tubes of a 10-gauge shotgun with both hammers cocked.

Jackson had never looked into a meaner, more self-assured face. Walker White had the drop on him, and yet he might have tried to duck and weave his way through in a quick fight had it not been for the girl and the old man, who would be directly in line of fire. White and his gang were nervous devils, and when powder suddenly burned, anything was apt to happen.

"The last of the Jackson breed!" White could laugh now. "Seven of us followed Fighting Sam out here, and now the last one stands at the bar of judgment! It's nice to catch you like this, Cousin Fate. Your daddy killed my father and two uncles back in Virginia. I swore I'd be the one to wipe out the last Jackson!"

Walker White was having it pretty much his own way out here these days. Like Sam Jackson, he had had money when he came, and he had found thieves and gun-hawks of every brand ready to pawn their souls for it. He had always had dreams of becoming a king of his surroundings. Land here was cheap, much of it for the mere taking over the barrel of a six-shooter or a rifle. With the law bought and paid for to back him, such a man could not lose.

"You're looking good, Cousin Fate," he grinned. "The pen must have done well by you."

"I went there alone," nodded Jackson. "Not with a gang of gunmen surrounding me to do my fighting! In other words, I kept it in the family, Walker."

"Take his fighting tools!" White snapped. "Tie his hands behind him, and I'll see how he talks after he goes through what's ahead of him."

Men were already coming forward from the lower level, each with a six-shooter ready, their faces tense, eyes flicking to the old man and the girl.

"No monkey business, Day!" snarled one, a short, dark-bearded lout with a square of black felt over the right eye. "Yuh ain't wantin' that purty gal shot in case somethin' fast starts. An' you stand hitched, Jackson. Yuh killed my brother before yuh left these parts."

"I remember you well enough, Hatch Collbran," Jackson said. "You were always the loud-mouthed tough with a gun's muzzle in a man's back, but you'll never have half the guts your brother Grubber had when he came at me head-on—"

Hatch Collbran jammed his six-shooter hard against Jackson's spine. "One more word, one more yip"—his voice was getting a half-crying tone to it—"an' I'll blow yuh down!"

"Dry that sick-dog whine, Hatch!" The order came from Walker White. "Do as you're told, damn you!"

"You haven't changed much, Walker." Jackson was watching White. "You still handle men like some people handle snakes, don't you, cousin? Kick them, curse them—"

"And make them mind!" snapped White. "That's right, his guns, Hatch! Then strap their hands behind them and hump them forward. Keep your paws off the girl, Bert Stacker! She's not carrying any gun!"

Hands behind them, Jackson, the old man and the girl were being ushered into what had once been one of Hell Bender's trade-rooms. It was a huge room, high-ceilinged with a balcony all around where trusted men with cocked guns could watch mobs of Indians trading at the counters below. The counters and stout tables were still there, the empty shelves behind the counters staring where looting red hands had stripped them bare after the massacre.

The moment Jackson entered the room, the hillbilly in his blood told him there was a moonshine distillery somewhere in the ruins. The unmistakable smell of mash came to him, and at once he realized that this would be the most ideal place in the country for whiskey-making. No one would dare to come prowling about up here to discover what was going on and make a report of it to the government.

"Follow me!" Hatch Collbran, very important now, was strutting on ahead. He had picked up a lantern from the counter, and at the rear of the room he swung open a door. They walked along an evil-smelling corridor for about eighty feet. Two gunmen ahead unbarred a second door and swung it open. Here Hatch Collbran stood to one side, a six-shooter again slipping quickly into his hand.

"Right on down, damn yuh!" he snarled. "If it wasn't for Walker yuh'd already be dead, Fate Jackson. Right after 'im, Day. Yuh, too, gal!"

Jackson walked on, down an old stone stairway, down into what had once been one of Hell Bender's vast store rooms rammed full of overland wagon train loot. As soon as Day and the girl cleared the top step, the door was slammed behind them, the heavy bars shooting back in place. As they rounded a bend, light glimmered ahead and a low mumble of voices came up to them.

Two more burly gunmen were here, sullen bullies at a big table with a jug on it in the center of a square chamber cut from solid rock. Beyond, through a lattice door made of stout wooden bars, were cell-like dens out of which eight men had come pouring to stare with hopeful eyes into the outer room.

"So, by Gawd," a gunman arose unsteadily, "the prize-winner has come! Folks, the company's royal now—accordin' to Walker White. That is *him*, ain't it, Hutch?"

"Bloody Fate, it is!" Collbran's voice lifted behind the girl. "Poke all three in the hole. Now that he's got his paws on 'im, Walker may turn human agin. He's been a damn fool since the word come through that this hellion was gettin' back to his old haunts. If I had my way I'd kill 'im right here."

"Yuh ain't got yore way," grinned one of the gunmen. "This

dude can be sorter thankful for that. Straight ahead, you!'' He caught Jackson by the shoulder, giving him a jerk forward, a shove and a quick kick. ''There is some folks inside that tiger cage what'll be glad to see yuh.''

The moment the door slammed behind him Jackson saw that he was in for it. The first prisoner he recognized was Dobbs Parker, a bald-headed sharp-faced old whelp who had been the foreman of his jury. Parker immediately took himself back into a dark cell, a rat that had suddenly spotted the cat, but a big blackbeard came forward, a snarling ape-man.

''I've waited a long time for this, Fate Jackson!'' he rumbled, voice the low bellow of a bull. ''Yuh may not know me, 'cause I'm Anvil Clark an' yuh never saw me, but yuh did see my brother— Phil Clark. Yuh shot 'im in the back just before yuh went to jail. Now I've got yuh at last!''

Jackson had never heard of Phil Clark, but there was no stopping this lunging ape-man. He came in, fists flying. Hands behind him and helpless, Jackson ducked, throwing himself to the left just as a long-drawn splinter of laughter came down on him from somewhere overhead in the darkness above the lanternlight.

CHAPTER FOUR
Song of the Rattlers

Anvil Clark was on the kill, nothing going to stop him, but his half-sane fury was his undoing. Jackson dived under the flying fists, and got in a furious kick to the shins. Clark let out a yell and went down. Jackson hurled on, stumbled and went down in a rolling fall. He was fighting desperately to get back to his feet when another man darted forward, pounding him on the back as he came up.

Half the men among the lot here were old enemies, men who had ridden for Walker White in the past and had taken his orders without a question. What they were doing here now, locked in like wild animals, was something one did not have time to ask himself.

''Get off, damn yuh!'' Clark tore the bully off Jackson's back and knocked him sprawling with one sledge-swinging blow to the jaw. Then he was after Jackson again. ''He's *my* meat now!''

The high voice of Bill Day now filled the corridor. ''At least untie his hands! Give 'im that much of a chance or, damn it, yuh ain't the man me an' Lane thought yuh was!''

"How do you like it, Cousin Fate?" Walker White's voice was coming down out of the darkness now. "I don't intend to let them kill you. I'm only letting them rough you up a little. I like fights, as you know, and this should be a good one.''

"I see it now, Walker!" snarled back Jackson as Clark followed him, still mauling like a grizzly with those big fists. "You're having somebody else do a job you could never do!''

"Maybe I am." White mocked him with another laugh. "I never spoil my hands in a dog-fight, Fate.''

Anvil Clark was seeing nothing and hearing nothing except the man he wanted to kill. Jackson drove another furious kick to his shins. Clark again stumbled and fell, this time feeling only the jar. He came up, a spasm of laughter tearing from him in a wild jackal's howl when he saw that one of the straps on Jackson's wrists had broken and he was about to free his hands to fight. But he was roaring like a lion a second later when a bull-necked redhead darted in to kick Jackson from behind.

Broken straps still clinging to his wrist, Jackson was like a man who had dragged himself up through hell by his own bootstraps. He weaved in, taking the fight to Anvil Clark now. Clark was all bull and slinging mauls for fists, a near-crazy man hitting blindly. Jackson got in and under, every muscle buckling and straining as he landed his first blow, a driving left uppercut to the jaw, then a fast swinging right to the heart with all his powerful weight behind it.

Clark rocked back, a look of surprise filling his face. Before he could recover, Jackson was driving him to the wall. Another right and left found his jaws. He sagged, powerful arms dropping. In a fury of blows Jackson attacked the big face. With a grunt as if all the air were rushing out of him, Clark went down, and then Jackson was wheeling to face Ruddy Anderson, the bull-necked redhead.

As far as Jackson knew, Ruddy Anderson had always been a near-harmless, slow-thinking work-horse. In partnership with a brother Tobe he owned a strip of well-water grassland to south-ward, and that was about all Jackson knew of him or his brother. But now Ruddy was cursing and sputtering something about Tobe being killed like a dog without a chance. He came wading in, all bull, like Anvil Clark.

It was another fast-hammering battle to put Anderson down and out of the way, but it was not over yet by a long shot. A third man was boring in now, a long, lanky fellow of forty-odd with immense shoulders and hamlike hands.

Jackson did not know him at all, but he was smarter than the other two—a fighting man who had waited for the opportune moment, and a flying buzz-saw from the time he started until the finish. Instead of swinging his fists like powerful weights on the ends of poles, he came in crouching, a puncher who wasted no wind by sputtering and cursing.

Laughter came down on their heads a number of times as they fought, rocking back and forth. Jackson was downed twice, but he literally tore his man off his feet each time he came up, then a hitch-hunch blow with every ounce of strength and weight behind it caught the man on the point of the chin. He went down this time with his heels in the air, his head striking the rock floor a blow that left him limp and flat. As Jackson leaped back, expecting an attack from anywhere now, Bill Day's voice came into it and the old man stumbled forward after somebody had unstrapped his hands from behind him.

"Can't nobody see a thing? Can't yuh hear Walker White up there laughin' at yuh?" Bill Day was half crying now. "Jackson's been outa the pen only a few days. Tobe Anderson was found shot more'n a month ago! Jackson was in the pen miles away from here when that was done. Can't none of yuh stop an' think?"

"Keep out of it, you old buzzard!" That was Walker White's voice, half choked with laughter. "Your turn will come, and you won't like it when it does, you fool!"

"My turn may come, yeah." Day stepped back, trying to look up in the blackness above the light. "Still, Mr. White, I don't want to see a fella ganged up on an' beat to death just because a lot of lies has been told. It's been said that Anvil Clark's brother was ridin' for yuh when he got shot. That's old, too, damn it. Folks say that a man either quits the country mighty quick on a fast hoss or gets killed when he knows so much about yore business."

"That's right, Walker." Jackson was standing against the wall, both hands bloody and gasping for breath. "You've always managed to pile your sins on somebody else—a neat little trait as far back as I can remember anything about you. I never had a cross word with Tobe Anderson in my life, and I never once heard of Phil Clark. I—"

"I know that, cousin." Another one of those nervous splinters of laughter came down. "In the meanwhile cool your ire and wait for something really big. I have a lot of things in store for you. And that will include the rest of the damned fools down there with you."

He was gone with that. Jackson was looking up. He saw the flash of an opening somewhere up there high in the darkness, a blade of daylight coming through. The light vanished as suddenly as it had come, and all was dark up there again.

Laughter was still shaking Walter White when he closed the door of a hut over the mouth of an old shaft and turned away to mount a winding line of stone steps. Hell Bender had once lowered barrels of rum, gunpowder and heavy cases of muskets on blocks and tackle through that shaft under the shadow of the east wall of his robber castle.

He had been a brawny man, that fellow, owning everything as far as eye could see by the sheer weight of his fist and the sudden death of his trigger fingers. Taking what he wanted, and asking neither God nor man for the right to it.

It might never be exactly like that again, but there was still room out here for a man to expand. Coming to the country at first only as a sneak-wolf looking for blood, Walker White had been a changed man within a week. He had seen opportunities for a vast empire at every hand out here. The people out here for the most part had been easygoing, those in power the kind money would buy. Without those Jacksons around he would have owned it all long before this, but Jacksons were always damned fools who wanted to be honest!

Not yet did he exactly know how he was going to dispose of Fate, the worst of the lot. Down there in the hole Fate would be safe enough, along with others who had become dangerous and were no longer to be trusted, and he could take his own good time to think out the rest of it.

Four of his brothers—Pat, Jake, Kit and Willie—had come to this country with him. In addition to the brothers an even dozen mountain gunmen had stepped off the train behind him that morning when he got his first look at Gun River.

The Jackson tribe had been a hard one to knock out. They had had their friends and a few relatives, and Pat and Jake White had been killed in the first battle. With them had died four of the mountain gunmen. A year later Kit and Willie had gone down in a last stand on Horsethief Creek; then one by one, the mountain men had vanished.

Only the smart one of the entire mob had lived, and he could pat himself on the back for it. Always the dramatic one, the wild tales he had heard out here about the Mexican and Indian way of disposing of an enemy now and then had appealed to his imagination. More than one man out here had died in a wet cowhide—and there were still plenty of hides around!

He stopped suddenly, the sun warm behind him. His face had gone white as if an invisible paint brush had swept across it. A tangle of vines was to his right and left, growing up the walls and spreading across the roofs. From the tangle to his left a low noise had come, sounding like dry seed being shaken in a metal box. Hand on the butt of a six-shooter, he moved on, lips still white.

Rattlesnakes on Hellfire Hill were beginning to crawl in the higher and warmer places. The one in the vines was the first White had heard on any of the roofs. Those vines would have to be cleared, and that would put an end to snakes up here. The infernal things belonged eastward, out there on those rocks with all the holes in them.

He turned, staring in that direction. A few diamond-shaped heads had already appeared on the rocks, and they would keep coming until they piled up out there like hundreds of coils of rope. There they would remain, a sight as ugly and evil as hell until the hot sun drove them below ground again.

When he reached the next roof, Telescope Hank Butler was there waiting for him, tobacco drooling down the sides of his mouth, dirty paw outstretched, the palm up.

"Mornin', Walker," he droned. "I come early. Boys below said I'd find yuh up here. Gimme ten dollars."

"You blood-sucking old buzzard!" snarled White. "Can't I ever look at you without your damned hand shoved out? Ten dollars this time—for what?"

"Twelve if yuh argue," grinned Butler. "It's about that thirty-mule pack-train loaded with whiskey yuh sent outa here last night for Chinaman Crick." He nodded toward a little town twenty miles to southward. "I reckon what I have to say won't exactly please yore ear. . . . Thank yuh, Mr. White, *thank* yuh!"

He pocketed the money White had suddenly handed across. "Yore mules are in the corral down there an' yore eight fellas what went with 'em are all in the calaboose."

"Jailed!" White's eyes widened. "Why—why, damn it—?"

"Yore marshal down there didn't do it." Butler still held his ugly little grin. "State an' federal men got 'em. Gimme another ten an' I'll tell yuh somethin' else to pin yore ears back, Walker. It's about Fate Jackson this time an' how he was let outa the pen so quick— Oh!"

"You damned blackmailer!" Walker White had suddenly lunged forward, right fist smashing into Butler's face, the left one swinging to the jaw, the two furious blows sending the old man flying backward and down. "I'll kill you!"

"Just about did, I reckon." Butler rolled over on his side and wiped blood from his mouth. "That ten is the only money yo've give me in a month, an' me tryin' to be kind to yuh. I didn't charge yuh for the telegram I got this mornin' at four o'clock from China-man Crick. I'm too old to fight yuh with my fists—don't kick me in the face, White!"

White stepped forward. His right foot had lifted and slammed down, the tall heel of the boot catching the old man's hand and pinning it to the roof. "Talk!"

"I—I will!" gasped Butler, squirming with pain. "The governor let Fate Jackson outa the pen only in time to get back here an' see yuh wiped out clean."

"Go on!" White stepped back, releasing the hand. "I'll drive that heel down your throat the next time!"

"What I've got to say is really worth fifty." Holding his hand, Butler arose to a painful squat. "Even you oughta been able to see that we've had a lot of cow-buyers 'round these parts of late. The most of them birds are straight from the governor's office to get the low-down on yuh. With yore whiskey-makin' money yo've been buyin' off Hog-Face an' Leadbelly, like Marshal Brown an' ever'-body else with a star. The state's got enough evidence on you dudes to hang yuh—"

"And you and your damned telescope!" snarled White. "You've been selling information to the state, I'll bet! Get up from there! I'm going to put you where you won't be able to do any more dirt! I'm sealing you up in a hole—"

A noise from below cut him off. It was a faint *plump* coming from deep in the old ruins. It was followed by another and another, then a distant but furious rush of feet and a wild babble of voices.

White wheeled, face suddenly long and gaunt. Six-shooters filled his hands as he started to run, leaving the old man squatting there with a slow look of growing alarm spreading across his face. Before he had gone forty paces, louder voices were lifting ahead and below in the panic of noise.

"Somebody besides Bert Stacker an' that fool of a Hutch Collbran oughta searched 'im!" a man cried. "He had two derringers in his bootlegs! He made the two boys below unlock the door for 'im, an' now he's comin' up with their guns an' the boys locked up behind 'im."

"But he can't get through the other doors!"

"The hell he can't! Can't yuh hear them .45's barkin' now? Man, he's shootin' his way through the doors!"

CHAPTER FIVE
Feudists' Settlement

Fate Jackson had not been fool enough to come back here without being prepared for such a trap. Had they searched his bootlegs they would not have found those wicked little guns. They were the shortest rimfire .41's he could buy, and the wide black belt had been enough to conceal them in their hidden pockets.

The two guards at the door had been standing there, grinning through the long wooden bars as they watched the fight. Behind them had been the strutting Hutch Collbran, a cursing and threatening maniac when Jackson strolled to the door. Quicker than they could have batted their eyes, the two guards had let out only a grunt of surprise when the muzzles of the derringers had suddenly been pressed against their stomachs.

Hutch Collbran had wheeled and run for it, taking the news upstairs as fast as his legs would carry him. Knowing death was staring them in the eye, the guards had opened the door and been disarmed. Then, with the others ushered out, they had been fastened in, and Jackson had made his dash for it, armed now with a broad pair of belts and two good six-shooters, while Bill Day— suddenly showing an amazing desire to fight—had let out a wild yell and grabbed the second guard's weapons.

Ordering the old man to keep close to the wall behind him and hold the others back and out of danger, Jackson was at work now on the remaining door. He roared six shots through it to scatter any gang beyond it, and he was now shooting at the places where he expected it would be fastened.

Hutch Collbran had evidently been too scared to fasten the door. The pound of bullets jarred it open much quicker than Jackson had expected. Suddenly he gave it a kick, sending it flying back. Then, he dived forward and behind a counter as a shot tore at him across the room.

It was Collbran again. Apparently afraid to go out and face Walker White, he was crouching in a corner with a six-shooter in each hand. A snarling wolf at bay, he started pouring lead into the wall of the counter. But the counter was like the wall of a block-house. Innocent looking knot-holes here and there in the outer planking were really revolver and rifle ports through which a suddenly attacked man could drop to the floor behind a bullet-proof barricade and open fire on a crowd in the trade-room.

One shot settled the score with Collbran and turned him half-around, a gasping, pop-eyed thing.

The room was clear now, and Bill Day came scooting forward with the big Anvil Clark at his heels. Beyond the door and windows everything looked clear, but Jackson yelled a warning as Clark started to dart forward and snatch up the dead Collbran's six-shooters.

"Keep down, Clark! They're in that building—"

He did not have to finish the rest of it. From the windows and doorway of the ruins across the courtyard the spouting flames of six-shooters were suddenly in action. Clark wheeled and went down, caught through the shoulder by a heavy slug of lead.

"Through the flesh!" he snarled. "I ain't hurt bad!"

Jackson had seen a double-barreled shotgun lying on the counter when he entered the room. Reloading his six-shooters, he crawled along the floor until he was just below the gun. Like a cat under a table and reaching up a quick paw to snatch something from the top, he had the weapon in his hands in a moment.

It was like swinging a cannon into the fight a few moments later. Thrusting the muzzle of the shotgun out the window and leveling it toward the doorway across the courtyard, he let go the double blast. Yells of pain and hoarse bawls of terror answered him. Before they could get over their surprise he was up beside the window, blazing away with both six-shooters until he emptied them and dropped back, while Bill Day opened up from behind the counter at the end of the room.

"Scatterin' 'em!" yelled the old man. "Just like we scattered 'em with the musket balls at Shiloh! *Whoop-ee!* I allus said there was another good fight left in me if I'd only let myself get started! Janet just oughta see ol' grayheaded granpa go now!''

It was a lost fight within fifteen minutes, and Walker White realized it. He was caught himself up there on the roof, unable to go down without running into the endless hail of lead ripping back and forth across the main courtyard. All he could do here was to stand and shout down his orders, and nobody in the entire lot below seemed to be paying a single bit of attention to him.

He turned back, the half-insane notion to finish his business with Telescope Hank suddenly upon him. It was about time, anyway, to wipe the old devil out of the picture. A man like Butler would be dangerous in any courtroom. He stopped before he got back to where he had left him, straining in his tracks, right hand dropped to the butt of a heavy Colt. Butler was taking his breath away.

Telescope Hank was taking himself to hell out of here. He had left his old horse down the slope beyond the rattlesnake den on top. Scores of the snakes were now out of their holes, the noise of their combined rattling making the air quiver. Butler, a long-legged scarecrow, fringed buckskins flapping, was making a run for it right out across the rocks, a leaping, side-slinging old fool with death striking at him and seemingly missing him only an inch each time.

White actually forgot the fight behind him. A man might live a thousand years without seeing half such a terrorizing sight. They almost had him. A row of coils now had him cut off, forcing him to wheel back. For a moment the old fool halted. He picked up a slender stick, a mere switch. Little good that was going to do him!

But Telescope Hank was of the kind to think himself out of trouble every time he landed in it. White saw him quickly fasten his hatband on the end of the stick; then he turned right around like a stark natal fool and headed straight back for that line of coils that had stopped him. In a moment Butler was giving an exhibition of snakesmanship!

Hat on the end of the stick, Butler was swinging it to the right and left. The coils flew into action, faster than lightning. Each time the hat was swept toward a snake it shot out of its coil, striking at the hat. Butler was simply making them move. In a few moments he had the way cleared, then he was flying on, a devil in danger flinging unhurt through until he was beyond the dens and fleeing on down the slope.

''Steady, cousin! I wouldn't shoot him in the back.''

The cold, jarring voice behind Walker White was like the painful stab of a knife squarely between the shoulder blades. His mouth flung open for a cry of alarm, but not a sound came from it. Cold perspiration buckled out on his forehead. Without a word he started lifting his hands.

"That's a nice crowd you had below, cousin." Fate Jackson laughed. "The moment the going got tough they started showing the white feather. Men in this country will ride for you, they'll die for you. They'll even steal for you if you're hungry. But you've got to have something they can think is on the level before they'll do that. You never hired anything but born thieves and born killers. They stick only when you're going strong. Turn around and look me in the eye. You know I can't shoot even you in the back."

"No—damn you—you can't!" The words jerked from White in croak-like gasps. "Jacksons never could!"

"Some of your men quit the fight cold, cousin." Jackson was laughing that whispery sound again. "They'll talk before they're done. . . . Come back here!"

Walker White had started to run. One shot tore at him, but nothing was going to stop him. He slung the bullet-splintered hand to his chest, gripping it with his left. Blindly, madly now, he was racing on.

Jackson stood there watching him, knowing nothing of the amazing feat Telescope Hank Butler had accomplished only a short time before. Walker was going to dare to cross those holes, and it looked as if there were ten thousand rattlesnakes out there.

A leaping, dancing thing, White was going on, to the right here, the left there. He was half across before his foot dropped to his calf in a hole and he stopped suddenly, a terrific squall of pain coming from him. He went down, twisted over on his back, foot still in the hole, the leg broken under him.

His voice was high and thin, shrieking at the top of his lungs. "You—you drove me into this, Fate Jackson!"

"It beats a wet cowhide, doesn't it!" yelled Jackson. "It beats dying a mite at a time. It—it—"

His own voice died away. A coil near White had slung forward, an ugly streak. White screamed like a woman, fighting now with both his good and his broken hand as other coils stirred and became striking streaks. The noise seemed deafening now. A thousand rattles were singing, the air quivering with them.

Bill Day was at Jackson's left elbow. "I won't be able to sleep for a month after this! Come! There ain't one thing yuh could do for him—if yuh wanted to."

"Look!" Jackson pointed to a sharp little peak in the distance, the only one in many miles as high as Hellfire Hill. On it something glinted like gold in the sunlight. "Telescope Hank's on the job. He'll charge a dollar a word for this!"

"Come on, Fate!" Day gave him a quick pull that almost jerked him off his feet. "Two of them fellas yuh let outa that hole are government fellas. We've got eleven prisoners down there now. Just quit cold an' dropped their guns an' come out with their hands up. Didn't even have to ask 'em to surrender.

"There's somethin' else, too. There's been a lot of government fellas workin' this country. One of them below says that this mornin' at sunrise was the time for them to throw Pike Redfern in his own jail an' Homer Ledbetter right in on top of 'im. They're in jail by now, an' all their cutthroats with 'em, yuh can bet. I'd give a purty to see 'em—an' maybe we will. They're sayin' down below that it's in the cards for yuh to take over Pike's job."

"Wouldn't have it at a thousand a month!" cut in Jackson. "Telescope Hank's the man for that job! In the meanwhile, how about you and Miss Hamlin coming to my house until all these things get straightened out? If—of course—"

"—Janet will go?" Day looked up and grinned as they started down the steps. "She'll jump at it! She sorter likes yuh, Fate. Yeah, she does, though she may not act like it. Wimmin are plumb peeculiar!"

THE END

BOSS OF
BUCKSKIN
EMPIRE

A Novelette of the Wilderness Fur Country

The night erupted into a volcanic spurt of red flame. . . .

By CLIFF FARRELL

Neither the buckskin courage of Captain Del Keech nor the loveliness of Sherry Chalfont, owner of the great Wilderness Fur, could halt for one brief moment Black Sul Romero's dream of Empire, as ruler of a land that knew no law!

CHAPTER ONE
Earmarked for Death!

Sullivan Romero, second factor of the mighty Wilderness Fur & Trading Company, believed in maintaining his reputation as a polished gentleman at all times on public occasions—even while he was seeking to break the body and spirit of a prisoner by slow torture.

He ordered that his afternoon repast be served outdoors, where he could enjoy the cooling breeze from the river on this hot July day, and he gave painstaking instructions to the French chef he had imported to White Stockade, the primitive stronghold here in the untamed heart of the upper Missouri River country.

Wearing a snow-white capote of unbleached elkskin, a powder-blue silk shirt, green sash, plaid breeches and high, beaded moccasins, he came from the factor's quarters and inspected the table which had been set beneath the shade of a gaily striped canopy in the open compound.

Italian glass, frail English china, and Flemish silver gleamed from a background of Irish linen. Thin-stemmed wineglasses stood in rich array, and a basket of the finest champagne was placed handy to his chair.

Sullivan Romero, whom some men referred to as Black Sul, seated himself and clapped his hands. His thick, wavy black Spanish hair, thin brows, and alert, black eyes all accented powerful, arrogant features which had the hard-cut quality of a cameo. A tinge of gray at his temples added a distinguished touch. Black Sul Romero had inherited all the outward quality—as well as all the worst of the blood—of his Spanish-Irish parentage.

Headed by the chef, a dozen comely half-breed girls, the *bois brulé* of the fur country, came from the kitchen bearing massive silver platters and bowls.

Corks popped, and wine bubbled against thin crystal. The long table groaned beneath the great, juicy joints of elk shoulder steamed there, alongside spiced, clove-dotted Virginia hams, and garnished platters of buffalo brisket, and thin-fried, breaded antelope and venison cuts. Roast wild turkey, broiled dove and partridge, crisp-fried mountain trout were uncovered for Black Sul Romero's inspection. There was golden young corn from the gardens around the fort, dishes of buttered, highly seasoned greens, and fresh salads in great mixing bowls.

Black Sul lifted a wine goblet, and spoke to the prisoner: "To your very good health, m'sieu'," he said.

"Gracias!" replied Del Keech. "May you have your reward in the deepest pit of hell!"

Del Keech's voice was a croaking rasp between swollen, cracked lips. Barefoot, wearing only buckskin breeches, he stood in the brassy glare of the relentless sun, spread-eagled, his outstretched arms manacled to cedar posts, his ankles chained to stakes.

Before him within reach, had his hands been free, was that loaded banquet table which held food enough to sate the hunger of twenty men. The fragrance of those steaming dishes swirled around him, arousing an almost unbearable desire in every fiber of his flat-muscled body.

"Perhaps you would care to join me, my friend?" Black Sul said blandly. "There is enough for both of us."

"I'm a mite particular who I eat with," Del remarked.

Del Keech had to use all his will to keep his voice casual, and to keep his eyes off that food, and especially off an ewer of cold, sparkling spring water that Romero pushed tantalizingly near.

Del Keech had not eaten in the forty-eight hours since he had been brought to White Stockade a prisoner. Worse yet, he had not tasted water in that time. His eyes were red-rimmed slits of dull slate against the background of his gaunt, unshaven jaws. He had stood here since sunrise, unable to change his position more than an inch or two.

Black Sul waved the servants back to their quarters, and turned his attention again to Keech.

"Where is this priest?" he demanded. "This Father Jean DuBois, who meddles in matters that do not concern the Church or himself."

"Don't tell me you're wanting a priest to hear your confession?" Del jeered. "That would be a full day's chore for any Black Robe."

Black Sul smiled faintly. There was within the man the vanity to feel flattered at that remark. He cast a glance around the compound as though proud of his handiwork.

Once the name of Wilderness Fur had commanded respect in the mountains, and a partisan who wore a company capote had held his head high. That was in the days of tough old Amos Chalfant, the granite-ribbed New Englander who had founded this independent organization.

But Amos Chalfant had been found with an Indian arrow in his back five years previously. Weeds now grew on the sod roofs of the storehouses, and the chinking was cracking from their sides. Fur sheds were beginning to sag, and ash heaps littered the compound.

The partisans and Indians who lolled at a respectful distance in the shade of the buildings were ragged, unwashed, evil-tongued. The majority of them were drunk, as were their Indian wives. Upstream from the post, an uproar drifted from a score of lodges pitched by a tribe of Crows. Black Sul saw to it that rotgut whiskey was always available for both his followers and visiting tribesmen.

This was the change that had been wrought since Amos Chalfant's death.

Black Sul's gaze returned to Del. "You are the one to make the confession," he corrected. "Not I. Where is Father DuBois?"

"Well," Del said reflectively, "he might be one place. Then again, he might be in another."

Black Sul's big fists clenched on the table.

"The priest is dead!" he snapped, watching Del, hoping to read some flicker of expression that would acknowledge that thrust in the dark.

"Are you *sure* of that?" Del asked mockingly.

Veins corded in Black Sul's temples. "He was shot during that fight when you helped him escape," he said between set teeth. "I myself saw the splotches of blood. You were not wounded. Therefore the blood must have come from the priest."

He paused a moment. "Lead me to his grave, so that I may be sure," he added softly. "And I'll make you a rich man."

"Sure," Del nodded heartily. "Just take these chains off me, and I'll be ready to travel."

Black Sul's mirthless smile glinted again. "You accede too easily, my friend. You would lead me on a wild goose chase, hoping for a chance to escape. I fear I must give you more time to consider the matter, my brave Captain Keech."

"So you know me?" Del asked grimly.

"I have suspected for a long time that the mysterious Tom Sloan, who posed as an army deserter, was a trifle too inquisitive about the operations of Wilderness Fur." Romero nodded. "But only a fortnight ago did I learn from one of my new recruits that Tom Sloan and a dashing United States cavalry captain named Delos Emmett Keech were one and the same."

Romero sloshed water into a goblet. He arose and extended it to Del. "Drink hearty, my spying captain," he said. "This sun must make one a trifle thirsty."

He snatched the goblet away, letting only a tantalizing trickle cross Del's parched lips.

"And the sun will make you thirstier by tomorrow," he added. "Perhaps your memory will improve by then."

They stood face to face; the hatred between them was a vivid, crackling force. They were of the same height, though Romero was heavier, and a dozen or more years older. But within Del Keech burned a grim, inflexible will as unyielding as the purpose that drove Sul Romero.

"Let's understand each other, Romero," Del said. "You can't afford to let me live. I know too much. And so does Father DuBois. I'm going to die here. I'll die slow and hard, for I'm unlucky enough to be tough. But I'll have my fun while I'm shufflin' off. I can stand here and watch you sweat right along with me, Romero. For you'll never have any peace of mind as long as you don't know whether the Black Robe is alive or dead."

Sul Romero struck the helpless prisoner with an open palm. The blow left Del half-stunned, a great bloodless welt forming on his cheek.

Del's head cleared. He spat and laughed again. "You won't sleep of nights, Romero," he jeered. "You'll pace the floor by days. You'll be wondering if the priest has reached St. Louis, carrying the letter that'll ruin you."

Sul Romero drew back a fist to smash Del in the face, then abruptly paused as a deep, alien sound echoed, like the mourning of a lost soul. A steamboat whistle!

Del Keech thought he must be dreaming. He had heard that one or two packets had ventured a considerable distance up the Missouri River in the past, but Fort Leavenworth was usually the limit of their voyage.

Then a single-stack steamboat, small in comparison to the Mississippi River packets, hove around a bend half a mile below the fort. Her whistle moaning again, the craft churned toward the keel-boat landing below the bluff, her twin wheel boxes leaving a long trail of ripples on the muddy Missouri.

Del made out the name on the near wheel box: *Queen of the Plains*. The pennant flying below the national colors on the jackstaff carried the insignia of Wilderness Fur.

The *Queen of the Plains* was a company boat. The dust of the plains country, through which she had come, filmed her decks and stained her sides, but she was beautiful to Del Keech, for her arrival had given him a reprieve.

Romero was staring in surprise at the packet, as the half-drunken rabble stampeded to the landing to await the oncoming craft.

And then a runner came panting into the fortyard, pointing to the steamboat. "De grand factor, m'sieu'!" he exclaimed. "It ees de Ma'moiselle Chalfant."

Romero ripped out an oath. He looked stunned. Then he too went hurrying down to the landing.

CHAPTER TWO
Satan's Hand-Maiden

Del Keech also stared in amazement. The name of Chalfant was now an epithet in the mountain country. The free traders and trappers who were left cursed it with fervent hatred whenever it was mentioned.

Sole heir to the great Amos Chalfant, his granddaughter Sherry now held the title of grand factor of Wilderness Fur, and it was the name of Sherry Chalfant that honest men cursed when they mentioned it.

For Sherry Chalfant evidently had not inherited her grandfather's rockbound character. She was said to be an irresponsible, pleasure-loving butterfly who preferred to spend her time flitting through the drawing rooms of St. Louis and Eastern society, or lavishing her money in the capitals and watering places of Europe in search of a husband with a title. She had never ventured west of St. Louis into the country her kinsman loved, and from which he had carved a fur empire.

Sul Romero, by the terms of Amos Chalfant's will, still carried the title of second factor, but was placed in full charge of Wilderness Fur, charged with operating it for the inexperienced heiress.

Once Black Sul was in the saddle he began systematically looting the company. While Amos Chalfant's granddaughter lived in her gilded paradise, Black Sul diverted the profits to his own pockets, and methodically made himself the arrogant lord of the wilderness. One by one he displaced honest sub-factors with cutthroats and renegades of his own choosing, who cleared the country of independent trappers and traders by terror and murder, their places on the trap lines taken by Romero's followers. With whiskey he debauched and enslaved the Crows, the Sioux, the Blackfeet, and the Northern Cheyenne.

And Romero had other, further plans. Only two men, outside of Black Sul's inner circle, knew the full details of the scheme the man had in mind—a scheme that would shake the young and troubled American nation to its foundations.

Del Keech was one of those who knew the secret. The other was Father Jean DuBois, the Jesuit missionary who had dedicated his life to the welfare and salvation of the Indian tribes.

Del wondered if Father DuBois, who had in his possession a letter that would smash Romero, would ever live to reach St. Louis and tell the story. He wondered if the Jesuit was alive even at this moment.

For Romero had partly guessed the truth. Father Jean DuBois had a bullet in his body, and he was lying in a hideout in a thicket no more than twenty miles down the river from White Stockade—lying there, probably at the point of death, too badly injured to move or help himself while he waited for Del Keech to return to his side.

Grimly Del watched the procession that came up the path from the landing. Black Sul led the way with a small, trim girl in a fashionable, tight-bodied, pink-flowered dress resting her lace-gloved hand lightly on his arm. A poke bonnet framed Sherry Chalfant's piquant face, and her eyes, big, autumn-brown as was the shade of her hair, were clear, self-possessed.

She quit smiling as she looked about and saw the shabbiness and squalor of this post which had been her grandfather's pride. Then her glance stopped with a shock on the spread-eagled prisoner.

Her eyes widened. "What—?" she exclaimed, horrified.

Romero tried to steer her onward toward the factor's quarters.

"It is nothing," he scoffed. "Only a mountain man who killed two of our partisans. He was caught red-handed robbing a trap line and resisted arrest."

The girl pulled away from Romero's detaining hand, and came hurrying close, staring with growing pallor.

"You—?" she said shakily. "It can't be!"

Black Sul stared. "You know this fellow?" he demanded sharply.

"Why—why, no," she stammered. "That is—"

"I had the pleasure of dancing with Miss Chalfant at a masked ball in St. Louis on all Saints Eve, nearly a year ago," Del explained. "There was no introduction. It was presumptuous of me. She does not know even my name. She may not remember me."

That night, Del, garbed as a river gambler, had danced again and again with a lithe, clear-voiced creature who wore a red-spangled Spanish dancing costume. He had fallen in love with her voice that night. And when the masks were dropped and he saw her face, he had never seen anything as lovely.

When she had told him her name, he felt a bitter shock. He had bowed, turned on his heel, leaving her standing there as he walked away.

For even at that time he was on his way into the wilderness, charged with investigating the vague rumors that he had heard in regard to Wilderness Fur, and this girl who was its grand factor. He had never seen Sherry Chalfant again until now. But he had never forgotten her. . . .

With an effort the girl gained command of herself. "What—what are you going to do with him?" she demanded of Romero.

Romero spread his hands. "He is a murderer. He must pay the usual penalty."

Sherry Chalfant shuddered, turning to Del. "Is there anything I can do for you?" she asked.

"Sure," Del said. "You can keep these cussed gnats off me. And shoo away the deer flies."

Suddenly she fled, hurrying ahead of Romero into the shelter of the factor's office.

The hunger and the madness of thirst came back upon Del with redoubled force. Sherry Chalfant's appearance in the wilderness at this time seemed patent evidence that she was a party to Romero's scheme.

Then a new probability drove through him. Sul Romero was a romantic, handsome figure, with a reputation for feminine conquests in St. Louis. The chances were that Sherry Chalfant was in love with Romero.

Birds of a feather, Del reflected bitterly.

He thought of Father Jean DuBois, and the letter in Black Sul's own handwriting the priest had inside his blood-stained cassock. That letter was evidence enough to send Black Sul before a firing squad or to the scaffold—along with all his accomplices.

Del had entered the wilderness the previous fall, roughing it through the winter, posing as an army deserter, while he sought for a clue to substantiate the vague rumors that had come out of the country.

In Father DuBois he had found the only ally he could confide in, for the priest was fighting to offset the debauchery of the Indians brought on by Black Sul's whiskey trading. Del one day waylaid a runner that Black Sul was sending to one of his sub-factors up the river. He found in the runner's pouch a letter written by Black Sul carrying instructions to his lieutenants. That letter gave full and complete proof of Black Sul's plot.

The letter also divulged that Black Sul suspected Del was a government agent, and Black Sul offered a reward for the delivery of both Del and the padre to him, dead or alive.

Del had located Father DuBois at an Indian village, warned him of the danger, and they had headed down the river together for civilization. But Black Sul and his partisans were already on their trail.

A running fight started, during which the black-robed Jesuit was hit by a bullet.

Del held off Romero and his partisans until dark, and then escaped, carrying the wounded prelate on his back.

But Father DuBois was too desperately injured to travel far. Del, as a last resort, made him as comfortable as possible in a new hideout that night, then went on alone, leaving a plain trail which Romero picked up at daylight.

Del succeeded in drawing pursuit miles from where he had left the wounded Jesuit, but luck turned against him. As he was cooling his trail, meaning to shake off the pursuit and return to Father DuBois, he was waylaid and overpowered by three half-breed trappers.

They brought him to the fort, and turned him over to Black Sul Romero, who gave them two kegs of brandy as their reward.

Sundown came, and Del's mind was beginning to wander. At times he imagined he was dancing again with a musical-voiced girl in a black velvet mask and a Spanish costume, whispering compliments in her ear. And then again he was hearing the weakening voice of Father Jean DuBois calling to him across the twenty wilderness miles that now separated them.

Footsteps sounded. Vaguely he realized Romero and two armed *bois brulé* were standing before him.

The heavy wrist clamps were opened, and the ankle chains removed.

"Here," Romero growled surlily, handing him a bowl of water.

Del expected it to be dashed from his hands. But Romero let him drink. He felt life stir within him again as that water coursed down his swollen throat, eased the agony of his dry, bloated tongue.

Then they handed him a platter of food. Del tried to wolf it down, but was forced to eat slowly because his throat was still giving him hell. That food was like a miraculous tonic. The madness faded out of him; even hope began to flicker within him again.

He was marched into a stone-built hut with a grilled iron door. The barred door groaned shut, and Romero fumbled at the big iron lock.

"Trust a woman to be squeamish," he grumbled as he went away.

Del understood then that he had Sherry Chalfant to thank for the food and water and his release from the chains. She apparently drew the line at torture, at least.

CHAPTER THREE
A Sprung Trap

The long twilight deepened. Candlelight flickered in the factor's quarters. The Crows up the river were pounding out a stomp dance, the hypnotic rhythm beating like a drum through the shadows.

Activity began at the river landing. Axes thudded in the timber downstream, and ox carts rumbled in the mauve dusk.

The steamboat was being refueled, and furs from the store-sheds were being loaded aboard. The Missouri was falling toward its mid-summer ebb, and Del guessed the packet was making ready to head downstream at once to avoid being stranded.

Del stood at the bars looking out. Then he made a startling discovery.

The big, clumsy iron lock which hung in the hasp, securing the door of his cell, was not entirely closed. The jaw of the lock had not been pushed home. And it was within reach of his hand through the bars.

Romero had been careless when he snapped the jaw of the lock, and it had not seated on its pin.

Or was it carelessness? Romero was not the man to overlook a detail of that importance. Romero had deliberately left that lock sprung. He *wanted* Del to attempt an escape.

The only person in sight was a *bois brulé* guard, who squatted against a stretching frame a rod away, his rifle across his knees, apparently dozing with his head bowed. The vicinity of the jail had remained strangely deserted, Del recalled. Not even the sticky-faced Indian and breed children, insatiably curious, had shown up to peer at this spectacle of a man in a cage.

Every sense of reason told Del that armed men were planted out there in the shadows, waiting to riddle him if he sprung this trap that was set for him.

Coldly, precisely, Del appraised the situation, mapping the points where danger likely lay. He decided there would be a rifleman crouching back of that fur-shed across the compound. Another should be in that clump of hazel brush which commanded a considerable area. The blockhouse roof with its rifle slots in the parapet, too, no doubt was manned.

His only advantage was that he knew it was a trap. His problem was to select the route that would draw the minimum of fire.

He made his decision, chose his route. Death by a bullet would at least be preferable to slow torture again.

Just why Romero had tried this, he did not know. The only answer was that Sherry Chalfant probably shrank from cold-blooded hanging, but took feminine refuge in excusing the shooting of an escaping prisoner.

Del reached out, jerked the lock free, threw open the door, and came out like a thunderbolt.

He took the *bois brulé* by surprise, even though the man had been only feigning sleep. Del knocked the rifle aside before the man could pull the trigger. He snatched the gun away then, and sent the stock smashing into the fellow's flat face.

The breed staggered, with a dazed grunt. Del caught him in his arms, held him as a shield, as he backed around the jail.

Swampy backwater from the river girded the area below the bluff at this point, and because of that swamp they had believed it was the one direction he would not head.

Del whirled with his shield as guns bellowed behind him. He felt the shock as a ball tore through the dazed guard. He snatched a pistol from the man's belt, and fired at a shadowy figure which reared up at the corner of the fur-shed to the left.

Then Del dropped his human shield, and went down the rocky, twenty-foot descent from the bluff and into the tules and muck of the swamp.

A bullet twitched at his hair, and others tore through the reeds, sending up snaky streamers of water.

He floundered into deep water, swam a few strokes, reached muddy bottom on the other side, and labored through it toward dry land. The tule growth and the darkness sheltered him now from bullets, but the post was in an uproar; already men were circling the swamp to intercept him.

He headed for the open river, two hundred yards to his right, a route which carried him between the fort bluff and the Crow camp.

He could hear men sliding down from the bluff and splashing across the backwater in an attempt to cut him off in that direction. It was too dark for gun-play, but they could hear him crashing through the tangled undergrowth.

Del put on an extra burst of speed, outdistanced them and saw the open glint of the river ahead.

He slid over a five-foot cutbank into the water. It was shallow, but he pushed out, drifted a rod or two downstream, then pulled himself beneath brush which overhung the water.

"He's in the river," Black Sul's voice, spiced with profanity, sounded near at hand. "Beat the brush along the shore. Kill him on sight. Fetch some pitch torches."

Discovery was certain if he remained there. Del sank below the surface, pushed himself away from the bank, and swam underwater out into the river. Forced to emerge, he drifted to the surface to replenish his lungs. Torchlight glinted in the brush on shore, and a silver radiance in the sky on the eastern horizon presaged a new danger—a rising full moon.

He was thirty feet or more out from shore, and above a rocky point which jutted out into the river just above the landing. The smokestack of the *Queen of the Plains* shone up against the stars a short distance beyond that point.

A wild shout sounded. "*Voilà!* The peeg is sweeming."

A gun gushed crimson flame on shore, and Del felt the burning sting of a graze on his shoulder as he dove under.

Del had been born and raised on the Ohio River, and as a boy he had learned the character of these big streams. He was in a slow-moving eddy here, set up by the outer current, crowding against that point of rock below.

He dove deep, out into the river. And as he had expected, he found himself suddenly seized by a chill, fast-running current that was sweeping on around the point. He let it carry him, conserving his lungs.

He had only one chance left now, and that was desperately frail. He was remembering the glimpse he had gained of the moored steamboat below the point. It had seemed far out of reach for an underwater swimmer, but this sub-surface current had a resistless force.

He began swimming inshore again. His lungs were constricting as he drifted to the surface. The bulk of the packet loomed up almost overhead. He took another gulp of air, sank, and swam until he touched its wooden hull. Surfacing, he found himself sheltered beneath the counter forming the foredeck above the prow.

Lungs laboring, he listened to confused shouting. Torchlight cast flickering reflection on the river above the point, but there was no indication that his escape had been solved. He heard men tumbling into boats at the landing and pushing upstream to join in the search.

Del drifted down the side of the steamboat. The starboard wheel box reared in a great arch above him, and he swam beneath its overhang. Grasping the slimy cedar blades, he climbed upward through the spokes until he was sitting on the hub.

Through weather cracks in the housing he watched the torch-light. But the search centered on the eddy above the point.

"By gar, he ees one dead man, I theenk," someone called. "Jules Deshon did not miss when he drew the bead on heem."

"Keep looking!" Sul Romero boomed from shore. "Make damned sure he won't come up! Maybe he got back to shore."

A flatboat came downstream, and torchlight burned brightly out there. The searchers probed desultorily near the packet, but it was plain they were losing interest, believing Del had been hit by that bullet and that his body was fishbait. It did not seem possible to them that he could have gone far underwater.

At last the torchlight gradually died away, and the boats returned to the landing.

Del was now in darkness. But in the faint light of the torches he had spotted a hatch in the side of the housing above him, evidently placed there for inspection purposes.

He climbed the wheel, felt for the hatch. It swung inward on hinges at his touch. A gust of steamy, oily heat assailed him.

The hatch opened on a crawlway above the boilers. Red lightning played over the engine room below as firemen, naked to the waist, stoked the boilers.

Del glimpsed a ladder at the forward end of the crawlway, which evidently led above. Waiting for a moment when the furnace doors were closed, he wriggled swiftly ahead and mounted the ascent.

He found himself in a passageway lighted by a single smoky whale oil lamp. Stateroom doors, three on each side, opened off this companionway. The *Queen of the Plains* was no passenger boat, and these quarters for officers occupied the full width of the deck, with this central entrance between.

Locks hung open on the hasps on all the doors. Del opened the nearest door, but saw that it was occupied, for men's clothing was strewn about. The adjoining stateroom also was plainly the quarters of one of the ship's officers.

Del turned to try a third door, hoping to find a vacant stateroom where he could hide. It was evident that steam was being made for immediate departure, and downstream was the direction Del wanted to go. Father DuBois might still be alive in that hideout twenty miles away. Riding the packet would be faster—and safer—than traveling by land over that distance.

He paused, listening to the sound of arrivals on the gangplank below.

"Thank you, Romero," Sherry Chalfant's clear voice floated up the forward companionway. "I regret my stay was so brief, but I prefer to return to St. Louis by packet. And the captain is very anxious to leave at once."

"I am desolate," Sul Romero said. "But I will not attempt to dissuade you further. *Au revoir*, my dear. *Bon voyage*."

Del heard the quick, crisp tap of her slippers mounting the companionway. He had no alternative but to hide in the cabin nearest at hand.

He opened the door, stepped in. A shock hit him as he glimpsed the interior, but it was too late to retreat, and he closed the door.

A faint, delicate perfume pervaded this cabin, and he had seen the trunk, open to reveal bright-colored silk finery. This was Sherry Chalfant's cabin.

A ringed curtain across a recess served as a clothes closet. Del stepped back of that curtain, pushing among filmy, gentle frocks and apparel which hung there.

Her quick step approached. Then she was in the cabin. He heard her lock the inner bolt. A sulphur match flared, and lamplight flooded the place with yellow glow.

From below came the grinding roar of the gangplank being rolled aboard. Orders were bawled, there was the sound of feet on the deck, and vibration hummed through the packet as the paddle-wheels came to life, backing her into the stream. They were under way.

Del chanced a glance through a slit in the curtain. Sherry Chalfant was delving into the trunk. She straightened with a cap-and-ball pistol in her hand which looked ludicrously huge in her slim fingers.

She leveled the gun at the curtain. "Come out, or I'll fire," she said in a level voice.

CHAPTER FOUR
Wilderness Rebellion

In spite of himself, Del felt a reluctant admiration for this girl. Sherry Chalfant, whatever she might be, at least had plenty of cold nerve beneath that young, alluring beauty.

He stepped out and bowed. "At your service, ma'moiselle," he said. "How did you know you had a guest?"

He was aware that he made a wild and fearsome figure. Blood that had dried with the river water on his bare upper body gave him a saturnine cast. The wound itself had stopped bleeding, leaving a darkening blotch of dried blood on his shoulder. Barefoot, clad only in soaked buckskin breeches which still dripped water, unshaven, his hair a tangled mat, he expected her to scream at once for help.

Instead she kept her voice down to a bare murmur. "I noticed a few drops of water leading to my door," she said. "And more of it leading toward that curtain."

He wondered at the enigma of this red-lipped, shapely girl, whose amber eyes were so cool and searching.

"Well?" he shrugged. "Let's get it over. Call the crew. Romero will be mighty happy when I'm brought back to him at White Stockade again."

"Is it true you killed two company partisans in a trap-line war?" she asked slowly.

"Well, I shot a couple of 'em, but it wasn't exactly a fur war, as you no doubt know," Del shrugged. "And I guess I sent one or two more of 'em under tonight after you and Romero were kind enough to arrange a quick death for me by your trap. Does that soothe your conscience any? I'm guilty—in the eyes of Sul Romero at least."

"I ordered Romero to take you under guard to St. Louis on this packet, along with the witnesses," she denied. "There you would have had a fair trial. If it wasn't a fur war that brought on the killing, then what was the cause?"

Her manner was astoundingly blunt, direct. Del studied her. She was probably trying only to lead him on, win his confidence in the hope of wringing from him the secret Sul Romero wanted to know—the secret of Father Jean DuBois's whereabouts. And it would be only too easy to fall under her spell.

"You know, I presume," he said slowly, "that they hang or shoot a man—or a woman—who conspires against his own government."

The gun wavered. "What do you mean?"

"As grand factor of Wilderness Fur you must know that Sul Romero has been using company funds to raise and arm an army of cutthroats and renegades here in the mountains, with the intention of seceding from the United States and setting up an independent nation. It's to be known as the Indian Federation. That name is a sop to the tribes, who are being won over to the idea. But it will be ruled by one man—Sul Romero. He will be king bolt."

"That—that seems impossible," she breathed.

She sank down on the bunk, letting the gun rest limply in her lap, while she stared at him with wide, lifeless eyes.

Del wanted to believe she might be on the level. But the stake was too big to make any error of judgment now.

"And you'll be the queen of this Indian Federation," he lashed at her harshly. "It's your money that is financing this business."

"You think that I—" she blazed in sudden fury. Then she buried her face in her hands. "I don't blame you for believing that. I've been such a fool. But I didn't suspect anything wrong until just lately. Romero's reports showed that the company was losing money. For two years I've been raising funds, borrowing on everything I could lay my hands on to keep the company going. I sold the home grandfather left me. I even went to England and France and sold jewels that were family heirlooms. And Romero was using that money for—for this awful scheme."

If Sherry Chalfant was acting a part she was a past master at the art. And if she spoke the truth she was absolving herself of the reputation she had as a gilded social butterfly.

Del was silent a moment. "Then why didn't you come into the wilderness to see your inheritance long before this?"

"Grandfather named Romero my guardian until I was twenty-one. I reached that age only a few weeks ago. He had directed in his will that Romero be placed in charge of Wilderness Fur. I trusted Amos Chalfant's judgment. And when I left the convent two years ago, the matter of raising funds to send to Romero kept me too occupied to come here."

Del lifted her to her feet, glared into her eyes as though hoping to read the truth there. "If I could only believe that!"

"It is the truth," she said. "I swear it, Captain Keech."

"So Romero told you who I am?"

"No. Romero said you were an army deserter named Tom Sloan. But I—I had made inquiries after—after the masked ball in St. Louis that night. I learned you were a cavalry captain."

"You still remember that night?" Del asked slowly.

Her eyes remained unwavering. "Yes."

Del forced himself to release her, and that took an effort of will. He moved to the cabin window. The full moon burnished the river with silver, etching out the horizon of low hills off to the south which served as a landmark.

The *Queen of the Plains* was making good time in the moonlight. The hideout in which Del had left the wounded Father DuBois was now only half a dozen miles away.

He turned to the girl. "I'll be leaving now. Give me fifteen minutes before you put 'em on my trail."

"You still don't trust me, do you? I would have called for help before this if I were what you want to think I am."

"Do you believe I *want* to think you're mixed up in this thing?" Del groaned.

"I'll prove it," she said. "Take me with you when you leave this boat."

She recoiled from the new suspicion that flamed in Del's eyes. "So I can lead you to Father DuBois?" he jeered. "So you can send word to Romero?"

Suddenly she slapped him. "I hate you," she sobbed. "Why do you insist on thinking this awful thing about me? What has Father DuBois to do with this? I never saw him in my life."

"Then why do you want to go with me?"

"Because—because I'm afraid here. Don't you understand? I saw the drunkenness and the vileness there at White Stockade. Sul Romero never wanted me to see things like that. And I saw the way he had tortured you with that terrible banquet he placed before you. Beyond a doubt Romero realizes that I knew who you really are, and that I will act when I get to St. Louis. I—I don't imagine he wants me to reach St. Louis alive."

She paused, her lips trembling. "Now you know why I'm afraid. Romero tried to talk me out of departing on this boat. I have a feeling that—that Sul Romero might be aboard right at this minute."

Del felt cold inside, for his mind had rushed far ahead of her explanation, seeing her true plight long before she had put it in words.

Then he made a gesture for silence, jerking his head toward the door.

The girl understood, even though she heard nothing. But Del's perceptions, tuned by weeks of danger, were keener. A stealthy presence was moving in the passageway.

The girl lifted the gun again. She began moving around, her skirts rustling, making a pretense of normal activity.

Del heard the soft rasp of metal out there. Then, after a moment, that intruder went away.

He began to breathe again. Evidently his presence had not been discovered after all. He waited five minutes, then moved silently to the door. He listened for minutes more. At last he slid back the inner bolt, turned the knob.

The door opened only a fraction of an inch, but it would open no farther. It was locked on the outside. Del remembered the click of metal.

Del looked at the girl. "I am a fool," he said, but there was a queer throbbing elation in his voice. "In thinking of myself, I might have let you stay here alone."

Her face lighted as she looked at him. "You do believe me now!" she choked.

He motioned toward the door. "That was the clincher. Someone locked you in. But he didn't know I was here, or he'd have taken other steps."

"Romero," she murmured, and there was stark fear in her for the first time. "I knew he was aboard. I felt it. Why would he want to lock me in?"

"No telling," Del said grimly, "except that he wants to know where you are at all times. Knowing Romero, I'd say that this is a hell of a good time to light a shuck out of here. Can you swim?"

"A little. Enough to stay afloat."

Dell opened the cabin window. It was small, but he believed he could squeeze through. The moon was on the opposite beam. The packet's shadow cruised along there below them. Black and oily in that shadow, the surface of the Missouri slid past and into the maw of the paddles, which cast it astern slashed into tattered shards of tumbling silver in the full moonlight. The shore Del wanted to reach was a quarter of a mile or more away.

Del watched the river until she spoke. He turned. She looked like a handsome boy. In that brief time she had changed to buckskin breeches and a dark-colored shirtwaist. She was tying a pair of moccasins about her neck.

"I'm ready," she said, and began tying back her hair. "I brought the buckskins and moccasins along in case I got a chance to do a little game hunting. I never thought that I'd be the one who was hunted."

CHAPTER FIVE
Night of Death

Del hated to think of the hardships and dangers that lay ahead for this clear-eyed girl. But like himself, like Father DuBois, she knew too much. And Sul Romero would not let anything stand in his way now.

Del wriggled through the window feet first and lowered himself to a toehold on a combing. He waited there, clinging to the window casing with one hand as he helped the girl who came agilely climbing out to join him. He guided her to the foothold, and they balanced there for a moment, fifteen feet above the water.

"Dive far out, and deep," Del instructed. "Stay under as long as you can to make sure you miss the wheels. Don't make any commotion when you come up."

Then they dove side by side, cleaving the water cleanly. Del reached out beneath the surface and shoved her farther ahead, even though that maneuver thrust him back into the danger zone.

He heard the paddles pass almost overhead with the roar of dull thunder, felt the sucking force of the upswept water. But he stroked clear of it and surfaced, swimming to the girl's side as they were tossed about in the steamer's wake.

She needed no help. She was swimming easily. "This convent you attended," Del muttered, "toughens 'em up. Did you wear buckskin breeches under your confirmation dress? I suppose you learned to swim when they baptized you. And the Mother Superior taught you how to ram powder and wadding and bullets home in a pistol!"

"Grandpappy Chalfant saw to it that my practical education wasn't neglected," she chuckled. "I learned these things long before my convent days."

The steamboat was receding into the moonlight. Del fancied that a formless, dark object moved in its shadow, and he saw a splash of water. A moment later he glimpsed a black dot in the tumbling wake of the packet. Evidently it was a floating log, cast astern by the paddles.

He and the girl struck out for shore. The *Queen of the Plains* churned onward, its riding lights growing fainter and finally vanishing beneath the fading plume of smoke from its stack.

Then the night downstream erupted a hideous, volcanic spurt of red flame that mounted hundreds of feet in the air. It came and went like a thunderclap while Del and Sherry Chalfant stared aghast.

In the next instant the heavy, sullen slam of the explosion hit their eardrums.

A confused rumble of debris rained back down upon the surface. Then silence. The throbbing peace of the wilderness night returned.

They knew they had seen the death of the *Queen of the Plains* there at that half-mile distance. The packet had been blown to pieces by that explosion.

Del looked grimly at the girl. "Boilers let go," he said.

Her wet face was gray as ashes. "You know better," she corrected. "Boilers wouldn't send up such a red flash. That was a powder explosion. That boat was deliberately blown up! Some of those bales of beaver plews that Sul Romero had carried aboard today probably had kegs of powder inside them—with fuses attached."

Del nodded. "Now we know why you were locked in your cabin. Romero didn't want you to miss his little surprise party."

Shaken, they struck out again. A dozen men probably had died there, and the majority had been loyal to Romero. It was a further grim insight into the implacable nature of the man that they were dealing with to know that he would sacrifice even the lives of his followers without compunction to gain his own objective.

That disaster was to go down in river annals as a boiler explosion, according to the way Romero had planned it. Sherry Chalfant's death could never be traced to him.

They headed for a sandbar which glinted gray-white in the moonlight ahead. They were still in deep water a hundred yards from their objective when Del touched the girl, with a murmured warning for silence. They drifted silently.

Eerily they heard the surge of water. Another swimmer was nearing them.

Not a dozen yards away, the head and shoulders of a man came into the bright path of moonlight, swimming strongly.

It was Sul Romero, stroking for that same sandbar. Del remembered the shadow he had seen alongside the packet. He knew the answer now. That had been Sul Romero diving into the river, leaving the packet by the same method by which Del and the girl had departed. Romero had taken to the water only a few minutes behind them, unaware that he had company in the river.

Del knew that before he left the packet Romero had touched fire to the fuse that had destroyed the steamboat.

Romero was heading for the shore and the river trail back to White Stockade, satisfied that Sherry Chalfant would never denounce him now.

Del swam ahead. Hearing him, Romero whirled, staring. And there he found himself swimming with ghosts—with the girl he believed he had just sent to death in that explosion, and with the man he believed had gone to the bottom more than an hour earlier.

"Take a good look, Romero," Del said icily. "It's the last sight you'll ever see on this earth. This is for every man you have had murdered, and every Indian you ruined with your rotgut whiskey. This is for the girl you robbed, tricked, and tried to murder. And this is for Amos Chalfant, too. I can't prove that you murdered him. I only know it. You murdered him so you could make yourself a king. And you probably forged that will which named you boss of Wilderness Fur and this girl's guardian."

Del's hands closed on Romero's throat. Sul Romero, weaponless except for the feral strength in his powerful body, was facing on even terms the man he had tortured.

As Del's fingers tightened, the man erupted from the stunned spell cast by those two ghostly faces there in the moonlight. And he met that challenge like a wild animal.

He broke Del's grip, clawing at Del, trampled him under the surface. But as Del went down he pulled Romero under with him. His fingers once more inexorably went to Romero's throat.

And again Romero tore free with a strength that was based on frenzy and desperation.

They came to the surface, and Romero smashed at Del with a fist. It was like beating at iron. Del closed again, and for the third time his hands clamped around the throat of the man who had aspired to power over the bodies of murdered men.

"Don't—" Black Sul Romero half-sobbed. "Don't, Keech! Have mercy!"

They went under together. Romero fought maniacally. But he could not break that grip again. They sank deeper into chill water.

Del felt that his own life was fading with each passing second, for his lungs were like iron bands. But Romero still fought, and Del still maintained that grip. He would never loosen it now. If he died there he meant for Romero to die with him.

Suddenly Sul Romero's struggles ceased, and he went limp. Del released the man who would have been a king.

It was over. But Del did not have the strength to stroke back to the surface. He was struggling feebly when he felt a hand grasp his hair. Sherry Chalfant, swimming down into the depths, had found him.

That aroused him. After a time, with the girl supporting him, he made his way to shore. She dragged him out on the sandbar, and he lay there a long time until he found the strength to get to his feet.

Then he bent and kissed her on the lips, as her arms slid around his neck.

"Del," she kept sobbing. "Oh, Del!"

Del led the way through the brush away from the river. He told her the story of Father DuBois as they traveled.

It was nearing midnight when they crawled through the brush up a little coulee and found the white-haired Jesuit lying on the bed of dry leaves where Del had left him.

Father Jean DuBois, wrapped in a single blanket, was still clinging to life. His eyes were open, and he looked up at Del and smiled.

"Bless you, my son," he murmured. "I knew you would come back if you were still alive."

The Jesuit lapsed into a coma then. He was clinging to life only by a thread.

And Sherry Chalfant went to work. While Del built a fire and brought water, she soaked away the bandage that had been on too long. She boiled strips from the missionary's own cassock, dried it over the fire and dressed his wound again.

She made a broth from the few scraps of pemmican in the pack Del had left with the missionary, and forced a sip or two between his lips whenever he aroused.

At daybreak she looked at Del, who had fallen into exhausted sleep, spent by three days of ordeal. She bent down, kissed Del's gaunt face, and placed a cool hand on the forehead of the sunken-eyed priest. Father DuBois was sleeping now. His fever was beginning to abate.

Del awakened after a time, watching her slim figure in the shrunken, drying buckskins and moccasins. She turned, and color rose happily in her cheeks as she saw him looking at her.

"We've got a gun now—and powder," Del said, nodding toward the long rifle he had left with the missionary. "The country is full of game. I cached an Ojibway canoe ten miles down the river last fall. When the moon wanes we'll head down the river. The good father will be able to travel by that time. He's a mountain man—tough as whang-leather. He'll be on his feet before you know it."

He took her hand, pulling her closer. "The history of the Indian

Federation is closed,'' he added. ''Things like that fall down of
their own weight once the foundation crumbles. Romero was the
foundation. A few troops of dragoons will scatter what's left of the
organization before fall.

''We'll be in St. Louis in a month. It'll be a nice honeymoon—
traveling down to St. Louis.''

Her eyes were dancing. ''Honeymoon?''

''We've got a priest right with us, haven't we?'' Del grinned.

''Apparently,'' she murmured, leaning her head against him,
''you have made all the arrangements. And who am I to upset the
plans of Captain Del Keech, next grand factor of Wilderness Fur?''

GOOD-BY, MIMBRES KID

By
FRANK BONHAM

From the rocks he looked
down upon the scene....

Only the return of the long-dead Mimbres Kid could free Sam Landers from exile in his hostile prairie hell.

AT ELEVEN o'clock, Landers and the Mexican harnessed the team and began to listen for the sound of the stage horn. From the Apache Creek station, the contours of the rugged foothills blocked to view all but a few hundred yards of the road in each direction, but in the clear dry air the note of the driver's horn could be heard for over a mile.

Landers went inside and stirred the frijoles and jackrabbit stew he had on the cranes. He took some pride in giving weary passengers the only good meal they got between La Mesilla and Tucson, and certainly there was not a place on the Butterfield route where they needed a lift more than at the start of the Apache Pass climb.

They were sick of the monotony of sand, sage and sky through which they had been dragged and jolted for days. They dreaded the high, Apache-ridden pass ahead. They could not even discuss the route without using such terms as Massacre Rock, Dead Man's Canyon, or Bloody Creek.

Sam Landers heard the Mexicans shout, and then the sound of a horse loping into the yard. He had his rifle off the rack and was glancing through the window before the horse pulled up. There was a box of cartridges below each vertical wall-loop and two extra rifles over the fireplace. There had been Indian and outlaw trouble on the Apache Pass run for six months without a letup, and only this morning he had observed smoke signals to the east.

But the man who rode up was an American, and he held his free hand shoulder high as he stopped, so that there could be no mistaking his intentions. He wore a denim jumper and black bullhide chaps, and there was a cowboy's sixty-foot rope tied to his saddle.

Sam Landers went outside. He said to the man: "Light down."

The cowboy gave his horse to the Mexican. "Seen any Injun sign?" he asked. He was a strongly built man in his thirties, with short arms and legs and thick-fingered hands. His face was square and dark, with a stubble of light brown whiskers.

Landers said: "Four bucks rode by yesterday. They were friendly. I gave them some eatin' tobacco and they went on."

"They got a little unfriendly up the line," the puncher said. "I came by Hill's Ranch last night. Old Man Hill had been scalped and all the stock driven off. This morning I saw smoke signals all the way through the Pass. Stage been through?"

"Due any minute."

"Better hold it up," the cowboy said.

Sam Landers glanced down the road. Apache Creek relay station lay among the scanty cottonwood and hackberry growths along the shallow wash that was dry nine months of the year. It had its back to the dry, broken hills of the Dragoon Range and looked out on a jumble of gaunt foothills beyond which spread the canyon-slashed reaches of Sulphur Springs Valley.

"It's up to the driver," Landers said. "But it sounds like massacre weather. Come inside and have some chuck."

"If it's all the same to you," the puncher said, "I'll stay overnight. I was headin' for the H-Bar round-up to rep for my outfit. Looks like a good time for some bunk-house riding."

While the station tender filled a plate for him, the puncher talked. His name was Tom Bartell and he had worked for the Pothook for six years. He didn't care much for this Dragoon country; it was all turned on end and every draw was an ambush.

"I'd go buggy, running an outfit like this," he said. "Nobody but a greaser to talk to . . . forty miles to nowhere."

"Depends on what you want," Landers said. "I want peace and quiet. I like it."

He didn't like it, but it was a means to an end. A man who couldn't live at peace with his fellow men could isolate himself from them and achieve the same result as self-mastery would have given.

Bartell's pale eyes, the paler for brows like black hedges, showed sudden comprehension. "Sam Landers! You must be the one that killed Denver Red, the Mimbres Kid, and . . ."

The sound of the stage horn came across the hills. Sam Landers said shortly, "Yes, that one." He went outside.

When the Concord stopped before the adobe buildings among the trees, Landers said to McCormick, the driver: "Indian sign all the way to Benson, Mac. Want to try it?"

"Got a lady aboard," McCormick said. "I'll hold over till morning and be sure to hit Benson 'fore dark." McCormick jumped down, a young man whose skin had been baked as red as his hair and was covered with a multitude of freckles. He opened the door of the Concord coach, and by the way he stood solicitously by Landers knew the lady was young and attractive.

Naco Bill Wood, the shotgun messenger, was pulling baggage out of the boot. A big cowhide bag went to a stout, massive framed

man whose jowls had a well-massaged look and who had the
appearance of a prosperous cattleman. A sour-faced man with a
checked gray suit and a high-crowned hard hat received a telescope
bag and went into the stage station. The girl accepted McCormick's
hand and stepped down.

Sam Landers glanced at her as he began to unhitch the team.
Suddenly he dropped the chain trace and stared. The girl was
blonde and small, and wore a gray traveling cape and a blue poke
bonnet. The features within the frame of the bonnet were regular.
And, to Landers, they were familiar.

Gail Baylor glanced at him and smiled, not at all startled at this
chance meeting after two years. She said: "Hello, Sam!" and
followed Feliciano, the hostler, into the station with her suitcase.
When Sam went back to his work, his hands were unsteady and
there was a breathlessness in him.

Landers and Naco turned the lathered horses into the corral and
went inside. Feliciano had taken the others to the bare little rooms
in which they would spend the night. They returned one by one as
Landers was placing plates of steaming frijoles and stew on the
long table.

McCormick said cheerfully: "Loosen the cinches and dig
in, folks. This is the last white man's chuck you'll get till we reach
Tucson."

During dinner Sam Landers did not speak to Gail Baylor. He
listened to the conversation of the others.

The big stockman from El Paso laughed easily and talked about
the deal he had put over on an Eastern syndicate in selling a herd of
second-rate cattle for ten thousand dollars. Weedin, the saturnine
little man in the checkered suit, talked little but his small eyes were
never at rest. Landers had run enough tinhorns out of town in his
marshaling days to know one when he saw him, and Weedin wore
the marks.

He finished his dinner quickly and went out to tend the stock.
While he was forking up hay for the horses, Gail came outside and
sat on a bench beneath a big cottonwood.

Landers went to her, and she put up her hands, and he took
them, seeing her tears.

"Did you know I was here?" he asked.

"Henry Lowdon said he saw you when he came through. I had

to come, Sam. I had to know whether you were ever coming back.''

Landers said, ''This is where a man like me belongs.'' He sat down, holding her hand.

Gail said, ''You didn't know yourself as well as we did, Sam. You thought they were beginning to call you a 'killing marshal.' If anyone ever did, it was a term of respect. You brought Piñon City through, when the silver boomers would have ruined it for cattlemen. Every man you ever killed forced you to kill him.''

Sam Landers wanted to say, ''Not the Mimbres Kid,'' but he could not bring himself to show a side of his nature to her that he had never betrayed to anyone. Then, as if she had known what was in his mind, Gail said: ''I helped nurse the Mimbres Kid before he died, Sam. I think I heard almost the last thing he said: 'Landers is a square lawman. He gave me the breaks. I asked for it.' ''

''I gave him every break but letting him live,'' Landers said bitterly.

''But that was your job!''

Landers stood up, the stab of old memories turning in him. ''It was a job I didn't want any longer. I'm not going back, Gail. I'm through with killing. And as long as I am in Piñon City there will be killing.''

He went back to work, finding jobs to keep him busy until dark, but he could not drive from his mind the ghosts that her presence had brought back to him. Not that he had ever escaped them. On cold nights they filed in and sat by the fire and showed him their bloody faces and torn breasts. They were sad, as men are who have had some great hope unseasonably killed, for life is the greatest hope of all, and Sam Landers had taken it eleven times.

And it was the eleventh man he killed who came back oftenest to sit with him. The Mimbres Kid was young. He had hit Piñon City with a theory of bank-robbing that nearly worked, and a gun he could almost use.

Landers had walked in on him while he was in the midst of robbing the Piñon City Trust, and when the Kid threw down on him he shot him through the wrist. The Kid dropped the sack he carried and pulled his other gun with an awkwardness that told the marshal it was carried for show. He could have shot the Mimbres Kid in the arm and taken him alive, but the Kid made his mistake by talking.

"You big-mouthed saloon-fighter!" he taunted. "Ten notches, and you never shot a man yet except in the back!"

Anger came raging through Sam Landers, the kind of fury that is master of the strongest of men, and he told the Kid: "Take your shot!"

He knew he was going to kill him, not because he had to, but because he hated him; because he wanted to see him die. Sam Landers shot when he saw the Kid's finger jerk. Then he walked out of the bank and went down to his office.

The next day he resigned, because it was time to get out. He had taken the job when the town needed him. Now he wanted to get away, to try to forget the terrible savagery when he confronted a man in anger.

So long as he kept his temper he could control it. When that slender thread broke, he had to kill.

That the Mimbres Kid had taught him.

After dinner Stallman, the rancher, produced a bottle of fine French brandy from his bag. It must have cost a cowpuncher's salary, Sam thought, but he poured each man a half-tumblerful and raised his.

Weedin, the gambler, sipped his brandy. He took a deck of cards from his pocket. "As long as we're stuck here for the night," he suggested, "what has more power to soothe the traveler's breast than the bright and shining pasteboards?"

Stallman rubbed his hands. "You may not know it," he said, "but I cut my teeth on a poker chip. Cut for deal."

Tom Bartell won the cut. Sam Landers went to his room. He came back to see McCormick win a little pile. Landers laid a fresh deck on the table.

"Try mine," he said.

Weedin's glance was quick and angry. "What's the matter with these?"

"Maybe nothing. But I'm a disinterested party."

Stallman watched them with frank, ingenuous eyes. "No matter," he said. "This'll just be a friendly little game."

Not the way you've been running off at the mouth, Sam thought.

He went outside to see that Feliciano had locked everything securely. It was a black night, and he scanned the yard carefully before returning. When he went back, the card game had warmed up.

Stallman had drunk somewhat generously of his own brandy, and he was backing two pair as though they were a full house and drawing to blind straights. Landers had known scores like him, too rich for their own good, and he had seen them get into trouble when they began to suspect, too late, that they were being fleeced. But this fleshy, smiling cattleman never seemed to tire of losing.

Sam had his eye on the tinhorn across from him. Weedin and Tom Bartell were taking most of the pots.

On Weedin's deal, Stallman finally drew some cards. That was evident in the way his eyes sparkled and he began to finger the bills before him. He opened with twenty dollars. Naco Bill Wood dropped out, Bartell raised five, and Weedin put the pot up to fifty.

Stallman grinned. "This is going to cost you money. Two hundred to see me!"

Weedin whistled, and he seemed to debate whether to stay in, but his eyes were too confident. Bartell met the rancher's wager. Weedin sighed and laid down his money, and he said: "What've you got?"

"Full house, on kings and eights!" Stallman said. He already had his hands on the money.

Tom Bartell threw down his cards in disgust. Weedin's crooked mouth smiled. "Aces and jacks," he said.

He pulled the money in. Stallman looked stunned. Then a brown hand came over Weedin's shoulder and took his wrist firmly, turning his hand over so that the palm was up.

Sam Landers said: "Your pot, Stallman. I make it a rule not to let any man that uses a flasher in this tavern win over five dollars."

Stallman stared at the silver ring which Weedin wore with the plain, mirror-like face turned inside, so that as each card left his hand he could read its value in the flasher. The tinhorn tore loose and stood like a coyote at bay.

"Flasher, hell!" he said. "It's a signet ring. Only I've never had my initials put on it."

"And you never will," Landers told him.

Weedin struck Sam in the face, and while he was still shocked with the suddenness of it, the gambler reached for a hideout gun.

Anger came into Sam Landers's brain, raw, savage fury such as he had not known since he killed the Mimbres Kid. His hand went to his side in a move that was purely reflex, for he had not carried a revolver in two years.

He saw Weedin's gun come out of his vest pocket. Landers smashed at the tinhorn's wrist with a backhand blow, and the belly-gun clattered on the table.

Sam Landers scooped the gun up, feeling the hammer under his thumb and the metal butt still warm from Weedin's body, and it was all like a picture he had looked at until he knew it by heart.

But something was wrong. Landers hesitated. The picture was not right. Weedin was unarmed; and, more than that, he was a cringing, sickening thing it would dishonor a man to kill.

He threw the derringer in the fireplace and said to Weedin: "Go to your room. If I see you out here again I'll hold you for the law."

He was sick and shaken. The tinhorn would never know how close to death he had been tonight.

He spoke to Stallman after the gambler had left. "A word of advice: Tinhorns like that are thicker than lice on the stages these days. Don't flash your roll unless you want to lose it."

The rancher looked shamefaced. "Man ought to know better at my age," he admitted. "Hell, I'm carrying over ten thousand! Figured to look over some copper mining property near Tucson."

It was nearly nine o'clock, and there was a jolting day of mountain travel ahead of them. McCormick yawned and reckoned he'd catch some shut-eye. Naco went with him to the room they shared, and Stallman followed.

Tom Bartell picked up the bull's-eye lantern by the fireplace. "Reckon I'll see that that pony of mine ain't into your grain shed."

"No lantern," Landers warned. "Makes too good a target in this country."

The cowboy laughed. "I'll risk it."

He started to light it, but Landers took the lantern and put it back in its place. "Maybe you're willing to risk it," he said, "but I'm not. I said this was bad country. I make it a rule to act as though I knew there were Apaches in the brush."

Bartell shrugged and went outside.

Sam Landers went to bed, wondering why a man like Bartell,

who was willing to stay at the tavern because of the outlaw and Indian menace, was so eager to risk his life with a lantern. And wondering, too, where an ordinary cowpoke got two hundred dollars to risk on a card game. . . .

In the morning, before the rest were up, Landers and the stage men harnessed the Concord and had everything ready to leave as soon as the light was good enough.

They were still working on the harness when Tom Bartell came out with his heavy work-chaps buckled on and his brushpopper jacket buttoned high because of the crisp air.

He said to Sam Landers: "Thanks for putting me up, pardner. I'll need an early start if I'm going to make the H-Bar."

Landers watched the puncher saddle and ride at a walk up the steep road into the forbidding Dragoon hills. While Naco and the driver loaded in the passengers' baggage, Sam Landers prepared hot coffee and eggs.

The men ate hungrily. McCormick finished and stood up. "That's it, folks. Let's go."

Stallman shook Sam's hand. He said: "Thanks, mister. If you're ever in El Paso, look me up."

There was always a sadness in seeing overnight passengers go, for Landers was not by nature a solitary man. But there was a sharper poignancy this time that stabbed him deeply, for he knew he would not see Gail again. He could not go back, and there was no life for a woman with a man who must live in the gloomy backwaters of the frontier.

After the others had gone out, Gail gave him her hand. Her eyes, which blended the soft blue and gray of her costume, were very sober.

"I suppose I was foolish to come, Sam," she said. "But I had to know. A woman can't wait forever. You won't be coming back?"

"Not while things are like they are," Landers said. "I'm as dead as any of the men I ever killed."

She started to go, but suddenly he pulled her to him. He kissed her on the lips, with all the hunger of a man who has starved for something. Abruptly he released her and went to his room, shutting the door hard.

He was sitting on his cot when the stage rolled up the road to Benson.

After a while Landers poured himself a cup of coffee and sat at the table watching the embers of the breakfast fire in the round corner fireplace. He was conscious of a vague discomfort. But it was nothing physical, and he came to the realization that something about the room was out of place.

When he discovered what it was, he came up out of his chair, staring at the fireplace. Something was missing—the bull's-eye lantern! He had put it back in its place beside the wood-box last night.

He went quickly to Tom Bartell's room, and, as he had thought, the lantern was on the window-sill. It was burning. The top was smoking hot, so that he knew the lantern had burned all night. Landers snuffed it out and slowly carried it back to the main room.

He remembered Tom Bartell's lame story about checking up on his pony, and saw again the war-smokes on Farewell Peak that he had observed yesterday morning. He was remembering other times he had seen smoke on the air, times when a stage-robbery had followed.

Sam Landers stepped out the door and bawled at Feliciano: "Saddle my Pancho horse pronto!" He went back and took his old Colt out of the trunk, frowning at the empty shells in two chambers.

They had been there since he had killed the Mimbres Kid, for he had not touched the gun since the hour he wrapped it in a cleaning rag and put it away. He dropped the shells in his pocket, buckled on the gun and tied the holster.

Landers hit the saddle and loped up the road the stage had taken fifteen minutes earlier. He took all the short-cuts, the flinty, climbing ridges that overlooked the road and straightened out the hairpin turns. The prints of the iron tires were clean and sharp in the soft red dust.

He went more carefully. Already he had an idea where the hold-up would take place, and when he got his first glimpse of Hanging Rocks he knew he had been right.

He left his horse ground-tied and removed his spurs. He did not yet know how many men he was up against, but he knew that two of them would be the little tinhorn Weedin and Tom Bartell. From the rocks he looked down on the scene.

The stage was lurching back and forth as the swing and wheel horses tried to break away from the dead leaders. Naco Bill Wood and McCormick were alive, but both lay on their faces in the dirt, with their arms outstretched. Tom Bartell and another man were standing over them, while Weedin kept a Colt on Stallman with one hand and tried to count the contents of a cowhide billfold.

Gail Baylor stood off to one side.

Sam could hear Weedin's complaints as he crept through the brush. "There ain't even five hundred pesos here! Where's the rest of it? Where's the ten thousand you been shooting off your mouth about?"

The cattleman's voice was sheepish. "That's all it was, friend—just the kind of money you shoot your mouth off about. I haven't had ten thousand dollars in my life!"

"You'll wish you had," Weedin said, "if I don't find the ten, pronto. Set down and take off your boots."

Weedin was so intent on Stallman that he did not see the station tender step from behind. Sam said quietly: "High and quick, boys."

The gun was pointed at Tom Bartell and the stranger, and Bartell cursed and dropped his carbine. The other outlaw tried to duck behind the horses, firing as he moved, and Landers dropped him under the rearing horses.

Weedin, filled with a crazy courage that was not backed by gun-skill, made a quarter-turn to bring the ex-marshal under his sights. He fired, the slug striking the Concord, and at the same instant Sam Landers dropped the hammer of his own Colt.

Weedin was sent back a step by the force of the .45 slug. Landers watched him falter and try to bring his gun up, and then collapse.

Bartell was not out of it. He had a sidearm, and now he was bringing the gun up fast, standing sideways, eyes flashing fire.

Sam fired, the outlaw's arm jerking with the impact of the bullet. He went to his knees and then rolled onto his side, groaning and gripping his shattered arm. McCormick got his guns.

Landers took a long breath. He was as steady, as calm, as a rock. And he knew that shot had not been a freak: It had been fired in anger, but he had been so sure of himself that he could take the time to send an aimed shot into the outlaw's arm instead of slamming a bullet into his heart.

They buried the dead outlaws beside the road and carried Bartell back to the station.

Stallman produced another bottle of brandy, and each man drank his liquor as though he needed it.

Landers said to the rancher: "This will show you why I advised you to keep still about your roll. Bartell and Weedin aren't the last of their breed, either."

"Feller," Stallman said, "I'm paid to shoot off my mouth. I've been riding the stages three months trying to get a line on how so many of our wagons were being stopped. I work for Butterfield. Weedin finally gave me the answer. He got on at El Paso, and I gave him the old line about being a big stockman. At La Mesilla he rushed over to the saloon and talked to a man. This man got word ahead to Bartell, I don't know just how."

"Smoke signals," Landers told him. "They must have been working short-handed, and Bartell used the Indian stunt to hold the stage up till another man was on hand, rather than try to go it alone."

Stallman smiled. "You ought to be working for Butterfield yourself. You aren't so bad at the pay-off, either. Done some shooting?"

"A little."

When Sam was able to speak to Gail alone, he said: "I'm sorry you had to see it, Gail. Killing is never pretty."

"I'm only sorry for you, Sam," Gail told him. "It seems that they won't let you rest, even way out here."

"I'm all done resting," Sam Landers said. "I've paid my debt to the Mimbres Kid. There's a little spread up near Wild Horse Mountain where I've always wanted to run a few head of cattle. If I can find a partner—who can cook and darn socks—I might try it."

She came into his arms, neither of them speaking. She did not ask how he had paid his debt to the Mimbres Kid. That was between him and the Kid, and she was satisfied that he had buried the ghost at last in his own way.

Landers was still trying to explain it to himself. He knew he owed a lot to Weedin, the tinhorn. He had seen himself in Weedin, last night—hot-headed, letting his hatred lead him into foolish moves, as it had led the tinhorn and the Kid to death. Letting his anger use him, instead of forcing that savage drive into channels that would make him steadier and stronger.

Twice in twelve hours he had met hatred, and twice he had taken it in his two hands and turned it to his own uses. Maybe that was what the Kid had tried to tell him, all those lonely nights on Apache Creek. If so, the outlaw had not died in vain.

Sam Landers took from his pocket two empty .45 shells. He flipped them into the brush, and he murmured: "*Adiós*, Mimbres Kid!"

THE END

Bearhide's Moonshine War

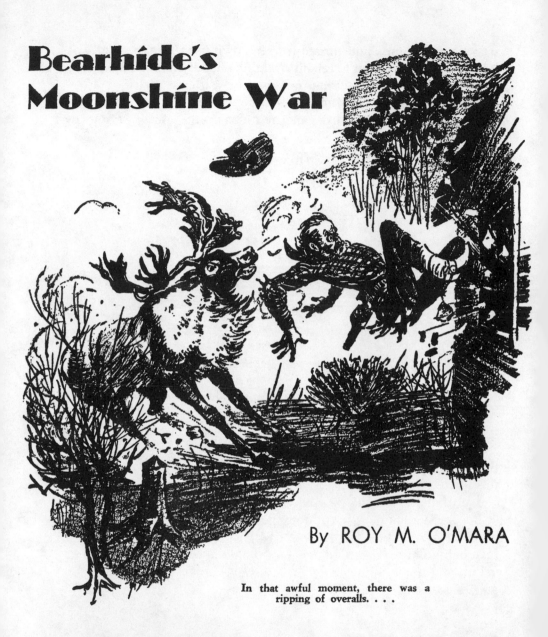

By ROY M. O'MARA

In that awful moment, there was a
ripping of overalls. . . .

Bearhide and Charley Pine Cone had put up with Ol' Jack's tromping
their corn patch, flirting with their mare, and helling around generally. . . . But when that locoed old devil got the idea that the pardners
were rival bull elk, that was the time when Bearhide—helped by
bottled brave-maker—declared his own kind of war!

THERE was a crashing at the timber edge, and Bearhide Judson broke into the clearing amid an aura of shattered buckbrush. Spurts of dust appeared rapidly at wide intervals in the parched grass. Close on Bearhide's flushing high-heeled boots, an evil-eyed quadruped lumbered in the dusty wake, with a cocked horn coming ever closer to a cringing posterior.

"Halp!" Bearhide Judson yodeled. He was mocked by the tranquility of the shale-spattered clearing, the age-darkened ranch cabin and the winding highway below. Tall firs on the opposite mountain took up the plaintive supplication and tossed it back— "Halp!"

For some time the childish antics of Ol' Jack, the bachelor elk, had been the subject of amused gossip among the wide-spaced citizenry of the Saddle Gap country. They chuckled at reports of the aged bull elk—banished for orneriness by his own herd— bedeviling truck drivers as the big rigs inched up the long grade to the Gap. Then too, no little amusement was derived from bewildered complaints by the agents at the agricultural quarantine station at the state line regarding an unearthly beast that often stood out in the darkness and made vulgar noises at them. Neither Bearhide Judson nor his partner, Charlie Pine Cone, was able to manifest any enthusiasm or appreciation for the humorous situation, however.

Being in the geographic center of Ol' Jack's sphere of activity, their spacious sidehill corn patch provided succulent and easily masticated fodder for stump-toothed outlaw elks—and corn, in the Judson-Pine Cone enterprise, was important indeed.

Bearhide's leather-sinewed arms pumped like piston rods as he grabbed morsels of atmosphere and tossed them into the mossy face behind him. There was a sharp nudge under a hip pocket that set his shoulders up beside wind-torn ears and inspired a flip in his gait that hadn't been used since his last run with the lawmen.

As reckoned over the sights of a .30-30 carbine, the distance from the edge of the timber to the weather-warped ranch shanty was about one hundred yards—a distance Bearhide covered in a rough eight seconds. The final spurt of speed tore an anguished yelp from deep within Bearhide's air-hungry being, and his remaining morsel of strength was used to hurtle a lanky body at the shack window.

During the awful moment the aperture loomed to greet his airborne carcass, there was a vicious ripping of overall material, a sound of sliding hoofs, a frustrated snort, and the feel of warm summer air—all behind Bearhide Judson.

An extended spur affixed to the foremost boot-heel preceded Bearhide to the rough lumber floor. Following the course of an erratic rowel, he made a zigzagging and destructive maneuver involving a blocked-up cookstove, a rickety board table and a clutter of saddles, traps, mining tools, and gallon jugs underneath Charlie Pine Cone's yellow wrought-iron bed. Charlie Pine Cone hung by both fat hands from the safety of a sagging rafter and surveyed the proceedings with round coal-black eyes.

"Damn lucky," Charlie Pine Cone observed, "me take window out!"

Bearhide extricated an overtaxed body from the rubble and retrieved a flop-brimmed black Stetson. Charlie came to the floor with a thud, and Ol' Jack trotted off toward Saddle Gap in the late afternoon breeze. A generous segment of faded blue cloth fluttered from a high-held antler.

Bearhide blinked watery eyes and swallowed rapidly. "Why," he demanded, "didn't yuh plug that murder-minded beast?"

Charlie Pine Cone recovered an over-turned bean kettle from under Bearhide's bunk and wiped it out on the tail of a red shirt. Before answering, he summoned an eager hound into the house to clean up a trail of sowbelly and beans generously spread during the recent influx of Bearhide Judson.

"You carry forty-five," Charlie mentioned, measuring a new batch of beans. "How come you no shoot?"

Bearhide grumbled in a three-week beard framing his loose-lipped mouth. "You know why I didn't shoot," he said, extending an exploratory finger to the nether region of a loose-jointed anatomy. "Why, even that pot-lickin' hound is so afeered o' th' game warden he won't yap at that elk!" He winced when the trembling digit encountered nothing but floor-burned hide.

There was a time, and not long before, when Ol' Jack would have been subjected to a hide-puncturing ceremony involving the use of a well-handled carbine. But Bearhide had been recently convicted for the planned murder of a deer at the wrong time and place, and had enjoyed a sixty-day free ride at the county jail. The partners' distaste for game laws in general was now tempered with a grudging respect. Moreover, they were behind in their work.

The smoke-blackened interior resounded to Bearhide's resonant profanity. Charlie Pine Cone threw a handful of bark on the fire and sagged an ever-weary body into a rawhide chair.

"Besides chasin' bug-station agents an' pesterin' truck drivers," Bearhide rumbled as he pounded the remnants of the table with a hairy fist, "that fool elk has been stompin' up our corn patch. But did we do any bellyachin' tuh th' law?"

Charlie Pine Cone's jowls flopped, indicating a negative answer. He hoisted a double chin and propelled a generous consignment of tobacco juice through and around a convenient knothole.

"And when that deluded bull heathen got tuh thinkin' my saddle mare was a cow elk—did we squawk?"

Charlie's jowls flopped again.

"But when that lovesick devil gets it in his head that I'm a competin' bull elk, an' won't let me near th' mare—an' runs me home from th' upper corral—"

"Time then," Charlie finished, "to raise hell."

"Yuh said somethin' there, redskin," Bearhide thundered. "We'll make a try at losin' that elk legal—otherwise we'll do it anyway, game warden or no game warden."

"You do," Charlie grunted. "Elk still think I'm bull calf."

In spite of Charlie's advice that he use a grain sack like a breech-clout to hide his nakedness behind, Bearhide donned a long black slicker that almost touched the shanks of his spurs.

"I'm gonna sashay in tuh th' county seat," he announced, "for another pair o' pants. While I'm there I'm goin' tuh have a showdown with th' law about that fool elk. I'll eat when I get back."

"Me be at—"

"Call it a factory—always," Bearhide interrupted. "Only reason why not is that it ain't licensed like a lot o' them hifalutin' places."

"Get sugar," Charlie suggested.

Bearhide flapped the slicker to dissipate the sweat popping out under the heavy garment.

"Won't be gone very long," he said. "Just long enough tuh pick up that stuff an' tell Perry Fletcher, th' game warden, tuh take care o' that elk. . . . If he don't, I'm goin' tuh murder him, even if I'm in th' pokey for a year."

"No!" Charlie Pine Cone groaned. "You in pokey all summer—me do work. Not all winter, too!"

It was dusk when Bearhide kicked a block of wood from under a

back wheel of his flop-fendered touring car, climbed over the door
and coasted from the corral. At the third bend in the fifteen-mile
downgrade to the county seat, the lunging vehicle broke into a
three-cylindered clatter, filling the dark canyons with an unmuffled
symphony of rusty combustion chambers—and clouds of acrid
black smoke.

All Bearhide's physical energy was devoted to herding the frac-
tious car within the confines of a twenty-two-foot pavement. All
mental energy was devoted to phrasing his part of the conversation
he planned to have with the game warden relative to the immediate
disposal of a feeble-minded bull elk. By the time the hiccoughing
car was anchored in front of the officer's home at the county seat,
eloquence bubbled within Bearhide Judson. Sternly, he pounded
on the door.

The door opened, and State Officer Perry Fletcher was framed in
the light from within. One eye roamed the dark, mountainous
horizon while the other regarded Bearhide Judson with suspicion.
The officer inserted a deft fingernail between wide-spaced buck
teeth to dislodge a morsel of the meal he had been eating. He was in
field uniform.

"Well," he remarked, looking at the long slicker, "must be that
the rainy season's set in early in the high country."

The mountain man eyed the five-pronged star adorning the chest
of the lawman. Bearhide's bulging Adam's apple moved rapidly up
and down beneath the wrinkled hide on his leathery neck. He
rubbed a rubberized sleeve across a long nose, and the angered
eloquence within him gave way to what is generally known as the
bull horrors.

"Please, Mr. Fletcher," he gulped. "That elk—that is—yuh
know—he's plumb ruinin' our corn crop!"

"Well?"

"Maybe—uh—I thunk maybe yuh could do somethin'."

"You mean Ol' Jack, the bachelor elk?"

Bearhide twisted the black sombrero in both hands. "Yeah," he
said hopefully.

Officer Perry Fletcher assumed his favorite stance, with feet
spread and knotted fists jammed against his hips. "Look," he
snapped, "that elk is property of the state. You touch one hair on
his hide and I'll have you back in the jailhouse—where you belong
anyway!"

Cold fear was clutching the vitals of Bearhide Judson, but not from the tirade of the blustering game warden. Bearhide's eyes were fastened on a huge, baldheaded man, bellied up to the table inside the house, stowing away great fragments of meat that looked and smelled like venison. It was "Mash" Merritt, the revenue man, known and feared by every illegal still operator from Phoenix to Seattle.

"Yes, sir!" Bearhide mumbled, and backed away.

Bearhide wheeled the car around in the street and headed up-grade for Saddle Gap without stopping for new pants or Charlie's sugar. His booted foot sprung the floorboard downward.

The county jail was one thing—and a Federal penitentiary was another. Bearhide's heart pounded out an accompaniment to the clanking connecting rods, for Mash Merritt could smell a can in operation for five miles, according to report.

At the ranch, he doused car lights and drove into the brush across the road from the shanty. He threw the slicker in the back seat of the steaming car and shuffled into the brushy canyon below.

There was a sliver of a moon off in the west, and the night wind made the trees uneasy. There was no other sound except an occasional clink of a spur rowel. The darkness was no handicap for Bearhide Judson. This trip was always made at night, and he usually carried a sack of corn or sugar. On a densely timbered spur ridge within a quarter of a mile from the highway, he paused and tapped the root of a towering snag with a short limb. He forced his way into a brush-pile. A spring bubbled in the darkness nearby.

He encountered a rough lumber door, stepped through into warm darkness. "Pine Cone!" he whispered.

"Hokay!" Charlie Pine Cone struck a match and applied it to a lantern hanging from the tree-roots that formed a roof to the enclosure. The Indian was stripped to the waist, and sweat stood out on his fat, brown body. He opened the draft on a glowing firebox.

"Injun," he observed, "wear pants like that all time— Where in hell is sugar?"

Water, from the spring outside, dripped in a washtub. Bearhide slumped to a block of wood in front of the fire. Charlie Pine Cone busied himself around a brimming vat beside a jumble of copper contrivances centered over the bright fire. Bearhide tried to calm a leaping Adam's apple.

"Pine Cone," he said ominously, "Mash Merritt is at Perry

Fletcher's place. There is hell tuh pay—not only does that game warden say lay off the elk, but we got tuh start dodgin' th' revenue boys!''

''Him no can see smoke from road,'' Charlie suggested hopefully. ''An' him never smell mash around here yet—mebbe hokay?''

Bearhide paced the dirt floor. ''I think,'' he suggested, ''that it'd be safe tuh operate th' factory tuhnight—them stool-pigeons won't feel like workin' after that meal. That way, we could have enough tuh fill this last order an' could shut down for a while. But that still leaves that red-eyed elk on th' loose tuh tear hell outa th' corn patch, pester my mare an' run me flat-footed.''

Charlie Pine Cone flavored the mix with a little tobacco juice. ''No law,'' he grinned, '''bout *scarin'* elks to death.''

A speculative gleam came to the watery eyes of Bearhide Judson. ''Warhoop,'' he said, ''yuh have just used yer yawp for somethin' besides soupin' tobaccy. I'm goin' tuh set a bait o' likker-soaked corn for that elk, an' when he gets good an' loop-legged I'll let 'im chase me or somethin' until he bashes his brains out agin' a tree!''

''Good idee,'' Charlie grunted. ''Only have no likker. Just fired up.''

''Then, by golly, I'll use mash! I'll mix green corn with part of it—he'll get th' idee from that an' eat th' rest raw. Whilst you're finishin' up here, I'll head for th' Gap an' set th' bait. You can come up later afore th' fun starts.''

Burdened with two wire-bailed five-gallon cans of mash, Bearhide made his cautious way to the corn patch, where he filled a sack half-full of tender corn ears and tied it to his belt.

There were two good reasons for him to scramble into the underbrush as cars or trucks approached. First, a natural modesty urged him to keep his frayed posterior from the public eye; and there was always a silly inclination of night-riding lawmen to make a fuss over any illegal materials—such as mash.

Choosing a vantage point in the underbrush at the Gap, he dropped his load and rested a weary back against the rough bark of a tall fir. Down on the other slope, half a mile away, he could see the illuminated quarantine building and the busy agents prying through the luggage of bus passengers for contraband agricultural products. Ol' Jack wasn't in sight.

''Oh well,'' the lanky mountaineer remarked, dumping the corn in the darkness beside him, "he'll be showin' up any time." He chuckled inwardly at the cleverness of his scheming.

There was an appetizing odor about the tender corn as he broke it in small pieces, dipped it in a sour-smelling can and returned it to the sack. The thought ran through his mind that he had missed his supper. He tried a bite of green corn.

"Not bad," he muttered, shifting unprotected hip joints where they were contacting the mossy ground beneath. "But I'm a swivel-necked hoot owl if it don't taste better dipped in corn-squeezin's fust! I'll just make out a meal whilst I'm fixin' for Ol' Jack."

At length there were only three ears of corn on the ground beside him. These he dipped and saved out for dessert. He arose. "Lemme see now," he breathed. "I'll dump th' corn out on that flat just across th' road, an' set th' cans alongside. Ol' Jack'll get th' corn fust, an' by then he'll have a taste for th' raw makin's. Shucks, it even tastes good tuh me. . . . Then I'll climb a tree an' wait for th' fun. Hope Charlie gets here in time."

There was a rattle of hoofs and an angry snort down toward the quarantine station as a bus roared through. Bearhide hurried to get loaded. The three ears of corn he was saving for dessert he put on his bald head beneath his floppy black hat. He noted that one five-gallon can was half-empty and the other about a third gone. "Doggone," he mumbled. "I must o' spilled some outa that one can—I ain't been usin' on it at all."

He lurched from the underbrush into the dark roadway, with the sack in one hand and the two cans in the other.

"Funny thing," Bearhide Judson said aloud. "I can see leetle balls o' fire dartin' ever' which way, an' my ears feel as big as a mule's—an' besides that, my thinker is all cluttered up with worryin' 'bout what happened to that can o' makin's which is supposed tuh be plumb full!"

The graveled shoulder of the highway felt strange to his scuff-booted feet, and the cool wind in the Gap caressing an unprotected rear brought a twinge of shame. The little balls of fire he was seeing broke for an instant into a sheet of flame, and Bearhide Judson swayed forward and crashed like a tall fir tree.

There was a jangle of dropped cans, and he felt the three ears of corn fall from under his hat; there was a numb sensation of his whiskered Adam's apple pushed against roadside gravel and his long midsection resting on the corn sack. Then he knew no more.

One eternity passed and another one was well started when Bearhide Judson lifted the lid from one weary eye. There was an impression of much light, the amused rumble of many voices, and directly in front of him, between two empty five-gallon tins, was the nightmarish likeness of a sprawled mossy-faced bull elk, high horns and all, with closed eyes and protruding tongue. In Bearhide's ears was a pulsating, dreamy rumble that sounded like idling truck motors. In his nostrils was the stench of burned diesel oil and—of all things—sour mash!

"Remind me, Pine Cone," he mumbled, "never tuh use any o' that stuff agin till it's at least three days old—I'm havin' th' darnedest night ever. Dreamin' about Ol' Jack—an' there's awful noises in my noggin an' I can't keep th' covers on my hind end!"

There had never been a time, during long association, that Charlie Pine Cone had manifested much sympathy, but there was always at least a grunt of acknowledgment when Bearhide complained. Instead a strange voice said, "They called the cops from the bug station—maybe they can figure this deal out."

Bearhide Judson opened both eyes and raised a gravel-dented Adam's apple from the ground. "Pine Cone!" he shrilled, before the full significance of his surroundings broke over fast-returning consciousness. And then he said, "Great gobs o' rang-tang sign— who said *cops?*"

Ol' Jack, the bachelor elk, heaved a weary sigh. He opened a dull eye that more or less focused on the tongue that extended at right angles to the side of his head. He tried to retrieve the dirt-spattered member and succeeded in flopping it across a gray nose. The other eye opened and regarded the rebellious tongue from that angle. A second later his range of vision extended another two feet to the supine body of Bearhide Judson, his arch rival. Bearhide was draped over a lumpy sack, big spurs sprouting skyward and a disgraceful expanse of exposed anatomy facing the same general direction. Fury glinted in Ol' Jack's crossed eyes.

Bearhide's equilibrium was fast returning. Up the road, approaching along a line of parked headlights, he recognized Perry Fletcher and Federal Officer Mash Merritt. Firm of jaw and officious in bearing, they marched through the gathered travelers.

Fear gripped Bearhide Judson. He knew a tight when he saw it. His Adam's apple quivered as he looked around. By reflected light from parked trucks and cars, he could see the cans were licked clean—but there was that sack beneath him, half-full of damning evidence. He moved fast.

"Elk," he growled, "yuh got me intuh this mess—yuh can get me out!"

Bearhide came to his feet, twisted the wire handle of one can into the now twitching tail of the awakening animal. Then he grabbed up the sack of corn and straddled the struggling bull elk.

"Come on, yuh corn-soaked bum," Bearhide gritted, slapping the animal on the rump with a free hand. "Make elk tracks—fast!"

There was a wild moment when the approaching lawmen broke into a run, yelling and drawing their guns—and when Ol' Jack's legs were too unstable for locomotion. Then the can banged him on the hocks. Bearhide let three loads go from his .45 and raked his mount from withers to flanks with big-rowelled spurs.

Ol' Jack's first jump took them into the brush and threw gravel in all directions. Bearhide Judson dug in with determined spurs, held on to the corn sack with one hand and used the other to gather up a fold of coarse elk-hide. Ol' Jack chose to make elk tracks in a wide circle through thick brush.

Then there was no more brush stinging Bearhide's face. Between the bobbing elk horns before him he could see the quarantine station approaching at a surprising rate of speed. For a moment there was pistol-fire from back up the highway, and then an earth-shaking explosion from the same general direction.

The white posts indicating the state line flashed by before the quarantine road barricade loomed before them. There was no change of tempo in the thundering hoofs and the clanking tin can. Ol' Jack took the barricade in stride, leaping high and far. Bearhide went somewhat higher, turned over once with a despairing yell and came to earth on the sack of corn. There was the fading clatter of tin on elk hocks for a few moments, and then silence.

Bearhide gathered his wits and the sack of twice-mashed corn and was making for the brush when an angry voice stopped him. He turned to face a quarantine official.

"I thought," the uniformed man said, "that I knew of every way of sneaking contraband into this state—but this is something new. Give me that sack!"

"Yes, sir," Bearhide mumbled, surrendering the sack and moving in a wide circle to where he could back up against the white building. The official carried the sack at arm's length to a small room at the other end of a long shed. There was a glow in the sky beyond Saddle Gap, and the headlights of a fast-moving car with a howling siren bore down on Bearhide.

"This looks like th' end of a glorious but unprofitable career," Bearhide mumbled. "At least they won't have nothin' on Charlie Pine Cone. He can hold our leetle household tuhgether until I get outa th' pen."

There was a grinding of brakes, a door flung open on a sedan and Officer Perry Fletcher stepped forth, alone.

"You," he said through clenched teeth, "are under arrest. Where is that sack of corn mash you're supposed to be carrying?"

"Th' inspector—" Bearhide faltered.

"That's fine!" Officer Fletcher smiled. "We've always had the finest kind of cooperation from these lads. Even though they're not particularly enforcement conscious, they're good at seizing and withholding evidence for police officers!"

Bearhide lifted his eyes to petition any Deity that would be interested in interceding for a repentant mountaineer with an evil past. Nothing happened, and he removed his gun-belt with dejected hands and exposed his wrists for encircling steel. The sound of the metallic ratchets shook him to the tips of sockless toes in shaking boots.

A door slammed at the far end of the quarantine building, and a beaming agent approached them. "Hello, Officer Fletcher!" he smiled.

"Where," asked Officer Fletcher, "is that—?"

"You know," interrupted the quarantine agent, "your prisoner here had the vilest contraband I ever saw. It even smelled worse when I put it in the incinerator."

"In the where?" Officer Fletcher almost screamed.

"In the incinerator—whatever it was, it was too smelly to be legal. We burn all contraband!"

Bearhide's shoulders straightened against the building. Bushy eyebrows arched, and he extended the handcuffs to be removed. "Looks tuh me, Mr. Fletcher," he remarked, "that there's durned little evidence tuh go on."

"Shut up!" the lawman snapped. "And get in the car. While we were back on the mountain, Federal Officer Merritt smelled mash and found a trail of it leading back toward your ranch. He probably has your still located and Charlie Pine Cone in custody by now!"

Bearhide slumped in the seat beside the officer. "Now," he muttered to himself, "I can see why that one can o' mash wasn't clear full. Was leakin' all th' way from th' factory up tuh th' Gap. Pore ol' Charlie Pine Cone—he's never been in jail more'n a week at a time. McNeil's Island will kill him."

A forestry truck zoomed past them as they rolled through Saddle Gap. "From here," the officer remarked, "it looks like there's a timber fire close to your ranch."

"Probably burn us out," Bearhide observed mournfully. "But there won't be nobody ther tuh mourn th' loss—not even Ol' Jack."

At the ranch gate, the headlights picked up Mash Merritt and Charlie Pine Cone in the glow of a forest fire in the canyon below, already confined to a twenty-acre area by fast-responding for-esters. Bearhide puzzled at the unmanacled wrists of Charlie Pine Cone. Moreover, there was nothing in the way the round-faced Indian turned and drenched a headlight on the police car with tobacco juice that indicated he harbored anything but gross indif-ference for lawmen of all types.

The door jerked open on Bearhide's side of the sedan, and Mash Merritt leaned a big body inside. "Give this hillbilly his gun," he rasped, "and get 'im out of those irons. And let's get moving before I blow up!"

When the two taillights were gone around the first bend down the mountain, Bearhide sought a gatepost for support and conceal-ment. "Pine Cone," he confided, "things is movin' too fast for me. Why ain't we headed for a big stony house?"

"No case," Charlie Pine Cone grinned. "Me hear big pow-wow in Gap. Think you havin' fun with elk. Build heap big fire under boiler, start up to look. Fire too big. Blow boiler up an' factory all over mountain. Rest burn up."

Bearhide Judson sat down suddenly against the gatepost. "Pine Cone," he said firmly, "right after I corner one o' them fire-fighters an' take his pants—we're goin' tuh embark on a life o' absolute honesty."

"You bet," Charlie Pine Cone agreed with enthusiasm. "Swipe some cattle. Start ranchin'."

THE END

By MURRAY LEINSTER

"Pull yore gun!"
howled Teetotal.

TEETOTAL AND THE
SIX-GUN SPIRITS

THE LIGHTS of Dos Almas glowed yellow in the moonlight, far below and far away. Teetotal Coombs came to a spot where they could be seen clearly. He spat. He halted until Suzy, the burro, ambled placidly up in his wake and stopped within arm's reach. Suzy was small and meek and of a placid disposition. Teetotal Coombs was small and bristling and truculent in looks and habit alike. He scowled down at the dully twinkling lights, small amber jewels in a world all silver beneath an incandescent moon. He jerked a horny thumb at the tiny settlement. Suzy flicked her large ears forward.

"Dos Almas," said Teetotal scornfully. "Huh!"

Suzy blinked.

"Sodom," said Teetotal, disparagingly, "an' Gomorrah! An' licker." He reached out a gnarled hand. He extracted a bottle from a convenient place in Suzy's pack. He held it up to the moon to estimate its contents. He tilted it toward the stars. The last drop flowed down his throat, and he tossed it over his shoulder and raised a solemn hand in Suzy's view.

"Nary another drop," said Teetotal firmly, "as long as we' in town! You heah that, Suzy?"

Suzy flicked one ear.

"It's bad stuff," said Teetotal sourly. "It's pizen in the mouth that takes away a fella's brains. In town, a fella needs brains if he's goin' to play poker an' git another grubstake. But out in the hills he's got to do somethin' to numb his brains or he'll quit prospectin'. Come along! Git movin'!"

He began the descent toward Dos Almas. Above, the sky was a sea of shimmering stars, in which the full moon floated grandly. Uneven rocks cast sharp black shadows on the earth, and an occasional cactus or yucca threw an angular or a foleated pattern on the sloping ground which slanted toward the little cowtown. There was a vast stillness. The small pugnacious figure of Teetotal Coombs and the rotund placid figure of Suzy the burro were the only moving objects in all the world.

Teetotal grumbled and grunted to himself as the town grew slowly nearer. He had been prospecting in the Borrachas for three years now and was about ready to call it a job. There were at least two reasons. One was that he had prospected every likely spot readily reached from Dos Almas as a headquarters. The other was that the poker games in the Deadline Saloon weren't what they used to be. Time was when he could amble into town at sundown, turn Suzy into the Acme Corral with a mountain of fodder before her, stuff himself full of town-cooked ham and eggs, and win a three-months' grubstake in poker in the Deadline Saloon, all within a matter of hours. Once he had his grubstake, he'd quit the game, retire scornfully to the Acme Corral, and sleep on baled hay no more than ten yards from Suzy. He'd be the first customer at the first general store to open in the morning. One more meal of town-cooked ham and eggs, and one stop for a supply of bottled liquid refreshment, and he was off to the hills again without having touched a drop of intoxicating liquid within the limits of the town. His first drink came solemnly, out of town.

Now, though, plodding truculently over alkali-dust-covered terrain, he snorted his low opinion of Dos Almas in these later days.

"Ain't worth a dinged whim-wham," he said disgustedly to Suzy. "Never see such close-fisted poker players in m'life. Took me two hull days to git a grubstake last time, and oncet I was twenty dollars in the hole. They ain't got no sportin' blood—got to be a passel of danged business men!"

He snorted. He had spent twenty-odd years as a prospector, and had a vast disrespect for persons of smaller views, even though his own labors had netted him no more than Suzy, the tools of his trade, the clothes he stood in, and three golden double-eagles as capital for the poker game in which to win his next grubstake.

"It's enough," he said darkly, "to drive a fella to drink. But I told you, Suzy, that I won't take nary a drink whilest we' in town. No, suh! Cagier those fellas get playin' poker, the more brains I got to have to git theah money. Don't worry!"

The first of the town's buildings loomed ahead. Even from the end of Dos Almas's almost solitary street, though, there was an oddity in the atmosphere. The town was not deserted. There were more than the usual number of patiently drooping cow-ponies at the hitching-racks. There were two or three times the normal number of buckboards in sight. But the street was empty of human beings. Marching challengingly down the dusty way, he saw saloons open to right and left, and not a soul but a lonely bartender or two. A general store was open, but in it—which should have been the town's busiest emporium—he saw only a single clerk looking wistfully down the street toward the Deadline Saloon.

Curiosity grew in him, and therefore he snorted scornfully. He turned into the Acme Corral. It was full of visiting horseflesh, but there was no one in attendance. He snorted more loudly. He put Suzy in a separate small box-pen, normally reserved for skittish or bad-tempered animals. He dumped her pack and himself heaped up a mountainous pile of hay before her.

"Feed up," he said sternly. "Put some flesh on y'bones."

He watched her begin placidly to eat. It was then the regular schedule for him to stuff himself with town-cooked ham and eggs, but he was too curious. As he reached the street again, he saw a stream of humans moving tumultuously from the Deadline Saloon to the Black Jack. They moved as if with a common purpose and with much hilarity.

He marched bristling to the Deadline. He had taken all his grubstakes for the past three years from the poker tables in the Deadline. Now he thrust his way in and stopped, incredulous. Very plainly, the place had been full a mere few moments since. The air was thick with smoke. The bar was lined with glasses. Discarded cigarettes on the floor still sent up thin trickles of smoke. But there were just two humans in the place—two bartenders, unhappily clearing away the glassware. There wasn't another living soul in sight.

Teetotal went up to the bar. It would have been only courtesy to order a drink, but he bristled.

"Huh!" he said truculently. "What's happened to everybody?"

A bartender said, "H'llo, Teetotal. The town's gone crazy."

"Crazy?" snorted Teetotal. "No more'n a skip an' a jump from normal. What druv it crazy?"

"Fella come in," said the bartender, "with some ore that'd make yore eyes bug out. Look!"

He lifted down a white quartz rock from a place of honor behind the bar. He placed it before Teetotal. Teetotal jumped. It was gold ore. But such gold ore! It was thickly studded with flecks of metallic yellow. There was a lump of actual golden metal plainly visible. Let the quartz rot away and there would be a sizable nugget from this one lump of stone. It was incredibly rich. It was preposterously rich!

"Wheah'd this come from?" demanded Teetotal fiercely.

"That's what the town's goin' crazy tryin' to find out," said the bartender resignedly. "This fella, name of Lucky Kane, he comes in an' says exultant that he's found the great-gran'mammy of all mother lodes an' he's got the ore to prove it. An' he has! There's a hunka it. The whole town's busy right now tryin' to get him drunk so's he'll talk."

Teetotal Coombs jumped again. He seemed practically rocked back on his heels.

"Lucky Kane?" he demanded furiously. "A tall lean drink o'

water with pinto whiskers? Prospectin' with a sway-backed hawss name of Gallagher? Fella looks mournful an' pious, like butter wouldn't melt in his mouth at midday? Lucky Kane?"

"That's him," said the bartender.

"It's a lie!" bellowed Teetotal, truculently. "He ain't found no mother lode! When I was young an' foolish I was partners with him one trip! He drunk my licker on the sly, et four men's grub, an' wound up cheatin' me outa half of a four-thousan'-dollar claim! He ain't found no mother lode! He's too durned lazy to bend over an' pick up a ore sample! It's a lie!"

He breathed heavily, glaring. He picked up the rock again. He studied it, fury exuding from each separate bristling whisker. He slammed it down again.

"Y'want to know?" he demanded in hot passion. "That there ore's from the Li'l Giant. I know that ore—it's from that freak pocket Tom Casey found, runnin' ten thousan' a ton! Kane got these samples from highgraders an' he's—" He stamped his foot. "An' this heah dod-whizzled pack o' ding-danged fools are quittin' poker-playin' to git him drunk! Y'durn tootin' this town's gone crazy—wheah they now?"

"Over to the Black Jack," said the bartender. "He's gettin' kinda softened up. Was talkin' about lettin' his friends in on his strike, so's he'd have good fellas around to git drunk with when his mine started workin'. Y'never see so many fellas tryin' to prove they was good fellas to get drunk with in y'life! An' one fella says the Black Jack's got some snakehead licker that beats ours, so he went over an' the whole crowd follered."

Teetotal Coombs seethed. He yanked his battered hat down on his head.

"They'll come back!" he said bitterly. "After I show up that thievin' bow-whingled jackass for the four-flusher he is, they'll come back an' play poker quiet like sensible folks. You'll see!"

He marched ominously out of the door, so completely filled with fury that the suicidal aspect of one man trying to undeceive a whole town bent on being fooled did not occur to him. For a matter of seconds he was out in the bright moonlight, a small and bellicose figure stamping down a dusty street between rows of false-fronted buildings. Then he turned in to the Black Jack and saw the booted legs of men crowding it to the very doors. Teetotal Coombs flung himself at the opening, forcing his way in by the simple process of shoving other men aside. He created a very considerable ripple.

"Lemme git through, dang-whizzle it! I got to git at that goat-faced jackass that says he's found th' mother lode! Lemme through!"

He bored at the solid wall of men. He heaved. He hauled, he squirmed and writhed and butted his way through a compact mass of humanity, most of it too tall to see the top of his head beneath the shoulders of the rest. As he practically forced a tunnel, he emitted outraged roarings.

"Git outa my way, dod-wham it! I'm gonna scorch them pinto whiskers! I'm gonna make 'im eat his own gall! I'm gonna—"

He burst into the open—a clear space no more than five feet across, respectfully kept clear about the long, lean, mournful and falsely benevolent figure of Lucky Kane. The lanky prospector's features beamed at those about him. His eyes were very slightly glazed. They dropped to the bristling, rage-purpled face of Teetotal Coombs, grew startled and scared for an instant, then glazed again. Lucky Kane beamed vacantly.

"You," shrilled Teetotal, beside himself with fury, "you four-flushin', thievin', prevaricatin' hunka buzzard-meat! What' you mean takin' folks away from theah poker playin' an' sensible drinkin' to listen to yore shenanigans? You got that there ore from highgraders outa Tom Casey's Li'l Giant! You didn't find no mother lode! You' a lyin', thievin' golly-whoopus, an' you' goin' to admit it right heah an' now or—"

Lucky Kane looked mournfully down upon the raging small Teetotal. He hiccoughed.

"M'old friend, Teetotal Coombs!" he said sentimentally. He raised a finger and seemed to brush away a tear. "M'old partner! We fussed in the old days, Teetotal, but I forgive you! I hit it rich now, Teetotal! I found the great-gran'mammy of all the mother lodes there is. Ain't nobody I'd ruther share my good luck with than m'old pal Teetotal! Put 'er there, Teetotal!"

Teetotal howled with fury.

"You' a ding-danged gol-swizzled liar!" he raged. He reached up a horny fist to shake it under Lucky Kane's nose. "That theah ore's from the Li'l Giant! You ain't found nothin'! All you want is for folks to git you drunk an' pay 'tention to you instead o' poker-playin'!"

Lucky Kane drooped. He seemed deeply, maudlinly hurt.

"Have a drink with me, Teetotal?" he asked pathetically. "You have drink with me an' I'll let you in on my strike. You'n all yore friends. These fellas, they my friends, but ol' friends are best. You have drink with me an' I'll let you in on my strike!"

"Pull yore gun!" howled Teetotal, "or I'll let daylight into you anyways, you—"

Men fell upon him. Lucky Kane had come into town a bare three hours before. For three hours enthusiastic and painstaking efforts had been under way to get him to the talkative stage, where he would tell at least the approximate location from which he had taken that completely incredible ore. He was visibly softening up. Any minute now he might grow confidential. And nobody would let anything happen to Lucky Kane while the secret of the great-grandmother of all mother lodes was his alone. Firm and sinewy hands seized Teetotal. He fought like a maniac, howling his wrath. Then half a dozen men held him while Lucky Kane regarded him mournfully.

Lucky Kane raised a visibly wavering arm.

"No frien' of mine," he said with dignity, "is gonna hurt m'old friend Tectotal. Gonna make Teetotal my partner 'gain. Teetotal, you have drink with me—"

Teetotal practically foamed at the mouth.

"I'll see y'—"

"Somebody," said Lucky Kane pleadingly, "somebody make m' old friend Teetotal have a drink with me." He appeared on the verge of tears. "Anybody's my friend, make Teetotal have a drink with me."

Willing voices cried, "I'm y'friend, Lucky! Best friend you got!" There was a milling uproar. At its end, Teetotal was down on the floor, spread-eagled and roaring furiously, while Lucky Kane looked on with all the appearance of tearful drunkenness. But Teetotal could see a wholly cold and calculating gleam in his eye. The little man was in a soul-searing fury. He bellowed unintelligibly. Someone bent over him with a drink. He clamped his jaws, his eyes glaring. Somebody held his nose. Reluctantly he opened his mouth. The drink went in. He gulped and roared again.

Lucky Kane beamed.

"My frien's," he said happily. "That's what he needs. Give'm another. M'old friend Teetotal! Don't never drink in town, only out in th' hills! Tell you what, fellas! Teetotal gits drunk with me an' we

all go partners in my strike, Teetotal an' all! 'Nough for everybody!
All of us git rich! Get'm drunk an' we'll draw up th' papers an' all
go stake out some more claims on that lode I foun'—''

Tumult approaching bedlam arose. Teetotal Coombs stayed on
the floor, firmly held. There were drinks all around. His nose was
held and he had his. There were more drinks and more drinks and
more. The town of Dos Almas saw, at last, the prospect of very
great happiness for everybody. There was not a man in town who
did not either have a horse ready saddled or one in mind to be
saddled the instant the location of Lucky Kane's strike was re-
vealed.

Festivity soared. Never was any Roman emperor more toasted
or fêted. Never was any nabob so flattered or so openly admired.
When Lucky, presently, grew indignant with Teetotal's howling
obstinacy even after repeated drinks of the best snakehead whiskey
to be had, his devoted followers shared his scorn. And when
Lucky, weaving markedly on his feet, announced sadly that he was
going back to the Deadline and draw up partnership papers, reveal-
ing the location of the strike to all his friends, the surging mob
which followed him practically trampled all over the prostrate form
of Teetotal.

In seconds, it seemed, the Black Jack was empty. For minutes
after, Teetotal lay still, grinding his teeth. Then he sat up.

"Listen heah!" he said ferociously to the two bartenders who
alone remained in the abruptly emptied saloon. "Did I heah that
bob-whingled jackass say that he was gonna make a partnership
an' everybody that kicked in fifty dollars was gonna be a partner?"

The fatter bartender looked longingly at the door.

"That's what y'heard, Teetotal."

"Huh!" said Teetotal dourly. He got heavily to his feet. "Th'
thievin' bothallifer! He ain't got the morals of a house fly!"

He hiccoughed. He started for the door. At the door he paused to
say sternly, if a trifle dizzily, "You fellas know I don't never take a
drink in town!"

The lean bartender said wearily, "Yeah, Teetotal."

"This time I couldn't help m'self," said Teetotal. He ground his
teeth. "Them ding-danged fools made me break my principles.
But—" he hiccoughed again and admitted generously— "it was
right good licker."

He went out the door. He moved a trifle unsteadily down the

street. He turned in the Dos Almas Cafe. He banged on the counter until the proprietor woke up. He filled himself with ham and eggs. As he ate, the slight vagueness of his manner diminished and disappeared. He was cold sober and quite comfortable when he heard the clattering of hoofs in the dust outside. He grunted and shoveled a huge mouthful between his teeth. There were more clatterings. There was tumult. There was a thunder of horses' hoofs upon the earth outside. He turned in his chair and looked out the window. The bright moonlight showed chaos. There was a racing, straining, hell-for-leather stampede of mounted men all headed in the same direction. Buckboards joined it. Dust rose in a monster, strangling cloud. Men ran frenziedly to their mounts tied to the hitching-racks. They mounted and spurred out into the blinding fog of stirred-up alkali dust.

The proprietor of the Dos Almas Cafe stared goggle-eyed.

"What's all this?" he asked blankly.

"Dos Almas," said Teetotal, snorting, "has gone crazy. Just a skip an' a jump from th' usual, though. Lucky Kane got drunk enough to tell 'em what they wanted to know."

He ate stolidly, while every piece of horseflesh in town headed off to the northward, until Dos Almas was empty, deserted, silent and still, and until the thick, impenetrable pall of dust had begun very vaguely to settle.

Then Teetotal Coombs paid for his meal. He went out into the fading moonlit dust-cloud, filled to repletion. He strolled through the peaceful, empty street until he came to the Acme Corral. There were just two animals left in it. One was Suzy, his own burro, still placidly gorging herself on the huge pile of provender he had placed for her. The other was a swaybacked gray. Teetotal knew the horse. It belonged to Lucky Kane.

Teetotal rolled a smoke and waited. Lucky Kane might, of course, be snoring loudly and realistically after having given away the secret of his lode. Or he might be weeping maudlin tears because all his new-found friends had deserted him once they knew the secret of his find. But Teetotal did not think so. He waited, his whiskers bristling. He watched the swaybacked horse.

Presently he grunted. Gallagher, the horse, favored one foot. Still later, moving, the horse limped noticeably. Teetotal Coombs puffed angrily. He went resentfully over to the gaunt, sagging animal.

"That ding-whizzled jackass don't even take care o' you!" he said wrathfully. "Gimme that foot."

He lifted the favored hoof. He felt around the shoe with a calloused forefinger. There was a stone caught there, a sharp one. Teetotal spat wrathfully and hauled out an over-sized jackknife. There was a hook among its many blades. He got the stone out of the horse's hoof. He was about to heave it away when something made him look at it in the moonlight. A moment later he struck a match. His acid muttering stopped short.

He smoked and smoked, concealing the glowing end of his successive cigarettes. A sea of stars shimmered overhead. The round full moon floated downward toward the western hills. Then Lucky Kane came sneaking furtively into the corral. He carried a duffel-bag and he moved through the moonlight toward the swaybacked gray.

His first knowledge of the presence of Teetotal was a gun muzzle against his spine.

"H'ist 'em!" said Teetotal grimly.

Lucky heisted. Teetotal took his gun and heaved it away. He turned the tall lean prospector about.

"How much'd you git?" he demanded scornfully. "How many dumb fools paid y' fifty dollars to be partners in that theah mother lode o' yours before you told 'em wheah to go hunt for it?"

Lucky Kane swallowed. He was as sober as Teetotal himself. His capacity had always been great—as Teetotal had bitter reason to know—and he'd had a motive for seeming drunker than he was.

"You come in town," said Teetotal savagely, "with them high-graders' samples an' let 'em try to git you drunk. You sold 'em a bill o' goods. They paid you off to be sent on a wild goose chase. How much'd you git?"

"I—I dunno," gasped Lucky Kane. "Teetotal! Don't kill me—I never done nothin' to you!"

"Nothin'," rasped Teetotal, "excep' filin' on a partnership claim in y'own name instead of partners, an' sellin' it for four thousan' dollars an' goin' off an' drinkin' it all up by y'self! Wheah's my two thousan' dollars?"

"I—guess I got that much t'night," panted Lucky in terror. "They were pourin' it in my lap. Y-yeah, I guess I got about that much. But—"

"I'll take it," said Teetotal grimly. "Whatever 'tis. If there's over, it'll be interest. Gimme—an' I'll take them ore samples, too, so's you won't go swindlin' other fellas outa money that they oughta lose happy playin' poker!"

He took what Kane handed him. Then he searched him, and the duffel-bag. He was thorough. He had two thousand and fifty dollars when he was through.

"Now git!" he commanded.

His eyes were baleful. Lucky Kane stumbled away. Then he said in a sickish panic, "I —got to go a long ways, Teetotal, an' travel fast. An' you took ever' cent I got. Teetotal—"

Teetotal Coombs spat. Then he said derisively, "Tell you what I'll do. You ain't never told the truth in y'life, Lucky. Never once. But you break yore rule—like you made those fellas break mine about not drinkin' in town—an' I'll grubstake you fifty dollars worth. Remember, now—I know which way you come in town. I was trailin' you. You tell me which way you come to Dos Almas an' if y'break y'lifetime rule an' tell the truth I'll grubstake you!"

Lucky stammered. Then he told.

"T'ain't enough," said Teetotal acidly. "Remember, I was foller-in' yore trail! Wheah'd y'hawss go lame?"

Lucky weakly, bewilderedly, gave details. Teetotal listened with every appearance of suspicion. At the end he said with every evidence of reluctance.

"A'right, It musta hurt to tell th' truth! Heah's yore stake. Now git!"

He stood, bristling, until the man and the swaybacked gray horse had departed into the fading moonlight. They would travel fast, and necessarily they would travel far.

Teetotal sat and smoked until the dawn. He was the first customer of the first general store to open up. He paused for bottles of liquid refreshment and for a fill-up on town-cooked ham and eggs. Then he headed out of town.

Two miles out, he looked back. Dos Almas was barely visible, a drowsy, sprawling small settlement in the morning sun. Teetotal extracted a bottle from Suzy's pack. He took a drink.

"Nary a drink in town," he said firmly, "of my own free will. But anyways, we grubstaked even if they was crazy an' not playin' poker, an'—h'm—"

He pulled a small piece of rock from his pocket. He regarded it fondly. It was gold ore. Not like the ore from the Little Giant mine, but very, very satisfactory ore just the same. And he knew where Lucky Kane's horse had picked it up.

He took one more drink and replaced the ore sample. He took a last look back at Dos Almas.

"Sodom," he said caustically, "an' Gomorrah! An' licker!" Then he said less disparagingly, "But it was pretty good stuff they poured in me at th' Black Jack. Come along, Suzy! Git goin'!"

THE END

Townsmen came
out, carrying
stretchers. . . .

Flatwheel Draws the Line

By TOM W. BLACKBURN

As bull-headed and tempera-
mental as the old iron teakettle
that drew his narrow-gauge train,
Flatwheel Clancy was double
damned if he'd risk hauling gold

bullion — but when it came
braving Black Canyon at f
flood with a cargo of wound
men, that was a different matt

CLANCY stalked up the street of Powder City, rocking on his heels with the ire of an Irishman prodded beyond endurance. Muckers and mill men glanced hastily at his face and gave him room as he passed. He plowed through the door of the Fall River Railroad office, kicked open a railed gate, and sailed into the private office of Samuel Smiddy.

Smiddy was a big man, both in body and importance. He was at once the president, board of directors, dispatcher, and agent for the one-train, narrow-gauge Fall River line. Smiddy looked up, saw Clancy's face, and began talking with hasty mollification.

"Now, Flatwheel, we're not starting this again!" he protested. "Sit down. Have a cigar. Go buy a drink on me. But don't give me no argument!"

"Argument!" Clancy yelped. "Why, you ding-busted, dad-gummed, dod-rotted old porcupine, I ought to bust your head with a crown wrench! I just seen my freight manifest. And what's on it? Bullion again—a whole damned chest of it!"

"It's freight, Flatwheel—" Smiddy offered placatingly.

"Freight, hell! It's suicide—practically murder—with me an' Lucy the goats! For ten years me an' Lucy've been haulin' supplies into this be-deviled, be-damned, be-thundered camp. Grub, machinery, chunks of iron that wasn't made to roll over the cock-eyed roadbed you put your sloppy track on. Miners in and miners out. We hauled raw ore when there wasn't nothin' here but holes in the ground. We hauled concentrates when you put in your blasted stamp-mill. But we got to draw a line. And bullion is where we draw it!"

Clancy was seeing red. The pleasant warmth of a shot of whiskey from O'Sullivan's bar was running commandingly through him. He was riled.

He hated bullion, and Smiddy knew that. He had reason to hate it, and Smiddy knew that reason, too. This was the second shipment of smelted metal turned out by the new community reduction plant the mines of Powder City had installed. The first had subjected Clancy—and his beloved engine, Lucy—to a harrowing experience.

A carload of raw ore wasn't good booty. Neither were bins of concentrate. Saddle bags didn't come big enough to carry any profit away from the robbery of a train carrying either one. But bullion was different.

Black Canyon, half the way down through the hills to Denver, was a bad place. Narrow, crooked, and Smiddy's roadbed had about been stripped of ballast by the storms and floods of past years. Right in the middle of the worst stretch of the canyon, divers gentry had dropped a tree across the rails and sat down to wait for Lucy, her engineer, and the golden freight in the single little car.

The memory was yet painful. Lucy didn't want to stop. Neither did Clancy. Professional pride, it was. Lucy had slowed, spooned the log off of the rails, and snorted on as Clancy shot her the throttle. The gents beside the tracks had not cared for this. Their bullets got Lucy in the headlight, a gleaming beacon Clancy had kept polished through the years with assiduous care. And they got her in the fire-box, scattering coals on Clancy through the fire-box door he habitually left open for draft. And one bouncing missile of death sheared the goggles Clancy always wore above his visor, clear of his cap.

Lucy lost no steam, Clancy no blood. But they had lived right and served Powder City well, or death would have claimed them both. And all because they carried the wrong kind of freight. . . .

Clancy jolted Smiddy's inkwell onto its side with the impact of his balled fist on the desk-top.

"The law says a man ain't required to jeopardize life nor limb without pay in keepin' with the risk, and your two-bit smelter won't turn out enough bullion to pay me for pullin' it! Get that chest off'n Lucy's car or we don't go down the hill!"

Sam Smiddy puffed his cheeks out and sucked them in three or four times. A sly look glazed over his eyes. Clancy watched it uneasily.

"You're a nervous man, Flatwheel," Smiddy said with syrupy concern. "You're wore thin an' jumpy, spookin' at a little trouble! You need time to get a hold on yourself. This keeps on, somebody's goin' to start hintin' Flatwheel Clancy's turned up a gun-shy yellow streak."

Clancy's face twisted in a black scowl. His hands knotted up. "You're that somebody?" he asked with deceptive softness.

Smiddy shook his head hastily. "Not me, Flatwheel. You and me is friends! Have been for ten years. That's why I want to do something for you. How about a vacation—a whole week at O'Sullivan's bar—on me?"

"On *you*—?"

Clancy was stunned. If Clear Creek had turned suddenly to whiskey to oblige a thirsty man, he could not have been more surprised. Smiddy nodded expansively.

Clancy's scowl weakened. His hands unflexed. "And no bullion on the manifest when I start the run again?" he asked suspiciously.

"No bullion," Smiddy agreed.

Clancy let the last of his truculence run out of him. It was bruited about Powder City that Sam Smiddy was a stubborn soul, not above cutting a man's throat from ear to ear, so to speak, if it meant profit for himself and the Fall River Railroad.

In substance, however, this was not wholly true. Smiddy had the makings of a white man, after all. A vacation . . . happy thought! A break in the ten-year routine of up one day and down the next, Powder City to Denver and back. He grinned at Smiddy.

"If it won't cramp you none, Sam. . . ."

Smiddy shook his head benignly. "It won't, Flatwheel. That kid, Spud Harris, had rid up an' down the line with you in the cab so many times I reckon him and Lucy'd get along while you're off."

"Him and Lucy—you mean you'd put a *kid* at Lucy's throttle-bar?" Clancy's face darkened afresh with hot blood. "Why, you wall-eyed old walrus, Lucy'd pound the seat off that kid's britches in a mile, and he'd take her over a turn! Serve you right, at that, if your rollin' stock ended up at the bottom of Clear Creek! But Lucy's stuck by me. I'll do the same by her. Put anybody else in that cab and you'll carry 'em out—with my crown wrench stuck atween their ears!"

Smiddy sputtered. "Listen, you whiskey-soaked old throttle-hog—!"

"I know—I know!" Clancy cut in savagely. "This is a one-man railroad. All right, Smiddy. And this is a one-man strike! Try rolling Lucy and see if I don't make it stick!"

Samuel Smiddy was a philosopher. He watched Clancy's retreating back out of sight, then rose with relief from behind his desk. He had done all right in this exchange, he reflected. It hadn't come to blows, at least, which left him moral victor, for Clancy, despite his rusty and aged appearance, had horsepower.

He was like Lucy in this respect. And when he was riled, he tossed his fists around with undiscriminating impartiality. When he connected . . . . Smiddy shuddered slightly at the thought.

What Flatwheel needed was a good drunk. Not that he wasn't

always slightly stoked on O'Sullivan's Irish dew. He just needed a good tear to sort of work the venom out of him. Once he had one—a couple of days, maybe—he'd be as meek as a lamb, as weak as a kitten, and as pious as a deacon.

He wouldn't even look at his freight manifests. That chest of bullion consigned to the Denver mint could wait a couple of days. By then, if Flatwheel was still ringy, something would turn up in the way of a trick by which it could be shipped out. Smiddy had confidence in himself and the good offices of fate.

Smiddy was without illusions, realizing that Flatwheel Clancy was not strictly an engineer. That is, he'd play hell throttling one of the big boomers running on the main lines these days. But he could handle Lucy, and that was an art.

Smiddy had forgotten when Lucy was built. She'd been old when he'd bought her. He was firmly convinced that with another man at her throttle, she'd come apart in the first mile. Drunk or sober, Flatwheel had a gift; with flattery, cajolery, and a patience as enduring as the old engine's stubborn iron, he could keep Lucy on the rails and pulling. This, in itself, was enough to balance off many faults. And Smiddy had been balancing them for years.

With a sigh of patience on his own account, Smiddy closed up the Fall River office and headed up toward the mill to explain to the boys at the cooperative that there would be a slight delay in the shipment of their freight. Cause—Flatwheel Clancy had struck again!

O'Sullivan was sympathetic. "'Tis a blitherin' shame when a honest man cannot work at his trade without a stuff-nosed white collar makin' troubles for him!"

"For a fact!" Clancy agreed lugubriously. "Them that has holds; them that hasn't hopes. And a man workin' with his hands, sweatin' like a slave an' pourin' out his heart, gets naught but abuse! Me and Lucy, keepin' this be-damned town on the map for ten years—and now we got to get shot at! You're a man o' rare understandin', O'Sullivan. Another bottle of McReady's Mayblossom. I'll drink ye to friendship o' the masses!"

"Ye'll drink me to wan dollar and forty cents, ye shpalpeen!" O'Sullivan corrected sharply. "Which is seven and twenty total."

Clancy shook his head in great sorrow. "It's a catchin' disease!" he mourned owlishly. "This camp has corrupted ye, O'Sullivan. An upstandin' man, poisoned by associatin' with them bloated rich mill men and that poker o' hell, Sam Smiddy. Ye've turned Scotch!''

O'Sullivan roared and seized the neck of the whiskey bottle sitting between them. Clancy ducked back a little, battle-light coming up eagerly in his eyes. He should have taken this out on that scheming Smiddy. But O'Sullivan could put up a better pair of dukes.

''Ye asked for it, bucko,'' Clancy rumbled. ''But lay down that bottle for the love of Heaven. I'll not be billed for broken glass!''

O'Sullivan came over his bar with practiced ease, when a man from off the street stopped it.

''The windows in your back room are wide open, O'Sullivan, and it's rainin' like hell outside!''

''Begorra, my bedding!'' the saloon man yelped.

Wheeling, he ran hastily to the rear door, leaving Clancy with his wounds unsalved by violence, and with the bottle of Mayblossom for solace. . . .

An hour or so, and Clancy had reached a stage where it was easier to sit than stand. He had moved to a back corner table, comfortably close to the stove, a fresh bottle of Mayblossom before him. His tally with his host and friend was now eight dollars, sixty cents. And he was very drunk.

He observed that O'Sullivan's customers were progressively more rain-soaked as the afternoon dragged out, evidence that Powder City was enduring one of the occasional cleansings to which the storm gods of the mountains subjected it. And he thought that the hand of a kindly fate had directed matters.

If the reduction mill had not readied a chest of bullion ingots for shipment to the mint, it would not have been on his manifest. If it had not been on his manifest, old Lucy and himself would even now be rocking through Black Canyon.

Clancy knew these storms and he knew Black Canyon. Water would be up over the rails. Clear Creek would be roaring from wall to wall. He and Lucy would be having a wet time, maybe even reversing and backing out of that Satan's mill race to higher ground to wait for the water to subside, as they'd done before. But this time he was snug beside O'Sullivan's stove, and Lucy was in her shed with a banked fire in her belly and her rheumy old iron out of the weather.

He had another drink when Samuel Smiddy came in with Arrow and Burton, a couple of boys from the miners' cooperative. The three were wet to their ears. Clancy grinned at their obvious discomfort.

By hell, he thought, this was a fine night! He had himself successfully maintained his fights in defiance of these soft-palmed tycoons of Powder City. He had demonstrated the right of an honest working man to speak his mind and stand his ground against titans of commerce. Single-handed, he had cut Powder City off from the world and paralyzed the ebb and flow of the trade by which these jackals of industry made their money. He had them by the short hair!

The rain was a fitting climax, and he liked it. Here he was dry, while Smiddy was wetter than a mudhen. The more Clancy thought about it, the more he decided that now was a good time to get tough. Now he should clamp down. It ceased to be a question of getting shot at. It became something more—something fundamental.

If Smiddy should show up in the morning with a couple of good riflemen for guards and a new lantern for Lucy and armor plate for her boiler, he'd turn him off cold. Lucy should have new grates. Ought to be a fireman ride the cab, too, to pitch wood into the fire-box. The roadbed ought to be re-ballasted and a couple of turns straightened out. And an engineer should be worth five bucks a day instead of three.

Why, his powers were unlimited! So long as he and Lucy stuck together, Smiddy and the whole damned camp were putty in their hands. The forgotten man at last was coming into his own.

Clancy could see himself and the old engine making history!

Muckers could take up their example; they could refuse to go underground. A new day was coming. Clancy was convinced of it. And the importance of his own part grew magnificently before his eyes. It was too much to keep to himself.

He rose unsteadily to his feet and started across the room noting that the crowd which had been in O'Sullivan's place had gone out. Curious—cock-eyed foolish—with the rain torrenting down outside. They should have stayed inside, dry and mellow.

Smiddy and the two cooperative men were hunched together at the bar like tyrants crushed before a just revolt. They were pallid and silent, their eyes and their faces preoccupied.

Clancy let a rumble of satisfaction stir in his chest. Tails down, were they? Good! Time they learned it was little men, honest men, horny-handed men, who were boss. Not clean-shaved gents, with soft-cushioned swivel-chairs and rear ends to fit them!

He rolled up beside Smiddy, hooked a calloused hand in Smiddy's shoulder, and pulled him around. "Listen, you busted piston," he said threateningly, "I'm makin' no more runs atall till you an' me have had a palaver. What's more, I—"

"Shut up!" Sam Smiddy said. He said it softly, quietly, firmly, like a man at a belly-achin' kid.

Clancy raised his voice. "*I* said—"

He stopped there. He sat down suddenly. He rubbed his jaw.

Smiddy had been holding out on him. Clancy thought of all the times he had been brash with the owner of the Fall River Line. And all the time Smiddy had been saving up a Sunday punch like that!

Clancy was impressed. He should have started off a little more gently. He came to his feet, groggily, and rubbed his jaw. So! Smiddy aimed to fight, eh? All right!

He started in again. But O'Sullivan had swiftly circled the foot of the bar and caught him. "You're drunk!" he charged swiftly. "Man, leave them boys be. Have ye not heard what's happened?"

Clancy nodded. "And sure! Clancy, engineer, has struck!"

O'Sullivan shook him roughly. "Listen, Number Three drift in the big hole has caught fire. Shorin' burnin' like hell and eight-ten boys caught back of it. Doc Weaver's gone down. They're tryin' to get 'em out now. They's the devil to pay. They're bringin' 'em here if they can get 'em out. Doc needs room to work. There's a pot of coffee on a table out back. Get it on a stove lid and a quart of it in your belly. Doc'll need help!"

Clancy shook his head. Doc wouldn't need his help. Not with a bellyful of McReady's Mayblossom under his belt! Was O'Sullivan out of his head, talking as though coffee—even O'Sullivan's acid brew—could kill the lusty flames Mayblossom built in a man? Clancy shook his head again and rolled back to his table and the half-finished bottle there. He poured himself another drink.

Shoring afire meant a cave-in, sooner or later. A cave-in meant boys badly hurt. His just bitterness of moments before toward the two mine operators and Sam Smiddy softened a little. These three were not so bad. He even felt a little sympathy.

He had another drink and pondered the catastrophe which had struck at Powder City, then the door of O'Sullivan's place swung inward ahead of a white-faced procession.

Doc Weaver, his hair rumpled, in his shirt sleeves despite the rain outside, and his lips pressed in a tight line. Muckers and mill men, coming in fours and carrying stretchers between them. Clancy counted one—two . . . . Nine of them, all told. Men in agony. Burned, crushed, biting blood from their lips and watching the doc with nerve-rasping hopefulness.

Doc went to work when the stretchers were set down on Sullivan's hastily arranged tables. He cursed the crowd and drove them out. Clancy was immobile at his little table in the corner—beyond notice.

Doc was frantic. Medicants and drugs from his satchel saturated the air, mingling confusedly with the fumes of Mayblossom back of Clancy's eyes. It lasted a half-hour, then Doc jerked his head at Sam Smiddy and the two men from the cooperative, motioning them away from the injured men. Doc and Smiddy and the other two huddled a scant yard from Clancy.

"These boys have got to have a hospital!" Doc said harshly. "I've got to have nurses and equipment and professional help! I ain't a magician—and this is bad!"

Arrow and Burton swung their eyes to Smiddy. The owner of the Fall River Railroad shook his head slowly. "With this rain running off, Black Canyon will be running eighteen inches over the rails. A saint couldn't get through there till it slacks. Tell me what I can do, Doc."

Weaver shrugged heavily. "Get your hands washed, Sam—clean. We'll do what we can."

The four turned back toward the laden tables. Flatwheel Clancy came slowly up out of his chair. He glowered at Sam Smiddy's retreating back.

So a saint couldn't go through Black Canyon at flood, eh? His lips twisted. Maybe not. But a throttle-hog! Clancy slid out of O'Sullivan's place, muttering to himself. . . .

Twenty minutes later a protesting chunk of iron with rising steam pressure in its belly clanked to a stop on the rails back of the saloon and flung a quavering whistle into the black, rain-washed night air. That whistle was off-pitch and uncertain—not much of a battle-cry—but it brought men on the run.

Among the first was Sam Smiddy. He loped up to the cab. "You blasted idiot, get out of there!" he yelped angrily. "You're drunk and interrupting us when we're trying to save men's lives!"

"So you set yourself up for a medical man now, eh?" Clancy jeered. "Sure, I'm drunk. But I'll save more lives than you, you scurrilous shpalpeen! Get them hurt men into Lucy's caboose. I've got cots from the bunkhouses in there for 'em, a tub of water, and fire goin' in the stove. They're goin' to Denver!"

It was a fine, large speech, only slightly impaired by two explosive hiccoughs.

Sam Smiddy stared upward in disbelief.

"You'll not make it!" he protested. "That's whiskey talking!"

Clancy nodded owlishly. "And what if it is?" he parried. "It's Irish whiskey, ain't it? We're goin', and what's more, you're goin' too! This is one run Clancy don't fire his own engine!"

Smiddy's face purpled with explosive derision. Doc Weaver shouted from the back door of O'Sullivan's, cutting him short. "Leave the blathering!" the Doc bellowed. "Crazy or not, it's the best chance. Give a hand in here—get these men into that car!"

The crowd behind Smiddy turned obediently into the saloon. Smiddy shot a sharp glance upward at Flatwheel, then spoke to Arrow and Burton beside him. The three went back into O'Sullivan's.

Townsmen came out, carrying stretchers. Smiddy and his two companions did not appear until nine stretchers had come out. They came carrying the tenth—apparently loaded with a large man. They staggered under its weight. Clancy was curious. He thought only nine men had been hurt. He tried to catch Smiddy's attention, but Doc Weaver waved a highball, and when Smiddy swung into the cab, he went immediately into the tender where Lucy's firewood was stacked. Clancy growled and shot steam to the old drivers.

Smiddy came out with a stick of wood under each arm and shoved it into the fire-box. He repeated the trip, monotonously, steady. Perspiration beaded his face, and the links slipped out of the cuffs of his shirt so that they flapped about his wrists. Each trip he was driven back on another by a baleful stab of Clancy's eyes. Finally Smiddy straightened.

"You crazy baboon!" he squawked wildly. "It ain't enough you've got to try to make this run, but you never covered the tender last night. This wood's wet and won't burn!"

Clancy shook his head. "It ain't me. It's Lucy. She'd burn mush if she wanted. She's miffed. Poor gal, she ain't been treated right!"

He unbuttoned the front of his shirt and brought out the better part of a bottle of Mayblossom. Bending, he knocked the neck from it and bowled it into the fire-box. Flame puffed out from the door, driving Smiddy back, cringing. And the roar of the draft took on an earnest tone.

Flatwheel Clancy laughed.

"Stoke, you crimp-backed seat-sitter!" he howled exultantly. "Stoke her full! She'll eat now. And we'll roll!"

It wasn't an empty prophecy. Flame shot out through the screen over the old engine's funneled stack as an inferno built up inside the open fire-box door. The creepy old pressure gauge pivoted upward at an alarming rate, and Clancy inched back on the throttle.

The rough, uneven track jolted past underneath, kicking one truck up, then the other. The engine rocked and pitched, and every loose joint in her piston linkage pounded threateningly.

Smiddy listened to these things and grew pallid of face. But Clancy, his head thrust pleasurably out into the rush of rain-swept wind, kept leaning back on the throttle.

They hit the head of Black Canyon like runaways on a dead downgrade. The track was two thin black lines, slanting down into a rolling mass of muddy water.

Smiddy shut his eyes. Clancy pulled his head in. And Lucy hit the water. A sheet flew up on either side of the cab, flooding in through the windows and falling like a cascade on the tender coupled behind. Clouds of steam hissed up where the splash wiped along the bottom of the fire-box.

Clancy glanced at the cascade on the tender and grinned wickedly. He stabbed an elbow into Smiddy's side. "Stoke, blast you!" he roared. "If the water damps out the bottom of the fire, we got to build the top higher—right into the dang-busted tubes!"

Like a man berserk with terror, Smiddy stumbled back into the flooded tender after more wood.

Clancy sighed and gave the drivers more steam. Lucy was walking into ten inches of rushing water over the rails. Any minute she might come to one strip which had been undermined. It would only take one, and over she'd go on her side. But Clancy ignored this possibility. So long as the engine was upright, keeping her moving ahead against the increasing drag of the water—that was the important thing.

At the halfway mark in the canyon, water was above any flood-marks Clancy could remember. He felt a faint stabbing of concern and regretted he had not shared that last bottle of Mayblossom with Lucy. She could have spared him a little. And he needed it now!

Water began sloshing across the floor plates of the cab. Smiddy, dancing about to avoid it, pulled at Clancy's arm, calling his attention to the slosh.

"Roll your pants!" Clancy advised in a thundering bellow. "Swim, if you've got to! But keep stoking!"

The last quarter mile Clancy had to inch his way to keep Lucy's wheels under her at all. Clear Creek was a giant's mill race of logs, brush, debris, and wet, roiling hell. Clancy wondered how Doc Weaver and the men in the ancient caboose tagging along were faring. All right, he hoped. The caboose was floored a foot higher than the engine cab. All right—if he could keep engine and car on the rails!

Clancy wanted to sing a song—a song like a man ought to have learned from his mother, having heard that such singing would keep the devil away. But he didn't know any such songs. He swore, instead—and in its way, it was as beautiful as any song. It gave him comfort and solace and bridged dragging minutes of uncertainty. Suddenly, ahead, the rails tipped up out of the water as they debouched from the narrows of the canyon into the wider valley below.

Clear Creek swung away to the right in a bend of its own and far down the line Clancy could see the lights of Denver through the clearing dark.

Reaching up, he caught the whistle-cord, twisted a fat knot into it, and hooked it into a bolt-head—tied down. He tugged the old throttle-bar to its limit, and gave off swearing. Twenty minutes later, leaking steam from every gasket and with her pop-off snoring away the excess in her boiler by the Mayblossom-inspired fire in her innards, Lucy clanked to a stop in the Denver yards.

Doc Weaver got yard men scouting. Swift buggies and commandeered hansoms rolled up and rolled away with freight on stretchers. Flatwheel Clancy and his boss hung out the window of Lucy's cab, watching these things. Smiddy spoke with obvious reluctance.

"You're a hero, Flatwheel—and a less deserving man I never seen! Ye had the devil's help, I'm not doubting, but ye did it. And my hat's off to ye!"

"I'm an engineer, Sam Smiddy!" Clancy corrected dourly, "and sweet-talk'll not make it different! An engineer with a grievance. There's yet a strike on this be-damned road. An' there'll be a strike till ye see sense!"

"About shipping bullion?" Smiddy asked mildly.

"And what else! It ain't human to ask old ones like me an' Lucy to risk our lives like that!"

"I'll make you a promise, Flatwheel," Smiddy offered. "We'll not talk about it for two months."

Smiddy swung down and started back toward the caboose. Arrow and Burton were standing there, talking to half a dozen armed men who had climbed out of a van pulled by four big horses.

Clancy scowled. Two months—it took two months for the mill at Powder City to get a shipment of bar metal ready. But what about the one which had been on yesterday's manifest?

The armed men went into the caboose. They came out carrying the stretcher Smiddy and the two men from the cooperative had loaded at Powder City—the stretcher with the heavy man under its blanket, the tenth victim of the accident in the big hole.

The armed men loaded the stretcher carefully into the back of the van. The van turned, started to roll away. A lantern shed light for a moment on its lettered side. Clancy started violently.

The legend was simple:

TREASURY DEPARTMENT
Denver Mint

Clancy yelled an oath which flashed in the night air like gunpowder. Samuel Smiddy heard it, turned and started to run, but he couldn't run fast enough to drown out the bellow of Clancy's lungs:

"Sam Smiddy, you hound of hell—!"

THE END

Though he lives to be a hundred, Pud will never forget that winter at the Y Cross line camp when, day after day, he had to act as decoy for the bushwhack death stalking the mad renegade who held him—a hopeless captive in a frozen cow-country hell!

THE LINE CAMP TERICO

It was brutal, crude surgery, but
the big man had guts. . . .

Gripping Cattle-Range Novel
★ By WALT COBURN ★

CHAPTER ONE
Winter Prisoner

Pud stood near the sod dugout, the burlap bed-tick still in one mittened hand. In the snow at his feet a shower of green and yellow bills lay scattered like fallen leaves. He'd never seen so much money in his life.

That was when the big black-whiskered man with a six-shooter in his hand came out of the dugout—the kind of place where, as Windy Bill put it, "the cowboy winters his spud." The man's big yellowish teeth were bared; the eyes that stared from under ragged brows were bleak as the Montana winter sky. His other hand and the arm above it were wrapped in a dirty, blood-spattered bandage, and he carried it in a sling made out of a black silk muffler. His voice had a croaking sound.

"There's exactly twelve thousand, four hunderd and two dollars in the jackpot you're starin' at, kid. The odd two bucks is one of them unlucky two-dollar bills. That 'un's yourn. Shove it in your pocket—fer bad luck!"

Then his yellow-toothed grin was gone, and the six-shooter in his hand clicked to full cock.

"Who in hell are you, button? And what fetches you here to this line camp that's a'ready snowed in fer the winter?"

Pud's Adam's apple moved up and down. His mouth was full of cotton. He tried to talk, and couldn't.

Try bucking snowdrifts all day, leading a bed-horse, swinging stiff arms across your chest, and slapping mittened hands and kicking numbed feet against your stirrups. That's when you pray that you'll get to the line camp before a blizzard catches up with you or, in the approaching black night, you have to lay out in the snow and maybe freeze to death.

Then you want to yell or sing when, just at early dusk, you sight the log buildings and pole corrals, half buried in the snow. There's smoke rising from the log-cabin chimney. That should round out a memorable day in your life, if you're an eighteen-year-old cowboy. And you get all set to grin it off like and old hand, because Windy Bill would hear you ride up, and he'd open the cabin door. He'd stare, slack-jawed, and then greet you with something loud-mouthed and comical.

But Windy Bill hadn't opened the cabin door. When he didn't

show up to help unload the tarp-covered bed from the pack horse, young Pud figured Windy must have sighted him coming through the high drifts and was hiding out somewhere for a josh. . . .

Pud had already unloaded his bed and shoved it into the warm, empty cabin. Then he'd watered and stabled his saddle horse and bed-horse. After that he'd come back to the log cabin. He'd shoved a stick or two of wood into the dying fire. He'd lighted a candle, then started to spread his bed on the extra bunk.

There was a fairly new bed-tick on the bunk, made out of a big burlap wool sack. Young Pud figured that a good way to work up some circulation into his chilled body was to dump out the old hay in the burlap bed-tick and then fill it with fresh hay at the barn.

So he had lugged the big burlap bed-tick outside, untied the buckskin string at its open end and dumped its contents on the snow. Then he had stood there, his blue eyes widening. Because mixed with the hay were packets of banknotes fastened together with paper tape or elastic bands. . . .

When he saw that ugly, black-whiskered face in the gray dusk, saw the gun in the big man's hand, young Pud had shoved both hands in the air.

This wasn't any kind of a josh.

"Talk up, you young whelp. You deef an' dumb?"

"They sent me here," Pud found his voice, "from the home ranch. To help Windy Bill out—here at the line camp."

"What's your name?" The big man's red-rimmed eyes glowered at him.

"Pud. That's short for Puddin' Head."

"Puddin' Head is right! Puddin' Brains!" The black-whiskered man stared at the scattered money in the snow. "Spillin' a man's life's savin's in the snow! Pick it up and put it back where you found it. Wait a second! You pack a gun?"

"No, sir. Where's Windy Bill?" Pud asked.

"Windy Bill," grinned the black-whiskered man, "was askin' too many damn-fool questions. So I sent him away. Now quit askin' them same kind of questions, and mebbyso I'll let you stay on here. . . .

"Somebody's got to feed them pore cattle yonder. I can't chop water holes in the ice er handle a hay fork with this bad hand. Run the tine of a hayfork plumb through it. Be lucky if it ain't blood-poison sets in. Now put my money back in that wool sack, and don't hold out nothin' but that unlucky two-dollar bill. Then git in there and cook supper.

"I'm awful perlite to git along with. Unless I'm crossed. Er double-crossed. Then I git harmful. Now commence to act busy, young Puddin' Brains."

Pud picked the money up and shoved it back into the big sack. The black-whiskered man let down the hammer on his six-shooter but still held it in his hand. His bloodshot pale gray eyes watched every move the young cowboy made. And he grinned mirthlessly when Pud picked up the crumpled-looking two-dollar bill and shoved it into the pocket of his heavy flannel shirt.

Young Pud was too excited and puzzled to be very badly scared. A range orphan, he had been kicked around a lot and he'd seen a few gun-plays. He figured he knew where all this money came from—all but the lowly and despised two-dollar bill.

There had been a bank robbery about ten days ago at Lewistown. Later—if this big gun-slinger gave him time to do some quiet thinking—he'd be able to remember more about what he'd heard and read in the newspapers. He kept wondering now what had become of Windy Bill. And thinking to himself what a whale of a big day in his life this was turning out to be.

The money made a skimpy bulk inside the big burlap wool sack. The man told him to lug it inside, and tomorrow he could fill it with hay. Black Whiskers made some kind of a joke about it being a mighty high-priced mattress to sleep on.

While Pud cooked supper, the man folded the big burlap sack with the money and shoved it under the tarp-covered bed on the bunk. It was Windy Bill's bed. Pud knew the tarp with Windy painted crudely on its canvas. . . .

They had steak and biscuits and fried spuds and beans for supper. The man drank half a dozen cups of the strong black coffee. Then after Pud had washed and wiped the dishes, the man told him to heat some water. He cut away the dirty bandage. The dried blood glued the soiled rags to the wounded hand, and it bled when the man jerked the cloth free. Then he shoved the hand in the basin of hot water and held it there, gingerly cleansing the wound with his other hand.

Pud hadn't seen too many such wounds, but he knew that a bullet—probably a steel jacket .30-30—had made that clean round hole through the thick muscle between the man's thumb and forefinger. No pitchfork tine had made that. But young Pud kept quiet.

He ripped a clean floursack dishtowel into strips and bandaged the man's hand. The man had guts. The only sign of pain he showed was the baring of his big yellow teeth, or the squinting of his bleak eyes. And he held his six-shooter ready in his other hand.

"You can call me Boss," the man told him. "An' you be awful keerful about rilin' my temper. Things always happen sudden when I git harmful."

Boss made young Pud empty out the contents of his warsack and shake out his blankets and soogans. Just to make certain, he grinned, that Puddin' Head didn't have a sneak gun hidden there.

He found no gun.

Pud had left his white angora wool chaps with his saddle at the barn. In the deep pocket of his chaps was a .45 six-shooter. He said nothing about it. He would try to get to his chaps before this Boss had a chance to look in the pockets. If the man found Pud's gun, he'd be most apt to get 'harmful.' That was Pud's risk.

Besides the extra socks and underwear and shirts and a new pair of blanket-lined canvas pants, a toothbrush and a shaving outfit, the contents of his warsack was mostly books—school text books.

"I'm missin' a winter's schoolin'," he answered the black-whiskered Boss's derisive grin. "So I aimed to do some studyin' of a night." Pud stacked the books and writing tablets and pencils on a shelf.

Boss told him that there were a couple of hundred head of Y Cross cattle to feed and water every day, besides the barn chores and cooking that he'd be doing before daybreak and after dark.

Pud looked a little light in the beam for heavy work, Boss went on, and chances was he'd lay on the bedground without burning up good candles to study by. Book learnin' was all right for women, but as for Boss, he couldn't read or write an' didn't intend to learn. He seemed almighty proud of that ignorance.

"But I kin tally money, button—carry the figgers in my head. So don't git no petty larceny notions."

Pud said he didn't want any of Boss's hard-earned money. He wondered if Windy Bill had tried to swipe some of that bank robbery wealth. Windy was always talking big about how some day he'd rob a bank and pull out for the Argentine with a South

American stake. That only boneheaded fools worked twenty hours a day punching cows for forty a month and beans. But that was the way Windy Bill always talked about everything.

Windy ran off at the head too much. Drunk, he was always running big whizzers until somebody got sick and tired of listening to his drunken fight talk and called his bluff. Then Windy would bellow with laughter. But there was the talk that Windy Bill had killed a man once and had traveled the Outlaw Trail till things cooled off. That for all his loud paw and beller, there was an ornery streak in him.

Now something had happened to Windy Bill. He wasn't here at the line camp where he was supposed to winter. He'd left his bed behind. And no man in his right mind was pulling out while the snowdrifts were piled deep and high, and the badlands along the Missouri River were snowed in until the warm Chinook winds cut the drifts next spring.

When it came time to go to bed, the black-whiskered Boss told Pud to skin out of what clothes he wasn't sleeping in.

"Till we git better acquainted, button, I'm hog-tyin' you of a night to your bunk. I sleep awful light—with one eye open, as the sayin' goes. If I was to ketch you tryin' to git loose, I'd be apt to act harmful." He grinned wickedly in the candlelight.

Boss took two nearly new red Hudson's Bay blankets from Pud's bed and threw him a pair of badly worn old blankets from Windy Bill's bed in exchange. Those bright red heavy wool blankets, with the broad-back stripe across each end and the black lines woven into the red wool to mark their "three point" excellent quality, were among the young cowpuncher's most prized possessions. He had worked across the Canadian Line last spring with the Circle Diamond round-up and had swapped a Mountie out of the blankets.

A drifting cowboy doesn't own many things of value. His private horse, his outfit that includes saddle, blanket and bridle, his chaps and spurs and bed and gun. The odds and ends in his canvas warsack. A pair of shop-made boots and a new hat which cost him a month's wages. And because his work is hard and his holidays are few and far between, his wants are not many, and his possessions are scantily numbered.

Pud had what the cow country calls an Injun's eye for color. He thought an almighty lot of that pair of red blankets. He took his loss with a white-lipped silence, but the big black-whiskered renegade had made himself an enemy.

Perhaps the man knew it, because it marked the first of a long string of studied insults and taunts that were to come. This Boss had a cruel, warped sense of humor.

Pud got his nickname because of his great fondness for a steam pudding known on round-up and cattle ranches as son-of-a-gun-in-the-sack. Somebody had called the range waif Puddin' Face or Puddin' Head and they'd shortened it to Pud and the name had stuck like a sand burr to a saddle blanket. But if this big black-muzzled bulldozer wanted to figure him as puddin' brained, that was all right with young Pud.

The cow country orphan had learned many a lesson the hard way. Long, long ago he had quit fighting his head like a bronc when the cowhands plagued and teased him. And in many ways the eighteen-year-old cowboy was as wise as a matured man, and he knew how to do his own thinking. So Pud marked off the loss of his precious blankets as a petty larceny deal and told himself that he'd get even with the black-muzzled Boss.

He figured it out that a man as big and tough as this Boss claimed to be had a yellow streak in him, or he wouldn't belittle himself with a low-down picayune trick like taking blankets from a kid.

Pud pulled off his boots and heavy wool pants and flannel shirt and went to bed in his socks and long wool underwear. Boss stood at the head of the bunk with a couple of hogging strings. He told Pud to lay over on the flat of his back. Then he tied each of the young cowboy's wrists to one of the heavy pole uprights of the bunk.

"Don't kick off your covers, Puddin' Brains," said Boss, and blew out the candlelight.

CHAPTER TWO
Pud—Gun-Doctor

Pud got a fairly good night's sleep in spite of the discomfort. And he used his intervals of wakefulness to good advantage. He had time to think now, and remember what the newspapers told and what the bunkhouse range gossip had to add to the story of the Lewistown bank robbery.

The newspapers had printed the story in bold black type. Three bearded men had ridden to town just before bank closing time in the afternoon, during a snowstorm that was turning into a blizzard. There had been no customers in the bank. While one man held the horses, the other two walked inside with drawn guns. The teller had been caught off guard. The two bank robbers had made the teller shove over twelve thousand dollars in currency into a gunnysack.

The bigger of the two men, a six-footer with thick black whiskers and wearing a black silk muffler that left only his slitted eyes visible, had taken the sack of money. Then, with what the newspaper termed wanton brutality, he had hit the teller over the head with the barrel of his six-shooter as they stood lined up facing the wall, their hands high.

The three bank robbers had then ridden away into the blizzard. Somebody had seen them head due south, the storm at their backs. It was a clean getaway, without a shot fired.

Beyond the meager description the three bank officials could give of the two men who had come inside, there was nothing in the way of accurate description to identify the renegades. The man who seemed to be the leader had black hair and whiskers and pale gray eyes. The other man's hair and beard were a drab, sandy color, and he was shorter and much slimmer than his big partner. There was no description whatever of the man who had stayed out in the storm with the horses.

Sheriff Tom Dickson, stated the newspapers, had nothing to say. He had been sick in bed with a bad attack of grippe the day of the bank robbery and had disregarded the doctor's orders by getting up out of a sickbed to organize a posse and take out after the bank robbers.

Sheriff Tom Dickson was an outspoken man and a poor politician. At some time or another he had locked horns with the editor of the Lewistown newspaper. There was a sharp, biting editorial in the paper that hinted that the sheriff stood a very poor chance of being re-elected if he failed to bring in the bank robbers, dead or alive.

When the law, the newspaper stated, permitted three men to ride boldly into town in broad daylight, rob a bank, crack the skull of an honest citizen—the teller's skull was badly fractured and his chances of recovering were fifty-fifty—and ride away scot free with twelve thousand dollars booty, then it was high time that there be a change in sheriffs. Thus the political enemies of Sheriff Tom Dickson turned it into their field day. While the cowman-sheriff's staunch friends could do nothing but cuss the newspaper editor for a man who kicked another man when he was sick in bed.

The bunkhouse version of that bank robbery was many sided and somewhat confused in regards to the identity of the three bank robbers, where and how it had been planned and executed, and what had become of the three hold-up men.

They named a score of black-haired cowpunchers who were ornery enough to grow a set of whiskers and ramrod a bank robbery and get the job done without a mistake. They could name that many more sandy-haired cowhands with faded blue eyes who had grown weary of punching cows and tried for a South American stake. And the man left outside holding the horses could be anybody.

The majority of the bunkhouse strategists agreed that three cowpunchers had thrown in together, waited for a stormy day, pulled off the job and made a slick getaway. They'd stopped somewhere long enough to split the money three ways, then had split up and had each gone his own way.

There were some of the bunkhouse wise men who said flatly that the three men were outlaws from the Hole-in-the-Wall country. They'd come to town during the storm, decided to rob a bank, had done so, and had ridden back together along the Outlaw Trail to some hideout like the Hole, there to sit around the stove and play poker with the proceeds.

It had all the earmarks of a job done by cool-headed professionals, they said. And Sheriff Tom Dickson knew it. There wasn't a damned thing Tom Dickson could do about it except mark it off to profit and loss.

Pud had taken no part in the bunkhouse arguments. He was only a bald-faced button whose opinions one way or the other had no weight. Pud had learned years ago that a kid around a cow oufit keeps his half-baked opinions to himself, unless he wants to get unmercifully joshed and hoorawed.

Now, roped to his bunk and listening to the broken snores of Boss in the darkness, Pud tried to figure it out for himself.

That black-muzzled bulldozer was, beyond all doubt, the same big black-bearded man who had been labeled as the leader of the bank robbers. And he had not headed south. This line camp on the Missouri River was about seventy-five miles northeast of Lewistown. It was badlands country that offered plenty of hideouts for a man on the dodge. But that man had better know his country and how to ride it, or those same badlands could trap him. So Boss must have known where he was headed for and how to get there.

He'd be certain to have his hiding place staked out and supplied with a winter's grub and a bedroll and a warm roof and thick log walls waiting for him when he got there. Unless he had gotten lost in the storm and blundered in here by mistake, this big black-muzzled Boss had figured on holing up here at the Y Cross line camp. And it wasn't at all likely that this tough renegade would make any mistakes about his getaway.

The yellow streak in the man would make him plenty cautious. So, figured young Pud as he eased his aching arms in the darkness, this Boss had planned to hide out here at the Y Cross line camp this winter until the Chinook winds melted the snow and the excitement of the bank robbery had died down. He'd be just another grub-line riding cowboy drifting across the cow country to squander his winter's pay in town and get himself a job with another outfit. Nobody ever bucked the deep drifts to visit a snowed-in line camp fifty miles from nowhere. A man on the dodge could want no safer hideout.

Yet Pud asked himself, where did Windy Bill figure into it? Windy was a big man, a little pot-gutted. He could have been the third member of the bank robber outfit. Windy Bill might have stayed out on the street and held the two horses and acted as look-out.

Those three men could have gathered here, planned the bank robbery, done the job, headed south to throw the law off their trail, then doubled back against the storm and reached here the next day, if they had a couple of relays of horses staked out along that seventy-five-mile ride.

For all his loud-mouthed bragging, which actually made him a good cover for a dangerous job, Windy Bill had the guts to get the job done. But figuring him into it, where was Windy Bill now? Where, likewise, was the slim gent with the sandy hair and faded blue eyes? And if all three of them had planned to winter here, where was at least one more bed?

The money from the bank robbery—all of it, including an un-wanted lousy two-dollar bill—was here in the cabin, intact. It hadn't been split three ways. The black-whiskered Boss had it all. And the only way Pud could figure out that angle was that Boss had killed Windy Bill and the sandy-haired man. There'd been no shooting when they held up the bank. But there was a bullet hole in Boss's left hand.

The black-whiskered renegade wasn't sleeping at all soundly. He'd barred the one door and hung strips of old tarp across the two small windows. The fire had gone out, and the cabin was pitch black inside. But the pain from Boss's wounded hand was, of course, tearing his sleep apart.

He'd snore for a few minutes, then jerk awake with a grunting groan. And Pud knew that the man was wide awake, gripping his gun, listening, tense as a coiled rattler. A dozen times or more during the night Boss rolled a clumsy one-handed cigarette and lit it, and the flare of the match would show his slitted bloodshot eyes.

"You awake, Puddin' Head?" he croaked.

"I am now, Boss."

"You hear anything?"

"Musta heard you, or the match light woke me. Or the way my arms feel."

"Hear anything outside?"

"It coulda bin some outside noise woke me," Pud lied, and grinned in the darkness. That black-muzzled son was spooky. Let him stay awake and sweat with worry. The big bulldozer had a yellow streak a foot wide down his back.

Pud was young enough to go back to sleep. But he knew that the black-whiskered man would lie awake for a long time, listening for outside sounds. That gave the young cowboy no little satisfaction. The big black-muzzled buzzard wasn't getting too much pleasure out of those handsome red blankets.

The late November night was long. Hours before daybreak that would be about seven-thirty or eight o'clock, Pud was caught up with his sleep. His arms were numb from the shoulder sockets to the fingertips of his hands, swollen from the tight ropes that cut into his wrists.

He was sweaty and cold by turns, and then his back or the sole of his foot would itch. He lay there motionless, enduring the torture of the itching, until he heard Boss snore. Then he wriggled and twisted to relieve the itching. The black-whiskered Boss heard him moving. The snoring choked off, and the man was wide awake, and

Pud was as motionless as a rock. And so the young cowpuncher forgot his own discomforts and made a game of dealing misery to the man who was his captor.

Before daybreak, Boss lit a candle and pulled on his pants and boots. He jerked loose the knots that tied Pud's wrists to the bunk uprights and told him gruffly to get up and light the fire and cook breakfast.

Pud couldn't move his arms. They were as numb and stiff as two wooden clubs hung from his shoulders. His wrists were rope burned and his hands purplish and badly swollen.

"You just naturally played hell, Boss," he said quietly, "tyin' my arms thataway. They're plumb useless for a while. I can't even pull on my boots."

"If I figgered you was lyin', you young whelp, I'd kick the guts outa yuh." His voice was gritty.

He stood over Pud as the young cowboy sat on the edge of the bunk shivering in his underwear. Without warning, he slapped Pud across the mouth and nose with his open hand.

It was like being cuffed by a grizzly. The young cowpuncher's head rocked sideways. Blood spurted from his nose. He could not lift his hands to defend himself. Boss slapped him again. Then his yellow teeth bared in an ugly grin.

"You ain't lyin'. You couldn't lift a hand."

He turned and walked over to the cold stove. Pud had whittled shavings and fixed kindling for the morning fire. Boss shoved the shavings and kindling into the stove. He kept holding his bandaged hand high, about the level of his shoulder. He bumped it against a shelf and cursed through gritted teeth. Then he yanked one of Pud's books from the offending shelf and shoved it in on top of the kindling.

Pud was sitting on the edge of his bunk, his head bent forward to let the blood drip from his nose. Tears of pain and rage half blinded him, and he bit back a groan as he saw the big black-whiskered renegade shove one of his books into the stove. He saw the ugly glitter in the man's bloodshot pale gray eyes and kept his silence. But he marked it down in his memory.

Boss managed a one-handed job of grinding some coffee. He dumped it into the pot and dippered in cold water. And put a tea kettle on to heat some water.

The circulation began to pound blood into Pud's arms, and the pain was something to make him grit his teeth. His nose quit bleeding about the time he could use his hands and arms again. The coffee came to a boil, and Boss shoved the blackened pot to the back of the little sheet iron camp stove to simmer. Then he poured hot water into the tin basin and began undoing the bandage on his injured hand.

Boss's wounded hand was badly swollen, and Pud knew it must be throbbing with pain. Above the black beard the man's weatherstained skin was tinged with a grayish pallor. His bleak eyes, seared with pain, glittered in the candlelight as he shoved the blood-crusted hand into the warm water.

Pud dressed and washed his face and started getting breakfast, while Boss sat on his bunk bathing his wounded hand.

"Whole damn' arm's swole up," the man gritted. "Be lucky if I don't git blood poison."

"Or lockjaw," said Pud quietly.

"Lockjaw?" Boss opened and shut his jaws experimentally.

"Jaws commencin' to ache, Boss?"

"What the hell's lockjaw?"

"It's a form of tetanus," said Pud glibly, slicing bacon from a slab on the table. "Caused by a wound like that one you've got in your hand. The jaws lock together. Unless you get the proper medical care, that form of tetanus is fatal. You can't unlock your jaws. You die."

"Where'd you git so damn' smart?"

"I'm studyin' up to be a doctor," Pud grinned flatly. "That was a medical handbook, dealin' with the treatment of such infections, that you burned in the stove. I remember seein' a long chapter on that form of tetanus called lockjaw. I've read it, but not enough to learn it. I aimed to look it up in the handbook, but you burned it. . . ."

The black-whiskered renegade sat there on his bunk, an ugly mixture of sheer panic and cold-blooded murder in his slitted bloodshot eyes.

He cursed Pud in a croaking whisper. "I got a mind to kill you, you smart aleck young whelp! Kill you, by the hell!"

"You made one mistake when you burned my handbook, mister," said young Pud flatly. "Mebbyso you'd make a worse mistake by killin' me. Little as I do know about tetanus, it's better than bein' plumb ignorant as you are. Let me know when your jaw hinges commence achin' worse."

Pud forked the slices of bacon into the skillet. He had the big black-muzzled bulldozer plenty scared. Boss had been gritting his teeth and clamping his jaws against pain for many hours. Naturally his jaws would be aching. He'd play on the man's fear and ignorance.

"If the black-muzzled son keeps on thataway," Pud told himself, "he'll worry himself into a purty case of line-camp lockjaw."

As he cooked breakfast, Pud's fertile young brain began to devise various torturous treatments to inflict on his victim. But he'd have to use cunning or the big bulldozer would kill him.

CHAPTER THREE
Bushwhack Trap

A mangy-looking old coonskin coat hung on the wall, and Pud recognized it as belonging to Windy Bill. Alongside it on a wooden peg hung a big shaggy buffalo-hide coat and a muskrat-fur cap with earflaps and lined with heavy red flannel. The buffalo coat and fur cap belonged to Boss.

"Put on that buffalo coat," Boss told Pud when the young cowboy had helped him cleanse and bandage his wounded hand, "an' that fur cap. Git your barn chores done. Then come back to the cabin afore you harness your team and commence feedin' the cattle. Chop open your water holes when you lead the horses to water."

Pud said he had his own sheepskin-lined canvas coat and a wool cap that fitted him.

"Put on that buffalo coat," snarled the man, "an' that fur cap."

Young Pud was six feet tall, but slimly built. The buffalo coat was heavy and the sleeves were too long and it came to the tops of his overshoes. He felt lost in it. The big fur cap was too large for his head. He wondered what kind of a locoed notion this was.

He got the idea quickly enough when Boss pulled a saddle carbine from under the bunk. It was one of the .30-30 saddle-guns issued to the line-camp riders and had the Y Cross burned into the stock. The hammer of the gun and the lever and part of the breech had been badly smashed. The gun was useless as a shooting iron.

"Take this along," grinned Boss, "to kill varmints."

Boss unbarred the door. "Try to rabbit on me and I'll shoot you loose from your saddle, Puddin' Brains,'' he said, and shoved the young cowboy outside into the gray half-light of daybreak.

Pud got the idea. Anyone hidden at the barn or cattle shed watching the cabin would see a man in a fur cap and huge buffalo coat with a Winchester in his hands. If the watcher was an enemy of the black-whiskered Boss and recognized the fur cap and buffalo coat, he'd shoot first and ask questions later. Boss, then, was using Pud for a decoy.

Young Pud was more angry than scared as he plowed through the drifts, handicapped by the cumbersome heavy bulk of the buffalo coat. But no hidden guns cracked. There was nobody hiding inside the log barn or the large low-roofed cattle shed.

There were seven horses in the big log barn. The work team, Pud's two horses, two Y Cross saddle horses that Pud knew were Windy Bill's two winter horses, and the big gelding with the blotched brand that the bank-robbing Boss had ridden here.

Pud took along an axe and shovel and led the horses, two at a time, to the river's edge. He chopped and shoveled the frozen-over long narrow troughs cut in the river ice to water the stock.

He fed the horses and cleaned the stalls and harnessed the work team. His first move when he came into the barn was to get his six-shooter from the pocket of his chaps. He'd packed it hidden under his shirt. Now he debated with himself a while before he decided what to do with the gun. He finally, reluctantly, parted with it, hiding it in the manger of the last stall, burying it under the hay.

He stood for perhaps a minute in the barn, eyes narrowed, scowling thoughtfully at a saddle and blanket and bridle hung on a long, thick saddle peg. It was Windy Bill's outfit. Windy's old coonskin coat was in the cabin. That could mean only one thing. Windy Bill must be dead.

Pud went back to the cabin, swathed in the huge buffalo coat and carrying the useless, broken saddle-gun. Boss unbarred the door and let him in. Then he barred the door.

''See ary sign of anybody?'' asked the man.

''Nobody.'' Pud shed the heavy coat and fur cap. ''Your jaw botherin' you much?''

''Jaw, hell! It's my hand!'' But he moved his jaws with his good hand, and there was an uneasy look in his pain-seared eyes.

Pud pulled on his own cap and coat. He said it would be an all-day job scattering hay for the cattle. He had to fork it from the

stack to the hayrack and haul it around in a wide circle, forking it
off in small bunches and handling his team as he went. It would
take a couple of loads.

"I'll try to git done," he said, "while it's still daylight. In a good
light I kin see to work on that hand of yourn, Boss. Got to swab
that hole clean, mebby cut away a little proud flesh. Then we better
cauterize it."

"What the hell you mean—cauterize it?"

"Burn the edges that might git infected. I'll rig a twisted balin'
wire, heat it red hot in the stove, an'—"

Boss's snarl interrupted. "Like hell you will!"

Pud shrugged his shoulders and smiled faintly. "It's your hand,
Boss. It'll be your jaws, not mine, that git locked. It's one hell of a
slow and painful way to die."

It was at least twenty below, but Pud worked up a sweat that
day, and it was still daylight when he quit. Now and then he'd
caught a brief glimpse of the black-whiskered Boss, going outside
for another armful of stove wood. But mostly the man stayed inside
the cabin.

Pud knew that the renegade was watching from the cabin windows. Watching for riders, watching to see that Pud did not try for
a getaway.

His work done, Pud went to the cabin before he did his barn
chores. Boss's eyes were slitted and glassy and the gray pallor of
his skin was flushed and feverish. He had the bandage off his hand
and it looked ugly, the skin puffy and tight, yellowish green and
purple.

"Have at it, button," he croaked. "You can't make 'er hurt no
worse. Damn' thing's drivin' a man plumb crazy."

"How's the jaws?" asked Pud callously, shedding his cap and
coat and kicking off his overshoes. He rolled up his sleeves and
washed his hands in warm water and strong yellow laundry soap.
Then he took a home-made harness awl from his warsack. He
shoveled out some red coals and shoved the awl into them, and
took a bottle from the pocket of his canvas coat. Covertly he
watched the man move his lower jaw.

"Carbolic," he said. "Found it in the barn. And a box of gall
salve. Git a tail-holt on yourself, Boss. It's gonna hurt."

Sweat glistened on the man's face and his eyes were glassy and
he gritted his big yellow teeth. There was the odor of burning flesh
as the white-hot steel awl cauterized the raw wound. It was brutal,

crude surgery, but the big man had guts. Pud was glad when it was over, and he bathed the hand in carbolic solution and daubed the wound with the horse salve. Then he bandaged it.

Pud had learned a lesson. He'd gotten no satisfaction from the big renegade's suffering. He was as glad as Boss when the job was done. He was glad to leave the man alone and get back to his barn chores.

An hour after dark, Pud got back to the cabin. Then the man made him go back to the barn and return, carrying a lighted lantern held high so that Boss could make certain from the window that he came alone. He let Pud in and told him to cook supper.

Neither of them slept that night. Boss walked the floor all night, holding his bandaged hand up to the level of his shoulder, gritting his teeth and cursing, drinking coffee as fast as Pud got it made. The man was a little delirious, and his cursing talk was rambling and disjointed.

"I dastn't git off guard. Gotta work out a system—gotta trust you, Puddin' Brains. But you double-cross me and I'll make you wish you'd bin born dead. . . ."

"Why should I double-cross you, Boss?"

"Why? You half-witted whelp, twelve thousand dollars reason why! Windy Bill tried it. Figgered this bullet hole had my gun arm handicapped. He fergot I was left-handed. I didn't shoot him. Just weaned him off his six-shooter and throwed it away. Busted his saddle-gun. Then I worked him over, good and plenty, with a gun barrel. Then he broke loose. That big wind-jammer rabbited on me. Never stopped fer his cap er coonskin coat. . . ."

Pud said nothing.

"Dark outside, and a hell of a blizzard. I sent him on his way with a few shots. He kep' driftin'. No human could live through the night out in that blizzard. When the big Chinook cuts the drifts, they'll find Windy Bill's carcass where he froze to death some-wheres. . . . You try ary monkeyshines, you young whelp, and I'll strip yuh stark naked and send you off like I sent Windy Bill!"

Later on that night, the black-bearded Boss cursed a couple of men he called Sandy Slim and Big Newt. And Pud, piecing together the bits of broken talk, figured that Sandy Slim and Big Newt were the other two bank robbers. That all three of them came from the Hole-in-the-Wall country where they'd planned the bank robbery. Their agreement had been to split up and meet at the Hole. But first they were to stop at a deserted cabin about ten miles south of Lewistown and split the money. And that was where Boss had given Sandy Slim and Big Newt the slip.

"What good is twelve thousand bucks when you gotta split it three ways? Chicken feed! Anyhow, them two sons had 'er made to kill me there at the cabin. So I slipped 'em. Got away in the blizzard. But one of 'em drilled my hand with a bullet. . . .

"Me'n Windy Bill used to work fer the same outfit. I knowed he was winterin' here at this Y Cross line camp. I'd bin here before. But I rode down three horses and like to froze to death gittin' here. Blood froze a inch thick on this damn' hand.

"I throwed in with Windy Bill fer the winter. Promised him a cut of the proceeds. But the big-mouthed hog wasn't satisfied. He made a gun-play fer all of it. I hazed him off to his grave in a snow bank. Windy Bill froze to death in a blizzard and thawed out in Hell! It'll learn him not to cross me!"

It wasn't the law that Boss was afraid of. It was Sandy Slim and Big Newt. Those were the two men he was watching for, dreading to meet unless he sighted them first.

"I'll kill 'em when they show up. Kill 'em like I'd shoot a pair of prowlin' wolves!"

And as he paced the floor he cursed them. "Why didn't I kill 'em and git done with 'em?" he kept repeating. "Why didn't I kill that ornery pair of hydrophobia wolves?"

The days and nights of that first week were torture for the pain-wracked Boss. And for young Pud, they were one long, fear-ridden nightmare. He got his sleep in brief snatches, wolfed his grub, did the work of two men around the line camp. And countless times he looked into the black muzzle of Boss's six-shooter and wondered if this was it. It took every shred of courage he had to face the gun without cringing. His sheer nerve was all that saved his life.

"Better not, Boss," he'd tell the half-crazed man. "I'm gittin' that hand of yours in good shape. You can't take care of it yourself. You'd die in a few days from that lockjaw. Put down that gun and let's change the dressin' on it. Killin' me is killin' yourself. Only you'll die slow. Quit actin' so locoed, Boss."

He saved the man's hand, and probably saved his life. Though a man less tough would have died or gone crazy from pain and killed himself to end his tortured misery.

Bad as the man got, he was never off guard. He never gave young Pud any kind of a chance to kill him. Pud didn't dare risk digging his own gun out of the manger. Boss was chain lightning with a gun. And he always had his six-shooter in his hand or within easy reach, night and day.

After a week, the man's hand was getting back to its normal size and the cauterized bullet hole was healing from the inside out. Pud cleansed the wound twice every day with carbolic solution and bandaged it with clean fresh dressings. Boss no longer walked the floor at night. But he slept fitfully, and whenever Pud stirred on his bunk the man snarled at him like an animal. The young cowboy never took his clothes off that week. Only his boots. He was worn out and his nerves rubbed raw.

After that first week it was different, but not much better for Pud. The man's pain was slacked off, but his temper got uglier and he was more sullen and brooding now, and more abusive.

More than once he slapped the young cowpuncher alongside the head with the barrel of his six-shooter. Once, for some fancied wrong, he beat young Pud senseless. The young cowboy's nose had been broken and one of his ears partly torn off. And inside Pud's heart grew a cancerous hatred and bitterness, and his hidden promise for revenge became a brooding obsession.

Pud did all the work—the barn chores, feeding the cattle, the wood chopping, the cooking. Boss stayed inside the cabin with his six-shooter and saddle-gun, like a prisoner.

Every morning, day after day, until Pud lost track of the days that lengthened into weeks, this went on. And every morning with the first gray of dawn, Boss would sent Pud outside, wearing that big buffalo coat and fur cap and carrying that useless, broken saddle carbine. He was a human decoy to draw the deadly fire of any bushwhacker guns. After a while, the fear wore off, and Pud got calloused to the danger of it.

And so there was no fear in his heart, nor any premonition of danger warning him, on that stormy dawn when he plowed through new drifts to the barn, huddled inside the huge buffalo coat and his fur-capped head lowered against the storm, carrying the broken carbine. He pulled open the barn door.

It was still dark inside. He was carrying the lighted barn lantern in his mittened hand. And it was not until he hung it on its peg, the yellow light in his face, that he knew he was not alone inside the big log barn.

"You ain't Boss Blucher," said a flat-toned voice, "But you could be his pardner. Reach high, feller, and keep 'em lifted."

A big man in a heavy mackinaw and black chaps stepped out of a stall with a gun in his hand.

"He's locoed, Newt, whoever he is," said a voice behind Pud. "Look what he's a-packin'. A busted gun. Like some button of a kid playin' cowboys and Injuns."

"Well, I'll be damned! Look 'im over for a six-shooter, Sandy Slim. He's bound to be heeled."

"Then you don't know the Boss," grinned Pud mirthlessly, "like you should by this time. I'm packin' nothin' but that busted gun he gives me of a mornin' when he dresses me up in his buffalo coat and fur cap and sends me to the barn. I'm the Boss's decoy."

The big man chuckled. It was an ugly sound. "And the trick came near workin'. Only Sandy Slim said mebby the Boss had hid the stuff, and we'd have to sweat him some before we killed him. So we let you come on in, thinkin' it was Boss Blucher walkin' into the bear trap. Decoy!" Big Newt chuckled again.

"The Boss in the cabin yonder?" asked Sandy Slim, when he'd yanked off the big buffalo coat and searched Pud for a gun.

Pud nodded. "He's in the cabin."

"Where's he hid the money? Or do we burn your eyeballs out with matches?" Sandy Slim had a nasal voice. It matched his bloodshot green eyes and the tobacco-stained yellow whiskers.

"The money is in a wool sack bed-tick stuffed with hay. It's on his bunk under his tarp and soogans. You don't need to work me over. Your Boss has bin doin' that for weeks. He's in the cabin and so is the twelve thousand dollars. Have at it."

Sandy Slim shoved his face close to Pud's. His breath stank of whiskey and chewing tobacco. There was treachery and murder in his green eyes. His gun prodded Pud in the belly.

"I think I'll gut-shoot him, Newt. Just fer the hell of it."

"Back off, you damn' fool. Shootin' would spook the Boss. Anyhow, he might be lyin'. The stuff might be hid somewheres else. Bend a gun barrel acrost his head. We'll hog-tie 'im and git 'im outa sight. When we're done with the Boss we'll come back to 'im."

The gun in Sandy Slim's hand lifted and chopped down before Pud could duck the blow. The gun barrel crashed down on his skull, and he went out like a light. Only the heavy fur cap had saved his skull from being caved in by the savage, vicious blow.

CHAPTER FOUR
Brand for a Maverick

Pud didn't know how long he'd been knocked out. He came alive slowly. His head was splitting with pain and his hands and feet were tied and they had used his silk muffler to gag him. He was lying in the back stall, and it was broad daylight now inside the barn. For a while he thought he was alone in the barn, but he did not move. Then he heard the nasal voice of Sandy Slim and the heavy growl of Big Newt talking in low tones at the front of the barn. They were cussing the Boss for not showing up. They were getting impatient and suspicious.

Pud began to work at the rope that tied his wrists behind his back. Whoever had tied him had done a careless and clumsy job. He worked the knots free. And he had his feet untied when Sandy Slim's voice halted Pud's cautious movements.

"He lied to us, Newt. It's near noon and nobody's come outa that cabin. I'll whittle him awake with a jackknife if he ain't dead. He'll talk turkey when I spill his guts out on the barn floor. I ain't waitin' all day on an empty belly—"

"Shut up!" Big Newt's voice was a hoarse whisper. "Cabin door's comin' open. . . . By the hell, it's the Boss. He's a-comin'!"

Pud freed his feet, then got the gag out of his mouth. He got to his feet and over to the manger. His groping hand found his .45 six-shooter in the hay. He gripped the gun, wiping it free of chaff and dust with his other hand, and crouched low.

He could hear Boss's ugly voice bellowing curses now.

"What in hell ails you, you Puddin' Brains whelp? You bedded down in there? If you've coyoted on me, you've gone afoot and I'll ketch up with you an' beat your puddin' brains out! You've had 'er made to rabbit on me, you gutless young coyote! You'll never git nowheres! I'll track yuh down and pound your brains out. Lockjaw, hell! There ain't no such damned thing. And I was fool enough to let you run that hot iron into my hand! Lockjaw!"

"Sounds like the Boss has gone locoed," whispered Sandy Slim.

"Shut up! Lay low. When he comes in, let 'im have it. Shoot fer his guts. I'll git his briskit. He's tough. Don't git yaller."

Pud shifted his position. The stalls were filled with horses. Nine horses now in the barn. He could see Sandy Slim and Big Newt, crouched, one on either side of the door, their six-shooters in their hands, ready to shoot down the big black-whiskered Boss without giving him any kind of a fighting chance. The barn door was closed, and they were peering out through broken places in the daubling and chinking between the logs. Pud could not see the big man coming, but he knew that Boss would have a six-shooter in his hand.

Pud had nothing but hatred in his heart for the big black-whiskered Boss. He'd sworn to kill him, but this thing he was about tổ watch was cold-blooded, bushwhacker murder.

Boss had guts. He'd never whimpered during the agony of that brutal surgery. Ornery as the big black-muzzled bulldozer was, he deserved some kind of a chance for his taw. Pud licked his bruised lips and watched the closed barn door.

Inside the barn the thirsty horses moved restlessly. Out yonder the hungry cattle walk-bawled for hay and water.

Boss figured that young Pud had tried for a getaway on foot. That the young cowboy had pulled out, risking freezing and starvation rather than the continual abuse he'd been getting here at the line camp.

Boss was not too far from right. Pud had been tempted a thousand and one times to try for a getaway, but Boss was guessing wrong now.

The door creaked open. Pud yelled as loud as he could: "Watch out, Boss! They're here!"

It was Pud's shout, far louder and shriller than he'd ever yelled in his life, that filled the log barn, spooking the horses into snorting, lunging action and startling the two waiting bushwhackers, whose nerves were pulled to the breaking point. That gave Boss his fighting chance.

As their first bullets missed him, Boss charged in, shooting as he came. There was no fear in the big man. Only an insane fury that nothing but hot lead slugs could stop. Sandy Slim screamed and pitched over on his side, rolling over and over, his gun spitting fire. Hit mortally, shot through the belly, he was dying with a blazing gun in his hand.

The burly, paunchy Big Newt was shooting as fast as he could thumb back the hammer of his gun and pull the trigger. But he had been hit twice in the paunch and his widespread legs were buckling at the knees and half of his shots were missing. Then a heavy lead slug tore through Big Newt's face and out the back of his skull. He toppled over like a big sodden sack of blubber.

Boss stood there, huge and black-bearded, his yellow teeth bared in a wolfish grin. The sunken eyes under black, ragged brows were bleak and slitted and murderous. He held his smoking gun gripped in his huge hairy hand. He must have been hit, but no blood showed.

"So you helped 'em set their gun trap, Puddin' Brains. Then lost your guts and squawled like a panther. You knowed I'd kill them two coyote things. Then where'd you be? Just where you are now, you gutless whelp. I'm gonna beat your puddin' brains out. Come outa your coyote hole or I'll drag yuh out!"

Boss's voice had a harsh, croaking sound as it came from behind his big clenched yellow teeth. Froth bubbled out from his mouth and clung to his black beard.

Then, for one nightmare moment as he stared at the big man, Pud seemed paralyzed. Then he knew that Death was standing there and that he had to kill it or be killed.

"I'm comin' out, Boss!" Pud's voice was shrill. "I got a gun!"

He stepped out of the stall and into the wide passageway. The thought flashed through his brain that if he was killed and Boss died there would be nobody left to take care of these horses. The horses were snorting and pulling back on their tie ropes and lunging wildly, spooked by the shooting.

Then Pud was standing there in the gray light, unprotected. The gun in his hand was blazing. He could feel the heavy kicking recoil of it in his hand. The gun in Boss's hand spat a streak of fire, but Pud felt no thud of a bullet. And Boss was weaving back and forth on his big long legs like a drunken man. It seemed like a million years before the black-bearded giant pitched over on his face. Boss must have been dead on his feet before he finally went down.

It was all over, Pud told himself. He sat down weakly on the dirt floor. He examined his gun and was bewildered to find that each of the six chambers in its cylinder held an exploded and empty shell. He had no memory of shooting six times. But there was the gun in his hand to prove it.

He thought maybe he was going to be sick if he didn't get out into the fresh air.

He had to stumble over three bullet-riddled bodies to get out the door. He rubbed snow on his face and into his mouth, and after a while he felt better.

Pud was still shaky and sort of giddy. Here he was, with three dead bank robbers on his hands and a burlap wool sack bed-tick stuffed with hay and twelve thousand dollars. He'd sleep tonight on that twelve-thousand-dollar mattress. Pud laughed aloud. But the rattling sound of his own dazed mirth yanked him rudely back into silence.

"I got a barn full of horses to water and feed. And it'll be way after dark by the time I git any hay shoveled into them bawlin' cattle," he muttered to himself. "You kinda fergot, Puddin' Head, that you're still workin' for the Y Cross."

He dragged the three dead men out of the way and went to work. They were still there, side by side in the open space at the front of the barn where the saddles and harness were kept, when he finished his barn chores by flickering lantern light.

He found a big old canvas wagon sheet and covered the dead men. Then he took the lighted lantern and shut the barn door and plowed through the heavy snow to the cabin.

He was lame and weary, and there was a big sore lump on his head where Sandy Slim had hit him with the barrel of his six-shooter. But he was too excited to feel sleepy. He made a pot of coffee and cooked supper.

When he'd washed his supper dishes, he moved the twelve-thousand-dollar burlap wool sack bed-tick in under his own tarp and soogans. Then he stretched out, fully clothed, even to his boots, on the bunk. Grinning like a schoolboy in the candlelight. Wide awake with excitement and boyish dreams. Solving as best he could the problems that lay ahead of him.

The cabin was close, and the stale air with its mingled odors of stale sweat and dead tobacco smoke and cooking reminded him of Boss. He'd air out the cabin in the morning, first thing. Prop open the door and leave it open.

The drifts were too deep and the ground too hard frozen to dig graves. He'd haul the three dead men into the old blacksmith shop and wrap their frozen carcasses in that big wagon sheet and shut 'em in till he could get word to Lewistown for Sheriff Tom Dickson to come and get 'em. And would that be something to tell around the bunkhouse!

Maybe Sheriff Tom Dickson would make him a deputy. Pud had his bellyful of this doctor business. He hoped he never had to patch another bullet wound or smell blood again. Pud was all cowboy.

Forty a month and grub. Save his money. Have his own brand some day. P U D on the left ribs on the cattle. A smaller PUD horse iron on the left thigh. . . . Young Pud dropped off to sleep.

He was in the middle of a dream when he came awake with a jerk. And then he was not certain he was awake, or whether it was a part of the ugly nightmare. Because a short, blocky, gray-mustached man in a bearskin coat and black angora chaps stood beside the bunk, a gun in his hand.

Then a voice from the doorway said, "Take 'er easy, sheriff, it's young Puddin' Head." And the owner of the voice came in, limping a little, a bewildered look on his frost-blackened face.

Pud swallowed and found his voice. "Long time no see yuh, Windy Bill."

"We cold-trailed two men here," said the man in the bearskin coat, "and there should be a third man. They're outlaws."

Pud nodded and swung his legs over the edge of the bunk. His heart was pounding against his ribs, and he tried to make his voice sound casual. The candlelight threw flickering shadows on the log walls.

"You mean Sandy Slim and Big Newt. They laid a bushwhacker trap, but I hollered and Boss killed 'em both. Then Boss got what he calls 'harmful,' and I had to kill 'im. They're laid out in the barn under a ol' wagon sheet. There's twelve thousand and four hundred dollars in the bed-tick under my tarp here on this bunk. And a two-dollar bill the Boss give me, for bad luck."

Pud's young face, blackened by frostbite across his cheekbones and short nose, spread in a wide grin. He pulled the crumpled two-dollar bill from his shirt pocket and smoothed it out. Until right now he'd forgotten all about it. Now it was the most valued thing he owned. Far more precious than the text books Boss had burned one by one during the long black nights. Much more valuable than the fine "three point" red Hudson's Bay blankets.

"I'd kinda like to keep it," he said earnestly, "if I could."

Windy Bill let out a grunting gasp. The gray-mustached man in the bearskin coat grinned faintly and nodded.

"I'm Sheriff Tom Dickson from Lewistown. Windy Bill sent word from Rocky Point Crossin' above here that he was laid up with a couple of frozen feet and wanted to see me on business. So I met him there and heard his story. Then we waited for Boss

Blucher's two pardners to show up. One of the river 'breeds has bin watchin' this line camp. He said the stock was bein' fed. But he never saw more than one man here.

"We got word this mornin' that two riders was headed this way. I taken Windy Bill and headed up the river. The goin' was slow on account of the storm. Looks like we got here a little late.

"There's a two-thousand-dollar reward on Boss Blucher. A thousand apiece on Sandy Slim Baker and Big Newt Rucker. Every dollar of it goes to you, son. And I reckon the Lewistown bank won't begrudge you that two-dollar bill—that turned out to be good luck, after all!"

Pud folded the crumpled, lowly two-dollar bill that was supposed to bring bad luck. He was a little bewildered and inarticulate.

"Gosh! Four thousand dollars. . . . I'll put up your horses. There's a fresh pot of coffee! . . . Gosh!"

"We'll put up our own horses," said the sheriff. "You're a real cowhand, Pud, thinkin' of leg-weary horses at a moment as important as this. What's your real name, son?"

"Just Pud. Short for Puddin' Head. That's all the name I got."

"He's just like a mammyless calf at a round-up, Tom," said Windy Bill. "No folks. No name."

"Then," said Sheriff Tom Dickson, who had a habit of making quick decisions, "it's time you got one, legal. How'd Pud Dickson fit you, son?"

Pud looked into the cowman-sheriff's twinkling blue eyes and read something there that tightened a lump in his throat. He nodded.

"I'd be proud, sir. . . ." Then the words seemed to choke up inside him.

On his bed tarp in bold black letters was that brand he'd dreamed of. P U D. He looked down at it now.

Sheriff Tom Dickson seemed to read the boy's thoughts. "You kin have that P U D brand registered, Pud. Four thousand dollars will buy you a good little bunch of cows. You kin run 'em on my range. I just closed the deal for the Y Cross outfit.

"You'll git your pick of the remuda for a string of top horses. I'm turnin' in my badge and whuppin' a newspaper editor and then we'll stick to ranchin'. Windy Bill kin stay here at the line camp. Me'n you will have to load them three dead outlaws on their horses and take them and the bank money to Lewistown. Think you kin do it?"

"I'll be a kind of a deputy then, won't I?"

Windy Bill unpinned a nickeled deputy's badge from his shirt. His moon face beamed as he pinned it on Pud's faded blue flannel shirt. "I'll tell a man," he grinned.

"Keep the coffee warm, Pud, while me'n the sheriff put up our horses and look over the three dead outlaws. You kin tell us the story when we git back. If I hadn't bin tough I'd froze to death. Only one thing I want outa this—a big warm buffalo coat. Boss Blucher won't need it where he's at."

When they had gone, Pud shoved wood in the stove and washed up and began mixing up a batch of biscuit dough. He'd have biscuits in the oven, spuds and meat in the skillets, strong coffee simmering on the stove when they got back to the cabin.

"Pud Dickson," he said aloud. "The P U D outfit! Goshamighty!"

THE END

By **MURRAY LEINSTER**

The report was thunderous in the small saloon....

HELL TRAII
—PILGRIM—

RIDING into the light of kerosene lamps on either side of the town's single street, the man on the dun horse reminded himself that his name was Bob Powers for the present, and that he was just riding the chuck-line until he felt like working for a spell. He ought to be safe enough, this far from where anybody really knew him, but in spite of himself he was wary. The rows of drooping cow ponies at the hitching-racks, the smell of horses and dust and once a whiff of that pungent smell which is saloon and nothing else on earth—all these things were familiar, and should have been reassuring. But caution was an instinct now.

There was the stage office. There was a bulletin-board beside the door, and there were WANTED posters on it. He carefully didn't look at them, but he savored the atmosphere of the town very delicately and very intently. He could tell the feel of a town to a nicety, now. Maybe it was the way men left their ponies, or the number of filled rifle-holsters in sight—when things were all right there weren't any—or the way men grouped in the saloons, as he saw them through the windows when he went riding by.

There was something tense here tonight. Tense and deadly. But nobody was watching the street. Men talked, very quietly and very grimly. They watched each other with elaborate unconcern but great wariness. In every saloon was a strong tendency for its occupants to be separated into two groups, with plenty of clear space between them. Nobody paid special attention to a lone rider trotting sedately between the double row of houses. The rider himself seemed to be minding his own business with a studious care, but he knew something was happening in this town, or was about to. The sensation of strain was so sharp that it was like an electric tingling in the air. But the town wasn't waiting for somebody. It was waiting for something.

Once the man who called himself Bob Powers was sure of it, he relaxed. He drew a deep breath of relief. He felt in his pockets and rolled a cigarette and almost struck a match to light it with—but not quite. He wasn't foolish enough to make a light out in the street so that eyes would turn to him and see his face clearly while he was dazzled by the match-glow.

With his unlit cigarette in his hand, the temporary Bob Powers kneed his horse to the almost empty rack before a general store. He dismounted a trifle stiffly. He stood still a moment. He didn't tie his horse. It was too well trained to need it, and if he needed to leave in a hurry, he didn't want to have to stop to untie knots. Especially as he might need both hands for shooting.

He went into the store. There wasn't a customer in it and only one clerk. So he lit up, then said, drawling, "I need some coffee an' flour, an' some beans an' bacon. I been ridin' the chuck-line an' sometimes I don't hit, come sundown."

"That's right," agreed the clerk.

He made up the order and put it in a sack, wedging the articles in place very neatly. Without asking, he added some lengths of cord that would be just the thing for tying it in place behind the cantle. The stranger in town grinned slightly.

"Looks like a regular thing."

"'Tis," said the clerk. "Fellas go up to the railroad with shippin' cattle an' stay behind for a little hellin'. Then they trail back single."

He didn't ask any questions, which might be a good sign or not. The pseudo Bob Powers nodded toward the street outside.

"Plenty folks in town, but to a stranger like me it looks pretty quiet."

"Quiet, hell!" said the clerk. "You are a stranger—an' it's a right good thing to be, just now. Not buttin' into your business any, if I was you I wouldn't even stop for a drink. I'd move on. An' I'd keep goin' for a while too. Wish I could."

The supposed Bob Powers raised his eyebrows.

"There's a coupla hundred men in town tonight," the clerk told him. "There's forty Circle Bar men and maybe thirty Lucky Seven hands, and the rest are just dumb fools come in to see hell pop. It's ten to one they pitch in on one side or t'other when she starts. If I was you I'd keep ridin' tonight."

His customer perched himself on the counter instead. It began to seem that this was the safest town—for him—that he'd been in for a long time. At least these people had something to occupy their minds besides matching up strangers with wanted posters. He inhaled pleasurably.

"Sounds right lively," he said with interest.

The clerk opened his mouth to reply. Then the store door opened, and he jerked about to face it. The man at the counter turned his head. One hand hovered casually close to a sixgun butt.

A girl came in. A burly, grizzled cowman followed her. He looked uneasy and flustered. The girl looked with pale defiance at the stranger before she realized that she did not know him. Then she spoke to the clerk.

"Forty-five shells, please. All you have."

"Ain't got so many, Miss Anne," said the clerk regretfully. "Had right much of a run on shells today. Ain't but four-five boxes left."

"I'll take them," said the girl. "Give them to Mr. Gray, here. I'll pay for them." She turned to the burly man. "You pass them out to your men. I'm not asking you to fight for Ted. I'm asking you to fight for law and justice and decency and everything that honest men do fight for!"

The burly man took the boxes of cartridges without remarkable happiness.

"I don't hold with the lynchin', ma'am," he said gloomily, "but I can't ask my boys to fight. I'll pass these out to any that'll take 'em."

The pseudo Bob Powers watched with interested eyes. The girl turned suddenly to him.

"You're a stranger," she said abruptly. "Which way did you come from?"

He jerked his thumb.

"Up thataway, ma'am," he said politely.

The girl tensed.

"Have you ever seen Ike Houghton?"

"Yes, ma'am," he drawled. "Reckon I have. He's a right famous character."

The girl's eyes flashed.

"Then you'd know him if you saw him?"

"I sh'd think so, ma'am," said Bob Powers dryly. "Yes, ma'am."

"Then come along with me!" cried the girl. "They're planning to lynch an innocent man tonight, because they think he's Ike Houghton. And other men will be killed trying to stop it, unless something can be done! Come with me and look at him. If you know the man you'll be able to prove that Ted Brown isn't Ike Houghton!"

"Ted Brown?" demanded the supposed Bob Powers.

The girl nodded. There was silence. The stranger looked at his cigarette, frowning.

"I'll pay you," said the girl, angrily, "anything you like. They won't believe me—"

"Ma'am," said Bob Powers reasonably, "why should they believe me?" Then he got down from the counter. "I ain't yearnin' to be in the public eye, ma'am, but I'll look at the fella who's to be lynched for bein' Ike Houghton when he ain't."

He strolled to the door. There were four men outside. They regarded him alertly. The girl explained swiftly and they relaxed. Bob Powers tied his parcel to his saddle and mounted. The cavalcade of six—the four men, the girl and Bob—went trotting down the street. Heads jerked in the windows as six horses went by. The girl in their midst identified them, though. The heads turned back.

"It looks," drawled Bob Powers, "like I'm in the middle of somethin' without knowin' what. D'you elucidate, ma'am?"

The girl told him, breathlessly and almost incoherently. But the first part of it was familiar enough. Feuds between rival ranches were as old as the cattle business itself. Enmity between ranch owners communicated to their hands and ultimately to a whole neighborhood maybe fifty miles across—such things were old stories. It was only toward the end that this tale took a new turn. There had been cattle run off from both ranches, and each believed the other guilty.

Under normal circumstances gun-play would have begun long since. The situation really called for hired gunmen. But the girl who owned the Lucky Seven had fiercely resisted advice to this effect, and the Circle Bar—being a bigger outfit—had been reluctant to admit the need for mercenaries. So up to now there had been no actual bloodshed. But it looked like tonight would more than make up for it.

Ten days since, a new hand had come to the girl's ranch, the Lucky Seven. She'd sent for him. His name was Ted Brown, and he took over as foreman. But he wasn't a hired gunman. He was the man the girl was going to marry. She'd sent for him because she was scared. And two days ago the owner of the Circle Bar had been found by his men. He'd been shot off his horse, and then deliberately murdered by someone who rode up to him as he lay on the ground and deliberately pumped lead into him. And today the deputy sheriff who held sway in this part of the county had arrested Ted Brown for the murder. And he'd announced that Ted Brown wasn't really Ted Brown, but was actually Ike Houghton, gunman, hired killer, and all-but-proven stage robber and rustler.

"The Circle Bar men went wild," said the girl bitterly. "We found out hours ago they were going to come to town tonight to lynch Ted, so we came in to stop them. The deputy is wrong! Ted can prove who he is. Given time, we can prove that and everything else. But the Circle Bar men think he's a hired murderer, and they're going to try to lynch him and—we've got to try to stop them!"

She sobbed suddenly.

Bob Powers said slowly, "My swearin' he ain't Ike Houghton might be right useful—if you can get somebody else to swear I'm tellin' the truth."

They reached the jail. There were saloons opposite it, and heads suddenly crowded their windows. The lights were behind those heads, so that there were no faces but only ominous silhouettes with lamp-lit empty space behind them. There were two men sitting at ease before the jail. As the sextette rode up one man stood up suspiciously. The other merely raised his head.

"Here's a man," said the girl tensely, "who knows Ike Houghton! May he see Ted, Mr. Shawn? Mr. Shawn is the deputy sheriff," she explained jerkily to Bob. "If you explain to him—"

The suspicious deputy said harshly, "Listen here, ma'am! If you an' these fellas try to sneak him outa jail an' away—"

"I'm trying to keep people from getting killed!" the girl told him fiercely. "Maybe you among them!"

Bob Powers said softly, "His feelin's are reasonable, ma'am, an' you don't want to start the shootin'. You an' these fellas pull back. The deputy an' me, we'll go in, if he's willin'."

The deputy stared hard at Bob as he dismounted. The girl hesitated, and then reined aside. She and her four followers withdrew to the far side of the street, a hundred yards away.

It was an odd sort of scene, there in the darkness before the jail. There was the long, wide, dusty street which was practically all of the town. There were twinkling yellow lights in the windows, wavering as figures moved inside the buildings. There were cow ponies in long rows, drooping drowsily and rarely stirring, even to switch their tails. The man who called himself Bob Powers stood still, almost smiling. The Circle Bar man scowled. The deputy sheriff glanced from one to the other, uneasily.

"If anybody starts shootin'," remarked Bob Powers dryly, "everybody does. Maybe it's goin' to start anyhow, but I ain't anxious to begin it. All I want is to see this fella Ted Brown, to see is he Ike Houghton or not."

The deputy said uncomfortably, "I don't give a damn. I'll show him t'you—if the Circle Bar don't mind."

The Circle Bar man, who'd been sitting with the deputy as they rode up, spat.

"If he says that murderer ain't Ike Houghton," he said shortly, "he's lyin'. If he says he is, maybe the lynchin' can go ahead without gun-fightin'."

"That last," said Bob mildly, "is part of the idea."

The deputy rose and took out a huge key. He opened the jail door. He locked it behind him when he and the stranger were within. He struck a match and lit a lamp. They were in his office, and the whole jail had been utterly dark. He moved through a door, and the shadows of iron bars shifted against walls. Silently, he held the lamp so its light shone into one of the cells.

There was a young man inside the cell. He had dark hair and steady eyes. He couldn't know what this inspection could mean. It might be only a preliminary to his lynching. But he looked out defiantly. He blinked because of the light in his eyes, but Bob Powers's face was in deep shadow. After an instant he turned and went back through the door into the deputy's office. The deputy followed him. He set the lamp on his desk.

"Well?" said the deputy challengingly.

"It ain't Ike Houghton, o'course," said Bob. "Why'd you say it was? Who you workin' with?"

The deputy swore.

"What d'you mean?" he demanded angrily. "If he ain't Ike Houghton, who is he? An' what—"

The supposed Bob Powers said softly, "You got some WANTED posters around. I want to show you somethin'. Wheah are they?" Then he said, "Mmmh! I see 'em."

He reached forward with his left hand. On the desk a batch of crudely printed sheets had been impaled on a spike which served as a file. Bob Powers leafed through them quickly, with his left hand. His right hung near his holster. And his eyes were on the papers he glanced at, but there was no doubt that he noticed every move the deputy made.

"Heah 'tis," he said in the same soft tone, which would not carry through the window to the Circle Bar man outside. "This's the one. H'm—five-eight, dark brown hair—scar on left wrist. Look!"

He laid the poster squarely in the brightest part of the lamp light on the table. And he laid his left wrist beside it. There was a scar on that wrist. His right hand was close indeed to the gun at his right hip.

The deputy stared at the poster. The color left his face. He looked up, his hands twitching, and saw the supposed Bob Powers grinning at him.

"Kinda humorous, o'course," he said, "but you ain't goin' to tell. You can't. It'd sound too funny. Who're you workin' with, fella? They got things organized pretty. I might throw in with 'em."

The deputy sheriff gradually smiled a sickly, uncertain smile.

"I heard the Clantons was down this way," said the pseudo Bob Powers. "This sounds kinda like them. Makin' a range war first, so's they can nibble at the herds o' two ranches, an' then a trick like this one. Every fightin' man in twenty miles is in town tonight for a lynchin'—an somebody's due to make the biggest haul o' beef-cattle this country ever heard of, tonight. An' if the fight heah in town's as big as it looks to bc, there won't be anybody whole enough to chase 'em. Who is it?"

His tone was cordial—and amused. The deputy licked his lips. Then he said under his breath, "You guessed it. The Clantons." But he glanced at the poster on the table as if for reassurance.

"Old friends o' mine," said the stranger, smiling. "How'll I find 'em?"

"They—they crossin' the border at Littleman's Pass," said the deputy. "You—uh—you took a long chance ridin' into town. You goin' on to join 'em, or you goin' to stay—"

The stranger said humorously, "Stay wheah lead'll be flyin'—for nothin'?"

"Uh—what you goin' to say about—him?" the deputy asked.

The stranger laughed soundlessly. "You guess! Might's well go along now. Long ride to Littleman's Pass. Come along!"

They went out of the jail together. The Circle Bar man greeted them suspiciously.

"You two were in there a mighty long time!"

Bob Powers mounted. As he swung his horse aside he heard the deputy's voice.

"It's him, all right. An' when he seen this fella he broke down—"

Bob Powers's lips tensed. He rode to where the girl and her four followers waited, a hundred yards away. She spurred forward to meet him.

"Did you see—" she asked urgently. "Can you swear he isn't Ike Houghton? You can, can't you?"

"Naturally," he said in a dry voice. "But listen heah, ma'am! The deputy arrested this Ted Brown for killin' the Circle Bar owner. What evidence was theah, besides him sayin' Ted Brown was Ike Houghton, a known hired gunman?"

"Why—I don't know!" said the girl. "He didn't say! He just—arrested Ted, and brought him in town, and talk of lynching began, and we came in to prevent it."

"Okay," said Bob Powers. "Another thing. Had this Ted Brown ever seen this man he's accused o' killin', before the killin', that is? You said he was only heah ten days—"

"N-no. Of course not!" said the girl. "There's been so much hard feeling between the ranches that nobody on one would dream of going on the other. And Ted didn't have time to come to town—"

Two men, together, marched across the street. They went from before the jail to a saloon just opposite. One was the deputy. The other was the Circle Bar man from in front of the jail. The supposed Bob Powers turned his head and regarded them.

"Listen to me, ma'am," he said evenly. "Theah goin' to be some surprises around town in the nex' ten minutes. You get word to all your friends not to be took back too much if Circle Bar men start cussin' with 'em instead of at 'em. I'm goin' to try to stop this lynchin'. Maybe I won't manage it. But anyhow I'm goin' over yonder an' talk right disillusionin' to those Circle Bar fellas."

He wheeled his horse and rode toward the saloon the deputy and the Circle Bar man had just entered.

He dismounted before the door. And earlier, when he'd stopped at the general store, he'd left his horse untied because a tied horse can't be ridden off in a hurry if a man needs both his hands for shooting. Now, though, he tied the animal firmly, either so it couldn't be stampeded if other mounts around it raced away, or because he didn't expect to be shooting when he came out.

He went in.

The saloon was small and filled with men, but they were not divided into two groups with clear space between them. This was the unofficial but actual headquarters of the Circle Bar in town, and from here the lynching party would set out, fighting its way if necessary into the jail and after. There was nobody here but Circle Bar men and their avowed partisans.

The temporary Bob Powers went in quietly. The place was thick with cigarette smoke and the mingled spirituous odors inseparable from saloons. But it was oddly quiet. Only one voice was going, and all eyes turned toward its owner, the deputy sheriff.

"Yes, suh!" said the deputy. "He looked in them bars an' he seen the fella that's been callin' himself Ted Brown an' he says, 'Hello, Ike!' An' that fella says, 'Damn you! I been usin' another name heah!' An' I says, 'Then you admit you're Ike Houghton, an' he kinda snarls, 'What's the use o' denyin' it now—' "

Bob Powers rapped heavily on the bar with a silver dollar as a growl ran through the room.

"Bartender!" he called sharply. "You got a cash customer!"

There was a grunt above the savage murmuring all around.

"That sounds like that fella—"

Heads turned to the stranger in town. A clear space opened along the bar, against which Bob Powers leaned as he ordered a drink of a reluctantly attentive bartender. There was no one between him and the deputy sheriff, who stood and stared with an expression of dazed, incredulous amazement on his face.

"Hey!" said the Circle Bar man who'd been before the jail. "You tell 'em, fella! The deputy took you in an' you saw him."

Bob Powers carefully poured an exact drink from the bottle slid to him along the bar.

"Sure," he said. "I know the fella that's in jail. His name's Ted Brown. His pa owns a kinda small ranch up Nogales way. He's got two sisters an' three brothers, only one of 'em is dead, I b'lieve."

His tone was utterly matter-of-fact. It was so casual that it was ten times as convincing as a more vehement assertion would have been. He picked up his drink.

"What's that?" gasped the Circle Bar man, aghast. "The deputy says you identified him as Ike Houghton!"

"That's a lie," said Bob Powers mildly. "He ain't any more Ike Houghton than you are. I never said he was."

Heads jerked to the deputy. This was bewildering. The deputy's reaction was more bewildering still. His face was slowly going gray. He opened his mouth, but no words came out of it.

His hands began to shake.

"Somebody told me," said Bob Powers mildly, "that this whole business is queer. They tell me that this fella Brown never saw the man he's accused o' shooting. That fella didn't even know Brown by sight. But the fella that did the killin' pumped him fulla lead after he was knocked off his horse, same as if he knew he'd been recognized and had to make sure nobody lived to tell who'd done what he was surprised at. It was the kinda trick a—uh—a crooked deputy sheriff mighta done, but it don't seem like Ike Houghton, either."

He leaned casually against the bar, his left elbow not raised upon it, but comfortably enough for all of that.

"It'd be right likely it was the deputy," he added dispassionately. "He's a friend of the Clantons. Ask 'im. An' they're havin' a party tonight. With every Circle Bar an' Lucky Seven man in town tonight, there's a lot of cows that ain't bein' watched. So the Clantons are lookin' after 'em—headin' for the border," he added precisely, "to cross at Littleman's Pass. An' theah's supposed to be enough shootin' in town tonight so's theah won't be anybody on either ranch fit to chase after 'em in the mornin'. You might ask him. He sure knows."

He nodded toward the deputy sheriff, not ten feet away along the bar. And the deputy was not a credit-inspiring sight just then. His face was a haunted mask of terror.

"That's a lie! It ain't so! Look who's tellin' you! He's—"

The temporary Bob Powers waited politely. He held his drink in his right hand. He watched the deputy with a sardonic interest. The deputy had identified Ted Brown as Ike Houghton. He'd said the supposed Bob Powers had identified Ted Brown as Houghton. And now, if he said what he had been about to say, the results would be interesting.

"Tell 'em," he suggested mildly.

The deputy quit. He was trapped and—though he alone saw it at the moment—doomed. Bob Powers lifted his drink to his mouth. There was but one slim hope for the deputy.

While the stranger drank, with the snake-like speed of desperation the deputy snatched out his gun.

The report was very loud. It was thunderous in the small saloon. And then the supposed Bob Powers put his glass back on the bar with his right hand, and re-holstered his left-hand gun. The deputy crashed to the floor. He lay still.

"Now," said Bob Powers evenly, "you fellas better do some checkin' on your herds, or they'll be through Littleman's Pass an' into Mexico while you're foolin'."

And this was, of course, the most ticklish moment of all. This was the decisive instant. There was nothing more that one man could do. A lynching was still possible, though it was not nearly as likely as it had been. Doubt had been sown, now. A gunfight between forty men on one side and thirty on the other, with friends and sympathizers drawn in unpredictably, was still most desperately conceivable.

But in the tense, grim instant when the accomplished fact of the deputy's killing was still fresh and startling, there came the rapid, dust-muffled hoofbeats of a horse flogged into the town at breakneck speed. A man yelled in the street outside.

"Rustlers! Circle Bar! Rustlers—"

There was a roar, and men plunged for the door. Other saloons erupted men who raced toward the yelling man—a Circle Bar man with splints on his leg, who'd stayed cursing behind when a lynching was in order, but had ridden nevertheless when rustlers tried to drive off a herd of prime shipping-cattle held near the ranch house for an early trip to market.

Men peeled off from the crowd and raced to their horses. The horses raced for the open beyond the town. There was a pounding, a thundering, a drumming of hoofs. The town drained empty.

The man who called himself Bob Powers did not join the rush. He waited, watching interestedly, until the exodus was over. Then he watched two men and a girl batter valiantly at the jail door until it yielded. They went in, and doubtless found a key to the cells inside. The two men came out and jumped on their horses and pounded out of town after their fellows. The girl stayed in the jail with the man she was going to marry, but not before she'd seen the stranger.

"Me," said the man who'd ridden into town rather less than an hour ago, "me, I'm a stranger heah, so I didn't think I'd better join in. I think I'll have just one more drink an' mosey along."

He did. And some time later, many miles away and out in the darkness of the open range, the man who'd called himself Bob Powers, but whom the WANTED posters called Ike Houghton, heard infinitely faint, far-away poppings. The riders who'd gone roaring out of town had caught up at last with the Clanton riders.

And Ike Houghton said, marveling, to his horse, "It sure beats all! Kids sure do pop up! Who'd ha' thought that kid brother o' mine would be a grown-up man already, almost gettin' lynched an' thinkin' of getting married! It sure beats all!"

THE END

**A Parson Picka
Novel**

All that the hell-bending Parson Pickax wanted was to make a decent town out of roaring Owl-hoot Junction, and build a meeting house for his flock. . . . All that Big George McWhorter wanted was to make a decent corpse out of the Parson before the Reverend started backing up his Bible-talk with bullets!

WL OOT JUNCTIO

y Charles W. Tyler

Parson Pickax jerked his old Colt from under his long-tailed coat. . . .

CHAPTER ONE
Owlhooter Paradise

Parson Pickax cleaned and oiled his venerable Colt, his long jaw set with stiff determination. When he was done he examined his conscience, searched the Scriptures with scrupulous attentiveness and sallied forth to make medicine with Seco Snyder, gun-tough and killer.

With his gun-belt looped around his gaunt middle under his long rusty black coat, a worn, much-thumbed Bible clasped against him like a staunch shield, the Parson left the boarding house of Launcelot Jenks and stalked slowly down Chadron Street toward the den of perdition that was Rick Ringgold's saloon.

The Parson had been christened Philander Pickarts, but somewhere down the U. P. trail the wild Irishmen of General Dodge, with whom he had worked shoulder to shoulder, had called him Parson Pickax. Not only had this strange man proved himself to be a hardy son of toil, who had labored diligently for his daily bread, but a student of the Scriptures as well, finding there quotations to fit every situation.

Parson Pickax was a broad-minded, worldly man, as one must be who rubbed elbows with the raw frontier. A Godly man, too, the Parson, hating the wicked and unjust, and working always to further law and order.

He had played a prominent part in the reformation of Hungry Junction; he had been instrumental in whipping the ruling toughs of Jericho City to their knees, and had arrived recently in Saint David to lend what aid he might in the taming of this Purgatory of the plains.

Peal Ivy, the militant and crusading editor and publisher of the *Saint David Blade*, had sent for the Parson, feeling that the town needed the sobering influence of a church, but now Ivy regretted it, fearing for the life of his friend. Two days ago Maury Dines, the town marshal, had sprawled down before the blazing gun of Seco Snyder, and Saint David was without law.

Marshal Dines had been a good man, and a courageous one; his cardinal sin was that he was slow on the draw. Already it was being whispered about that his successor was likely to be a man chosen by the toughs, who were bossed by Big George McWhorter, representing the whiskey and gambling interests.

The seamed face of Peal Ivy looked out from the grimy window of the *Blade*, and, seeing the stiff-walking Parson, quick apprehension kindled in his eyes. He hurried to the door.

"Evenin', Parson."

"Evenin' to ye, Brother Ivy."

"Seco Snyder come in on the stage," said Peal Ivy. "He went into Rick Ringgold's place."

"So I heerd," said Parson Pickax, stroking his long chin.

"You aren't lookin' for him, by any chance, Parson?" The editor's troubled eye touched the other's gun-belt with its sagging Walker Colt.

"Seek an' ye shall find," quoth the Parson sonorously. "I go to convert a sinner from the error of his evil ways."

"Good Lord!" gasped Peal Ivy. He went on, "There isn't a man can stand up to Seco in a shoot-out. He'll kill you, as he did Maury Dines. I'm sorry I asked you to come to Saint David."

"It is written in the Book of Job to tread down the wicked," intoned the Parson. "An' I am a right pert treader."

Peal Ivy shook his head resignedly. A look at the Parson's determined jaw was enough to convince a man that there was no use arguing. Already blood had been spilled in the county-seat fight; there would be more.

Yesterday the Parson had preached Maury Dines's funeral sermon, and the closing words of that sermon had been a warning to Big George McWhorter, Seco Snyder and the rest that the smoking wrath of God was about to descend upon them.

The trouble was that the sheriff over at New Babylon was lined up with the wrong crowd. Big George and Seco Snyder had little concern with the wrath of God, just so long as they had the sheriff with them.

Parson Pickax continued on down Chadron Street. His angular frame was heightened by the battered stovepipe hat he wore; his long coat flapped about his bony shanks. His free right arm was loosehung, while a ham-size fist reached far below a too-short sleeve.

Everything about him spelled bungling awkwardness. His scarecrow figure held no hint of speed or dexterity; rather, it gave the impression of indolence. A bone-rack, it seemed, that might easily fall apart under the first breath of violence.

Long shadows lay on Chadron Street as the westing sun wheeled home below the prairie rim. The supper hour was past, and groups were gathered on gallery and sidewalk.

Grinning faces watched the Parson. Now and then a lounger addressed him with thinly veiled ridicule.

"Hi, Deacon."

"Make any converts today, Parson?"

"Well, well, if it ain't John the Baptist!"

To each, Parson Pickax gave a benign smile and a lazy flip of that big right paw. "Howdy, neighbor. Howdy to ye, brother. Don't fergit the Friday night prayer meetin' in the Belly-Up Bar."

And so the Parson came to Rick Ringgold's place, the Hell's Delight Saloon. He pushed through the batwing doors like a rangy longhorn steer thrusting incautiously through a brush thicket.

The high drone of voices tapered off, and a hush fell that was like the silence in a forest after the quitting of a gusty wind. Eyes hit at the figure angling up to the bar, and somewhere a voice said, "Hell, it's that old gospel-shouter."

"Howdy, gents," the Parson offered amiably. "I was jist makin' a little razoo, like Paul told the Romans, an' I bring redemption to a place of iniquity."

Seco Snyder, standing midway down the bar, pulled around, his eyes hot with whiskey. He had heard from friends of the Parson's sermon of vengeance. Seeing the gun-belt under the coat of the preacher, his right hand moved stealthily toward his holstered six-gun.

Western Nebraska was wild and tough, and Saint David had sprung out of the weeds with the coming of the railroad. Parson Pickax was its first minister, and the citizenry regarded him with mingled doubt and disdain.

Rick Ringgold, thumbs hooked in the armpits of his ornate vest, stood at the end of the bar talking to Big George McWhorter. He eyed the Parson tolerably, and winked at Big George. The latter grunted, scowled. He didn't know about this old coot who came sashaying into the Hell's Delight, packing a Bible and a six-shooter.

A bull-chested bartender gaped at the preacher, then flung a look at Ringgold for the signal to throw him out. However, the proprietor seemed to prefer to let matters run their course.

Parson Pickax took his place at the bar a few feet from Seco Snyder. Here he turned and held up his toil-worn hand.

"My text this evenin', gents," he began with deep-toned solemnity, "is taken from the twentieth chapter of Job: 'The triumph of the wicked is short as Ringgold's drinks, an' the sinner is slapped down in his bloom.' " The Parson revised the quotation slightly, as he frequently did. He went on, "Followin' a few words, there will be prayer an' benediction. Any hombres wishful to take part in the services are plumb welcome to indulge, no end." He regarded Seco Snyder benignly and from twinkling eyes.

"What the hell are yuh lookin' at me for, yuh old buzzard?" snarled Seco.

"The sinner I chastise," said the Parson, "an' the errin' son shall have coals heaped on his head; hence I call on you to repent, or get your unworthy hide scorched."

Somewhere there was a hoot of derision and raucous laughter. A hard-bitten figure at the bar said, "How about a drink, Parson?"

Parson Pickax said, "An' now let us pray: Dear Lord, be merciful to the transgressor. His name is Seco Snyder, an' the blood of innocent men is on him. For mercy sake, be charitable, for unless he mends his ways I aim to convert him—either by hot lead or by hell-fire preachin' of the Word!"

Seco Snyder uttered a roar of rage and jerked at his six-shooter. Men lurched away from the bar and out of the line of fire. Rick Ringgold yelled at the bartender, who grabbed for a bung-starter. Big George McWhorter yapped a startled oath.

The Parson was handicapped by his position, and his Walker Colt was draped around by the long coat, making it difficult to draw quickly. Seco Snyder, seeing that he had the other at a disadvantage, moved with cold deliberation, his beady eyes savage, malignant.

The distance between them was no more than two paces. Parson Pickax made a half-move for his gun, then dropped into a crouch and launched his bony frame at Seco Snyder's middle with amazing speed in his lanky frame.

The gunman fired, but the Parson was under the screaming missile and coming in like a thunderbolt, his long, angular arms flung out for a hold. His shoulder hit Seco Snyder in the stomach, and the killer uttered a gusty grunt as he was driven backward and off balance.

Years of hard labor had toughened the Parson, where soft living and whiskey had taken their toll of the burly gun-tough. He lifted

Seco, then dropped him like a sack of oats. A clawlike hand closed on the six-shooter and wrenched it free.

The bartender made a swipe at the Parson's head, but missed. The Parson straightened, and smacked the fat man leaning across the bar fair on the nose with the barrel of Seco Snyder's Colt, eliminating the gentleman from the fray.

Seco heaved to hands and knees, but the descending six-gun caught him on the skull, flooring him again. A big bouncer circled warily behind the Parson, but the maneuver was tardy and ill-timed, for the preacher had a full head of steam up and was covering ground like a runaway train. He dragged the bulky choreman of the Hell's Delight and heaved him out onto the sidewalk, unhinging one of the batwing doors in the process.

Parson Pickax retrieved his Bible and his hat and stood there then, balancing Seco Snyder's six-shooter in his right hand. "I can hear the devil groanin'," he said.

"That ain't the devil, Parson," said an onlooker. "It's Baldy Johnston," indicating the beefy bartender.

This worthy was sagged against the bar, holding onto his nose, while blood dripped onto the polished surface. Both of his eyes were swelling shut, and he sounded like a mourning dove.

Rick Ringgold was cursing softly. Big George McWhorter chewed hard on his fat cigar, at last finding words. "You're diggin' your grave, Parson," he said darkly. "This is the toughest town on the Union Pacific, but it suits us. If you don't like it, you can take the seat of your pants in your hand an' vamoose."

"I have heard that the town is called Owlhoot Junction," said Parson Pickax, "an' that it is besotten with sin. Truly it is a fertile vineyard, an' here I will build a church." He turned toward the door. At the threshold he paused to flip a jaunty paw at this, his first congregation. "Hallelujah! Revive us ag'in!" And he stalked away up Chadron Street.

CHAPTER TWO
Hell in Nebraska

Peal Ivy gave the affair in the Hell's Delight Saloon a place on the front page under a flaring black banner.

FIGHTING PARSON BRAVES LION'S DEN!

As Moses brought water from the rock, manna from Heaven and raised up the fiery serpent, so has the man who calls himself Parson Pickax performed a great deed in our community. Already has he struck terror in the hearts of the forces of evil in our fair town. Saint David, shunned by decent people and populated with toughs and crooks, has been derisively labeled Owlhoot Junction, a name we resent, however much it is deserved.

The *Blade* stands for law and order; we have championed the fight for right, but our feeble efforts have not been enough. We need honest and fearless men to join the fray. If we have to have whiskey, we want good whiskey. If we have to have gambling, we want a square deal. We are not snooty as concerns tarnished ladies, but we must make the streets safe for our wives and our daughters.

Saint David is well located; it is on the railroad, and we can offer every advantage to settlers. We deserve to be the county seat, but we cannot hope for that honor until we have washed our dirty linen. This fall election will decide whether we are to take our rightful place in the sun, or whether New Babylon is to retain this cherished plum.

Now is the time for all good men to put their shoulders to the wheel of progress. A churchless community is like a body without a soul, a cart without a horse. Parson Pickax has shown what a fearless man can do. Congratulations to you, Parson. And now, to quote from the Right Reverend Philander Pickarts, "Let's get together and kick the devil to hell out of Owlhoot Junction!"

The story of Saint David, or Owlhoot Junction, was as old as the first Judas; it was the story of blood and greed and men crucified. The town sprang into being with the laying of westward steel, and, when railhead moved on, somehow managed to survive the swift exodus of camp followers and parasites.

A few stayed—a few good men, a few bad. The cockle and the wheat. Peal Ivy and his wife put down their roots, as did Maury Dines and young Andy Pike, blacksmith, and Launcelot Jenks and Matilda. And there was Prudence Parmlee, pretty as a new-minted dollar. Some said Prudence stayed on account of Andy, and some said Andy stayed on account of Prudence. . . .

And there were others. They were from Vermont and Ohio and New York State and Missouri; they were the children of the West, each with a story as long as your arm—stories mostly of hardship and privation and sorrow.

They had settled in Saint David for various reasons. First, there was the river, the South Platte. Sometimes it wasn't much of a river, but it was a river. And there were a few cottonwoods. Not much like the elms and maples and good old shagbark walnuts back home, but they were trees. And there was grass, lots of it. Lastly, there was the railroad—not much of a railroad, but it had ties and rails, and trains ran on it. A kind of a steel link, it was, with civilization.

What was yonder in Wyoming, and beyond—besides redskins and trouble—they didn't know. And so Saint David looked pretty good. And so old man Jenks and Matilda built a boarding house, and Peal Ivy started his pioneer newspaper, and Andy Pike set up his blacksmith shop.

And everything looked as fine as a field of growing corn.

Settlers started drifting in, and Texas trail herds rolled up the dust in their northward trek. There were bearded miners, heading for the Black Hills, and freighters, and land sharks and cowboys—and toughs. Freight and stage lines made junction there.

With Saint David on the way to becoming a booming prairie metropolis, a movement was begun to make it the county seat.

Immediately a howl of protest arose from New Babylon. While admitting that Saint David possessed the advantage of being on the railroad, the citizenry of New Babylon pointed out that their town already had established suitable accommodations for county offices, that they had a school and church, and, above all, were a people of peaceful pursuits.

Saint David, on the other hand, New Babylon declared, was a sink of iniquity, populated largely by toughs and renegades of the worst sort, with only a makeshift school, no church of God, no law.

This struggle for the county seat was, even in these roaring seventies, an old story in Kansas, Nebraska and the Dakotas, leading frequently to turbulence and bloodshed, just as now fierce hatreds blazed, with politics, greed and graft playing their part.

The killing of Maury Dines was another nail in the coffin of Saint David, and the New Babylon partisans cried that it was a further example of the unbridled wickedness of Saint David. It was rightly called Owlhoot Junction, they said.

To add to the complications, sentiment in Saint David itself was sharply divided. The better element, favoring the county-seat movement, were strongly opposed by the gambling and whiskey interests, as represented by Big George McWhorter and Rick Ringgold, who claimed that a wide open town brought in more money.

Realizing that unless something was done, the county-seat movement was doomed to go down in defeat at the coming election, Peal Ivy had sent for Parson Pickax.

The Parson, filled with a holy zeal, and being an old battler from away back, had promptly accepted the call, arriving in Saint David just in time to preach Maury Dines's funeral sermon.

The affair in the Hell's Delight Saloon, serving as a preface to the challenge in the *Blade*, threatened to touch off the powder keg, and everybody held his breath, waiting for the explosion.

The first task that now confronted the town fathers was the selection of a new marshal. It was, clearly, a job for a man with courage and a fast gun.

Doc Byler said they ought to import a professional town-tamer—somebody like Bat Masterson or Wild Bill Hickok. Gideon Crowningshield, who ran the general store, suggested the Parson.

The Parson, however, protested. He said it would cramp his style, for a marshal was bound by certain civil laws and restrictions, where a preacher's activities were limited only by the blue sky and the Kingdom of God.

Peal Ivy then presented the name of young Andy Pike, the blacksmith. After some discussion, he was approached on the subject.

Andy was shoeing a mule. A fine, strapping fellow he was, in his leather apron, blue-eyed and tawny. He had learned his trade at his father's forge back in Vermont. He was sober, industrious, and as honest as homespun wool.

Peal Ivy told him why they had come, feeling a little guilty, for asking a man to step into the boots of the late lamented Maury Dines was like inviting him to make his peace with God and prepare for the worst.

The mule was a whacking big brute with a mean eye, but Andy slapped the beast around, said "Whoa!" brusquely, and picked up and straddled a hind leg, without giving the obstreperous animal a chance to decide whether or not to let fly.

"You know what the job is," said Peal Ivy. "Just keep the peace of an evening, and see that the boys don't overstep themselves." He mopped his worried brow.

Andy peeled off the old shoe. "What's the job pay?"

Peal told him, and Andy said, "When do I start?"

"Well, today is Friday," said Peal. "I guess this evenin'."

There were those who questioned the propriety of having a prayer meeting in a saloon, but Parson Pickax held to his decision to hold services in the Belly-Up Bar.

"There ain't no percentage in preachin' to four walls," the Parson said. "A lot of churches have died a-bornin' on empty pews. Yuh don't go up the trail with a few strays; yuh got to have a herd. There'll be a right smart crowd in the Belly-Up, an' the boys will have pelfry in their pokes. One collection, an' we get the foundation for a house o' God."

"'Tain't fittin'," Mrs. Jenks protested, "raisin' up funds in a saloon to build a meetin' house."

"The church I aim to build," said the Parson, "will be for saints an' sinners, an' I figger to make the sinners help pay for it."

The Belly-Up was a little out of the ordinary run of saloons in that it was bossed by a lady, one Belle McGee. A widow-woman, the Parson termed her. Her late spouse, following an embroglio with a tough gentleman, had taken wing for a fairer land.

Mrs. McGee was big and rangy and tough, and she could swear like a mule-skinner, but many a poverty-stricken sodbuster and his family had been the recipient of her generosity. She sold a good brand of whiskey and refused her girls the privilege of rolling drunks. In addition to whiskey, she sold Hostetter's Bitters, good for man or beast.

Parson Pickax had made the acquaintance of Belle back up the U.P. trail. Mrs. McGee liked the Parson, and she had an idea that a prayer meeting in her place would be good advertising. Further, it was bound to steal trade away from the more pretentious Hell's Delight for one night, at least. It tickled her to think that she would be putting something over on Rick Ringgold and Big George McWhorter, both of whom she despised.

At the hour set for the services, the Belly-Up Bar was jammed to the doors, and a most cosmopolitan gathering it was. There were many, like Prudence Parmlee, Mrs. Jenks and the station agent's wife, who had never been in a saloon in their lives, just as there were those who had never been to a prayer meeting.

The few who owned hymn books brought them. Belle McGee's piano player didn't know much about church music, but what he lacked in technique he made up for in enthusiasm.

The opening song was Onward Christian Soldiers, which seemed prophetic. The bullet-nicked piano fairly quivered, while the rafters rang to, "Onward, Christian Soldiers! Marching as to war. . . ." And on through, "Gates of hell can never 'Gainst that Church prevail. . . ."

Young Andy Pike, wearing his marshal's star, shared a hymn

book with Prudence Parmlee. The girl's eyes were shining, but in her heart a dread fear cast its shadow. She had been happy in Saint David, happy in her work of teaching school in an abandoned box-car. She was proud to be a part of this settlement of the frontier.

Behind her were sad memories and tragedy. Her mother had died of cholera at a wagon camp on the Missouri; her father, never strong, had slipped away from her during the journey across the prairies. Young Andy Pike had helped and befriended her in many ways. They were in love, and would one day be married and build a home here in Saint David.

Something told her that trouble was close. She had scolded Andy for accepting the job as marshal, even though he was so big and strong it seemed that nothing could hurt him, but he had made light of her fears, saying the extra money thus earned meant that their dreams would become reality so much the sooner; besides, being marshal was a kind of civic duty and an honor.

Andy Pike slanted a downward glance at the shiny star now, there on his homespun hickory shirt, and gave Prudence a reassuring grin.

The girl smiled bravely, but she could not help but feel that her happiness was too good to last.

Parson Pickax prayed, loud and earnestly. "Dear Lord, lend an ear. This voice yuh hear is comin' from Belle McGee's place in Saint David, Nebraska. Mebbe all yuh know it by is Owlhoot Junction. Or, likely, yuh never heerd of it at all, on account I reckon this is the first church service that was ever held in these diggin's.

"We're due west on Omaha on the Union Pacific, an' all trains stop here, includin' the Glory Train. I tried to get in a word with yuh over to the Hell's Delight a few days back, but the devil was a pawin' sod an' I couldn't scurcely make myself heard above the vast multitude."

At this point, two tough-looking men entered and swaggered to the bar. Guns were slung at their hips. They appeared not to notice the bowed heads, or hear the Parson.

"Whiskey, ol' girl," one demanded.

"Ain't no whiskey served until after prayer meetin'," hissed Belle McGee. "An' take off your hats, ye damn' heathen! Don't ye hear the Parson a-talkin' to the Lord A'mighty?"

"A prayer meetin'!" hooted the taller of the pair derisively. "Don't make me laugh."

"We want a drink," snarled the other, "prayer meetin' or no. Come on, set out yore red-eye." He banged on the bar with his fist.

"Plenty other saloons," said Belle McGee. "Git out!"

"The Belly-Up suits us," persisted the tall tough.

Men and women scowled at the disturbers, and someone said, "Quiet."

Peal Ivy recognized the intruders as two of Big George McWhorter's satellites, Alf Walker and Nick Dunn. It was easy to guess that they had been sent here to break up the prayer meeting, and, possibly, put the new marshal to test. The editor of the *Blade* glanced nervously at Andy Pike.

The Parson, standing near the piano, opened one eye, but continued to pray. "We are sore tried, Lord. Give us patience to bear with the transgressor an' the unbeliever, an' if yuh can't give us patience, give us strength to cuff 'im to a peak."

Alf Walker and Nick Dunn swung around and put their backs to the bar, thumbs hooked suggestively in their gun-belts.

"Listen to the ole rooster!" jeered Alf Walker.

"Hell, there ain't no God in Nebraskie," said Nick Dunn, "an' there ain't no law in Owlhoot Junction."

Young Andy Pike stiffened. He felt Prudence Parmlee's fingers tighten on his arm. He found voice at last. "There *is* law here," he said, "an' there's a God in Nebraska. An' if you fellers don't like our way, get out of town."

"Git out of town?" snarled Alf Walker. "You try an' run us out," he boasted belligerently.

"He can't even run us out of the Belly-Up," rasped Nick Dunn.

Andy Pike pulled away from the girl and started forward.

Alf Walker's hand drifted toward his gun-butt. "Stay back, or I'll blast yuh out from under yore hat!"

CHAPTER THREE
Medicine for a Killer

Parson Pickax, his hands clasped behind him under his coattails, rocked on his heels and rolled up his eyes, "Yea, verily, it is a wicked world," he said in a sepulchre-like tone.

Horrified, Peal Ivy suddenly became aware of the fact that Andy Pike was unarmed; yet he kept on coming, just as he had approached that mean-looking mule. When there was a job to be done, the young blacksmith was not one for dallying. With that big shock of taffy-colored hair and those blue eyes, kindled now with the fires of determination, he looked like a prairie Viking.

Alf Walker was a killer, while Nick Dunn leaned more to the crafty side. Observing that the new marshal wore no gun-belt, and aware that the shooting of a defenseless man was bound to arouse public feeling to an ugly pitch, Nick Dunn resorted to a trick.

"All right, Marshal," he said, "I quit." He pulled his six-shooter, reversed it and thrust the butt toward Andy Pike.

Unwittingly the young, inexperienced marshal walked into the trap. He accepted the proffered Colt—and in that act became an armed man, and legitimate prey for Nick Dunn's companion, standing there braced for action, not two paces away.

Alf Walker threw his gun. Andy Pike froze, looking stupidly from the weapon in his hand to the gunman.

In that instant, the right hand of Parson Pickax jerked from under his rusty-black coat, bearing his old Walker Colt, its hammer eared full back.

The piano player let out a screech and dove for shelter. Women screamed, and men flung out of the way. The sudden action of the Parson caught the attention of Alf Walker, as his startled eye jumped in that direction. Belatedly he pulled his gun around.

The old six-smoke in the hand of Parson Pickax bellowed mightily, and its snarling slug belted Alf Walker's .45 from a mangled fist.

"Smite a scorner," thundered the Parson, "an' the simple will beware. Proverbs 19:25."

"Up jumped the devil!" cackled Belle McGee. "Durn my hide, Parson, you're as handy with a hawg-laig as ye are at spoutin' Scripter."

Prudence Parmlee breathed again, and there were tears in her eyes when she looked at the Parson. "Thank God! Oh, I was afraid they were going to kill him."

"The Lord was a-figgerin' ways to warp it to Satan two thousand years ago," said the Parson, "an' he's got it all writ' down in the Book. A man jist wants to read what it says; an' when the ruckus starts, commence a-prayin' an' a-shootin'."

"I guess I was pretty much a fool," said Andy Pike ruefully.

"Live an' learn," said the Parson. "It tells in Genesis how

Abram armed his servants an' pursued the gun-toughs an' hard-cases thereabouts way back to the hills."

Belle McGee set out glasses for Alf Walker and Nick Dunn and filled them to the brim from a bottle on the back bar. "You two hellions come in here fer a drink. All right, have one on the house."

Cursing, the bullet-stung Alf caught up his glass and had the contents well down before he realized that he was drinking Hostetter's Bitters. He let out a howl and flung the glass to the floor.

Men in the saloon roared with glee. "Look at Alf takin' his medicine!"

"Haw, a dose o' lead an' a dose o' bitters."

Alf Walker and Nick Dunn headed for the door, muttering oaths and vowing vengeance. One or two good ladies who had mercifully fainted were revived, and the services were resumed.

They sang Old Hundred, and Parson Pickax expounded concerning the needs of a church house. "Askin' the Lord to join us in a saloon," he said, "may shock a few of ye, but directly we figger to build a church house. There's them as are ag'in' a church, the same as they're ag'in' law an' order. They're all for whiskey an' gamblin' an' hell-raisin'.

"Come a-Sunday, all ye got in Owlhoot Junction is a mess of hangovers an' empty pokes. It's like ridin' a merry-go-round—yuh spent your money, an' where you been?

"Paul, he says the church is purchased with blood. An' Saint Luke allows yuh got to do your enemies, an' do 'em good. So let's have at 'em. The purtiest sight that ever blessed the eye of man is a church spire a-standin' over a town. An' we goin' to build one, come hell or high water."

After leading in, "Hark! the Herald Angels Sing!" the Parson passed the hat. "All right, ladies an' gents, kick in. Feed the kitty." There was the pleasant jingling of silver and gold coins. Painted ladies, hard-bitten Texas cowboys, bearded miners, plainsmen, merchants and tinhorns, all contributed.

And so the first church of Saint David took root, there in Belle McGee's Belly-Up Saloon.

Big George McWhorter, ruddy-faced, heavy-joweled, snake-eyed, had, at one time or another, been engaged in almost every manner of shady enterprise known to the Nebraska prairies. As a trader, he had sold whiskey and guns to the Indians; he had engaged in claim jumping, he had been a land shark, dealing in false abstracts; he had promoted boom towns and peddled worthless lots.

He had no conscience or scruples and, more than once, had found killing a convenient shortcut out of difficulties. And yet he had never even been close to a hang-noose, for he had hirelings ready to do his bidding.

Big George had holdings in New Babylon which would continue to be valuable only so long as New Babylon remained the county seat. In Saint David he had invested money in saloons and gambling halls. The whiskey was bad, the games were crooked, and the "take" was high.

Further, Mr. McWhorter had political ambitions. Hence he preferred to manage his affairs in Owlhoot Junction from the side lines. He owned an interest in the Hell's Delight and here made his headquarters, with Rick Ringgold his lieutenant.

From the early fifties, gangs of thieves had holed up along the Overland Trail. At first they had preyed on the wagon trains, but later turned their attention to stage coaches and steam trains.

Saint David, from the day it had been a tent city at railhead, had been a haven for many of these renegades, as they squandered their ill-gotten gains in Big George McWhorter's fleshpots. The town boss gave them protection, in return for which men like Seco Snyder, Alf Walker and others performed his little chores, including murder.

At election time they went to the polls, voting as Big George directed, with the result that the sheriff and many county officials were corrupt. Following the shooting of Maury Dines, Seco Snyder had surrendered to the law in New Babylon, a mere matter of formality. No one appeared to prefer charges, and the sheriff had no urge to mess around in Owlhoot Junction investigating so common a thing as a shooting scrape; so the doors of the local bastille were thrown open, and Mr. Snyder returned to his former haunts, pure as the driven snow.

He was in the Hell's Delight, catching up on the late gossip, including news of the arrival of the Parson in town, when the gent in question hove over the horizon.

Seco was prepared not to like the preacher, having been informed that the pious one had lambasted his name and reputation in the course of Maury Dines's funeral sermon.

Having been physically belted around by the Parson, Mr. Snyder liked him even less, and had vowed loudly that he would kill this elongated disciple the next time that he saw him. However, Big George ordered him to hold his horses, pending the initiation of the newly appointed marshal, Andy Pike.

When the Parson had not only properly lambasted the devil at the prayer meeting but had violently thwarted Alf Walker's and Nick Dunn's attempts to hasten the demise of the new marshal, Big George McWhorter became aware of his first vague stirring of uneasiness.

Apparently, they had a wildcat by the tail. Peal Ivy had been fighting for law and decency ever since the Union Pacific had given birth to the town, but his had been a small voice in the wilderness. Every time a few stout souls rallied around, Mr. McWhorter cracked the whip, and these good men and true scrooched down in their pants in fear and trembling.

The Parson, however, didn't scrooch for shucks. On the other hand, he gave every indication of being a rampaging old sin-twister, and not at all averse to battling it out with man or the devil, from hell to breakfast.

Beside winning the confidence of the decent citizens, he was on his way to earning the grudging respect of a lot of hard-cases, men who admired courage in any man and had an inherent liking for fair play.

It was a feeble straw in the wind, and Big George had a feeling that unless the Parson was properly squelched—and soon—Owlhoot Junction was headed for a day of judgment. So he immediately formulated plans to settle the hash of the warring sky-pilot once and for all.

Saturday morning found Saint David a-foam with conversation. There was talk of Parson Pickax, the new church movement and the pleasant memory of Alf Walker, gun-tough and bully, his claws clipped, gagging down Hostetter's Bitters.

There was, too, considerable speculation regarding the fitness of the new marshal. None could deny that Andy Pike possessed courage, but it had been all too evident that he lacked the ruthless, iron-fisted qualities necessary to his office, else he would have killed Alf Walker in his tracks when he had the chance.

The toughs, men said, would make short shrift of the young blacksmith. It was like leading a lamb to slaughter.

When Andy Pike fired up his forge and donned his leather apron, the sun was shining and the birds were singing and the air was clean and sweet, but he was aware of none of this. Standing in the wide doorway of his shop, he saw only the utter ugliness of the sprawled buildings down Chadron Street.

Saint David, indeed! The town was a blot on the face of the earth, a dwelling place of ruffians. The cottonwoods were an insult to trees; the South Platte was a muddy imitation of a river; the prairie was a hateful expanse of nothing.

Andy thought of the town he had left back in Vermont, of the stately elms, of the green and friendly hills, of the white church spire there, of the majestic, tree-bordered Connecticut, and wondered why he had ever come west.

He thought of Maury Dines, gunned into the dirt. He thought of Nick Dunn and Alf Walker, making him look the fool before all of those people. He thought of Prudence Parmlee, so sweet and pretty, devoting herself to teaching a mess of brats, there in an old box-car.

He loved her and had dreamed of making a home for her, of having kids of his own. The sing-song patter of his hammer on the anvil had, to him, been the sound of carpenters driving nails in that new house he was planning.

But that had been yesterday. He had been a smithy then, strong and capable and well thought of. Today he was a dumb, slow-witted marshal, with a cheap tin star. He was alive, only by the grace of God and because a bony-shanked old freak, who called himself a parson, had unlimbered a shooting-iron, pulling his chestnuts out of the fire in the nick of time.

He must have been crazy, Andy told himself, to take the job in the first place. He had been busy shoeing that evil-tempered mule, and hadn't taken time seriously to consider what he was letting himself in for.

The funny part was that the thought that he might turn in his badge and quit never entered the head of Andy Pike this Saturday morning. He turned from his dour contemplation of those unpainted false fronts, thrust some irons into the fire and began to pump the bellows vigorously.

"By the great horn spoon!" he cried suddenly to the empty shop. "Who am I to show the white feather? My forebears cleared the forests of New England, with an ax in one hand and a gun in the other. They went armed to church, and neither the savages nor the red-coats were able to turn them from their purpose of living as free men."

"Well spoken, my young friend!" a voice called from the broad-arched door.

It was Parson Pickax. Prudence Parmlee stood beside him. Andy thought he had never seen her looking so vividly radiant.

"Bravo!" exclaimed the girl. "A mighty man, the village blacksmith!"

Andy regarded them sheepishly. "By golly," he said, blushing, "you gave me a start."

"Behold, I have created the smith," intoned the Parson, "that bloweth the coals in the fire, and that bringeth forth an instrument for his work; and I have created the waster to destroy."

"By golly, does it say that in the Bible?" said Andy.

"Isaiah, 54:16 are the tally numbers."

"By golly!"

Prudence Parmlee said, "The Parson is looking for a job, Andy. I told him you said you needed a helper, particularly on Saturday when so many settlers bring in their teams to be shod and have other blacksmithing done."

"I need a helper all right," said Andy, " 'specially since I took up with this marshal job." There was a twinkle in his blue eyes like the glimmer of sun on a lake. "The Parson comes real well recommended."

"I labor for modest wages," said the Parson, "for my needs are few."

"Don't you get any pay for bein' a minister?" asked Andy.

"No," said the Parson, "not bein' a circuit rider, an' it would be unfair to ask my little flock to support me in idleness. I am healthy and able, an' honest toil is good for any man."

"By golly," said Andy, "you just peel out of that coat. You'll find a leather apron hangin' on the peg in the corner there."

While the Parson prepared to go to work, Andy went to the door with Prudence. Off to the south a smudge of trail dust lifted against the horizon.

"Another trail herd," said Andy. "A lot of Texas cattle are comin' to Nebraska. One day this will be a great range country."

"As soon as the cattle are on the bedground at the river," the girl said, "those Texans will come whooping and ki-yipping into Saint David. I wish their folks had taught them better manners."

The Parson came forward, an incongruous spectacle in his high hat and leather apron, his sleeves rolled past his bony elbows. " 'There will be cattle on a thousand hills',"said he, quoting from the fiftieth Psalm. "A man named Asaph writ it, an', dollars to doughnuts, he had a vision of the Chisholm Trail."

"Guess I'll have my work cut out tonight," Andy said, running his fingers through his great mop of yellow hair. "Cowboys are tough, by golly."

"Yuh can't hooraw a Texan none," said the Parson, "but, man to man, he'll give an' take with yuh, for fun, money or eyeballs."

"I hate them!" the girl cried. "They're drunken bullies."

"It wa'n't cowboys that give Owlhoot Junction its name," the Parson reminded her. "They do honest work; they're not thieves an' murderers. They like to blow off steam when they git to town, but mostly they're jist full of paw an' beller."

"The Parson's right," said Andy. "McWhorter's toughs are the ones we have to fear." He went on, "Rustlers have been stampedin' an' runnin' off cattle. The drovers blame it on the settlers, but more likely it's Seco Snyder an' his crowd. An' then the saloons an' gamblin' halls rob the cowboys right an' left, which makes for a sight o' hard feelin'."

"Shorely," said the Parson. "Bound to." He waxed thoughtful then, eyes on the distant dust cloud. At length, he said, "The cattle trails are p'intin' north. Saint David is goin' to be a big cow town, like Dodge an' Caldwell was down in Kansas."

The Parson rubbed his hard-calloused palms. "Next to bein' on the railroad, give me a trail town, with hell a-smokin'. Then give me a marshal, brawny an' tough, an' a few God-fearin' souls, an' a few sinners. An', by the seven-toed prophets, I'll give yuh a goin' town fitten for all o' God's children—with a church spire a-p'intin' straight to heaven."

Prudence Parmlee stared at this strange Parson and was caught by his pioneering enthusiasm. Then she looked at Andy Pike, starry-eyed. They three represented the things on which this new frontier was founded—a church, a school and a lawman's star. They were building for a future generation.

"You're right, Parson!" she cried. "One day Saint David will be a good place to live in."

"Then we'll laugh about the wild days," said Andy Pike, hooking his thumbs in the armpits of his vest and swelling out his chest, "an' we'll tell our children how their maw an' paw tamed the West, by golly! Shucks, if we had it easy now, we wouldn't have a durned thing worth talkin' about when we're old."

And he kissed her, right there in front of the Parson.

Parson Pickax proved to be a right handy man around a blacksmith shop. Men of the plains had need to know many trades, and the Parson was no exception. Too, he was strong and willing.

They made a strange pair—Andy Pike, blond, square-built, big-muscled; and the Parson, his scarecrow figure enveloped in that flapping leather apron.

There were the usual hangers-on, together with cowboys from the trail herds held at the river. Lean and bronzed, they were, these Texans, bringing their wants and their Texas drawl to the Yankee blacksmith shop in Saint David. A chuck-wagon was needing a wagon tire shrunk on and a new doubletree. There were horses to be shod, small jobs of smithing.

Some of the cowboys had been at Belle McGee's the night before, and they joshed the Parson about his six-shooter religion, but he was always ready with an answer.

"It's all in the Book," he told them.

"Yuh mean it tells in the Bible about shootin'?" said a lank puncher.

"For sartin," declared the Parson. "Things back in them times was like in Owlhoot Junction now. Jist look at the sixty-fourth Psalm. It says, 'They encourage themselves in evil . . . they lay snares. . . . But God will shoot them, an' they shall be wounded, an' light a shuck."

The Texan grinned, shook his head. "Yuh got a job to tame this town."

Between shoeing horses and oxen, sharpening plowshares, bending and shaping hot iron and fitting spokes to wagon wheels, the Parson, from time to time, spoke of wild times on the Union Pacific and hell-roaring nights in Julesburg, Cheyenne and other towns at railhead. He expounded sixgun lore and told of tough gents who took departure from this mortal vale with their boots on.

"What are yore ideas on killin', Parson?" asked a Texan.

"I'm ag'in' it," said the Parson solemnly. "When a gent waxes too simultaneous, I jist favor shootin' 'im in the right eye, which disturbs his aim."

Big George McWhorter had come along Chadron Street with a man named Pete McCoy, a card-sharp and gun-slick. They stopped to join the loungers in front of the blacksmith shop, unaware that the Parson had taken employment there.

At the sound of that familiar deep-toned voice within, McWhorter stiffened. His hatred of the preacher had become an obsession that goaded him relentlessly. His eye hit at the ungainly figure, poised at the anvil to strike at a red-hot iron held by Andy Pike, and his lids pinched down.

"Still shootin' off your mouth, I see," boomed McWhorter.

"I shoot other things beside my mouth," said the Parson, casting a glance at the pair outside of the broad-arched door.

"They buried a man here the other day who popped off out of turn," said Pete McCoy maliciously. "You might be next; who knows?"

The Parson had never seen this man before, but he knew the breed, and it was enough that he was with the town boss of Owlhoot Junction. Still standing with his sledge cocked, Parson Pickax gave them his attention, while the iron on the anvil dulled, lost its cherry red.

Many times the Parson had walked hand in hand with death, and he sensed its spectre, hovering like a dark shadow there now. It leered from behind the slitted lids of Big George McWhorter; it glinted with cruel intensity in the eyes of his sleek-dressed companion.

This wasp-waisted, bleak-faced man with Big George had flung his threat, and it left the Parson no alternative but to challenge the remark. That, or be branded a quitter before these Texas men and the loungers.

No gun was in evidence on either McWhorter or his companion, but that they were armed there was no doubt in the mind of the Parson. Men of their ilk were like to pack sneakguns.

Slowly the Parson put down his sledge and walked to the place where he had hung his coat and holstered Colt. He buckled the scuffed gun-belt about him over the leather apron and went then to stand watchfully in the threshold of the shop.

"As you were sayin'," said the Parson, resting his faded blue orbs on the man who was called Pete McCoy. "About this gentleman who popped off. I take it yuh refer to the late marshal, a kindly an' honorable citizen, I am told. I pop, right considerable—you weasel-eyed, snake-crawlin' prairie rat!"

Pete McCoy smiled wickedly—and waited, his slim, lady-white hands clasped in front of him. "That's fightin' talk, my friend."

"Shore is," said the Parson. "An' if yuh got openers—have at it!"

Pete McCoy's right hand darted with lightning speed just inside of his left sleeve, where a derringer nestled in a special-made holster.

Startled faces watched. Andy Pike gasped, "By golly!"

It seemed that never in the world could Parson Pickax clear the enormously long barrel of his old Walker Colt in time to compete fairly with the gun-fanged killer before him, but already he was in action.

The Parson drew and fired in one fast, smooth motion. For so awkward-looking a man, he showed incredulous speed. The tight bark of the derringer was swallowed by the tremendous bellow of the jerking .44.

Pete McCoy's shot was wide of the target, for the reason that his aim had been disturbed by the slug that slapped him fair in the right eye.

The gunman wilted, fell forward. Big George McWhorter, his ruddy features turned chalky, gulped a startled oath, shuddered at the sound Pete McCoy made when he hit the ground and hastily backed away from the inquiring eye of the preacher.

"Lord," said the Parson, holstering his gun, "here's a pore, repentant sinner a-gittin' on the train."

CHAPTER FOUR
Hell-Town Invitation

Owlhoot Junction was shocked, stunned. The toughs and decent citizens alike stood aghast. This was sixgun redemption with a vengeance. No doubt now of the Parson's courage, or of his fighting ability.

A Texan in the Belly-Up Saloon said, "I don't sabe what brand of religion that old gospel-shouter ramrods, but if I lived in this man's bailiwick I'd git in the fold."

There were those in Saint David who now were for publicly declaring themselves on the side of Peal Ivy and the Parson in the fight for law and order. Many, however, thought the Reverend was not long for this world, for Big George McWhorter had left the scene of the shooting foaming oaths and threatening to send the Parson to hell a-fluking.

Peal Ivy took new courage and dashed off some red-hot copy for the next week's issue of the *Blade*.

The towers of Babylon were tottering. The county-seat fight was half won. All rightful-thinking citizens were behind the preacher. Owlhoot Junction was due for a clean-up, even if it took a vigilance committee to do it. A few hangings in Nemaha, Nebraska, he wrote, had discouraged thieves and hard-cases.

Doc Byler said the thing that had happened might take the pressure off the new marshal, Andy Pike, for a little, but that the roughs would be out for revenge.

Rick Ringgold lamented the death of Pete McCoy solely for the reason that he had lost the services of a top card-slick. Seco Snyder and some of the others saw in the killing a prediction of disaster for the gun-slinger foolhardy enough to brace the Parson's game head-on.

Alf Walker, his smashed right hand an aching reminder of his recent encounter with the Parson, considered himself lucky to have escaped being a one-eyed corpse.

Great as was the furor caused by the shooting of Pete McCoy, there was not one in Saint David to express genuine sorrow over his death.

Almost before the body of Pete McCoy was cold, Big George McWhorter was shaping a plan for the removal of Parson Pickax. Already the Parson's flaming lamp had burned too brightly and too long.

To a man of Mr. McWhorter's accomplishments, extinguishing the Parson's light presented no great problem. It merely meant a little scheming, plus a few guns in the right place at the right moment. . . .

*   *   *

Saturday night in Owlhoot Junction was a time when men died handily. They died on the turn of a card, because of the fickle whims of a spangled lady, because their bellies were full of red-eye and their heads were full of butterflies.

Cowboys, miners, freighters, honyaks, Saturday night was their night to howl. Rustlers, road agents and slickers, they jammed the saloons and gambling halls; they overflowed to gallery and sidewalk—the joyful, the quarrelsome, and the taciturn.

Children, women and dogs stayed off Chadron Street on Saturday night.

Parson Pickax, a hard day's work done and a dollar earned, relaxed in sprawled comfort on the gallery of the boarding house of Launcelot Jenks and meditated on tomorrow's sermon.

At the end of Chadron Street, where deep shadows lay, Andy Pike and Prudence Parmlee stood, thinking for the moment of nothing but each other. There was the smell of coolness on the earth, the whispering of wind in the prairie grass. Star dust sprinkled the sky.

Yonder a light glimmered from the window of a sod house. Close by cottonwoods rustled their skirts.

Down Chadron Street a fiddle squeaked. The piano in Belle McGee's place was banging out its tin-pan harmony. There was the galloping rhythm of a hurdy-gurdy, the sounds of shrill laughter, of harsh-pitched voices, with now and then a drunken howl.

Neither Andy Pike nor the girl heard these things, or remembered the killing at the blacksmith shop. They lived in these moments in a world that was no part of Owlhoot Junction. Theirs was a small and wonderful heaven, here in the night of the Nebraska prairie, the heaven that lovers know.

And Andy kissed her—the soft, tender kiss of an awkward, bashful sweetheart. . . .

The shot came from the direction of the Hell's Delight Saloon. Brief and hard was the sound it made—a brutal reminder that this was Owlhoot Junction, the town that boasted that it knew no law and no God.

A grimness was suddenly carved on the face of Andy Pike. His hand slid from the girl's waist to his gun-belt. Prudence uttered a small, frightened sound.

"Oh, Andy!" Her pale face was like marble in the night.

Twice had Andy Pike made his rounds, down one side of Chadron Street and up the other. There had been the friendly greeting of acquaintances; some had joked with him about his new job; there had been a few sullen stares.

This last time, Prudence had come from the boarding house to walk with him to the edge of town.

"By golly," said Andy, "I've got to go see what's up."

The girl was afraid, but her voice was steady now. "Yes," she said, "that's your duty." After all, they had faced hardships and death on the trail, and they must go on, as bravely as they had come, until this frontier was settled up and safe for those who would come after.

Prudence Parmlee walked with Andy as far as the boarding house. From there he went on alone. . . .

They called it Dead Man's Alley. Other towns had had their Dead Man's Alley, but none had been so bloodstained as this dark-walled gulch.

On the one side it was bounded by the Hell's Delight, and on the other by a long, rambling building containing a honkytonk and gambling hall. Doors from both the saloon and honkytonk opened into the alley. These provided handy exits when bouncers tossed out troublesome gents. Fist-fights were frequent in the alley, and often there was gun-play that ended up in new occupants for boothill.

The pistol shot that attracted the attention of Andy Pike had come from Dead Man's Alley.

A short time before, Big George McWhorter had gathered certain of his henchmen around him in a back room of the Hell's Delight. A jug and glasses were on the table, and whiskey flowed freely.

Seco Snyder, Nick Dunn, Alf Walker and several others were there. McWhorter, thumbs hooked in the armpits of his vest, was backed against the wall, puffing at a big black cigar.

"You're a hell of a pair of gunslingers," Big George snarled, looking at Seco and Alf. "That damned parson made monkeys out of both of you."

"He made a corpse out of Pete McCoy," said Alf Walker. "A helluva lookin' one, too, if yuh ask me."

"You had plenty chance to paunch 'im," Seco Snyder said sulkily, "when he gunned Pete."

"Shut up!" thundered Big George. "An' stay shut. I'll do the talkin'. Tonight we're goin' to kill two birds with one stone, an' in the mornin' this psalm-singin' old badger is goin' to be camped on the doorstep of hell, along with Andy Pike."

"Simple as that," said Nick Dunn with a crooked grin.

"There will be a pistol shot out here in the alley," said Big

George. "That's to suck in the marshal. He's made a couple of rounds, and he won't be far off. Rick will be on the lookout for him, and he's goin' to say one of them riders from down in the Skillet killed a man in here. Rick's goin' to point him out.

"It ain't in the craw of a Texas man to take any guff from a blue-bellied abolitionist. When this Yank marshal tries to arrest the man Rick says did the shootin', guns are goin' to start blastin'.

"You boys circulate around in the crowd. Keep an eye out for the Parson. He sided the new marshal in Belle McGee's last night, and I look for him to buy into this game. When he does, let him have it."

Seco Snyder nodded, fortified himself with another slug of red-eye. "I'll fog the old buzzard to a cinder," he said thickly. "Cracked me on the skull with my own sixgun. I never did git it back."

Big George McWhorter went into the main saloon then and gave Rick Ringgold the nod. The proprietor of the Hell's Delight spoke to a rheumy-eyed hanger-on. This man eased out of the side door into Dead Man's Alley, and a moment later the sound of a shot ripped the night. . . .

Parson Pickax liked peace and quiet. He liked to sit and dream and watch the moon silver the prairie. He could see it shinin' on the spire of Saint David's new church this blessed minute.

Yes; the church he was a-goin' to build here in Owlhoot Junction would have a steeple, a-pointin' the way to Glory. There would be benches an' a real pulpit an' a hay-burner stove. There might even be a melodeon with treadles.

There would be buryin's in this church, an' baptizin', an' marryin', an' singin' of a Sabbath morn. Yuh take that yaller-haired blacksmith now, Andy Pike, an' the schoolma'm, with her dimples an' her freckles an' her uppity nose—like as not they'd be the first couple j'ined in the holy bonds o' wedlock in this here meetin'-house. . . .

Then the sound of a shot stopped the Parson's daydreams cold. He scowled at the lights down Chadron Street, then erected himself like a sooky old steer getting up to look for boogers.

"A hell-born town," said the Parson. He went into the house and buckled on his gun-belt. When he came out, Prudence Parmlee was standing by the steps, her hands clasped against her breast, staring after Andy Pike.

"You'll look out for him, Parson?" she said, anxiously.

"Th' Almighty looks after his own," said Parson Pickax. And he went along the plank sidewalk in great strides.

Rick Ringgold, sleek as a snake, stood outside of the Hell's Delight, his hard, narrow features set with a look of craft.

The blocky bulk of Andy Pike appeared, the marshal's star glinting.

Rick Ringgold purred, "Ah, there you are, Marshal. I was lookin' for you. A little trouble in the back room. One of them Texans killed a man. Come along; I'll point him out."

"A lyin' man is an abomination in the sight of the Lord!" boomed a voice close behind Andy Pike.

Rick Ringgold jerked around and saw there the towering form of Parson Pickax. Hatless he was, with the light from the door shining on his high, bald dome.

"That shot never come from inside four walls," cried the Parson. "It was fired from outside."

"You're a liar!" snarled Ringgold.

The Parson instantly swung a gnarled, ham-size fist, which popped against the jaw of the proprietor of the Hell's Delight with a sound like that of a gourd dropped on a rock. Ringgold swayed, started to fall, but before he hit the planking the Parson seized him and pitched him through the saloon doors.

At that instant the black mouth of Dead Man's Alley blossomed with muzzle-flame, and a slug creased the Parson's bony ribs. Another gun howled, and death crooned past the ear of Andy Pike.

The suddenness of this leaden tempest confused the young blacksmith.

It was the voice of the Parson that whipped him into action. "Strike while the iron's hot, my son! Th' day o' judgment's at hand!"

Andy Pike lowered his head and charged into the Hell's Delight. Partly he was motivated by the instinct to dodge the lead screaming from the alley, but more by righteous wrath because of the trap that had been set.

Baldy Johnson, his nose held in shape by strips of courtplaster, hung over the bar, his jaw agape. Everything had been set to shuffle the marshal and the Parson off to boothill, but something had miscued.

Here came his boss, Rick Ringgold, head-first through the batwing doors; and here came this young blacksmith, built like a bull buffalo, his huge fists swinging.

Big George McWhorter was standing at one end of the bar, the lord-mayor of Owlhoot Junction, all primed to enjoy the sight of a pair of festering disciples of law and order getting bludgeoned down by hot lead. His face turned pale.

Guns were slugging it out in Dead Man's Alley. Chadron Street was coming to a boil. A wild bullet hit a horse at a hitch-rail, and the animal went down screaming. Other snorting, plunging ponies jerked free.

Except for the gay melody of a hurdy-gurdy, a stunned hush briefly gripped the Hell's Delight; then there was bedlam. The shrieks of spangled ladies mingled with the yells and curses of men. Tables were upended; cards, chips and whiskey glasses were spilled in all directions.

Andy Pike knew little of gun-slinging as an art, and his holstered Colt sagged forgotten at his hip. His was a trade that called for muscle and brawn and the use of stout hands. These things he employed now.

He saw a man wrenching at a six-shooter, and he seized an overturned table and with it cut a swath that not only mowed down the gunman but all in his path. He snatched up a chair and found only one fragment in his grip after he had brought it down on the head of a hulking rough who tried to close with him.

Seco Snyder, bully and killer, took a half-crouch at the far end of the long bar, waiting for his chance to blast Andy Pike.

In Dead Man's Alley, Parson Pickax had gone into action with his old cap-and-ball Walker Colt. Six bullets he had to spend, no more, for it took a week to load one of these guns. But the Parson had always contended that six shots were a-plenty in any fight, his notion being that the gent who failed to down his opponents after thumbing the hammer six times was a dead man anyway.

Alf Walker was there in the alley, shooting left-handed. He missed the Parson in two tries and then went up the flume with a lead package in his belly. Nick Dunn had too much red-eye aboard to be at his nimble best. Moreover, once bullet-burned, Parson Pickax was on the peck.

Four unhatched hunks of lead nested in the chambers of the Walker-gun when the Parson popped through the side door of the Hell's Delight and presented his credentials at the portals of this, the devil's own rendezvous.

Rick Ringgold's place had been the scene of a lot of hectic brawls, but never one with the promise of a harvest like this. Men of the wolf-breed were rallying under the command of the fury-choked voice of Big George McWhorter.

All law they feared and hated—the law represented by the shiny star on the vest of this tawny blacksmith, Andy Pike.

The leathery-faced Texans seemed to sense that this was a grudge battle between local factions and called for no meddling by outsiders; hence they remained aloof, content to have a grandstand seat for the show. Too, they admired courage, and the sight of the young blacksmith taking on all comers with his two bare hands was something for the book.

Big George McWhorter jumped behind the bar and grabbed a sawed-off shotgun from a shelf under the counter. Baldy Johnson came up with a .45. A Bowie knife flashed in the hand of a big bouncer. Rick Ringgold crawled to the wall and staggered to his feet, a snub-nosed derringer gripped in his hand.

Seco Snyder saw his chance now and drove a bullet at Andy Pike. The impact half turned the smithy around, but it didn't drop him. A knife whistled through the air. The yellow-haired young giant threw up his arm, stopping the blade.

With the knife still in his arm and his shirt reddening, Andy flung himself at his nearest antagonist, his six-shooter still unholstered. With his bare hands, he picked up the man and crashed him down across the bar, breaking his back.

Seco Snyder snarled a curse and again eared back the hammer of his six-shooter. In that instant, the black-frocked Parson burst through the door that opened on Dead Man's Alley. . . .

The hurdy-gurdy against the back wall was still grinding out music, a gay refrain for red death's parade.

Big George McWhorter, fingers crooked against the triggers of the double-barreled shotgun, saw the Parson. He saw more, for he saw Pete McCoy, with a crimsoned hole where an eye had been, kneeling slowly in eternal reparation for his sins, there in the dirt in front of the blacksmith's shop.

Parson Pickax had found Jordan a hard road to travel, a road where only fighting men stood the ghost of a show. This was the toughest saloon in the toughest cow town of the new cattle trail to the north. Here there were only the quick and the dead.

Parson Pickax, looking through the gauzy banners of smoke, saw that the time was short. Seco Snyder was readying to throw a second shot at Andy Pike, bloodied but still fighting. The guns of Baldy Johnson and Rick Ringgold were spurting flame.

Big George McWhorter was crouched behind the bar, with only his flat-crowned hat and his evil eyes showing above the twin-muzzles of his murderous little weapon.

The Parson, his bony shanks spraddled, steadied to the task of converting sinners. The battle-scarred old Walker shouted, and Seco Snyder, the fruits of a misspent life ripening fast, swayed against the end of the bar, his six-shooter oozing from his fingers.

The Walker swung then and laid its frowning eye on Big George. With the trigger pressed home, the Parson loosed the long hammer-piece under his thumb. The bullet took McWhorter in the center of the skull.

Both barrels of the shotgun vomited buckshot, but already Big George was sliding over the brink and the twin charge only tore a gaping wound in the ceiling.

Rick Ringgold dropped the derringer and threw up his hands. Baldy Johnson burrowed behind the bar, content to still be alive.

That night the Hell's Delight Saloon stood as a tombstone over the grave of Owlhoot Junction. The fight for the county seat was done long before an election ballot was cast. A town, men said, with a marshal like Andy Pike and a preacher like Parson Pickax was likely to be a decent place to live in.

Anyway, Saint David was on the Union Pacific, and, as the Parson said, all trains stopped there, including the Glory Train.

Andy Pike had a close call, and for a time it seemed that he'd never survive his several bullet wounds. But he was rugged and tough, with the vitality, Doc Byler said, of a Texas longhorn.

Further, the whole town was praying for him, and with Prudence Parmlee for a nurse—well, as Belle McGee put it, it would have been "durn ungrateful of him to up an' kick the bucket."

Parson Pickax did the blacksmithing during those weeks that Andy was laid up and managed very well.

Rick Ringgold and Baldy Johnson, along with most of the hard-cases, quit town. Folks cleaned out the Hell's Delight and put in some benches, and held services there through that first winter.

When the frost was out of the ground in the spring, work was begun on the new church. Too, a suitable school was built, and a court house. And Saint David was on the way to becoming a thriving town.

Trail herds moved north in increasing numbers, and cowboys whooped it up in town, but there was law and order now, and a deadline which separated the sheep and the goats, as it were.

Andy Pike continued as marshal until the court house was finished and the new sheriff had established himself in Saint David.

Peal Ivy strutted and bragged until folks could hardly stand him. Beside being a deacon in the church now, he claimed credit for having sent for Parson Pickax and said the *Blade* had helped kick the devil to hell out of Saint David.

Andy and Prudence were married that summer. The ceremony took place on the steps of the new church, with the whole town looking on. Belle McGee said it couldn't have been a bigger crowd if it had been a hanging.

The Parson kissed the bride, and the bride kissed Andy, who blushed and said, "By golly!"

Down the years the first thing the traveler saw upon approaching the town of Saint David, there in western Nebraska, was the white spire of the church that Parson Pickax built, pointing like a finger straight up the Glory Trail. . . .

THE END

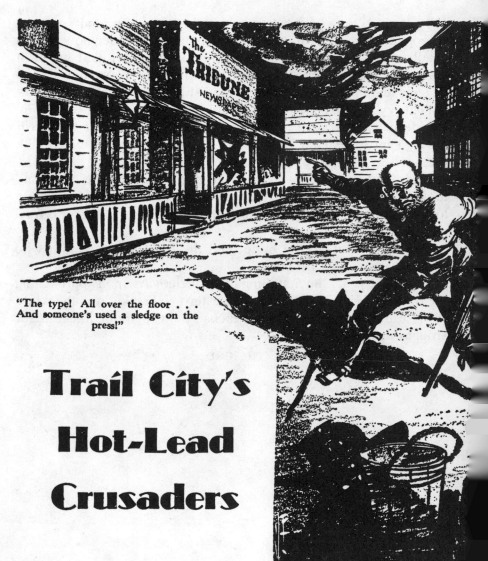

"The type! All over the floor . . .
And someone's used a sledge on the
press!"

Trail City's

Hot-Lead

Crusaders

By
CLIFFORD D.
SIMAK

Novel of a
Hell-on-Earth Cowtown

Fighting editor of the *Tribune*, Carson saw in Trail City the honest, prosperous town that it might someday become. . . . But now, deserted by the friends who had staked him, could he buck Byron Fennimore's vicious gun-army—who saw in Trail City, instead of Carson's shining dream, only a vassal outpost of his crooked cattle empire?

CHAPTER ONE
Hit the Trail, or Die!

Morgan Carson, editor of the *Trail City Tribune,* knew trouble when he saw it—and it was walking across the street straight toward his door.

Dropping in alone, either Jackson Quinn, the town's lone lawyer, or Roger Delavan, the banker, would have been just visitors stopping by to pass the time of day. But when they came together, there was something in the wind.

Jake the printer clumped in from the back room, stick of type clutched in his fist, bottle joggling in hip pocket with every step he took, wrath upon his ink-smeared face.

"Ain't you got that damned editorial writ yet?" he demanded. "Holy hoppin' horntoads, does a feller have to wait all day?"

Carson tucked the pencil behind his ear. "We're getting visitors," he said.

Jake shifted the cud of tobacco to the left side of his face and squinted beneath bushy eyebrows at the street outside.

"Slickest pair of customers I ever clapped an eye on," he declared. "I'd sure keep my peepers peeled, with them jaspers coming at me."

"Delavan's not so bad," said Carson.

"Just pick pennies off a dead man's eyes, that's all," said Jake.

He spat with uncanny accuracy at the mouse-hole in the corner.

"Trouble with you," he declared, "is you're sweet on that dotter of hisn. Because she's all right, you think her old man is too. Nobody that goes around with Quinn is all right. They're just a couple of cutthroats, in with that snake Fennimore clear up to their hips."

Quinn and Delavan were stepping to the boardwalk outside the *Tribune* office. Jake turned and shuffled toward the back.

The door swung open and the two came in, Quinn huge, square-shouldered, flashy even in a plain black suit; Delavan quiet and dignified with his silvery hair and bowler hat.

"This is a pleasure," Carson said. "Two of the town's most distinguished citizens, both at once. Could I offer you a drink?"

He bent and rummaged in a deep desk drawer and came up empty-handed.

"Nope," he said, "I can't. Jake found it again."

"Forget the drink," said Quinn. He seated himself on Carson's desk and swung one leg back and forth. Delavan sat down in a chair, prim and straight, like a man who dreads the job he has to do.

"We came in with a little business proposition," said Quinn. "We have a man who's interested in the paper."

Carson shook his head. "The *Tribune*'s not for sale."

Quinn grinned, pleasantly enough. "Don't say that too quickly, Carson. You haven't heard the price."

"Tempt me," invited Carson.

"Ten thousand," said Quinn, bending over just a little as if to keep it confidential.

"Not enough," said Carson.

"Not enough!" gasped Quinn. "Not enough for this?" He swept his hand at the dusty, littered room. "You didn't pay a thousand for everything you have in the whole damned place."

"Byron Fennimore," Carson told him levelly, "hasn't got enough to buy me out."

"Who said anything about Fennimore?"

"I did," snapped Carson. "Who else would be interested? Who else would be willing to pay ten thousand to get me out of town?"

Delavan cleared his throat. "I would say, Morgan, that that should have nothing to do with it. After all, a business deal is a business deal. What does it matter who makes the offer?"

He cleared his throat again. "I offer that observation," he pointed out, "merely as a friend. I have no interest in this deal myself. I just came along to take care of the financial end should you care to sell."

Carson eyed Delavan. "Ten thousand," he asked, "spot cash? Ten thousand on the barrel-head?"

"Say the word," said Quinn, "and we'll hand it to you."

Carson laughed harshly. "I'd never get out of town with it."

Quinn spoke softly. "That could be part of the deal," he said.

"Nope," Carson told him, "ten thousand is too much for the paper. I'd sell the paper—just the paper, mark you—for ten thousand. But I won't sell my friends. I won't sell myself."

"You'd be making a stake out of it, wouldn't you?" asked Quinn. "Isn't that what you came here for?"

Carson leaned back in his chair, hooked his thumbs in his vest and stared at Quinn. "I don't suppose," he said, "that you or

Fennimore could understand why I came here. You aren't built that way. You wouldn't know what I was talking about if I told you I saw Trail City as a little cow-town that might grow up into a city.

"Gentlemen, that's exactly what I saw. And I'm here, in on the ground floor. I'll grow up with the town."

"Have you stopped to think," Quinn pointed out, "that you might not grow up at all? Might just drop over dead, suddenlike, someday?"

"All your gunslicks are poor shots," said Carson. "They've missed me every time so far."

"Maybe up to now the boys haven't been trying too hard?"

"I take it," said Carson, "they'll try real hard from now on."

He flicked a look at Delavan. The man was uneasy, embarrassed, twirling the bowler hat in his hands.

"Let's stop beating around the bush," suggested Carson. "I don't know why you tried it in the first place. As I understand it, Fennimore will give me ten thousand if I quit bucking him, forget about electing Purvis for sheriff and get out of town. If not, the Bar Y boys turn me into buzzard bait."

"That's about it," said Quinn.

"You don't happen to be hankering after my blood, personally?" asked Carson.

Quinn shook his head; "Not me. I'm no gunslinger."

"Neither am I," Carson told him. "Leastwise not professionally. But from now on I'm not wearing this gun of mine for an ornament. I'm going to start shooting back. You can noise that around, sort of gentle-like."

"The boys," said Quinn, sarcastically, "will appreciate the warning."

"And you can tell Fennimore," said Carson, "that his days are over. The days of free range and squeezing out the little fellow are at an end. Maybe Fennimore can stop me with some slugs. Maybe he can stop a lot of men. But he can't stop them forever.

"The day is almost here when Fennimore can't fix elections and hand-pick his sheriffs, when he can't levy tribute on all the businessmen in town, when he can't hog all the water on the range."

"Better put that in an editorial," said Quinn.

"I have," declared Carson. "Don't you read my paper?"

Quinn turned toward the door and Delavan arose. He fumbled

just a little with his hat before he put it on. "You're coming to the house tonight for supper, aren't you?" he asked.

"I thought so, up to now," said Carson.

"Kathryn is expecting you," the banker said.

Quinn swung around. "Sure, go ahead, Carson. Nothing personal in this, you understand."

Carson rose slowly. "I didn't think there was. You wouldn't have a man planted along the way, would you?"

"What a thought," said Quinn. "No, my friend, when we get you, it'll be in broad daylight."

Carson followed them to the door, stood on the stoop outside to watch them leave. They crossed the street toward the bank, the dust puffing up from their boots to shimmer momentarily in the slanting rays of the westering sun.

A horse cantered down the street, coming from the east, its rider slouching in the saddle. A hen scratched industriously in the dust and clucked to an imaginary brood. The sun caught the windows of the North Star Saloon directly opposite the newspaper office and turned the glass to glittering silver.

Trail City, thought Editor Morgan Carson, looking at it. Just a collection of shacks today. The North Star and the bank and sheriff's office with the jail behind it. The livery stable and the new store with the barber shop in one corner.

A frontier town, with chickens clucking in the dust and slinking dogs that stopped to scratch for fleas. But someday a great town, a town with trains and a water tower instead of a creaking windmill, a town of shining glass and brick.

A man was coming down the steps of the North Star, a big man stepping lightly. Carson watched him abstractedly, recognized him as one of Fennimore's hired hands, probably in town on some errand.

The man started across the street and stopped. His voice came quietly across the narrow stretch of dust.

"Carson!"

"Yes," said Carson. And something in the way the man stood there, something in the single word, something in the way the man's face looked beneath the droopy hat, made him stiffen, tensed every nerve within him.

"I'm calling you," said the man, and it was as if he had asked for a match to light his smoke. No anger, no excitement, just a simple statement.

For a single instant time stood still and stared. Even as the man's hands dove for the gun-butts at his thighs, the street seemed frozen in a motionlessness that went on forever.

And in that timeless instant, Carson knew his own hand was swooping for his gun, that the weapon's butt was in his fist and coming out.

Then time exploded and took up again and Carson's gun was swinging up, easily, effortlessly, as simply as pointing one's finger. The other man's guns were coming up too, a glitter of steel in the sunlight.

Carson felt his gun buck against his hand, saw the look of surprise that came upon the other's face, heard the blast of the single shot ringing in his ears.

The man out in the street was sagging, sagging like a slowly collapsing sack, as if the strength were draining from him in the dying day. His knees buckled and the guns, still unfired, dropped from his loosened fingers. As if something had pushed him gently, he pitched forward on his face.

For an instant more the stillness held, a stillness even deeper than before. The man on the horse had reined up and was motionless; the scratching hen was a feathery statue of bewilderment.

Then doors slammed and voices shouted; feet pounded on the sidewalks. The saloon porch boiled with men. Bill Robinson, white apron around his middle, ducked out of the store. The barber came out and yelled. His customer, white towel around his neck, lather on his face, was pawing for his gun, swearing at the towel.

Two men came from the sheriff's office and walked down the street, walked toward Carson, standing there, still with gun in hand. They walked past the dead man in the street and came on, while the town stood still and watched.

Carson waited for them, fighting down the fear that welled within him, the fear and anger. Anger at the trap, at how neatly it had worked.

The door slammed behind him and Jake was beside him, a rifle in his hand.

"What's the matter, kid?" he asked.

Carson motioned toward the man lying in the dust.

"Called me," he said.

Jake shifted his cud of tobacco to the north cheek.

"Dang neat job," he said.

Sheriff Bert Bean and Stu Leonard, the deputy, stopped short of the sidewalk.

"You do that?" asked Bean, jerking a thumb toward the dust.

"I did," admitted Carson.

"That bein' the case," announced Bean, "I'm placin' you under arrest."

"I'm not submitting to arrest," said Carson.

The sheriff's jaw dropped. "You ain't submittin'—you what?"

"You heard him," roared Jake. "He ain't a-going with you. Want to do anything about it?"

Bean lifted his hands toward his guns, thought better of it, dropped them to his sides again.

"You better come," Bean said with something that was almost pleading in his voice. "If you don't, I got ways to make you."

"If you got ways," yelped Jake, "get going on 'em. He's calling your bluff."

The four men stood motionless for a long, dragging moment.

Jake broke the tension by jerking his rifle down. "Get going," he yelled. "Start hightailing it back to your den, or I'll bullet-dance you back there. Get out of here and tell Fennimore you dassn't touch Carson 'cause you're afraid he'll gun-whip you out of town."

The crowd, silent, motionless until now, stirred restlessly.

"Jake," snapped Carson, "keep an eye on that crowd out there."

Jake spat with gusto, snapped back the hammer of the gun. The click was loud and ominous in the quiet.

Carson walked slowly down the steps toward the sidewalk, and Bean and Leonard backed away. Carson's gun was in his hand, hanging at his side, and he made no move to raise it, but as he advanced the two backed across the street.

Quinn pushed his way through the crowd in front of the bank and strode across the dust.

"Carson," he yelled, "you're crazy. You can't do this. You can't buck law and order."

"The hell he can't," yelped Jake. "He's doing it."

"I'm not bucking law and order," declared Carson. "Bean isn't law and order. He's Fennimore's hired hand. He tried to do a job for Fennimore and he didn't get away with it. That man I killed was planted on me. You had Bean sitting over there, all ready to gallop out and slap me into jail.''

Quinn snarled. "You got it all doped out, haven't you?"

"I'm way ahead of you," said Carson. "You used a man who was just second-rate with his guns. Probably had him all primed up with liquor so he thought he was greased hell itself. You knew that I'd outshoot him and then you could throw a murder charge at me. Smart idea, Quinn. Better than killing me outright. Never give the other side a martyr.''

"So what about it?" asked Quinn.

"So it didn't work."

"But it'll work," Quinn declared. "You will be arrested."

"Come ahead, then," snapped Carson. He half-lifted the sixgun. "I'll get you first, Quinn. The sheriff next—"

"Hey," yelled Jake, "what order do you want me to take 'em in? Plumb senseless for the two of us to be shooting the same people.''

Quinn moved closer to Carson, lowered his voice. "Listen, Carson," he said, "you've got until tomorrow morning to disappear.''

"What?" asked Carson in mock surprise. "No ten thousand?"

CHAPTER TWO
Gunsmoke Goes to Press

Jake scrubbed the back of his neck with a grimy hand, his brow wrinkled like a worried hound's.

"You sure didn't make yourself popular with the sheriff," he declared. "Now he ain't going to rest content until you're plumb perforated." '

"The sheriff," announced Carson, "won't make a move toward me until he's heard from Fennimore."

"I'm half-hoping," said Jake, "that Fennimore decides on shootin'. This circlin' around, sort of growlin' at one another like two dogs on the prod, has got me downright nervous. Ain't nothin' I'd welcome more than a lively bullet party.''

Carson tapped a pencil on the desk. "You know, Jake, I figure maybe we won that election right out there on the street. Before tomorrow morning there won't be a man in Rosebud County that hasn't heard how Bean backed down. A story like that is apt to lose him a pile of votes. Fennimore can scare a lot of people from voting for Purvis, but this sort of takes the edge off the scare. People are going to figure that since that happened to Bean, maybe Fennimore ain't so tough himself.''

"They'll sure be makin' a mistake," said Jake. "Fennimore is just about the orneriest hombre that ever forked a horse.''

Carson nodded gravely. "I can't figure Fennimore will take it lying down. Maybe you better sneak out the back door, Jake, and tell Lee Weaver, over at the livery barn, to do a bit of riding. Tell the boys all hell is ready to pop.''

"Good idea," agreed Jake. He shuffled toward the back, and a moment later Carson heard the back door slam behind him.

There was no question, Carson told himself, tapping a pencil on the desk, that the showdown would be coming soon. Maybe tonight, maybe tomorrow morning . . . but it couldn't be long in coming.

Fennimore wasn't the sort of man who would wait when a challenge was thrown at him, and what had happened that afternoon was nothing short of a challenge. First the refusal of the offer to buy the paper off, then the refusal to submit to arrest, and finally the bluffing that had sent Bean skulking back to the sheriff's office.

In his right mind, Carson told himself, he never would have done it, never would have had the nerve to do it. But he was sore clear through, and he'd done it without thinking.

The front door opened and Carson looked up. A girl stood there, looking at him: a girl with foamy lace at her throat, silk gloves, dainty parasol.

"I heard what happened," she said. "I came right down.''

Carson stood up. "You shouldn't have," he said. "I'm a fugitive from justice.''

"You should skulk," she said. "Don't all fugitives skulk?''

"Only when they are in hiding," he said. "I'm not exactly in hiding.''

"That's fine," said the girl. "Then you'll be able to eat with us tonight.''

"A murderer?" he asked. "Kathryn, your father might not like that. Think of it, a murderer eating with the banker and his charming daughter.''

Kathryn Delavan looked squarely at him. "I'll have Daddy come over when he's through work and walk home with you. Probably he'll have something to talk with you about.''

"If you do that," Carson said, "I'll come.''

They stood for a minute, silent in the room. A fly buzzed against a windowpane and the noise was loud.

"You understand, don't you, Kathryn?" asked Carson. "You understand why I have to fight Fennimore—fight for decent government? Fennimore came in here ten years ago. He had money, cattle and men. He settled down and took over the country—free range, he calls it now, but that's just a term that he and men like him invented to keep for themselves things that were never theirs in the first place. It's not democracy, Kathryn; it's not American. It isn't building the sort of country or the sort of town that common, everyday, ordinary folks want to live in."

He hesitated, almost stammering. "It's sometimes a dirty business, I know, but if gunsmoke's the only answer, then it has to be gunsmoke."

She reached out a hand and touched his arm. "I think I do understand," she said.

She turned away then, walked toward the door.

"Daddy," she told him, "will be over around six o'clock to bring you home."

Carson moved to the window, watched her cross the street and enter Harrison's store. He stood there for a long time, listening to the buzzing of the fly. Then he went back to the desk and settled down to work.

It was almost seven o'clock when Roger Delavan came, profuse with apology.

"Kathryn will be angry with me," he said, fidgeting with his hat, "but I had some work to do, forgot all about the time."

Outside, dusk had fallen on the street, and the windows of the business places glowed with yellow light. There was a sharp nip in the rising wind, and Delavan turned up the collar of his coat. A few horses stood huddled, heads drooping at the hitching post in front of the North Star. Up the street a dog-fight suddenly erupted, as suddenly ceased.

Carson and Delavan turned west, their boots ringing on the sidewalk. The wind whispered and talked in the weeds and grass that grew in the vacant space surrounding the creaking, groaning windmill tower.

"I want to talk with you," said Delavan, head bent into the wind, hat socked firmly on his head. "About what happened today. I am afraid you may think—"

"It was a business deal," Carson told him. "You said so, your-self."

"No, it wasn't," protested Delavan. "It was the rankest sort of bribery and attempt at intimidation I have ever seen. I've played along with Fennimore because of business reasons. Fennimore, after all, was the only business in Trail City for a long time. I blinked at a lot of his methods, thinking they were no more than the growing pains of any normal city. But after what happened today, I had to draw the line. I told Quinn this afternoon—"

Red flame flickered in the weeds beside the tower, and a gun bellowed in the dusk. Delavan staggered, coughed, fell to his knees. His bowler hat fell off, rolled into the street. The wind caught it, and it rolled on its rim, like a spinning wagon-wheel.

A man, bent low, was running through the weeds, half seen in the thickening dark.

Carson's hand dipped for his gun, snatched it free, but the man was gone, hidden in the thicker shadows where no lamplight reached from the windows on the street.

Carson slid back the gun, knelt beside Delavan and turned him over. The man was a dead weight in his arms; his head hung limply. Carson tore open his coat, bent one ear to his chest, heard no thudding heart.

Slowly he laid the banker back on the ground, pulled the coat about him, then straightened up. The bowler hat no longer was in sight, but a half-dozen men were running down the street. Among them, he recognized Bill Harrison, the new store owner, by the white apron tied around his middle.

"That you, Harrison?" asked Carson.

"Yeah, it's me," said Harrison. "We heard a shot."

"Someone shot Delavan," said Carson. "He's dead."

They came up and stood silently for a moment, looking at the black shape on the ground. One of them, Carson saw, was Caleb Storm, the barber. Another was Lee Weaver, the liveryman. The others he knew only from having seen them about town. Men from some of the ranches.

Harrison glanced over his shoulder at the North Star. "Guess they didn't hear the shot in there. Probably helling it up a bit."

"I'm thinking about Kathryn," said Carson. "Delavan's daugh-ter. Someone will have to tell her."

"That's right," declared Harrison. He considered it a moment, a square, blocky man, almost squatty in the semidarkness of the street.

"My old woman will go and stay with her," he said, "but she can't break the news to her, not all alone. Someone else will have to help her do it."

He looked at Carson. "You were going there just now. Kathryn told me when she came in to buy some spuds."

Carson nodded. "I suppose you're right, Bill. Let's get Delavan in someplace."

Storm and two of the other men lifted the body, started down the street.

"Come down to the store for a minute," said Harrison. "The old lady will be ready to go in a minute or so."

Carson followed Harrison. Weaver lagged until he fell in step with the editor. He stepped close to Carson and pitched his voice low.

"I got word to Purvis," he said. "He sent out riders. Some of the boys will be coming into town."

"I'll be back at the office," Carson told him, "as soon as I can gct away."

Feet pattered on the sidewalk behind them and a woman's voice cried out: "Daddy! Daddy!"

Weaver and Carson spun around.

It was Kathryn Delavan, running across the street, sobs catching in her throat. She would have rushed by, but Carson reached out and stopped her. "No, Kathryn," he said. "Stay back here with us."

She clung to him. "You were so late," she said, "that I came to see—"

He held her close, awkward in his comforting.

"You don't know who—"

Carson shook his head. "It was too dark."

Robinson lumbered through the dusk toward them. "Perhaps," he said, "she might want to come to the store. My wife is there."

The girl stepped away from Carson. "No," she said, "I want to go back home. Martha is there. I'll be all right there with her."

She dabbed at her eyes with a handkerchief. "You will bring him home, too?"

Robinson's voice was understanding, almost soft. "Yes, miss, just as soon— In an hour or two."

She moved closer, took Carson's arm, and they moved west up the street, toward the house where supper waited for a man who would not eat it.

The clock on the bar said ten when Carson pushed open the door of the North Star.

The place was half-full, and in the crowd Carson singled out a handful of Fennimore's riders—Clay Duffy, John Nobles, Madden and Farady at the bar; Saunders and Downey at a table in a listless poker game. The rest of the men were in from other ranches or were from the town.

Carson walked to the bar and signaled to the bartender.

The man came over. "What'll it be?"

"Fennimore around?" asked Carson.

"You don't give a damn for your life, do you?" snarled the man.

Carson's voice turned to ice. "Is Fennimore here?"

The man motioned with his head. "In the back."

For a moment the room had grown silent, but once again it took up its ordinary clatter of tongue and glass and poker chip. One or two men smiled at Carson as he walked by, but others either turned their heads or did not change expression.

Without knocking, Carson pushed open the back door, stepped into the smoke-filled room.

Three men stared at him from a single round table decorated by two whiskey bottles, staring with that suddenly vacant, vicious stare that marks an interrupted conversation.

One was Fennimore, a huge man, wisps of black hair hanging out from under his broad-brimmed hat. Quinn and Bean were on either side of him.

For a moment the stare was unbroken and the silence held. Fennimore was the one who broke it. "What do you want?" he asked, and his voice was like a lash, hard and cold and with a sting in every word.

"I came," said Carson, "to see what was being done about Delavan's murder."

"So?" said Fennimore slowly. "So, what do you want to be done about it?"

"I want the man who killed him found."

"And if we don't?"

"I'll say that you don't want him found. On the front page of the *Tribune*."

"Look here, Morgan," said Quinn, "you're in no position to say that—when you yourself are wanted for murder."

"I'm here," said Carson. "Go ahead and take me."

The three sat unmoving. Fennimore's tongue licked his upper lip, briefly. Bean's whiskey-flushed face drained to pasty white.

"No," said Carson. "All right, then—"

"Quinn," interrupted Fennimore, "gave you until tomorrow morning to get out of town. That still holds."

"I'm not getting out," said Carson. "The day when you can tell a man to get out and make it stick is over, Fennimore. Because in another week we're electing a new sheriff, one who will uphold the law of the country and not the law of one cow-boss."

"It's your damned paper," snarled Fennimore. "You and your lousy stories that give me all the trouble. Stirring up the people—"

"What Fennimore means," said Quinn, smiling, "is that you'll never go to press again. . . ."

"But I will," said Carson. "Tonight. I'm not waiting until tomorrow. We go to press tonight instead of tomorrow afternoon. And I'm going to tell how Delavan was shot down from ambush and nothing's being done about it. And I'm going to point out that when I killed a man on fair call this afternoon, you wanted to run me in for murder."

"You can't blame any of my boys for killing Delavan," said Fennimore. "Delavan was my friend."

"He was your friend, you mean," said Carson, "until he told Quinn this afternoon that he was all through. After that, Fennimore, you couldn't afford to let him live."

Fennimore hunched forward in his chair. "If you think you can get me to raise the ten thousand ante," he declared, "you're wrong. It was worth that much to get you out of the way, but it's not worth any more."

Carson laughed at him, a laugh that came between his teeth.

"You're still willing to pay that ten thousand?"

Fennimore nodded. "If you leave within the hour. If you get a horse and ride. If you never go back to the office again."

"I knew I had you scared," said Carson, "but I didn't know I could scare you quite so thoroughly."

Slowly he backed out of the door, closed it and strode across the barroom.

CHAPTER THREE
One Against the Town

Light glowed in the windows of the *Tribune*, and Carson, hurrying across the street, saw the tiny office was filled with men.

Cries of greeting rose as he stepped through the door, and he stopped for a moment to recognize the faces. There was Gordon Purvis, the candidate for sheriff, Jim Owens, Dan Kelton, Humphrey Ross and others. Lee Weaver was there and so was Bill Robinson.

Jake shambled out of the back room, stick of type clutched in one hand, gunbelt joggling on his hip.

"Ain't you got that damned editorial writ yet?" he demanded. "Holy hoppin' horntoads—"

"Jake," snapped Carson, "how soon can you get out a paper? An extra?"

Jake gasped. "A whole paper? A whole danged paper?"

"No, just one page. Sort of a circular."

"Couple, three hours," said Jake, "if I can use big type."

"All right," said Carson, "get ready for it. I'll start writing."

Jake shifted the cud of tobacco to the left side of his jaw, spat at the mouse-hole.

Owens had risen, was making his way toward Carson. "What you planning to do?" he asked, and his question quieted the room so that Jake's feet, shuffling to the back, sounded almost like a roll of thunder.

"I'm going to blow Fennimore sky-high," said Carson. "I'm going to force him to produce Delavan's murderer or face the assumption that it was he himself who ordered the killing."

"You can't do that," said Owens softly.

"I can't?"

"No, you can't. This thing is getting out of hand. Range-war is apt to break wide open any minute. You know what that means. Our homes will be burned. Our families run out or murdered. Ourselves shot down from ambush."

Purvis leaped to his feet. "You don't know what you're saying,

Owens," he shouted. "If they want to shoot it out, we have to shoot it out. If we back down this time, we're done. We'll never—"

"You're safe enough," snarled Owens; "you're all alone. You haven't any family to be worried about. The rest of us—"

"Wait a minute," yelled Carson. "Wait a minute."

They quieted.

"Do you remember when you came in here six months ago to talk this thing over with me?" asked Carson. "You told me then that if I went with you, you'd string along with me. You swore you wouldn't let me down. You agreed this was the showdown. You said you wanted Purvis for sheriff and you'd back him—"

"We know that," yelled Owens, "but it's different now—"

"Let me talk, Owens," snapped Carson, his voice like a knife. "I want to tell you something. Something that happened this afternoon. Fennimore offered me ten thousand if I would sell you out—ten thousand, cash on the barrel-head and a promise that I'd get safely out of town. I turned him down. I told him I wouldn't sell you fellows out. And because I told him that, I have a murder charge hanging over me and Delavan is dead. . . . ."

He looked from one to another of them in the deadly quiet, each of them staring in turn at him.

"I refused to sell you men out," said Carson, "and now you're selling me out. You won't back my play. I should have taken that ten thousand."

Their eyes were shifty, refusing to meet his. A strange fear was upon them.

Kelton said, "But you don't understand, Morgan. Our wives and kids. We never thought it would come to this—"

From the street outside came wild shouts and the sound of running feet.

"Fire!" the single word ran through the startled night, crashed into the lamp-lighted *Tribune* office. "Fire! Fire!"

Carson spun toward the window, saw the leaping flames across the street.

"It's my place!" yelled Bill Robinson. "My store! Every dime I have—every dime—"

He was rushing for the door, clawing at the jamb, sobbing in his haste.

The room exploded in a surge of men leaping for the door. Across the street dark figures of men, silhouetted against the windows, hurdled the porch railing of the North Star, hit the street running. At the hitching posts the horses reared and screamed and pawed at the air in terror.

Flames were leaping and racing through the store, staining the whole street red. Smoke mushroomed like an angry cloud, blotting out the stars. Glass tinkled as a window was shattered by the heat.

Carson pounded through the dust. Running figures bumped into him. Voices bellowed—yelling for pails, for someone to start the windmill.

The flames shot through the roof with a gusty sigh, curled skyward, painting the pall of smoke with a bloody hue. One peak of the roof crumbled in as the fire raced through the seasoned timber. In the back something exploded with a *whoosh*, and for a moment the street was lighted by a garish flare that seemed to illuminate even the racing flames; then thick black clouds of smoke blotted it out.

The kerosene drum had gone up.

The building was dissolving, tongues of fire licking through the solid wall. Someone screamed a warning and the building went, the upper structure plunging in upon the flame-eaten nothingness that lay beneath it. Burning embers sailed into the street, and the men ducked as they thudded in the dust.

For a moment the crowd stood stricken into silence, and all that could be heard was the hungry soughing of the fire as it ate its way into oblivion.

Men who had been rushing from the windmill with water to douse the side and roof of the sheriff's office to keep it from catching fire, lowered their buckets, and as the fire died down a new sound came: the clanking of the windmill.

Through the crowd came Bill Robinson, face white, shirt smouldering where a brand had fallen. He stopped in front of Carson.

"Everything is gone," he said, almost as if he were talking to himself. His eyes were looking beyond Carson, scarcely seeing him. "Everything. I'm ruined. Everything. . . ."

Carson reached out a hand and gripped the man by the shoulder, but Robinson wrenched away and shook his head and plodded down the street. Men stood aside to let him pass, not knowing what to say.

Gordon Purvis was at Carson's elbow. He said quietly: "We'll have to figure out something. Pass the hat—"

Carson nodded. "We may as well go back to the office. Nothing we can do here."

A man came leaping through the open door of the *Tribune*, saw them and headed toward them at a run. Carson saw that it was Jake. And as the man drew near he knew there was something wrong.

"The type!" gasped Jake. "All over the floor and throwed out the door. And someone's used a sledge on the press—"

Carson broke into a run, heart down in his stomach, his stomach squeezing to put it back in place, the cold feet of apprehension jigging on his spine.

What Jake said was true.

The back shop was a shambles. Every type case had been jerked out of the cabinets and emptied, some of it heaved out of the door into the grass along the path that ran to the livery stable. The press was smashed as if by a heavy sledge. The same sledge had smashed the cans of ink and left them lying in sticky gobs upon the floor.

The work of a moment—of just the few minutes while the fire was racing through Robinson's store.

Carson stood slump-shouldered and stared at the wreckage.

He finally turned wearily to Purvis. "I guess," he said, "we don't print that extra after all."

Purvis shook his head. "Now we know that fire was no accident," he declared. "They wanted us out of here, and they picked a way that was sure to get us out."

They went back to the office and sat down to wait, but no one came in. Outside, hoofs pounded now and again as men mounted their horses and headed out of town. The hum of voices finally subsided until the street was quiet. Sounds of occasional revelry still came from the North Star. The windmill, which no one had remembered to shut off, clanked on in the rising wind. The embers of the fire across the street still glowed redly.

Purvis, tilted back in his chair, fashioned a smoke with steady fingers. Jake hauled a bottle from his pocket, took a drink and passed it around.

"I guess they aren't coming back," said Purvis finally. "I guess all of them feel the way that Owens felt. All of them plumb scared."

"What the hell," asked Jake, "can you do for a gang like that? They come in here wantin' help, and now—"

"You can't blame them," said Carson shortly. "After all, they have families to think of. They have too much at stake."

He picked up a pencil from his desk, deliberately broke it in one hand, hurled the pieces on the floor.

"They burned out Robinson," he said. "Cold-bloodedly. They burned him out so they could wreck the shop. So they could stop that extra, scare us out of town. A gang like that would do anything. No wonder the other fellows didn't come back. No wonder they hightailed for home."

He glanced at Purvis. "How do you feel?" he asked.

Purvis's face didn't change. "Got a place where I can stretch out for the night?"

"Sure you want to?"

"Might as well," said Purvis. "All they can do is burn down my shanty and run off my stock." He puffed smoke through his nostrils. "And maybe, come morning, you'll need an extra gun."

Carson awoke once in the night, saw Jake sitting with his back against the door, his head drooping across one shoulder, his mouth wide open, snoring lustily. The rifle lay across his knees.

Moonlight painted a white oblong on the floor, and the night was quiet except for the racing windmill, still clattering in the wind.

Carson pulled the blanket closer around his throat and settled his head back on his coat-covered boots which were serving as a pillow. In the cot, Purvis was a black huddle.

So this is it, thought Carson, staring at the moonlight coming through the window.

The press broken, the type scattered, the men he had been working for deserting, scared out once again by the guns that backed Fennimore. Nothing left at all.

He shrugged off the despair that reached out for him and screwed his eyes tight shut. After a while he went to sleep.

It was morning when he awoke again, with the smell of brewing coffee in his nostrils. Jake, he knew, had started a small fire in the old airtight heater in the back. He heard the hiss of bacon hit the pan, sat up and hauled on his boots, shucked into his coat.

The cot was empty.

"Where's Purvis?" he called to Jake.

"Went out to get a pail of water," said Jake. "Ought to be good and cold after running all night long."

Somewhere a rifle coughed, a sullen sound in the morning air. Like a man trying to clear a stubborn throat.

For a moment Carson stood stock still, as if his boot-soles were riveted to the floor.

Then he ran to the side window, the window looking out on the windmill lot, half knowing what he would see there, half afraid of what he'd see.

Purvis was a crumpled pile of clothes not five feet from the windmill. The pail lay on its side, shining in the sun. A vagrant breeze fluttered the handkerchief around Purvis's neck.

The town was quiet. The rifle had coughed and broken the silence and then the silence had come again. Nothing stirred, not even the wind after that one solitary puff that had moved the handkerchief.

Carson swung slowly from the window, saw Jake standing in the door to the back room, fork in one hand, pan of bacon in the other.

"What was it?" Jake demanded. "Too tarnation early in the morning to start shootin'."

"Purvis," said Carson. "He's out there, dead."

Jake carefully set the pan of bacon on a chair, laid the fork across it, walked to the corner and picked up his rifle. When he turned around, his eyes were squinted as if they already looked along the gun-barrel.

"Them fellers," he announced, "have gone a mite too far. All right, maybe, to shoot a hombre when he's half-expectin' it and has a chance at least to make a motion toward his own artillery. But 'taint right bushwhackin' a man out to get a pail of water."

Jake spat at the mouse-hole, missed it. "Especially," he declared, "before he's had his breakfast."

"Look, Jake," said Carson, "this fight isn't yours. Why don't you crawl out the back window and make a break for it? You could make it now. Maybe later you can't."

"The hell it ain't my fight," yelped Jake. "Don't you go hoggin' all the credit for this brawl. Me, I've had somethin' to do with it, too. Maybe you writ all them pieces takin' the hide off Fennimore, but I set 'em up in type and run 'em off the press."

A voice was bawling outside.

"Carson!" it shouted. "Carson!"

Stalking across the room but keeping well away from the window, Carson looked out.

Sheriff Bean stood in front of the North Star, badge of office prominently pinned on his vest, two guns at his sides.

"Carson!"

"Watch out," said Jake. "If they see a move in here, they'll fill us full of lead."

Carson nodded, stepped out of line of the window and walked to the wall. Drawing his gun, he reached out and smashed a window-pane with the barrel, then slumped into a crouch.

"What is it?" he yelled.

"Come out and give yourself up," bawled Bean. "That's all we want."

"Haven't got someone posted to pick me off?" asked Carson.

"There won't be a shot fired," said Bean. "Just come out that door, hands up, and no one will get hurt."

Jake's whisper cut fiercely through the room. "Don't believe a word that coyote says. He's got a dozen men in the North Star. Open up that door and you'll be first cousin to a sieve."

Carson nodded grimly.

"Say the word," urged Jake, "and I'll pick 'im off. Easy as blastin' a buzzard off a fence."

"Hold your fire," snapped Carson. "If you start shooting now, we haven't got a chance. Probably haven't anyway. As it is, they've got us dead to rights. Bean, over there, technically is the law, and he can kill us off legal-like. Can say later we were outlaws or had resisted arrest or anything he wants to. . . ."

"They killed Delavan and Purvis," yelped Jake. "They—"

"We can't prove it," said Carson bitterly. "We can't prove a thing. And now they've got us backed into a hole. There's nothing we can gain by fighting. I'm going to go out and give myself up."

"You can't do that," gasped Jake. "You'd never get three feet from the door before they opened up on you."

"Listen to me," snapped Carson. "I'm going to give myself up. I'll take a chance on getting shot. You get out of here, through the back. Weaver will let you have a horse. Ride out and tell the boys that Purvis is dead and I'm in jail. Tell them the next move is up to them. They can do what they want."

"But—but—" protested Jake.

"There's been enough killing," declared Carson. "A bit of gunning was all right, maybe, when there still was something to fight for, but what's the use of fighting if the men you're fighting for won't help? That's what I'm doing. Giving them a chance to show whether they want to fight or knuckle down to Fennimore."

He raised his voice. "Bean. Bean."

"What is it?" Bean called back.

"I'm coming out," yelled Carson.

There was silence, a heavy silence.

"Get going," Carson said to Jake. "Out the back. Crawl through the weeds."

Jake shifted the rifle across his arm.

"After you're safe," he insisted. "Until I see you cross that street, I'll stay right here."

"Why?" asked Carson.

"If they get you," Jake told him, "I'm plumb bent on drillin' Bean."

Carson reached out and yanked the door open. He stood for a moment in the doorway, looking across at Bean, who waited in front of the North Star.

The dawn was clean and peaceful, and the street smelled of cool dust, and the wind of the day had not yet arisen but only stirred here and there, in tiny warning puffs.

Carson took a step forward, and even as he stepped a rifle barked; a throaty, rasping bark that echoed among the wooden buildings.

Across the street something lifted Bean off his feet, as if a mighty fist had smote him—struck so hard that it slammed him off his feet and sprawled him in the dust.

At the sound of the shot, Carson had ducked and spun on his heel, was back in the room again, slamming shut the door.

The windows of the North Star sprouted licking spurts of gun flame, and the smashing of the *Tribune*'s windows for an instant drowned the crashing of the guns. Bullets snarled through the thin sheathing and plowed furrows in the floor, hurling bright showers of splinters as they gouged along the wood.

Carson threw himself toward his heavy desk, hit the floor and skidded hard into the partition behind it. A slug thudded into the wall above his head and another screamed, ricocheting, from the desk top.

Thunder pounded Carson's ears, a crashing, churning thunder that seemed to shake the room. Out of the corner of his eye he saw Jake crouched, half-shielded by the doorway into the back shop, pouring lead through the broken windows. Shell cases rolled and clattered on the floor as the old printer, eye squinted under bushy brow, tobacco tucked carefully in the northeast corner of his cheek, worked the lever action.

From the corner of the desk, Carson flipped two quick shots at one North Star window where he thought he saw for an instant the hint of shadowy motion.

And suddenly he realized there were no sounds of guns; no more bullets thudding into the floor, throwing showers of splinters.

Jake was clawing at the pockets of his printer's apron, spilling cartridges on the floor in his eagerness to fill the magazine.

He spat at the mouse-hole with uncanny accuracy. "Wonder who in tarnation knocked off Bean," he said.

"Somebody out in the windmill lot," said Carson.

Jake picked up the cartridges he had dropped, put them back in the apron pocket again. "Kind of nice," he declared, "to know you got some backin'. Probably somebody that hates Fennimore's guts just as much as we do."

"Whoever he was," declared Carson, "he sure messed up my plans. No sense of trying to surrender now."

"Never was in the fust place," Jake told him. "Damndest fool thing I ever heard of. Steppin' out to get yourself shot up."

He squatted in the doorway, rifle across his knee.

"They didn't catch us unawares," he said. "Now they'll be up to something else. Thought maybe they'd wipe us out by shooting the place plumb full of holes." He patted the rifle stock. "Sort of discouraged them," he said.

"It'll be sniping now," declared Carson. "Waiting for one of us to show ourselves."

"And us," said Jake, "waiting for them to show themselves."

"They'll be spreading out," said Carson, "trying to come at us from different directions. We got to keep our eyes peeled. One of us watch from the front and the other from the back."

"Okay by me," said Jake. "Want to flip for it?"

"No time to flip," said Carson. "You take the back. I'll watch up here."

He glanced at the clock on the wall. "If we only can hold out until dark," he declared, "maybe—"

A furtive tapping came against the back of the building.

"Who's there?" Jake called out guardedly.

A husky whisper came through the boards. "Open up. It's me. Robinson."

The man slipped in, dragging his rifle behind him, when Jake eased the door open. The merchant slapped the dust from his clothes.

"So you're the jasper what hauled down on Bean," said Jake.

Robinson nodded. "They burned my store," he said, "so they could bust up your shop. They burned everything I had—for no reason at all except to let them get in here and stop that extra you were planning."

"That's what we figured, too," said Jake.

"I ain't no fighting man," Robinson declared. "I like things peaceable . . . like them peaceable so well I'll fight to make them that way. That's why I shot Bean. That's why I came here. My way of figurin', there ain't no peace around these parts until we run out Fennimore."

"Instead of coming here," Carson told him, "you should have ridden out and told the ranchers what was happening. Told them we needed help."

"Lee Weaver is already out," said Robinson. "I was just over there. The stable boy told me he left half an hour ago."

A flurry of shots blazed from the North Star, and bullets chunked into the room. One of them, aimed higher than the rest, smashed the clock, and it hung drunkenly from its nail, a wrecked thing that drooled wheels and broken spring.

"Just tryin' us out," said Jake.

To the north, far away, came the sound of shooting. They strained their ears, waiting. "Wonder what's going on up there?" asked Jake.

Robinson shook his head. "Sure hope it isn't Lee," he said.

After that one burst there were no further shots.

The sun climbed up the sky and the town dozed, its streets deserted.

"Everyone's staying under cover," Jake opined. "Ain't nobody wants to get mixed up in this."

Just after noon Lee Weaver came, flat on his belly through the weeds and tall grass back of the building, dragging himself along with one hand, the right arm dragging limply at his side, its elbow a bloody ruin bound with a red-stained handkerchief.

"Came danged near lettin' you have it," Jake told him. "Sneakin' through them weeds like a thievin' redskin."

Weaver slumped into a chair, gulped the dipper of water that Carson brought him.

"I couldn't get through," he told them. "Fennimore's got men posted all around the town, watching. Shot my horse, but I got away. Had to shoot it out with three of them. Laid for two hours in a clump of sage while they hunted me."

Carson frowned, worried. "That leaves us on the limb," he said. "There isn't any help coming. They got us cornered. Come night—"

"Come night," suggested Jake, "and we fade out of here. No use in tryin' it now. They'd get us sure as shootin'. In the dark we'd have some chance to get away."

Carson shook his head. "Come night," he declared, "I'm going into that saloon the back way. While you fellows keep them busy up here."

"If they don't get us first," Weaver reminded him. "They'll rush us as soon as it's dark."

"In that case," snapped Carson, "I'm starting now. That weed-patch out there is tall enough to shield a man if he goes slow, inches at a time, and doesn't cause too much disturbance. I'll circle wide before I try crossing the street. I'll be waiting to get into the North Star long before it's dark."

CHAPTER FOUR
The Plans of Mice and Men . . .

The doorknob turned easily, and Carson let out his breath. For long hours he had lain back of the North Star, his mind conjuring up all the things that might go wrong. The door might be locked, he might be seen before he could reach it, he might run into someone just inside . . .

But he reached the door without detection, and now the knob turned beneath his fingers. He shoved it slowly, fearful of a squeaking hinge.

The smell of liquor and of stale cooking hit him in the face as the door swung open. From inside came the dull rumble of occasional words, the scrape of boot-heels.

Holding his breath, he moved inside, slid along the wall, shoved the door shut. Standing still, shoulders pressed against the wall, he waited for his eyes to become accustomed to the dark.

He was, he saw, in a sort of warehouse. Liquor cases and barrels were piled against the walls, half-blocking the lone window in the room. Straight ahead was another door, and he guessed that it opened into a hallway that ran up to the barroom, with another room, the one in which he had faced Fennimore the night before, off to the side.

A gun crashed ahead of him. A single shot. And then another one. Then a flurry of shots.

He felt the hair crawl at the base of his scalp, and his grip tightened on the gun in his hand. There had been occasional firing all afternoon, a few shots now and then. This might be just another fusillade, or it might mean that the kill had started, that the office would be rushed.

On tiptoe he moved across the room, reached the second door. And even as he reached for the knob, he felt it turn beneath his hand before his fingers gripped it.

Someone else had hold of the knob on the other side—was coming through the door!

Twisting on his boot-heel, he swung away, staggered back against the piled-up cases. The door swung open and a figure stepped into the room.

With all his strength, Carson swung at the head of the shadowy man, felt the barrel of his sixgun crash through the resistance of the hat, slam against the skull. The man gasped, pitched forward on buckling knees.

Moving swiftly, Carson scooped the guns from the holsters of the fallen man. He bent close to try to make out who it was, but in the dark the face was a white splotch, unrecognizable.

He straightened and stood tense, listening. There was no sound. No more shots from up in front.

He reached up to place the two guns he had taken from the holsters on top of the whiskey cases, and as he stretched on tiptoe to shove them back away from the edge, something drilled into his back, something hard and round.

Rigid, he did not move, and a voice that he knew spoke just behind him.

"Well, well, Morgan, imagine finding you here."

Mocking, hard—the voice of Jackson Quinn. Quinn, hearing the thud of the falling body, coming on quiet feet down the hallway to investigate, catching him when he was off guard.

"Mind if I turn around?" asked Carson, trying to keep his voice easy.

Quinn gurgled with delight. "Not at all. Turn around, by all means. I never did like shooting in the back." He chuckled again. "Not even you."

Carson twisted slowly around. The gun-muzzle never left his body, following it around from back to belly.

"Drop your gun," said Quinn.

Carson loosened his fingers, and the gun thudded on the floor.

"You've given me so much trouble," Quinn told him, "that I should bust you up a bit. But I don't think I will. I don't think I'll even bother." He chuckled. "I think I'll just shoot you here and have it over with."

Iron squealed against iron, an eerie sound that leaped at them from the dark.

Quinn jerked around, and for the first time his gun-muzzle lifted from Carson's body.

Carson moved like lightning, clenched fist coming up and striking down, smashing against the wrist that held the gun; striking entirely by instinct, for it was too dark to see.

Quinn cried out and the gun clanged to the floor.

The back door was open. A figure stood outlined against the lesser dark outside, a crouching figure that carried a rifle at the ready.

Shoulders hunched, head down, one foot braced hard for leverage against the whiskey cases, Carson hurled himself at Quinn. He felt the man go over at the impact of the blow, knew he was falling on top of him, hauled back his arm for a blow.

But a foot came up, lashing at his stomach. He sensed its coming, twisted, caught it in the ribs instead and went reeling back against the whiskey cases, limp with pain.

Quinn was crouching, springing toward him. A fist exploded in his face, thumped his head against the cases. He ducked his head, ears ringing, and bored in, fists playing a tattoo on Quinn's midriff, driving the man out into the center of the room.

A vicious punch straightened Carson, rocked him. The white blur of Quinn's face was coming toward him and he aimed at it, smashed with all his might—and the face retreated as Quinn staggered backward on his heels.

Carson stepped in, and out of the dark came piledriver blows that shook him with their viciousness.

The face was there again. Carson measured it, brought his fist up almost from the floor in a whistling, singing loop. Pain lanced down his arm as the blow connected with the whiteness of the face, and then the face was gone and Quinn was on the floor.

Feet were pounding in the hallway and shouts came from the barroom. Behind him a rifle crashed, thunderous in the closeness of the room, the red breath of its muzzle lighting the place for a single instant.

The rifle crashed again and yet again, and the room was full of powder-fumes that stung the nostrils.

"Jake!" yelled Carson.

"You bet your boots," said the man with the rifle. "You didn't think I'd let you do it all alone?"

"Quick!" gasped Carson. "Get in here, back by the door. They can't reach us here!"

A sixgun blasted and bullets chunked into the cases. Glass crashed and the reek of whiskey mingled with the smell of gun-smoke.

Jake came leaping across the room, crouched in the angle back of the door.

Scraping his feet along the floor, Carson located his sixgun, picked it up.

Jake's whisper was rueful. "They got us bottled like a jug of rum."

Carson nodded in the dark. "Been all right," he said, "if Quinn hadn't found me."

"That Quinn you had the shindy with?"

"That's right."

"Had a mind to step in and do some work with the gunstock," Jake told him, "but decided it was too risky. Couldn't tell which of you was which."

Guns thundered in the passageway, the explosions deafening. Bullets thudded into the cases, chewing up the boards, smashing the bottles.

Carson reached up and grasped a case from those stacked behind him. Jake's rifle bellowed. Carson flung the case over his head. It smashed into the doorway. He heaved another one.

Jake blasted away again. The guns in the hallway cut off.

"Keep watch," Carson told Jake. He heaved more cases in the doorway, blocking it to shoulder-height.

From across the street came the sound of firing—the ugly snarling of a high-powered rifle.

"That's Robinson," said Jake. "Some of them buzzards tried to sneak out the front door and come at us from behind, but Robinson was Johnny at the rat-hole."

"Robinson can't stop them for long," snapped Carson. "They'll get at us in a minute or two—"

A gun hammered almost in their ears and something stabbed Carson in the face. He brushed at it with his hand, pulled away a splinter. The gun roared again, as if it were just beside their heads.

"They're in the back room," gasped Jake, "shooting at us through the partition!"

"Quick!" yelled Carson. "We got to get out of here! Here, you grab Quinn and haul him out. I'll take the other fellow."

He grasped the man he had struck down with the gun-barrel, started to tug him toward the door.

"Why don't we leave 'em here?" yelped Jake. "What in tarnation is the sense of luggin' 'em?"

"Don't argue with me," yelled Carson. "Just get Quinn out of here."

The gun in the back room was hammering, was joined by another. Through the holes already punched by the bullets, Carson could see the red flare of the blasting guns. One of the bullets brushed past Carson's face, buried itself with a thud in the stacked cases. Another flicked burning across his ribs.

Savagely he yanked the door open; hauled his man through and dumped him on the ground. Reaching in, he gave the panting, puffing Jake a hand with Quinn.

"Pull them a bit farther away," said Carson. "We don't want them to get scorched."

"Scorched?" yipped Jake. "Now you're plumb out of your head!"

"I said scorched," declared Carson, "and I mean scorched. Things are going to get hot in the next five minutes."

He plunged his hand into a pocket, brought out a match, scratched it across the seat of his breeches. For a moment he held it in his cupped hand, nursing the flame, then with a flip of his fingers sent it sailing into the whiskey-reeking room.

The flame sputtered for a moment on the floor, almost went out, then blazed brilliantly, eating its way along a track of liquor flowing from one of the broken cases.

Carson lit another match, hurled it into the room. The blaze puffed rapidly, leaping along the floor, climbing the cases, snapping and snarling.

Carson turned and ran, Jake pelting at his heels. In the long grass back of the North Star they flung themselves prone and watched.

The single window in the building was an angry maw of fire, and tiny tongues of flame were pushing their way through the shingled roof.

A man leaped from one of the side windows in a shower of broken glass. Beside Carson, almost in his ear, Jake's rifle bellowed. The man's hat, still on his head despite the leap, was whipped off as if by an unseen hand.

From the *Tribune* office across the street came the flickering of blasting guns, covering the front windows and the door of the burning saloon.

"Listen!" hissed Jake. His hand reached out and grasped Carson by the shoulder. "Horses!"

It was horses—there could be no mistaking that. The thrum of hoofs along the dusty street—the whoop of a riding man, then a crash of thunder as sixguns cut loose.

Men were spilling out of the North Star now, running men with guns blazing in their hands. And down upon them swept the riders, yelling, sixguns tonguing flame.

The riders swept past the North Star, whirled and came back, and in their wake they left quiet figures lying in the dust.

Jake was on his knee, rifle at his shoulder, firing steadily at the running, dodging figures scurrying for cover.

A running man dashed around the corner of the flaming saloon, ducked into the broken, weedy ground back of the jail. For a moment the light of the fire swept across his face, and in that moment Carson recognized him.

It was Fennimore! Fennimore, making a getaway.

Carson leaped to his feet, crouched low and ran swiftly in the direction Fennimore had taken. Ahead of him a gun barked, and a bullet sang like an angry bee above his head.

For an instant he saw a darting darker shape in the shadows and brought up his own gun, triggered it swiftly. Out of the darkness Fennimore's gun answered, and the bullet, traveling low, whispered wickedly in the knee-high grass.

Carson fired at the gun-flash, and at the same instant something jerked at his arm and whirled him half-around. Staggering, his boot caught in a hummock and he went down, plowing ground with his shoulder.

He tried to put out his arm to help himself up again and found he couldn't. His right arm wouldn't move. It was a dead thing hanging on him, a dead thing that was numb, almost as if it were not a part of him.

Pawing in the grass with his left hand, he found the gun and picked it up, while dull realization beat into his brain.

Running after Fennimore, he'd been outlined against the burning North Star, had been a perfect target. Fennimore had shot him through the arm, perhaps figured he had killed him when he saw him stumble.

Crouching in the grass, he raised his head cautiously. But there was nothing but darkness.

Behind him the saloon's roof fell in with a gush of flames, and for a moment the fire leaped high, twisting in the air. And in that moment he saw Fennimore on a rise of ground above him. The man was standing there, looking at the flames.

Carson surged to his feet.

"Fennimore!" he shouted.

The man spun toward him, and for an instant the two stood facing each other in the flare of the gutted building.

Then Fennimore's gun was coming up, and to Carson it was almost as if he stood off to one side and watched with cold, deliberate, almost scientific interest.

But he knew his own hand was coming up, too, the left hand with the feel of the gun a bit unfamiliar in it.

Fennimore's gun drooled fire and something brushed with a blast of air past Carson's cheek. Then Carson's gun bucked against his wrist, and bucked again.

On the rise of ground, in the dying light of the sinking fire, Fennimore doubled over slowly. And across the space of the few feet that separated them, Carson heard him coughing, coughs wrenched out of his chest. The man pitched slowly forward, crashed face-first into the grass.

Slowly, Carson turned and walked down to the street, his wounded arm hanging at his side, blood dripping from his dangling fingers.

The guns were quiet. The fire was dying down. Black, grotesque figures still lay huddled in the dust. In front of the *Tribune* office the horses milled, and inside the office someone had lighted a lamp.

Voices yelled at him as he stepped up on the board sidewalk and headed for the office. He recognized some of the voices. Owens, Kelton, Ross—the men who had ridden away the night before, afraid of what might happen to their homes.

Owens was striding down the walk to meet him. He stared at Carson's bloody arm.

"Fennimore plugged me," Carson said.

"Fennimore got away. He isn't here."

"He's out back of the jail," Carson told him.

"We're glad we got here in time," said Owens gravely. "Glad we came to our senses. The boys feel pretty bad about last night. It took Miss Delavan to show us—"

"Miss Delavan?" asked Carson, dazed. "What did Kathryn have to do with it?"

Owens looked surprised. "I thought you knew. She rode out and told us."

"But Fennimore had guards posted!"

"She outrode them," Owens declared. "They didn't shoot at her. Guess even a Fennimore gunman doesn't like to gun a woman. They took out after her, but she was on that little Star horse of hers—"

"Yes, I know," said Carson. "Star can outrun anything on four legs."

"She told us how it was our chance to make a decent land out here, a decent place to live—a decent place for our kids."

"Where is she now?" asked Carson. "You made her stay behind. You—"

Owens shook his head. "She wouldn't listen to us. Nothing doing but she'd ride along with us. She said her father—"

"You left her at the house?"

Owens nodded. "She said—"

But Carson wasn't listening. He wasn't even staying. He stepped down into the street and walked away, his stride changing in a moment to a run.

"Kathryn!" he cried.

She was running down the street toward him, arms outstretched.

Jake, prodding Quinn and Clay Duffy toward the *Tribune* at rifle-point, saw them when they met. He watched interestedly and spat judiciously in the dust.

"Beats all hell," he told Quinn, "how that feller gets along with women."

THE END

Crazy Springs' Write-In Vote

By ROY M. O'MARA

"Seeing as you are repentant—" the sheriff began, but Stub interrupted him.

In durance vile for a crime he'd never heard of, Stub Woffard took cards in a strange game—whose object was, not to take the pot—but to get rid of it! A hilarious tale of the most unorthodox frontier election ever held!

UNMINDFUL of the three stealthy figures approaching from behind, Stub Woffard studied the panorama before him with back braced against a saddle bag and scuff-toed boots extended toward the embers of a brush-root fire. In the glare of a late September sunset, there was little to set Crazy Springs apart from a hundred other places he had visited during a long and idle career—unless it was a small weatherbeaten structure across from the stone courthouse. It was a two-story shiplapped building, without the usual false front, topped by a big square water tank bearing the red-painted sign: "Two-Handled Crockery Items—With Lid—Bolivar Sneed, Owner." It meant nothing to Stub Woffard.

"All right," a nasal voice boomed out behind him, "grab 'im, boys!"

Stub used one hand to help whirl a short body from the ground. The other was whistling in a vicious arc before he saw the big nickel-plated star on a hump-backed man at one side.

Before he could stop himself, Stub's fist connected with a hairy jaw and cracked like a board on a pack mule's rump.

Stub gasped. "Par'n me!" he gulped, as the bewhiskered victim landed on his neck. "Lawmen usually approach me from in front, formal-like. Don't tell me I'm arrested for somethin'."

"You shore are!" snapped the hump-shouldered man. He motioned with a skinny hand for the remaining man to relieve Stub of his gun. "Never mind what for—move!"

"But my hoss!" Stub protested. "An' my outfit—"

"Move!" the sharp-faced official fluted through a hooked nose. "Deputy McFootle will take care of that, when he wakes up."

As Stub stumbled along ahead of the escorting lawmen, he realized that he should have been more cautious in his approach. It wasn't that he had not been forewarned. Didn't the most road-hardened boomers get red in the face, confused and silent at the mere mention of Crazy Springs?

And what had become of his own partner, Boxcar Bailey, who had left Reno two months before for the avowed purpose of figuring prominently in local poker games? He hadn't been heard from since. Now Stub could see that the sprawling, windswept town kept its secrets well.

A kerosene lamp was burning in the cluttered office of the justice of the peace when Stub and his convoy reached the dusty street. As they entered, he noticed that the dirty-eared judge was blotting fresh ink on a complaint form, and was puzzled.

"Name?" the judge croaked.

Stub hesitated a split second. "Jimmy Smith," he answered, pulling his floppy hat from a gleaming bald head.

The judge scratched the name in the space provided on the

form. "Jimmy Smith," he read rapidly, "you are accused by this complaint of the crime of mopery, committed as follows: That on or about this date, in or around the county of Blackfoot, over, around or upon the township of Crazy Springs, you, the defendant, willfully and wantonly with malice aforethought, did deliberately and intentionally mope against the peace and dignity of this state. . . ."

Stub shifted his feet. "It's this way, Judge," he said, "Yuh see—"

"Guilty as charged!" snapped the judge. "Thirty days in the county jail!" He blew out the light, and Stub, marveling at the speed of local justice, was propelled roughly across the street. They went up the courthouse stairs and into a smoke-filled sheriff's office, where six more deputies made themselves comfortable on a rickety counter, a spur-marked desk and a cigarette-littered floor. The sheriff fumbled with his jail keys.

"Convention?" Stub inquired amiably, "or just a hold-over from th' Fourth of July?"

"Shet up!" a deputy admonished as he hoisted Stub through the door of the adjoining jail.

The steel door clanged shut. Then a match flared, illuminating a big arm stretched from a steel bunk at the far side of the cell. The match touched the wick of a candle stuck in a bottle. Even before Stub's eyes were entirely accustomed to the gloom, he could see piled cases along one wall and a cluttered table near the jail door. There was a strong smell of fresh paint.

"Mopery," he mumbled. "I've been in jail for a lot o' things— but never mopery. Must be somethin' like arson."

"Stub!" a joyous voice yelled as the other occupant of the cell rolled from the bunk. "I'd know that voice in hell!"

"Boxcar!" Stub yelped. "Boxcar Bailey! How long you been here?"

"Shhh!" Boxcar Bailey warned. "Don't let them stool-pigeons hear nothin'." He pulled jeans over muscle-knotted legs and thrust sockless feet into cold boots. "I been in about two months."

They made a strange pair—Stub being hammered-down, smooth in features, action and speech, while Boxcar Bailey was a slow-witted, rough, battered-faced ex-prize fighter. Moreover, he was built big enough to get Stub Woffard out of many scrapes with his hamlike fists or ready gun. Not that Stub was a slouch, but the diminutive loafer was prone to bite off more than he could chew at times. It was a convenient tie-up.

Stub twisted a brown-paper cigarette and leaned on the opposite bunk. "When yuh due out?" he wanted to know.

"About thirty more days," Boxcar Bailey replied mournfully. "This makes th' second time my sentence has been upped."

"Howcome?" Stub inquired.

Boxcar was silent for a moment. In the light of the flickering candle Stub could see the big man's face flush and his lips tremble.

"Yesterday," he blurted out at last, "I dropped another— item—and they gave me thirty days more!"

"I don't get it," Stub said. "What d'yuh mean, *item?*"

Boxcar indicated the cases piled high against the far wall and several objects now visible on the table, beside paint cans and brushes. "Them things," he explained, "is items. I has tuh stencil red roses an' bronc-busters on 'em—an' so will you."

"Why?"

"Because," Boxcar said, "nobody in their right mind will stoop low enough to be a item painter, an' as Sheriff Bolivar Sneed owns th' Two-Handled Crockery Items—With Lid—Company acrost th' street, he manages tuh keep fellers in jail tuh keep up on th' paintin'. Why, even them sheep-herdin' bums he has workin' for 'im won't paint items!"

Stub held one of the finished products to the yellow candlelight. Two curving handles, an ornate lid and a scalloped base adorned the pumpkin-shaped crockery piece. On one side of the receptacle there were stenciled red roses, and on the other a red bronc-buster astride a plunging horse. Underneath were the words: "A Handle To Spare!"

"Now," Stub said slowly, "I see it all! No wonder th' boomers wouldn't talk about Crazy Springs—they was ashamed of paintin' these dingblasted—"

"*Shhh!*" Boxcar interrupted. "You're talkin' too loud. Call 'em Two-Handled Crockery Items—With Lid. If Sheriff Sneed hears yuh call 'em anything else, he cuts off th' grub, soap an' tobaccy!"

Crash! A two-handled item, given steaming impetus by Stub's full-armed swing, shattered against the jail door and threw powdered white crockery all over the lounging officials. "You've lost your fightin' spirit, Boxcar!" Stub yelled. "This is a dirty deal!" And he let drive with another festooned piece.

Wildly Sheriff Bolivar Sneed came to his feet, clawing fragments of porcelain from shirt collar and eyes. "Every time you break a two-handled crockery item—with lid—" he trumpeted through his adenoids—"you'll get thirty days more!"

Crash!

"That makes ninety days!" the sheriff roared.

Crash! Crash! Crash! Three deputies were stuck for a moment amid the ankle-deep litter as they rushed the outer door. "You'll *never* get out!" the sheriff screamed.

"Why, you long-nosed, whining, ring-boned billygoat," Stub raved as Boxcar grabbed wildly at him, "we'll be outa here within a week, an' you'll cuss th' day you ever heard of a—"

"Two-handled crockery item—with lid!" the sheriff shrieked. "And besides that—have those items in there painted by tomorrow night, or you'll get no food, tobacco or soap!"

"Blub!" Stub observed, with Boxcar's hamlike hand clamped over his twisting face.

The light went out in the sheriff's office and Boxcar let go. "Stub," he pleaded, "for th' love o' Pete, take it easy or we'll never get out o' here. This jail is break-proof—I know."

Pent-up air from within rumbled deep in Stub's throat. "What's th' all-fired hurry about gettin' this stuff done?" he asked, pacing up and down the length of the stone enclosure.

Boxcar sagged to the steel bunk and ran worried fingers through his tangled black hair. "Campaign stuff," he muttered. "Him an' his deppities takes three-four wagon-loads out a couple o' days afore each election an' gives a two-handled item tuh each voter."

The light of unholy inspiration rested on the cherubic features of Stub Woffard. "Tell me more about this election stuff," he said, shoving his head through the barred window.

The courthouse door, he noted, was under the jail window. There was an occasional glare of light from a false-fronted business house, and a high-riding moon cast a shadow of the Two-Handled Crockery Item—With Lid—building in the street before him.

"Nothin' much to th' election," Boxcar Bailey summed up. "This feller Sneed has been in for years. All th' stinkin' bums he has workin' for 'im across th' street is deppities. They all get out an' campaign, an' a couple of 'em usual runs agin 'im tuh bust up any opposin' vote. A lotta people is sick o' him, but they don't know what tuh do."

Stub pulled his head back into the jail. "C'mon, Boxcar," he said, "we got t' get about twenty feet o' wire spliced together off th' tag ends of th' balin' wires around these cases. Might be a day or two before we can use it, but we'll be ready tuh go when things is right."

Boxcar came up standing. "Go?" he said. "Go where?"

"Spring out," Stub grunted. "Jail-break—nuthin' to it."

Boxcar was jubilant. "Tuhnight?" he asked.

"Nope," Stub replied. "We gotta do this legal—I don't know how much of a crime mopery is, but we can't afford tuh have this ol' snaggle-toothed bum advertisin' us from Anaconda tuh El Paso."

"How yuh goin' t' get around it?" Boxcar asked.

"Simple—just get elected sheriff," Stub replied, flipping a cigarette through the window. "They can't keep a sheriff or his deppity in jail, can they?"

Stub fashioned a big loop in one end of the wire, coiled it and stuck it in his bunk. Boxcar sat back on his bunk, kicked his boots away and rested massive shoulders against the cold stone wall. He said, "I never knowed of a man tuh get stir-crazy so quick."

Even as day was breaking over the flat country around Crazy Springs, Stub and Boxcar rolled from damp blankets and were soon plying deft brushes to two-handled crockery items—with lids. Stub was singing in a low voice:

> Roses are red;
>   Cowboys are too.
> If this is a item,
>   I'm a Hindu!

There was an expression of pleased surprise on the pinched face of Sheriff Bolivar Sneed when he shoved half a loaf of bread and a pot of coffee through the bars of the jail door. "Seeing as you are repentant," he droned, "and entirely industrious, something might be done about cutting your time. . . ."

Stub was fishing an unpainted item from a packing case. It splintered on a steel plate in front of the sheriff's face, and the two rooms resounded to the crash of shattered white pottery.

"Stub!" Boxcar Bailey wailed.

"You—you bandy-legged, hog-spavined, bit-lipped ol' maverick," Stub exploded, "git yer weasel face outa that door!"

The sheriff retreated hastily through the litter on the office floor, and Stub took up his brush.

The noonday meal was warm water and two hunks of stale bread; the evening meal was two hunks of bread and cold water. Later, with Stub and Boxcar herded at gun-point into a corner, the finished crockery items were removed. Fresh stock was left in its place.

"Just something to do," the sheriff explained, "until election is over."

"Stub!" Boxcar warned. "Keep yer trap shut!"

At daybreak the following day, Boxcar piled from his bunk to investigate a sound of activity in the street. "Why, them lowdown, unorthodox sheepherders," he fumed, "has got our hosses hitched to one o' them wagon loads o' campaign crockery!"

"It's only fair," Stub remarked.

"Yeah," Boxcar replied, "I s'pose that's right."

There was only a skeleton crew at the Two-Handled Crockery Item—With Lid—factory that day. Election day, nobody worked. One deputy was delegated to swamp the shattered pottery from the sheriff's office in preparation for the inaugural brawl. The sheriff donned a too-small derby and engaged in drooling over babies and giving away a few unpainted two-handled crockery items—with lids. He spent much time around the office of the Crazy Springs *Weekly Bugle*, where the votes were counted. Stub Woffard guessed, by the supercilious expression worn by the sheriff, that the local vote was in his favor.

It was late in the evening when vote reports started coming in from the outlying districts. Sheriff Bolivar Sneed lighted the big hanging lamp in his office and sat back to await the final vote tally and the plaudits of his supporters. In anticipation of the event he settled the derby firmly on his pointed head and took a long pull on one of five black bottles he had set up on his desk.

Stub licked dry lips. He said, "I'd like tuh smack that hump-shouldered monkey acrost th' face with a sockful o' stinkin' mud."

Boxcar Bailey touched a match to the candle. "Who wouldn't?" he asked reasonably.

Stub was pushing the big loop on the wire through the jail window and tying a smaller loop in the other end when there was the sound of running footsteps on the stairs. A wild-eyed deputy sheriff burst into the office. The sheriff inserted thumbs in his suspenders, lowered his beady eyes, blushed and waited for the good news.

"Sheriff!" the deputy yelled. "You done got whopped—some feller named James Sylvester Woffard took all th' outside votes an' nosed you out!"

The deputy rushed down the stairs without closing the door. The smirk on the derbied sheriff gave way to a sickly stare. He arose with uncertain movements and started through the door. "No!" he yelled at the departed deputy. "No! No!"

"Now!" Stub hissed, pushing his head between two of the window bars and his arms between others. "Hand me a two-handled item—with lid—an' we're ready tuh go! Wrap your hands in a blanket an' grab that small loop."

The sheriff came through the door below the jail window. Above, Stub Woffard poised a two-handled crockery item—with lid.

"Sheriff!" he called softly.

Sheriff Bolivar Sneed paused long enough for Stub to arc the crockery item downward. There was a resounding crash, and pieces of pottery flew in every direction. The derby was jammed over the sheriff's eyes and he staggered in a dazed circle on wobbling legs. A wire loop settled over his weaving body to a point below groping hands and jerked under his armpits.

"Heave!" Stub yelled.

By the time the sheriff was hoisted to window level, he was beginning to chirp feebly. Stub's darting hand relieved him of his gun and jail keys. By the time the jail door was opened and they had found their guns in a drawer, their hostage was making the town ring with terrorized yelling. A crowd gathered.

"Watch th' office door, Boxcar," Stub yelled, hurrying back to the jail window.

"Feller citizens," Stub yelled, "this is James Sylvester Woffard, th' newly elected sheriff, talkin'. When all th' deppities o' this lowlife Sheriff Sneed line up in the street an' throw their guns in a pile, I'll cut th' baboon outa th' winder!"

"Doggone," Boxcar commented from out front, "your ol' brain is beginnin' tuh locomote agin!"

Stub was thinking the same thing, until a howling slug from across the street ripped through a case of crockery stock, glanced on a jail bar and thudded into the office wall. There was a sodden thump outside, followed by a raging whoop.

Stub rubbed the stubble on his round chin and eyed the bullet-severed wire where Sheriff Sneed had been hanging. By the yelling in the street, he knew the sheriff was fixing to eliminate political competition.

"Two or three o' you deputies get over back o' the courthouse," the sheriff yodeled. "Everybody else get in the factory. Shoot to kill. James Woffard ain't the name this jailbird gave to me. It's nothing but a attempted jailbreak!"

"This," observed Stub to his woeful partner, "is a doggoned mess. They don't dare tuh tackle us, an' we'd be crazy tuh rush them."

Braving the smashing lead that poured through the windows, Boxcar doused the lights. "Might be," he gulped, "that we should lock up th' jail an' throw th' key an' our guns in th' street. After that we could take up paintin' crockery items where we left off, an' hope for an earthquake or Sheriff Sneed's sudden death."

"You forget," Stub said, "that we have several personal grudges to settle before we take this shebang over, th' first o' th' year."

"Yuh mean like runnin' that sheriff till his ankles smoke?" Boxcar inquired as he stepped into a safe corner to ignite a cigarette.

"Yeah—him an' that dirty-eared judge."

The sheriff's office yielded two double-barreled shotguns, one sawed-off, and a carbine. The stone wall was turning lead from across the street, but better-aimed slugs tore through the windows and made them flinch as they carried the guns and a case or two of ammunition into the jail. The biting smell of burned powder blended with the stench of paint as Boxcar raised up now and again to blast the crockery item building with No. o buckshot. Orange flashes streaked from every window of the opposite structure. Townspeople huddled in tight knots out of the line of fire.

Boxcar peered through the gloom. "Got somethin' figured out?" he asked hopefully.

"Yep," Stub replied. "Take a safe position here by th' window an' start shootin' at that nearest upright over there—see? I'll be behind th' office safe, doin' th' same thing."

All available guns were blistering hot and about two cases of ammunition were gone before a supporting timber under the big

water tank over the Two-Handled Crockery Item—With Lid—
plant began to crumble.

Boxcar let both barrels of his sawed-off go at the main part of the
building, just to hear the crockery crash when the buckshot
ploughed into reserve stocks. *"Timberrrr!"* he whooped joyfully as
the square tank settled more on the bullet-riddled support.

The added weight of water slopping to the low side was too much
for the weakened structure, and with a grinding roar the tank tipped
forward and crashed halfway through the roof below.

"If yuh can't shoot 'em," Boxcar yelled, "drown 'em!"

"Keep me covered!" Stub yelled back. "Here I go!"

Stub paused in the darkness of the courthouse door at the street.
There was no sound from the building across the way, except the
occasional yell of a waterlogged deputy. Water was pouring out of
second-story windows.

Suddenly there was the sound of feet splashing through water,
and Sheriff Bolivar Sneed leaped from the main entrance into the
moonlit street, watersoaked and wild-eyed. Holding his derby
aboard his head with both hands, he broke into a one-man stampede.

Stub, with a bloodcurdling shout, dumped a cargo of buckshot
ahead of the speeding lawman. Boxcar, in the jail, maneuvered his
sawed-off around and sewed a pattern behind him. The effect was
immediate. Sheriff Sneed almost tore boot-heels off, stopping.

"Come here!" Stub commanded, dropping another load in the
overworked shotgun. "Come here with your hands up, yuh
yeller-bellied gully lizard, before I plumb lose my temper and
ventilate your mangy carcass!"

He came. Stub noted that the lawman's holster was still empty,
and when he nudged him from behind with the snout of the twin-
bore, he took the courthouse steps three at a time. Boxcar had
watched the procedure and was lighting the candle over near the
outside stone wall. His pockets were bulging with shotgun ammunition. "I'm goin' over an' supervise th' extricatin' business," he
announced.

"Okay," Stub agreed, "but don't stick your neck out. Tell 'em
yuh're goin' tuh set th' place on fire if they don't pile out, an'
quick—an' if yuh see ol' Judge Dirty-Ears, bring 'im back."

Sheriff Bolivar Sneed was blinking his little eyes, shifting his feet, licking dry lips and twirling his derby. "Wh—what you want?" he stammered.

"My proposition," answered Stub, "is simple. . . . It's about ninety days before I take over here—so tuh make things quicker, all you have tuh do is sign my deputy's commission an' your resignation!"

The sheriff staggered backwards. "No!" He almost wept.

Stub took a step forward, and the sheriff cringed away. His angular elbow hooked into a pile of leftover painted two-handled crockery items piled on the counter. He leaped wildly to one side when three of them crashed to the floor.

"Hmmmm," Stub reflected. "Thirty days per. Now look, podner," he continued, "either you get busy with them documents, or I stand you in the corner and bust every cockeyed piece of pottery around here on your misshapen skull!"

Sheriff Sneed capitulated. With palsied movements the sheriff penned the two brief documents and then settled back, bathed in cold sweat, as the door suddenly burst open.

Stub grabbed the shotgun and was ready to go until he noted that Dirty-Ears, the judge, was being ushered in by a triumphant and grinning Boxcar Bailey, laden with rifles and sixguns taken from the embattled deputies in the Two-Handled Crockery Item building.

Stub unshouldered the shotgun. "Good evening, Judge!" he smiled. "We're about tuh hold a little court session. Thought maybe you'd like tuh write out a couple o' pardons for th' new sheriff an' his deppity—an' besides, we want tuh sign a mopery complaint agin' th' ex-sheriff an' git him salted away for about ninety days, so's he can ketch up a little with th' pottery paintin'."

Gulping and wild-eyed, the judge cringed back, and Boxcar's presented sawed-off touched him. The judge sprang forward again. "No!" he breathed.

"Judge," Stub asked pleasantly, "did any ornery maverick ever bust you over th' head with a piece o' painted pottery?"

"Or," contributed Boxcar, "did yuh ever have nightmares about runnin' through town without any clothes?"

The judge had never been victimized by lawless citizenry to that extent, but the idea horrified him. With fevered alacrity he guided justice in a hurried course and loped through the door. Stub ushered the ex-sheriff into the jail and set him up in business among bullet-riddled paint cans and shattered two-handled crockery items. By the aid of the bottled candle, Sneed did a shaky but thorough job.

Stub lighted the big lamp in the office. "That's th' only way tuh do business," he remarked, pinning the sheriff's badge on a plaid red shirt. "Legal, all th' way around."

There was another knock on the door.

Under the cold stare of four shotgun barrels a small, brisk individual with thick glasses and a pencil pushed in at Stub's invitation.

"I'm Charley Spencer," the newcomer announced. "Editor of the Crazy Springs *Weekly Bugle,* and chairman of the election board." He looked at the star on Stub's barrel chest. "I take it," he continued, "that you are James Sylvester Woffard—but can you prove it?"

The shotguns were lowered. Stub blushed and pulled at his shirt-tail. " 'Bout th' only thing," he confessed, "is a tattoo on my middle."

"Let's see it," grunted the efficient newspaperman. Squinting through the thick glasses, he studied the tattooed name inscribed across Stub's bulging mid-section.

"Something wrong," he said. "The name here is Wooffard!"

"Shucks, mister," Stub giggled, "one o' them o's ain't what yuh think it is!"

"Oh," said Mr. Spencer, blinking his eyes. "Oh!" Apparently satisfied, he pulled scratch-paper from his pocket. "We go to press tomorrow," he said, "and would like the story of your campaign, especially as to how you managed to get your name in the pot!"

"Simple!" contributed Boxcar, grabbing up one of the spare campaign items on the counter. "Just wrote it there—look for yourself!"

Mr. Spencer blinked his eyes again before thrusting his chin over the edge of the gay-colored receptacle. He read aloud: "Vote for James Sylvester Woffard for sheriff—the people's choice!"

Inside the jail, a two-handled crockery item—with lid—slipped from suddenly numbed fingers and crashed on the floor.

THE END

"There's two of our beef in there," Joe called from the fence. "I seen the brands."

Action-Packed Saga of the Cattle Frontier

In Piojoso, McBride figured to swap his money belt for a herd and m
on. But all that leather-necked cattle buyer could get for his clink
cartwheels in that man-for-breakfast Border town would be a lor
boothill plot, just big enough to hold one hundred and eighty pound
fighting man!

COL. COLT BUYS
A BORDER HERD

By

BENNETT FOSTER

CHAPTER ONE
Ride Out, Stranger!

McBride reached Piojoso as the sun went down, a compact, hard-twisted man upon a compact, hard-twisted horse. The day's dust mantled him, and with the dust he carried an air of calm assurance, the certainty of a man who knows he is a man. Dust and assurance were visible; hidden were the money belt about his waist and a .45 caliber Bisley model Colt in a shoulder holster.

Five buildings made Piojoso. Two stores confronted each other across a dusty space. Beside the smaller of the two was a saloon, beside the larger, a blacksmith shop with wagon yard attached. McBride left the horse, Shorty, in the wagon yard, grain in the feed box, hay in the manger.

The store by the saloon was old, the porch roof sagging, the porch floor uncertain. In its interior a single coal oil lamp struggled against the growing darkness, and the man who appeared as McBride opened the screen seemed feeble as the lamp. A small man, a wispy man, with a fringe of white about his bald spot and a long, shrewd face.

"The hostler told me I might be able to get a bed here," said McBride. "Is that right?"

"Depends," the wispy man said, "on what you call a bed. You can sleep on the counter."

"Suits me," McBride agreed, and advanced into the store. "I need supper, too. Sardines and crackers, and a can of tomatoes."

The storekeeper moved, his wooden peg thumping on the floor. McBride, easing himself up on the counter, used an expert hatchet on the tomato can.

"Any cattle for sale around here?" he asked.

"Nope." The storekeeper's eyes were bright and quick. "You buy cattle?"

"Not if there's none for sale." McBride drank tomato juice. "It's cattle country, ain't it? I passed some little outfits on the way. *Paisanos*, I took 'em to be."

"Cattle country, but there's no cattle for sale." Now that the cans were opened, the storekeeper replaced the hatchet beneath the counter. "Mister Norwood buys the cattle." There was heavy emphasis on the word Mister. He paused, then: "The grub's six bits. Nothin' for the bed. Pay for the grub now."

228

McBride put a half-dollar and a quarter on the counter. The money was pocketed. "I'll leave the lamp," the storekeeper said. "Blankets are on the shelf. Throw your cans out the door." He stumped toward the rear of the room, pausing at the door. "You won't sleep nohow," he said. "It's Saturday night."

The door slammed. McBride could hear the peg thump as his host moved about. He finished the last of his tomatoes. Piojoso, he thought. *Piojoso* means lousy. Lousy is right.

Six blankets on the counter made a bed; a seventh made a pillow. McBride put the Bisley Colt beside the pillow, added his coat for padding and placed his boots beside the counter. He cupped his hand behind the lamp chimney, puffed, and in the ensuing darkness stretched out, adjusting himself to the familiar burden of the money belt, the familiar lump of the Colt. In the darkness a cricket took up an endless song. From the saloon came a murmur of voices. Horses trotted up and stopped, and the murmur was augmented. Tomorrow, McBride thought sleepily, he would move along. He had six thousand dollars, and in a country this far away from a market that would buy a bunch of cattle. He yawned and remembered what the storekeeper had said: "Mister Norwood buys the cattle." Somebody had a lead-pipe cinch around Piojoso, McBride thought. Somebody named Norwood was doing all right. Maybe he wouldn't go on in the morning. Maybe he'd stay and . . . The endless song of the cricket seemed to fade. McBride slept.

He awakened bolt upright, the Bisley Colt in his hand, the echo of a shot still ringing in his ears. A shrill yelling sounded from the saloon, high pitched and raucous. McBride grunted and lay back again. Some fool celebrating. Now he knew why the storekeeper had said he wouldn't sleep. The yelling rose in pitch, and another shot thudded. McBride swore. If this kept up, his host would have the right of it. High spirits and a Saturday night celebration were all right in their place, but he wished the place was far away. He wished—

A third shot tore through the thin boards of the store wall, splintering them, and a can just above McBride's head gave a mournful chug. McBride slid down from the counter, pulled on his boots and possessed himself of hat and Colt. Fun was fun, but the store walls were too damned thin. He rubbed his hand over his beard-stubbled chin and strode purposefully to the door. After all, a man was entitled to his rest.

The saloon, when he walked in, was bright with light. There were three men, riders by their dress, against the bar, their faces uncertain. The bald-headed bartender was looking ruefully at broken bottles on the backbar. Four natives were collected sullenly at the end of the bar, and in the center of the room was a youngster, blond-haired, well dressed, a whiskey glass in one hand, a long-barreled gun in the other. The blond-haired man was laughing, but there was nothing mirthful in the laugh, nothing mirthful in his pale eyes, either.

"I'm goin' to take one more drink an' then kill me a Mexican," the blond man stated. "One of these here Mexicans. Fill 'er up, Curly."

He was, McBride decided, not nearly so drunk as he pretended, but he was drunk enough to be mean. The bald bartender, Curly, moved uneasily, and one of the men at the bar said: "Now, Reeder," placatingly.

McBride walked forward. "Give me that gun," he said.

The blond man turned. The pale blue eyes narrowed. "Who are you?" he demanded. "What'uh you mean, 'Gimme that gun?' Nobody gets my gun!"

"I'm a man that likes his sleep," McBride stated. "Give it here." His left hand was extended. He was close to the blond man. The gun swept up.

"To hell with you!" Light in the slitted blue eyes, sudden cruelty in the sullen mouth. McBride, agile as a cat, moved in and aside. The Bisley Colt, produced from nowhere seemingly, thudded against blond hair. The sullen mouth flew wide open, the blue eyes glazed. The blond-haired man went down, sprawled on the floor.

McBride faced the room. "I'm sleepin' next door," he said apologetically. "I've come a long ways today and I'm tired. Suppose you fellers go home now."

Curly, the bald bartender, craned across the bar. "Did you kill him?" he demanded; then seeing the blond man's legs move: "No, damn it! That's too bad. All right, boys, I'm closin' up."

At the bar the riders moved, the shock of the sudden action dissipated now, their wits recovered. One went out, but two lingered, looking questioningly at McBride.

"If he belongs to you," McBride said, "you're welcome to him. Only don't get any fool ideas." The Bisley Colt was still prominent in his hand.

"We work for his old man, mister," one of the riders said.

"Go on an' take him home, Joe," Curly ordered.

Joe and his fellow lifted the blond man. The natives had already disappeared, flitting silently through the door. With the blond man sagging between them, the two burden bearers walked out.

"You want a drink?" Curly asked.

McBride shook his head. "I just want to sleep," he said. "Good-night."

A rattling and banging of tin wakened McBride. He heard the thump of the storekeeper's peg, and daylight filled his sight. Sitting up, he rubbed his sleepy eyes, then arose from behind the counter where he had moved his bed.

The storekeeper looked at McBride reproachfully. "A wash-basin an' a tub balanced against my door," he said. "A half-dozen buckets an' a twenty-gallon can against the front door. You call that friendly?" The voice was chiding, but there was a change in the storekeeper's manner. He seemed more spry, more full of life.

"Did you," McBride asked, "ever hear the story about the man in the insane asylum? He was naked except for a derby hat. When they asked him why he was naked, he said nobody ever come to see him. When they asked him why the hat, he said that somebody *might* come."

The wispy man nodded. "You wasn't expecting nobody," he said, "but you was fixed to receive 'em. I see. Know who it was you buffaloed last night? That was Reeder Norwood."

McBride's eyes said that the name meant nothing. The storekeeper said: "Reeder's daddy, ol' Berry Norwood, is the he-coon of Piojoso."

"Oh," said McBride. "The man that buys cattle, huh?"

"An' runs most of the country. What's your name, mister?"

"McBride."

"Mine's Jim Sledge. There's a pump out back you can wash up at, an' I'm makin' coffee. Better come an' have some." The storekeeper stumped away.

Times change, McBride thought as he pulled on his boots.

The pump water was cold, the coffee hot, the ham and eggs that accompanied it filling. Tobacco was sweet in the morning. Sledge, pouring McBride's third cup, gave testimony.

"Curly Lerch, him that runs the saloon, tol' me what happened. Reeder didn't have all his bunch along last night. Noone Padden was missin'."

"Padden?" McBride savored the coffee.

"Norwood's foreman at his ranch. Reeder's kind of Padden's student, you might say. Padden's the teacher when it comes to hell raisin'."

McBride absorbed the knowledge. What Sledge meant to say was that, had the teacher been present, McBride would not have had so easy a time with the pupil.

"Do you," said McBride, "know any cattle that are for sale this mornin'? You said last night that Norwood bought around here. A little competition helps the prices an' that's good for business, you know."

"I was comin' to that. I know where you can buy mebbe a hundred head in one bunch; cows, calves, mebbe some steers an' bulls."

"Where?"

" 'Bout fifteen miles from town. At the Diamond Bar. Lewis Titus has got 'em. You go this a-way." Sledge's finger outlined a patch on the oilcloth.

"I'll look at 'em," McBride decided.

"You can come back here tonight," Sledge said, "I got an extra bed. Better'n the counter."

"Fine," McBride got up.

"You want I should get your horse?"

"Why?"

"It's Norwood's wagon yard. Mebbe—"

"It's my horse," said McBride. "Thanks. I'll see you tonight."

Shorty, McBride saw, had been fed. There was still grain in the box. The bay horse munched philosophically on the bit while McBride smoothed the saddle blanket in place. He had reached for the saddle when a tall man, gray-haired, blank-faced, walked into the wagon yard. McBride swung the saddle up, shook it and reached under Shorty for the cinch.

"Leavin'?" asked the tall man.

"For a while," McBride answered.

"No," the tall man refuted. "For good. That was my boy you hit last night."

Then the tall man was Berry Norwood. McBride paused in his saddling and surveyed the man. Blond Reeder Norwood was a minor copy of his father. Berry Norwood's eyes were pale blue, as were Reeder's, his mouth more cruel, his face harder, the lines deeper cut. A dangerous man, McBride thought; a man to watch, a man to be afraid of, if you wanted to be afraid.

"Your boy was drunk," McBride said. "And dangerous. And I was tired."

"You made a mistake," Norwood said. "But you didn't know. Ride out, now. Don't come back."

"I'm goin'," McBride said, foot in stirrup, reins in hand, "to look at some cattle. Maybe I'll buy 'em. I travel where I please. When I please. How I please. I stay where I want to stay. *Hasta la vista*, Mr. Norwood." He swung into the saddle. Shorty walked toward the gate.

"I've told you," Norwood warned as McBride passed.

"That's right," McBride agreed. "You told me."

He rode south out of Piojoso. Five miles and he left the mesa top. Below him the country spread, cut by canyons, red rimrock riding the bluff tops. Shelter here, timber and canyons, water, grass. Cattle country. Three miles down the canyon McBride came to a house, a bunch of calves weaning in the pen behind it. He turned and rode in.

Spanish was McBride's second tongue, learned along the border, perfected in Mexico. Juan Villareal, coming from the corrals, met his visitor. Villareal's face was familiar, and McBride placed the man as one of the natives he had seen in Curly's saloon. The calves, Villareal said, were not for sale.

Gently McBride pressed his point, not seeming to pry, not too eager, just talking. Mr. Norwood bought the calves, Juan said. Well, not exactly bought them, but he, Juan Villareal, owed money at the store and in a way the calves were security. How much for the calves? Ten dollars perhaps . . . perhaps twelve.

McBride said that he might be able to offer a more attractive price. He would return. He rode on down the hill.

He had the story now, and it was simple enough. Men worked on credit from one fall to the next. They owed money at Norwood's store, and they sold their calves to Norwood. McBride had seen peonage work in Mexico. It would work here. Only one menace to Norwood's system: if a cowbuyer came in, offering fair prices, Norwood was hurt. Such a man must be disposed of, driven out. McBride smiled thinly.

The canyon leveled off and widened. The sun was high. Shorty and McBride watered at a tank, went on. The road split and

McBride checked. Right hand or left hand? He had forgotten what Sledge said. Had Sledge mentioned the road fork at all? Rock rattled and McBride looked up.

A kid, riding on a red steer, came down the hill. The kid was black-headed, like McBride. His eyes were gray, like McBride's. He wore overalls, a denim shirt and a straw hat, nothing else. Tanned hide showed through rents in shirt and overalls. He was whirling a sling and, as McBride watched, let go. The stone clunked into a yucca. The red steer had a ring in its nose, two rope reins extending from it, but as the kid bent his mount to join McBride, it was evident that the steer had been bridlewise for a long time.

"Mornin'," McBride greeted.

"Mornin'." The two pairs of level gray eyes met, and the kid grinned suddenly. Full-mouthed, McBride thought. He's over twelve.

"I'm kind of mixed up," he said. "I'm lookin' for Lewis Titus's place."

"Lois Titus? She lives yonder." The boy pointed.

"Lewis," McBride corrected.

"There ain't no Lewis. Lois owns the Diamond Bar."

Mentally McBride swore. Sledge had said Lewis. McBride disliked doing business with women. Women, his experience said, didn't know their own mind. They'd make a bargain one minute and then back out the next.

"I'm goin' down there," the kid said. "I'll take you."

The red steer ambled down the right-hand road. Shorty caught up.

"My name's Fairweather," the kid said. "Dave Fairweather. What's your name, stranger?"

"McBride. Your folks in the cow business?"

"I ain't got folks." The small face frowned. "I own cattle, though. Red's mine, an' I got two cows, too."

"Calves on the cows?" McBride repressed his grin.

"Heifer an' a steer calf. Best two you'll ever see."

"I buy cattle," McBride stated. "Want to sell your calves?"

"I'll sell the steer. What are you payin'?"

"I'd have to look at him," McBride answered. "I'll pay from fifteen to eighteen dollars, dependin' on the calf."

Mental arithmetic went on behind the boy's gray eyes. "That's more'n Norwood pays,'' he said finally. ''You bought a calf, mister.''

One calf bought in the Piojoso country. ''I'll let you know where to deliver,'' McBride said. ''Here's earnest money.'' He extended a five-dollar bill.

''Thanks. Here's where we turn off fer Lois's place.''

CHAPTER TWO
Noone Padden's Sixgun

They went through a gate and crowned a rise. Before them lay a low rock house with sheds and pens, a windmill tower and a tank. ''Used to be a good-sized outfit,'' the boy said. ''There's Lois, comin' in.'' A rider was approaching the house from up canyon.

McBride, the boy and the rider met by the corral. The girl was not large, not small either, dressed like a man, with a man's sureness and competence in her movements. McBride raised his hat.

''My name,'' he said, ''is McBride. Mr. Sledge, in town, told me you might have some cattle to sell.''

The girl's eyes, level, dark, searched McBride's face. ''Uncle Jim sent you out to me?''

''Mr. Sledge. Yes.''

A little puzzled frown furrowed the smooth brow. The girl took off her hat. Her hair was auburn, not a fiery red, but dark, with a tinge of copper.

''I'm afraid Uncle Jim was mistaken,'' she said. ''He knows . . . I haven't but thirty head of calves.''

''Mr. Sledge said that I might get around a hundred,'' McBride stated. ''He mentioned cows and calves, maybe some steers and a bull or two.''

The puzzled look deepened in the girl's dark eyes. ''That would be all my cattle,'' she announced. ''What are you paying, Mr. McBride?''

''That depends on the cattle.''

''I sold my steer calf,'' Dave Fairweather said importantly. ''He's goin' to give me fifteen.''

''Would you like to look at the cattle?'' the girl asked suddenly. ''I can show you.''

"I sure would," McBride agreed.

"I'll go with you," the boy said.

"You go to the house and get something to eat," Lois Titus directed. "And you'll find your shirt and overalls in the kitchen. I washed and mended them. Leave the ones you have on, Dave."

"I'll do that," Dave agreed, and slipped down from the steer as McBride and the girl mounted their horses.

"He's an orphan," the girl explained as they rode off. "We all try to look after him. I've tried to get him to stay with me, but he won't. He just visits around."

"Don't go to school or anything?"

"There isn't any school," Lois Titus replied, her voice bitter. "There isn't anything in the Piojoso country. There are some of my cows, Mr. McBride. You can get an idea of the kind of cattle I have."

McBride looked at the cows, good-grade cattle with big calves sucking. They rode on, viewing more cattle. At noon they were back at the corrals.

"I can give you," McBride said, "thirty a round for everything. Or, if you want, we can class them and I'll price the classes."

"I'll let you know," Lois Titus said. She did not look directly at McBride.

"I'm staying in town with Mr. Sledge," McBride informed her. "You can get word to me there."

"I'll let you know, Mr. McBride," the girl assured, and went to the house.

Shorty's running walk ate into distance. McBride passed Villareal's without stopping. Piojoso, when he reached the place, seemed just the same. Asleep, apparently deserted. Sunday, McBride thought. He had not remembered the day. He put Shorty's reins over the hitch-rack in front of Sledge's store.

Sledge was busy. He had a can of paint, a brush and a stack of cardboard squares. The storekeeper looked up as McBride entered. "Buy them cattle?" he demanded.

"I don't know yet," McBride said. "Maybe. Why didn't you tell me that was a girl? You said Lewis."

"Sure. That's her name."

"Lois is her name. You want to learn to speak plain. What are you goin' to have? A sale?"

The sign Sledge was working on read: "Tomatoes, 15¢ a . . . . ."

"Maybe. Anyhow, I'm tired of Norwood settin' my prices. You can put your horse out back in my shed. I got some feed."

"Thanks." McBride turned toward the door, took a step and stopped. Curly was standing in the doorway.

Curly's face showed signs of wear. Curly's lips were puffed and bruised, and there was a discolored spot high on the cheekbone.

"Say," said Curly, "do you want to buy a saloon?"

"I buy cattle," McBride said. "What happened to you?"

"Noone Padden happened to me," Curly snapped. "I shot off my big mouth when I said it was too bad you hadn't killed Reeder last night. I'll sell cheap."

"A man that runs a saloon," McBride stated, "ought to be able to look after himself. I ain't interested in saloons." His voice was cold.

"You don't do much fightin' when one man holds a gun on you an' the other beats you up," Curly growled. "You stand still an' take it."

"An' don't do anything about it afterwards." Contempt in McBride's drawl. "Crawl under your bed if you're afraid."

"I ain't—" Curly began. Steps sounded on the porch. Curly moved quickly from the doorway. Jim Sledge's hands disappeared under the counter. Two men came through the door.

One of the two was the blond youth, Reeder Norwood; the other was a big man, bulky, hard face pitted with smallpox scars, eyes small and close set.

"That's him, Noonc," Reeder snarled. "That's the feller that slugged me from behind."

"We been waitin' for you, mister," the big man growled. "People don't come into Piojoso an' hit a man from behind an' get away with it. You're—" He broke off. He was staring into the muzzle of the Bisley Colt.

"People don't come walkin' in an' beat me up, neither," McBride said pleasantly. "Stand still. You too, Blondy. Stay right together. I like to look at both of you."

The Colt made a little circling movement. Noone Padden and Reeder Norwood stood still.

"Look here," Padden blustered. "I'm a deputy sheriff. You can't—"

"You're a deputy skunk!" McBride's voice carried a snap and a ring that was unmistakable. "You've beat up a man for doin' somethin' he couldn't help. We'll see how it works on you. Take that gun off him, Curly. Go behind him an' get it."

Like a man in a daze Curly moved to obey. "Throw it out the door!" McBride ordered. "No. Leave Blondy's alone. He ain't dangerous."

The gun thumped on the porch. Curly came back from the door.

"Now," McBride ordered, "slap his face. Slap it hard. He hit you when you were under a gun, didn't he? Let's see how well you can do it!"

"I don't want to," Curly said. "I ain't sore at you, Noone. I ain't—"

"You damned coward!" McBride spat out the words. "You come in here wantin' to sell out. You're scared of your shadow. Hit him!" The Bisley Colt swung to cover Curly.

"You hit me, Curly, an' I'll—"

"Shut up, you! Hit him, Curly. Hit him in the face!"

Curly half-lifted his hand. Lowered it again. "I ain't goin' to," he said. "I won't."

McBride holstered the Colt. "Yellow," he said. "You had your chance. Get out! You too!" His eyes centered on Padden's. "All three of you."

He took a step, and Curly backed away. McBride took a second step, and Curly went through the door. Padden, his face white under the tan, said: "You got my gun. You—"

"It's on the porch," McBride snapped. "Walk out. Pick it up. Try to use it!"

"Come on, Noone." Reeder Norwood caught Padden's arm, pulling him. "Come on!" For an instant Padden rebelled against the pull and then, giving way, went through the door. McBride followed. The two men crossed the porch, went on across the street and through the door of Norwood's store.

McBride picked up Padden's gun and came back. He put the gun on the counter. Jim Sledge was finishing his sign. "Can" he finished with a flourish. "There," he said, and stood back to survey his handiwork, "that ought to do. You was a little hard on Curly, McBride."

"He's a gutless wonder," McBride said.

"Nope. He's been here quite a while, that's all. Some things get to be a habit."

"Like knucklin' under to a bully? How come you ain't infected?"

"Maybe I am." Sledge's voice was dry. "I wonder why Norwood didn't come himse'f?"

"You don't," said McBride, "play your ace when you think the bowers will take the trick. You ain't a damn' bit scared, Sledge."

Sledge put the sign by the tomato cans. "There," he said. "An' that still leaves me a nice profit. I believe you're right about competition, McBride. It ought to be good for business."

He picked up a shotgun from under the counter and, cradling it familiarly, stumped toward the rear door.

McBride's eyes crinkled, and the corners of his mouth drew down in a sardonic grin. He would bet that old Jim Sledge hadn't lost that leg to a sawmill or by falling off a haystack. Shotgun, likely, or maybe a rifle slug.

"I'm scared to death," Sledge said, pushing the door open.

"Don't jump if I say 'Boo!' " McBride advised.

Monday morning McBride did not ride. He stayed in the store, watching Jim Sledge. Old Jim was not particularly active, but when he did move, he took the shotgun with him. There was no trade, none at all. Two wagons stopped at Norwood's, but their occupants did not come to Sledge's. A rider stopped at Curly's saloon and then went on again. About ten o'clock a buckboard came into town.

"Mail," Sledge announced. "I'll go see if I got any." He took the shotgun and crossed the street. When he came back he had a bundle of newspapers and a letter. "Advertisin'," he said. "Want to read the paper?" He tossed an *El Paso Record* to McBride.

McBride read the paper. An hour passed. A horse pulled up in front of Sledge's store. Lois Titus came in.

"I've decided to sell you my cattle, Mr. McBride," she announced. "I'll take the flat price you offered: thirty dollars a round."

McBride slid down from the counter. "That's fine," he stated. "I can go back with you this afternoon. Tomorrow I'll receive 'em."

The girl flushed, hesitated an instant. Then: "Could you pay me half now?" she asked. "I've got an even hundred head. I'd like— If you could pay me part, it would save me a trip to town."

"Sure. Excuse me a minute."

He walked back to the living quarters. As he removed money from his belt, he could hear Jim Sledge talking. It was impossible to make out the words.

"Here you are," McBride said, returning, money in his hands. "There's fifteen hundred dollars. I'll make out a receipt for it."

The girl's hands trembled as she took the bills.

"Count it," Sledge advised. "I got a pen an' ink someplace. I'll find 'em." He stumped along behind the counter. The girl counted currency.

"Fifteen hundred, right?" McBride said when the counting was finished. "Here's the receipt form made out. You can sign it."

Lois Titus read through the receipt, signed her name, gave the pen to Sledge. "You eat dinner with us, Lois," Sledge said. "I'm goin' to cook it right away."

"I've some business—" Lois hesitated. "I—yes, I'll eat dinner with you, Uncle Jim." She thrust the roll of bills into a pocket of her levis, stared at McBride for an instant, then hurried to the door. McBride and Jim Sledge watched her cross the street and enter Norwood's.

"Nice girl," McBride said.

"Mighty nice." Sledge's voice was drawling, absent-minded. "Lost her folks sometime back an' tried to make things go herself. It's been hard sleddin'."

"I expect."

"She went away to school. Come back here intendin' to teach. We was goin' to set up a little one-room school here in Piojoso. Then her daddy got kilt by a horse an' her mother just pined off an' died."

"And what happened to the school idea?"

"It died, too. 'Tend store awhile, McBride. I'm goin' to get dinner."

McBride seated himself on the counter. The El Paso paper had lost its flavor. He watched the street. Lois Titus appeared at Norwood's door. From the way she walked as she crossed the street, she was very angry. "That Reeder Norwood!" she said, letting the screen slam. "That—"

"I'll talk to Reeder," McBride said, and came to his feet.

"No!" Alarm filled Lois Titus's face. "Please don't. It wasn't anything. Please, Mr. McBride." She held out her hand to detain him.

Jim Sledge came into the store. "Where do you think you're goin', McBride?" he asked.

"Across the street."

"No!" The girl's voice was sharp.

"You damn' fool! What for?"

"Reeder Norwood—" McBride began.

"You leave Reeder alone!" command in Sledge's voice. "You're a cow buyer, remember? Come on an' eat. It's ready."

"Please, Mr. McBride," Lois said. "Please." Her hand was on his arm. McBride hesitated, then reluctantly moved toward the living quarters.

The meal was silent. Twice Jim Sledge started to speak, then thought better of it. They had finished eating and were drinking a final cup of coffee when steps sounded in the store.

"Customer," Sledge said, and went out.

He returned within brief seconds. "Man out there wants to see you, Lewis," he announced. "Says it's important."

The girl got up as Sledge sat down. She was gone for perhaps ten minutes. When she returned, her face was white. McBride eyed her curiously, but she said nothing and Sledge had no comment.

"I'll saddle up and we'll go," McBride said. "It'll be all right for me to come down this evenin'? I won't put you out?"

"Certainly not." Lois's voice was stiff. "You can stay in the bunkhouse, Mr. McBride."

"I'll go with you," Sledge announced. "You wrangle my horse, McBride. He's in the little pasture an'—"

"I don't need you, Uncle Jim," Lois said. "I can take care of myself, and this is a business matter between Mr. McBride and me."

Sledge sat down again. "Go on then," he growled. "You can get the Villareal boys to help you move them cattle, McBride."

When Shorty was saddled, McBride found that the girl had brought her horse around. They rode off side by side, passing the back of the saloon. The girl's horse was gaited and kept abreast of Shorty's running walk.

For a time McBride said nothing, and Lois, too, was silent. Then: "Mr. Sledge seems to think a lot of you," said McBride.

"He was a friend of Dad's." The girl was abstracted. She was thinking.

"He's a pretty salty old man," McBride ventured.

"Uncle Jim? When I was a little girl he was the sheriff. I remember sitting on his lap and playing with his star."

"How did he lose his leg?" McBride was trying to make conversation.

"That happened when I was six years old," Lois said. "I've heard Dad tell about it. Uncle Jim had arrested some men and had them in jail. A crowd came to lynch them. Uncle Jim was alone. There was a fight and he was shot. The doctor amputated his leg."

"And now he runs a little store in Piojoso," McBride drawled. "That's a comedown."

"Uncle Jim never had much money," the girl said. "The store makes his living. Everybody trades with him—when they can. But he can't give much credit and—"

"An' Norwood gets the business," McBride completed. "How long has Norwood been around?"

"Not long. He came while I was away at school. He bought a place and put up the store and the wagon yard."

"Ummmm," McBride said.

CHAPTER THREE
Clear Leather!

Silence again save for the plop of horses' hoofs in dust. They were at the lip of the mesa now, the broken country below them. Lois Titus reined in suddenly. McBride also checked, and the girl swung her horse to confront him. "I'm not going to sell you my cattle, Mr. McBride," she announced. "I've been thinking it over."

"You've changed your mind?" McBride drawled.

"I have." The girl brought the roll of bills from her pocket. "Here. Take this and give me the receipt. Go away. Don't go back to Piojoso. Go away—somewhere a long way off."

McBride made no movement to accept the proffered bills. "Why did you decide to sell in the first place?" he asked gently.

"Does that matter? I've changed my mind, that's all."

"Look," said McBride, "that was Norwood that come to the store, wasn't it?"

The girl nodded wordlessly.

"An' he told you," McBride's voice was still gentle, "that if you sold to me I'd be killed. Wait! Let me finish. He didn't use just those words, but that was what he meant, wasn't it?''

The girl nodded, her face miserable.

''An','' McBride went on inexorably, ''Reeder Norwood's been hanging around you, makin' you trouble. An' you're in debt to Norwood, an' when I offered you a decent, fair price for your cattle, it looked like a way out. So you took it, an' then you got to thinkin'. So now you want to back out. On account of me. A stranger.''

Lois remained silent. She would not meet McBride's eyes.

''You're good people, Lois Titus,'' McBride said, ''but I've bought your cattle an' paid you earnest money. The deal goes through.''

''But,'' the girl looked up now, her eyes wide and frightened, ''what—?''

''What about all the things I've just heard?'' McBride's voice turned clipped and hard. ''About killin' me an' all that truck? Don't let it fret you. I don't kill easy; it's been tried. No, ma'am. Our trade goes through.''

He started Shorty and, perforce, the girl gave way, swinging in beside him. A hundred yards they traveled, and then McBride spoke again. ''That old man—old Jim. He was just waitin' till somebody come along, somebody that would go with him. You wouldn't want me to back out on him, would you now? Why, that old man planned all this.'' McBride chuckled grimly. ''An' what about Dave Fairweather? I bought a calf from him, remember? I got to receive it, too. Don't meddle with men's business, Lois Titus.''

Dave Fairweather was at the Diamond Bar when they rode in. The boy came to meet them, riding the red steer, playing with his sling. ''Let me try that,'' McBride requested, and when Dave passed the sling over: ''I used to work one of these when I was a kid.''

He fitted a rock into the pouch and whirled it around his head, but time had dulled his cunning. The sling caught on his thumb, the rock knocked off his hat. ''Every man to his own weapons,'' McBride said, returning the sling to the grinning Dave. ''Here, you take this; I'll get my hat.''

At the Diamond Bar, McBride went to the deserted bunkhouse, Dave accompanying him. He would, McBride announced gravely, receive Dave's cattle in the morning, complete payment, and take a bill of sale. Dave was entranced. He had his two cows and their calves at the ranch.

"Why," McBride asked, "won't you sell me the heifer, too? I'm payin' good prices."

"I'm goin' to be a cowman," Dave replied. "Some day, when I get enough cattle, I'm goin' to marry Lois. Then her an' me'll run this outfit. I'll get her out of debt."

"I see," said McBride gravely, and shook dust from blankets on the bunk.

That night, while he smoked in the evening's cool, Lois Titus came from the house and sat beside him. Dave had climbed the windmill tower and from the platform was viewing the world. It was peaceful, and the girl's companionship was restful.

McBride, watching the boy, spoke suddenly. "No folks. No nothin' much, but he's happy."

The girl nodded. "But he needs someone to look after him," she said. "What will he grow up to be? What chance does he have?"

McBride's eyes twinkled. "He's got plans. He told me this evenin' as soon as he had enough cattle he was goin' to marry you. That's why he won't sell me his heifer calf. But you're right," McBride said seriously. "He needs somebody to look after him. I expect I'd ought to."

"More man's business?" There was just a trace of spite in the words. "A boy has a mother as well as a father, Mr. McBride."

"Some boys—if they're lucky," McBride said. "I hadn't neither one, no more than Dave." Standing, he called to the boy on the tower. "Come down now, kid. It's bedtime." He looked at the girl. "We'll gather 'em in the morning," he said. "Good-night, Miss Titus."

Dave came from the windmill. He had descended at McBride's call.

"The big nut is loose on the shaft," Dave said importantly. "I'd fix it if I had a wrench."

Lois Titus and McBride gathered cattle in the morning. The hundred head of Diamond Bar were scattered over a pasture big enough for many times that number, and the gathering took time. Dave Fairweather was as good a hand as any man would want, but hampered by his mount. Cattle will move for a man on horseback, but only their curiosity was aroused by a boy on a red steer. It was past noon before the last one was found and brought down to the herd.

"Why don't you," McBride said to Dave, "lope on down to the house? Me an' Miss Titus will bring these along."

Dave was loath to leave. He wanted to punch cows, but McBride was adamant.

The cows and calves were sticky, and the bulls were slow. The little herd would not string out and move freely. "I'd like to keep 'em gathered," McBride said. "I want to go up to Villareal's this afternoon and hire him to help me move these to the railroad. Have you got a trap we can put 'em in?"

Lois said that there was a little pasture, beyond the corrals and close to the road, that could be used.

When they reached the corrals, the red steer was inside. That helped in the penning. Cows bellowed for their calves, which had, of course, fallen behind in the drive. There was dust and a little hard riding.

Then McBride closed the gate. "That's it," he said. "I'll be up to the house in a minute."

Lois rode off, and McBride, letting Shorty stand, looked through the corral rails. For the moment his vigilance was relaxed; for the moment he rested, looking at the cattle. He could, he knew, make money with them. They weren't tops, but they weren't bottoms, either. He could drive to the railroad, sell them there and make a profit.

"Just stand easy, mister," a familiar voice commanded.

McBride turned slowly. Reeder Norwood, Noone Padden, and the two men who had carried Reeder out of Curly's place confronted him. Where had they come from? McBride demanded of himself. Where were their horses?

"We waited for you in the house," Padden said, answering the question in McBride's mind. "Are them your cattle, mister?" Padden's gun was centered on McBride. Reeder, too, had a weapon out. The two riders had not pulled their guns.

"You didn't bring the old man," McBride drawled. "You ought to play your ace."

"He's here," Reeder snarled. "He's in the house, tellin' that girl where she gets off."

"An' that's his size?" McBride marveled. "I figured you was the lady's man. I thought your dad was tough."

"Tough enough," Reeder began. "He's tough enough to handle six like you!"

"Lay off, Reeder," Padden commanded. "You say them are your cattle. We're goin' to look 'em over. If we find what we think, you're done. We hang cowthieves in this country, McBride."

"An' sure enough, you'll find what you want," McBride said. "Don't be funny, Padden."

"A rope ain't funny," Padden snarled. "The Mexicans around here will remember a rope. They'll know what happens to a man that steals cattle."

"An' they'll know what happens when a cow buyer comes in an' offers honest prices, too," McBride drawled. "That's important, ain't it? Here comes your boss, Padden. Here's the ace."

Berry Norwood was coming from the house, Lois, white-faced but steady, walking in front of him.

"What did you find, Noone?" Norwood demanded as he halted. "Any of our cattle?"

"We ain't looked 'em over yet." Padden glanced at Norwood. "We was just ready to. Get in the pen, Joe, an' see."

Joe climbed the fence. Lois said: "Those are all my cattle, Mr. Norwood."

"There's two of ours in here," Joe called. "I seen the brands."

"Come out then." Norwood's face was iron hard. "What have you got to say now, Lois?"

"I say this is a farce!" the girl flared. "I say if you go on with this, I'll have the sheriff out from Cisco. You aren't the law, Berry Norwood."

"I'm law enough right now," Norwood said. "Grab that cow-thief, boys, an'—"

He did not finish. There was a solid thud such as a butcher's cleaver makes when it strikes against flesh. Berry Norwood reeled, gasped, his hands flying to his chest. For an instant, for just a fractional second, every eye was fixed on Berry Norwood. It was enough. From McBride's shoulder holster the Bisley Colt leaped out and flamed in his hand.

Noone Padden, hit twice in the chest and belly, grunted and went down, his gun falling free. Crouching in his own smoke, McBride snatched up that weapon and fired again. Reeder spun half around, like a weathercock caught by a puff of wind. That much McBride saw, and had no time for more. Berry Norwood, recovered somewhat, had drawn his gun. It fell level, and McBride felt the bite and burn of flaming lead.

This was a different matter from men caught off guard and by surprise. Norwood was coming to him, running, weaving, closing the distance, firing as he came. The Bisley Colt kicked hard. Still Norwood came. Again the Bisley flamed. McBride dropped the gun, transferring Padden's weapon. There was no need. Norwood took two more lurching steps and sprawled, falling across Noone Padden's feet, hands reaching out, one still holding his gun. McBride came up, turned, and leveled off at the two riders.

Seconds had passed, only seconds. Joe, his mouth gaped with surprise, had his gun half out of the holster. The other man had not touched his weapon. By the fence Reeder Norwood sat groaning, gripping his shattered shoulder, blood dripping from his arm.

"Hold it!" McBride rasped. Joe let his gun drop back, and his hands went up, shoulder high. The other man took the example set.

On the windmill platform, Dave Fairweather stood up. His voice was like the crowing of a young game cock. "They're comin'," he yelled. "Ol' man Sledge an' Curly are comin' through the gate." He started down from the tower, the leather strings of his sling dangling as he climbed. McBride looked at Lois Titus. The girl had picked up Reeder's gun and was holding it competently, the hammer cocked and ready.

"Sit down, McBride," Lois ordered. "You're hit. You're bleeding."

McBride sat down cross-legged. Horses pounded up; Curly, cursing with every breath, a rifle in his hands, flung himself down. Jim Sledge was more deliberate. He dismounted, stiff on his wooden peg, his shotgun held carefully.

"Curly," said Jim Sledge, "couldn't ketch his horse, damn him. That's why we come so late. Git the guns off them thievin' skunks, Curly."

At six o'clock that evening, McBride was on the bunkhouse porch. Inside the bunkhouse were Joe and his sullen fellow, thoroughly tied. Reeder Norwood was in the bunkhouse, too, lying on a bed, groaning now and then with the pain of his wound. Reeder was not tied because there was no need of it. In the empty feed room of the barn were two bodies: Noone Padden and Berry Norwood.

McBride, stiff with the bandage around his middle, knew how Reeder felt. It would be some time, he thought ruefully, before he wore his money belt again. He fumbled for the makings.

"Lemme, will you, McBride?" Dave Fairweather held out his hand for the tobacco and papers. "Lemme roll it, will you?"

"The thing I can't figure out," McBride passed over the makings, "is why you didn't yell when we came in with the cattle. You were on the tower. You'd seen 'em hide their horses an' go into the house. Why didn't you yell?"

"I was scared." Dave's voice was candid and his fingers deft as he twisted paper around tobacco. "I didn't know what to do. I was askairt if I yelled they'd come out shootin'."

"They would have, too." Jim Sledge sat facing the door where he could keep a weather eye on the men inside the house. "The kid done right, McBride."

"He done good enough, anyhow," McBride agreed. "Throwin' that stone at Norwood—"

"It was the big nut on the shaft," Dave said. "It wasn't no stone. I twisted off the nut an' throwed it. I didn't have a stone with me."

"Whatever it was," McBride approved, "it did the business. That's a good cigarette, Dave. Where'd you learn to roll 'em like this?"

"I smoke," Dave boasted. "I can roll 'em with one hand."

"You'll quit smokin' till you're grown," McBride announced. "Curly ought to be gettin' back."

Curly had ridden to Juan Villareal's with orders. Juan was to saddle a horse and make the long ride to Cisco for the sheriff.

"He'll get back," Sledge said placidly. "Curly generally gets back. Him an' me are goin' to take turns watchin' them beauties inside tonight. An' quit frettin', McBride. You don't have a thing to worry about. Them boys are goin' to tell what Norwood planned. Hell, the sheriff an' the whole damn country's goin' to thank you."

McBride stirred irritably. Sledge said, "Why don't you go to the house? You ain't never paid the balance on them cattle yet. Ain't you goin' to?"

"That's right." McBride got up with feigned nonchalance. "I ain't, have I?" He walked toward the house. Dave Fairweather arose to follow, for he had attached himself to McBride.

"You stay here, kid," Sledge ordered. "All he was lookin' for was a half good excuse."

McBride knocked on the door. He heard the call, "Come in," and pushed the door open. Lois was sitting in a rocking chair, and about her the kitchen was neat and clean and homelike. "Sit down, McBride," she invited.

McBride did not sit down. "I come up about the cattle," he announced heavily. "Jim recalled it to me. I ain't paid you the balance on 'em yet."

"Is that all you came for, McBride?" In the dim light Lois's face was white and flowerlike, tipped up a little, still waiting.

"No," said McBride, "it ain't. Look, Lois, I ain't much good. I don't have much, but—"

"I don't even know your first name," Lois said softly. "Come here, McBride."

Down on the bunkhouse porch young Dave Fairweather asked a question. "You reckon McBride will take me with him when he goes? I'd miss Lois an' you an' Curly an' all, but I'd sure like to go with him."

Old Jim Sledge grunted and straightened his peg leg out before him.

"You ain't goin' to miss nobody, kid," he said. "McBride ain't goin' no place."

THE END

THE CORPS

By JOHN D. MacDONALD

He had no more breath for
screaming. . . .

IDES AT DAWN

Action-Packed Frontier Novelette

Seven hardcase killers awaited Dave Austin's return—to larn that stubborn rannihan proper respect for his brother's murderer!

CHAPTER ONE
Vengeance Trail

Dave Austin rode into the hot dusty little town of Oracle on the tall trail-weary black. He had hated the smallness and the sameness and the dullness of it when he had left four years before, his jaw sore and swollen from where his brother's fist had connected. He hated the town even more after the absence.

The hooves of the black kicked up little puffs of white dust as he rode by the store, the livery stable, Ike Andres's sadlery, the closed office of the deputy sheriff, the frame and adobe Oracle House, the Easy Do Saloon.

Two wagons were hitched in front of the Oracle House, and some hot saddle stock stood and fretted at the flies in front of the Easy Do and the Gay Gold further down the street.

He pulled up the black, and the pack horse, stupefied by the heat, walked into the black and dodged stiffly as the black kicked at it. He pulled around and went to the stable, swinging down from the black and peering into the dark hay-smell of the place. An old man in broken boots slept on a pile of hay.

Dave unsaddled and slapped the black into a stall; he grunted as he slid the bedroll off the pack horse. It thudded onto the board floor. The old man woke up, blinked at him bleerily and went back to sleep.

Dave walked over and kicked him lightly in the ribs. "Get up and take care of my stock."

The old man sat up. "I see you was doing everything yourself and—" The old man stopped abruptly. "Dave Austin, ain't you?"

"Yes."

The old man bounced up with surprising agility. "What you going to do about your brother Pete?" Dave looked at him steadily, didn't answer. "All right, forget I asked you. I know what I'd do."

"And what would you do?"

"I'd get to hell back on my horse and get out of here. Hawson'll send his boys onto you one by one until one of 'em guns you down."

"And what about Hawson?"

"He don't carry no gun no more. Best thing you can do is get on out of Oracle. Hawson has brought in maybe seven bad ones in the last two years. One of 'em got Pete. You haven't got a chance."

252

Dave Austin looked at the old man for a long moment, shouldered the heavy bedroll, yanked his carbine out from under the *rosadero*, and headed out into the sunlight. It was only a hundred feet to the wide porch of the Oracle House, but he was sweating heavily before he reached it.

An old man dozing on the wide porch took a long look at Dave, swallowed heavily, and the front legs of his chair thumped down onto the boards. As Dave walked in the door, the old man on the porch spat across the railing with great deliberation and little accuracy.

Martha Deen, the fat, pleasant, sloppy wife of Sid Deen who owned the Oracle House, came from the back of the place when Dave thumped on the desk.

She walked heavily to the desk, stopped suddenly and then walked toward him more slowly. "Hello, Dave."

"Hello, Martha."

"The town's been sort of waiting on you, Dave."

"I heard five days ago. I was about a hundred and forty mile down the line."

"You shouldn't have come back, Dave."

"I want a room, not advice, Martha. So far you're the second one I've talked to. And you both tell me to get out of town."

"You shouldn't be silly for Pete's sake, Dave. He was a mean, stubborn man, and forty people told him he shouldn't have set up his spread right in the way of Hawson."

"How about that room?"

She sighed. "Second floor. The one facing the stairs. Door's unlocked. Where do you want your stuff sent?"

"Sent?"

"After one of Hawson's boys kills you."

"You keep it, Martha. I was going to ride on through and stay out to Pete's place, but I figured this'd be handier."

She laughed. It was a flat, mirthless sound. "You wouldn't of liked it out there, Dave. Pete had lots of notes outstanding to Ryan over to the store. Maybe half again the value of the place after this hot spell. Stock dying all over. Hawson just upped and bought up the notes and foreclosed the place and sold it to himself. Using it as a line camp right now I hear. Intends to, anyway."

Dave shouldered the bedroll, trudged up the stairs and pushed the door to his room open. He dropped the bedroll on the floor, stripped, poured water into the basin and sponged the trail dust off his body. He squatted by the roll, opened it up and took out fresh clothes.

He was lean and hard and too thin for his height. A white puckered scar cut across the ridges of muscle on his back. His features were so regular as to have been characterless were it not for a deep hardness in his eyes, a rigidity about the set of his mouth. He dressed, strapped the gun-belt around his thin waist, sat on the edge of the bed and wiped trail dirt from the butt of his single-action peacemaker. The walnut grip fitted comfortably into his palm.

He sat for a long time and pondered what the old man in the stable had said. He thought of what Martha had said. Finally he unstrapped the gun-belt, tossed it into the open bedroll and threw a corner of the tarp over it.

Ike Andres came to the door of the sadlery, took Dave's right hand in both of his and drew him inside. Ike, in spite of his smallness, had been a foreman for Dave's father during the early days. A bronc he had been breaking had crushed him against the snubbing post in the middle of the round corral. He had mended, but he would never swing up onto a pony again. He was a gray little man with wide soft eyes and a bitter, twisted mouth.

"Dave, boy!" he said gently. "Dave!"

Dave permitted himself the first smile since entering Oracle. "Hello, you old horse thief!"

They went into the back room where Ike slept. Ike sat on the bed and Dave leaned against the wall and smiled down at him. They were both uncomfortable.

"How did it happen, Ike?" Dave asked.

"The dryness, boy. Hawson's holes dried, and he moved in on Pete. Pete and his two hands shot about thirty head, but Hawson's men pulled down the fence Pete had put up around his best hole and the Hawson beef trampled the hole to a mud wallow. The next day somebody found Pete over near Spike Ridge. Shot in the back of the neck. The horse had bucked him into the rocks. He wasn't pretty. I had him buried over on the hill next to your folks."

"I owe you whatever it cost."

"You don't owe me a damn thing!" Ike said angrily. "Your old man set me up in this place when I couldn't ride no more. So don't you try to talk slop to me."

"Where's Pete's stuff?"

"Over there in the corner. Clothes. And that box there is full of things I took out of the house. Some silver that belonged to your ma. The old man's books. Family Bible. Pete's roan is over to Louis Besa's place. I had it took over there before Hawson could grab it along with the spread. The horse and stuff belong to you."

Dave looked at the rough wooden box that held his patrimony and his inheritance. He rolled a smoke and found that he was pinching it so tight between thumb and finger that it wouldn't draw. He dropped it to the floor.

He thought of the bitter, back-breaking labor that had been the lot of his father and mother until they had gotten far enough ahead to hire ranch hands. He remembered the day during the long drought when his father, bone weary from trying to save weak stock, had been caught in the dry wash by a ten-foot flood wall coming down from the mountains. His mother had died a month later.

The foreman who had replaced Ike had been no good. The ranch had been sold to pay the debts. He and Pete had been too young to work it. Hawson, his saddle-bags heavy with gold from the Black Hills, had bought in. Pete and Dave had gone to stay with Ike, and one day Pete had hit the adobe wall with his hard young fist and said, "I'm going to get it all back. Every square foot of it. Every blade of grass!"

They had worked for day wages, and in the end Pete had insisted on claiming at the base of the hills just beyond the west boundary of Hawson's spread. They had argued about the location. At twenty, Dave had ridden out of Oracle, his jaw sore, his mind full of the harsh quarrel with Pete.

Dave looked at the box and said hoarsely, "That's about the same amount of stuff we had when the four of us first come out here. Haven't got far, have we?"

"What you been doing?" Ike asked quickly.

"Everything. Trapped and broke mustangs. Trail boss. Winter line camp. Deputy in a silver town."

"Can you shoot?"

"As well as most. Not as good as some that live off it."

"Hawson stayed right quiet until he started to make money. Then he began to elbow little spreads out of his way. Unexpected fires during the night. Brawls picked by his men. He's got maybe thirty regular cowhands now. He pays 'em good.

"But he's also got maybe seven men he's brought in. A rough string. He don't give those boys no cow work. Some of them ride with him wherever he goes. Hawson wants to be king of this country. Right now you might say he's crown prince. Where's your gun?"

"I hear Hawson don't carry one. I hear that if I carried one, his boys'd nudge me into a fight."

Ike looked thoughtful. "What are you fixing to do?"

"Damn if I know. Pete was shot in the back of the neck. I'd like to get Hawson the same way."

"You don't stand a chance, boy. Not a chance."

"Tell me more about Jud Hawson."

Ike scratched his lean jaw. His eyes were somber. "Not much to tell. His hair's gone white, and he's took to wearing it long. He's got kind of a wild look in his eye, and he talks to folks about seeing visions of people coming to him and telling him that he is the king wheel of this part of the country. Heard tell that out at his spread he makes the folks bow from the waist when they want to talk to him."

Dave was silent for long moments. He rolled another smoke, dragged deeply on it. His mouth was like a deep gash in saddle leather.

Ike said softly, "Going to miss Pete a lot, Dave. He was a stubborn fool, but he did what he thought right. Kind of vain about hisself, too. Wore that big old white-colored hat and had Ryan over to the store stock those yella shirts from Mexico.

"Maybe you better ride back out and forget this mess, Dave," Ike said. "In order to get to Hawson you'll have to gun your way through the seven rannies he's got, and by the time you've knocked off a couple he'd have more hired. Besides, it's a good bet that every damn one of them is faster than you."

Dave smiled tightly. "Look at this, Ike. See? Nothing in my hands." He yanked his right arm up, the elbow sharply bent so that his fist came close to his ear. The arm flashed down, and a lean knife with a slim blade and a rawhide handle buried itself in the doorframe with a chunking sound.

Ike said softly, "I'll be damned! How'd you do that?"

"Broke a leg in Mexico. While it was mending a *paisano* taught me. See how the right cuff on this shirt is loose? I got this piece of rubber around my arm. The knife goes under it with the hilt toward my wrist. It stays there until I snap my arm back. Then it slips out, and I grab the blade as it goes by.

"I've won over two hundred dollars with that little knife. Stand side by side with a gunfighter and somebody gives the word and I put the knife into a tree twelve feet away before he can get a slug into it."

Ike frowned. "Knife work is dirty."

"And shooting a man in the back of the neck is good clean fun!" Dave said hoarsely.

"I'm sorry, boy," Ike said. "I forget the kind of competition you got."

Dave walked across the room, kicked the wooden box gently, frowned down at it. "You say Hawson is maybe a little crazy?"

"He could be. Maybe is."

"You got Pete's clothes here?"

"That's right. Why?"

"Wait a minute. I'm doing some thinking." Dave frowned for a few minutes. "Is that roan fast?"

"One of the best."

Dave squatted on the floor close to Ike's bed and talked for ten minutes in a low tone. Ike looked at him incredulously for a long time, and then a slow grin crept across his face. "Dave boy, it just might. It just might. And there's not another damn thing you can do except wait with a rifle and try to bushwack him."

CHAPTER TWO
Buzzard Bait

Dave Austin shouldered his way through the swinging doors into the Gay Gold, Saturday night. Two games of pocar robado were going on at the round tables in the rear of the place. Fat Wesser, huge and red-faced with eyes like chilled skim milk, stood behind the bar. Two men stood at the end of the bar, and Dave realized immediately that they matched Ike's description of Hawson's men.

One was a kid too young to shave, with thin pale hands and dark eyes that were luminous and beautiful. They had the look of candles around a bier, of sunlight on silver coffin handles, of the raw metal of a filed sear. He had a quiet confidence far beyond his years. He stood with his back to the bar, his elbows hooked over it.

Thin white fingers dangled above the grip of the .44 in the shallow holster against his right thigh. His name, at the moment, was Randy Adams.

The second one was much older, a squat sandy man in his early forties with thick shoulders, no neck, freckled hands and small sleepy eyes. His underlip was severed by a vertical scar which bisected his square chin. Dave guessed that he would be Quinn. Dave glanced quickly around the saloon and decided that, of the seven Ike had carefully described, these were the only two in town. He had already stopped in at the Easy Do.

In a needlessly loud voice, Fat Wesser said, "Hello there, Dave Austin!"

Quinn lost his sleepy look, and the luminous eyes of Adams turned sharply toward Dave, flicked down to the empty holster and registered disappointment.

Before Dave had a chance to order a drink, Quinn hitched up his belt, swaggered over to him and said, "What's your business in town, Austin?"

Dave heard the silence that filled the saloon. There was no slap of cards, rattle of chips, from the tables in the rear.

"Who the hell is he?" Dave said to Wesser.

Quinn grabbed Dave's shoulder, yanked him around. "I'm talking to you, friend. Jud Hawson likes to know everybody's business. What's yours?"

Dave felt the quick red tide of anger and was glad he had left the Colt behind. He kept all expression off his face and said, "You look like the sort of scum that would work for Hawson."

Quinn went so pale that the freckles on his thick face stood out. He said over his shoulder, "Loan this punk your gun."

"I never use them, friend."

Quinn sneered at him. "What do you keep in that empty holster—knitting?"

"Suppose you haul that ugly nose of yours to your end of the bar and keep it out of my business."

Quinn was amazingly fast. Dave was braced for the punch and had hoped to duck it entirely. He slipped most of the blow, but enough of the force of it caught him high on the cheekbone to drive him back several steps. He shook his head clear as Quinn charged in.

Quinn's sledge-hammer blow went around the back of Dave's

neck. Dave pivoted and put all his lean strength into a short right hook into Quinn's middle. The diaphragm muscles that he hit were as hard as woven leather, but Quinn grunted and stepped back. Dave smashed Quinn's mouth with an overhand left and was in turn driven back, almost falling, by a thudding blow under the heart.

Blood ran down Quinn's chin. He shook his head and followed up his advantage. Dave was driven back by the grunting fury of Quinn's heavy blows. A hard fist caught Dave high on the temple, and, as he fell to one side, Quinn straightened him up with a blow to the jaw.

Dave was faced by two figures. Both of them were Quinn. They drifted apart and then together, refusing to merge into one opponent. Dave hit Quinn in the face with a feeble right and then went down as Quinn's fist hit him between the eyes.

He caught a flash of movement and turned his head sharply, putting his arm across his face. Quinn's heel dug deep into his arm with such force that he thought at first that the bone was shattered.

As the dimness faded away, Dave saw that Fat Wesser was holding a gun on Quinn, saying, "I won't have you killing him with your boots in here, Quinn."

"Get up, Austin!" Quinn roared.

Dave lifted his shoulders from the floor and gasped, "My legs! I can't move my legs!" He groaned and sank back to the floor.

There was a heavy buzz of conversation, and Dave caught the words, "His back . . . . Must have hurt his back when he fell. . . . Maybe he's just yellow. . . ."

"Get Ike Andres," Dave said, groaning again. . . .

Bart Case, who called himself a doctor, sat by the bed in Ike's back room and heated the end of a long needle in a match flame. He said, "Son, this sort of thing is a little over my head. I got to know if you got any feeling in them legs. Now I'm going to jab you in a couple of places with this here needle, and if you feel anything, you holler."

Ike stood close to the head of the bed. The light flickered on his gray face, his twisted mouth. "Sure, Bart," Dave said.

Bart, with odd deftness, jabbed Dave four times. Right and left thigh. Right and left calf. Dave said, "Come on, Bart. Stick me with it. What are you waiting for?"

Bart sighed. "I already stuck you, son. You sure enough got dead legs on you. I don't know enough to tell you what the answer is. Maybe after a few days the feeling will come back slow. I hope so. Maybe never. Hard to tell."

Dave bit his lip and said, "I'll be okay." His voice was flat and dead.

Bart left. Ike said gently, "He'll go right on back to the Gay Gold and tell 'em." Ike walked over and slipped the bolt on the door, drew the thick curtains across the one window.

Dave swung his feet over the side of the bed, stood up and stretched. He felt his jaw. "That Quinn had rocks in his hands."

"I was afraid that needle business would give you away."

"Got tossed into a hill of red ants once. Felt just about like that. Did you see Louis?"

"Sure, As far as Louis is concerned, the roan fought his way out and ran off into the hills. I got him up in that little box canyon a half mile beyond Pete's place. The place that Pete used to own."

Jud Hawson walked out onto his *placita,* yawned and stretched. In a few moments the Mexican woman would bring his breakfast out. He was a big man, thick-shouldered and tall, with a brown face too young for his long white hair. His eyes were a cold clear blue and his profile was taken from a Roman coin.

During the past three years he had trained himself to move slowly, speak slowly. He carried himself with enormous dignity. Each morning of his life he stood in his dooryard and looked at the distant blue of the mountains and thought of the day when his holdings would reach the edge of those mountains.

There was no limit, no ceiling, for a man with vision, with the guts to make that vision come true. The rest of them were stupid and lazy. They clung to their land and hoped for the best. He, Jud Hawson, would gobble up their little spreads and turn the range into bright yellow gold. The gold would buy more range, and what he couldn't buy he'd take.

They were stupid to resist him. The sheriff had bucked him, so he had bought the sheriff. If he couldn't have been purchased, he would have died. Ryan at the store resisted him for a time. He bought Ryan. Men could be either purchased or beaten or killed. They had small hearts and small visions. They lived with their stupid noses in the dust.

Hawson lived with the great men of the past who came to him during his long dreams at night and spoke softly to him. "You grow bigger, Hawson. Some day it will be impossible to ride across your land in a week's time. After you have all the land, there are other things. You will have many men then. You must raise and equip an army. The rest of them are weak. Only you, Hawson. Only you. Only you."

He stretched again and noticed that the golden sun of the dawn shone on a soft layer of mist that clung to the hollows, spread thinly across the flats. It was good land. The best.

He heard a faint shout, an unidentifiable sound that came from a great distance. He peered into the sun and saw a horse and rider. The horse cut through the mist in a slow lope, looking as if its hooves didn't touch the ground. He heard the distant thud of hooves.

He squinted into the sun, wondering who it was. Suddenly he was very still. The rider wore a yellow shirt that blazed in the sunlight. The big hat was dead white. There was something familiar about the way the man sat the horse. The horse itself . . .

Hawson gasped. The rider was soon lost in the mist.

Randy Adams stood with his hat in his hand in front of the table where his employer was having breakfast.

"Hell yes, he was dead!" Adams said flatly. "His horse tossed him into the rocks, and I went over and took a good look. The bullet went in the back of his neck and busted his chin all to hell on the way out the front. Besides, he landed on his head in them rocks."

"You say Louis Besa got his horse? Go see if Besa still has it. Send Quinn up here to see me."

When Quinn arrived, Hawson snapped, "Take off your hat and stand straight!"

Quinn looked sullen, but he removed his hat and straightened his shoulders. Hawson questioned him in detail about the episode with Dave Austin. When he had all the information, Hawson gave Quinn his instructions.

Both men were back within three hours. Hawson saw them together in the main room of the ranch house.

Adams said, "I saw Besa. He told me the roan got away from him and run off onto the open range. I backed him up against the gate to his corral and smashed his nose with the barrel of my gun. He got down on his knees and begged and blubbered and said that he'd told me the truth. He was too damn scared to lie. Why did you send me to see him?"

"Shut up! And how did you come out, Quinn?"

"Andres didn't want to let me in, but finally he agreed. I went in and told Austin I was sorry about his legs, and he cursed me for about five minutes. I let him rave. He looked sick as hell. I got over by the bed; and when Andres went out into the front of the shop, I leaned down and grabbed Austin by the throat.

"I watched his legs. He fought like hell with his arms. Knocked this here tooth loose. But he didn't move his legs at all. Finally he thumped on the wall with his fist and Andres came in and I had to leave go of him. He ain't faking, Mr. Hawson. His face was black as your boots, and still he didn't move those legs none."

Hawson stood up suddenly and paced over to the big fireplace. He looked down at the gray ashes of the previous winter and said, "I might as well tell the two of you what this is all about. But don't tell any of the others. This morning I saw Pete Austin ride across my range. Just to the east of the house."

Quinn gasped. Adams said, "Must have been somebody looks like Pete looked."

"It was Austin's roan. I know the gait on that animal. He wore one of those special yellow shirts and that white hat with the extra-high crown. He sat his horse like Pete Austin."

Hawson's back was turned to the two of them. Adams looked at Quinn and smiled crookedly, touching his finger to his temple. Quinn shrugged.

"Sun was pretty bright this morning," Quinn said.

Hawson turned and glared at him. "Damn it, man! I know what I saw! I saw Pete Austin ride by out there, and I want it stopped. You understand? Stopped!"

"Sure, sure," Adams said gently.

"Don't use that tone of voice on me, Adams!" Hawson yelled.

Hawson sat at breakfast again with Quinn and Adams standing in front of his table. He lifted a forkful of food with a trembling hand. His face was gray under the tan, and there was a new deepness to the lines bracketing his mouth.

He said gently, "I want to thank you gentlemen for following my orders so explicitly. This morning Pete Austin rode by here again. I trust that both you gentlemen were enjoying your sleep at the time?''

Hawson, for the first time in nearly two years, was wearing a gun-belt. Adams glanced at it and then looked at Quinn. There was quiet scorn in Adams's eyes.

Hawson continued in a louder voice, "When I give orders, I want them followed. Tomorrow morning you two will be out there on the flats before dawn. You'll both have rifles. You'll be on foot. You'll wait for Pete Austin, and when he rides by you'll fire. Understand?''

Quinn looked down at the flagstones. He said sullenly, "Pete Austin is dead. I'll be damned if I'll lay on my belly out there on the flats just because you start seeing things.''

The table upset as Hawson came up out of his chair. He swung his long arm, and his open palm cracked against Quinn's face. "You'll do as you're told!"

Quinn snarled and started to turn away. His hard palm slapped against the holster at his thigh and came up fast, levering the gun to bear on Hawson. The sound of the shot was flat and hard in the open air. Quinn took one step forward and fell onto his face. His gun slid, spinning, toward Hawson's feet.

Hawson's mouth worked. He turned toward Adams, who was shoving his gun back into the holster. "Thanks, Adams.''

"Don't thank me. You handle the payroll. That ought to be worth two hundred. I sort of liked Quinn. Better make it two-fifty.''

A Mexican woman came to the door to the *placita,* took a look at Quinn, threw her apron up over her head and ran back into the house.

"The hands are out. She won't say anything," Hawson said quietly. "Get Quinn's stuff out of the bunkhouse. Bury it with him. Keep any money you find on him. Get Miguel to dig the grave. That'll be worth three hundred to me.''

Adams grinned broadly. "I'll do all that, but I won't chase no ghosts for you, Hawson.''

"You'll call me Mr. Hawson!"

"I won't chase ghosts, *Mister* Hawson.''

In midafternoon Randy Adams rode out to the east of the ranch house. He swung down from his horse and walked until he came on the tracks. He squatted on his heels, rolled a smoke and looked at the tracks for a long time. There was a half-smile on his lips, but his eyes were puzzled. At last he went back and got Miguel. Miguel was very good at tracking. Just before dusk Miguel, panting with exertion, stood aside proudly while Adams rode into the little box canyon. The roan nickered. Adams grinned broadly and told Miguel to run along back to the ranch.

The door closed behind Bart Case. Dave sat up in bed and smiled ruefully at Ike Andres. "If that old fella don't stop coming around with that needle of his, I'm going to hire out for a pincushion."

"Needles feel better than bullets, Dave. I don't like the way you're pushing this thing. You can't show up at the same time again. Damn it, old Hawson'll be waiting with a rifle even if he doesn't get any of his boys to work on you."

Dave frowned. "I spoil the effect if I don't show up at the right time, Ike." He laughed. "I think I got the old boy going. His face looked as white as Pete's hat this morning. Just one more morning ride and then we try the hole ace."

"I don't like it," Ike said sourly. "Go along with me this far. Don't try it in the morning. Catch him just at dusk, and ride close enough so that he can catch a flash of the shirt. Then light on out of there."

Dave thought for long moments. "Okay. Maybe you're right. Maybe if he doesn't know what time to expect the ghost it'll rattle him worse. Did you bring back the thing from Louis's place?"

"It's out in the wagon bed. I'll get it."

Andres hobbled out and brought it in. Dave looked it over. Two pieces of strap iron bolted together in the form of a T. Bolt holes were drilled in the base of the T. It was about thirty inches high, and the cross-piece was about twenty inches long.

Ike said, "I didn't bother to bring the saddle in. We braced the horn the way you said and drilled through it."

Dave fingered the sharp curve in the base of the T. "You figure this curves enough?"

"Seems to when you get it set up. If it don't, we can wedge it between a couple of rocks and bend it just a little bit more."

"Tonight, Ike, after the town's abed, you better take the wagon and take all the stuff out to where the roan is. I'll go on out way before dawn as usual, and I'll stay in the canyon all day and hit Hawson's place at dusk. You better roll up some blankets and stick them in this here bed and tell folks I'm sleeping."

Jud Hawson sat in his big chair in the dark and looked out the window across the sighing plains, looked at the speckled infinity of stars. He sighed heavily. He thought of the dawn rider, and the palms of his hands grew clammy. He shivered. Lately the great men of the past hadn't come to him in his dreams. He had dreamed of the face of Pete Austin. There was a smile on Austin's lips. He had whispered, "You, too, Hawson. You, too. *You, too.*"

In his room Hawson lighted the lamp, took his favorite rifle from the gun cabinet. He spent over an hour cleaning and polishing it. At last he held it in his hands and snicked the bolt shut. It made a slick, heartening click.

He sat with the chill steel against his hands and thought of Pete Austin. He saw himself kneeling on the small terrace at dawn, the quick shots whipping the air, the butt thudding against his shoulder. He looked through the sights and fired shot after shot into the yellow shirt. He saw holes appear in the fabric. The rider laughed and kept riding.

Hawson looked toward the black square of his window and shuddered. He blew out the lamp and undressed in the dark. He stretched out, stiff and weary, and stared up at the dark ceiling. The muscles of his neck and back ached. He thought of the way Quinn's gun had spun at his feet. He thought of Adams's eyes.

CHAPTER THREE
Dead Man's Blood

Ike Andres saddled up the swaybacked gray with practiced fingers, climbed with difficulty up into the seat and slapped the gray's rump with the reins, clucked to it softly. The wagon started with a jolt. The horse clumped down the narrow alley, and he turned right on the main street. No light showed in all of Oracle. Andres guessed that it was about two o'clock. A pale moon rode near the horizon.

He swayed on the wagon seat and thought of Dave, whom he had left sleeping. Dave was a good boy. A little hard and bitter for his age. Couldn't hardly blame the boy. A tough deal all the way around. A no-limit game with death for the low hole card.

The slow rumble of the wagon made him sleepy. He swayed from side to side, peering through the night, clucking to the gray once in a while. It was a sad thing not to be able to ride after so many years in the saddle. He remembered the times he had rode the point on the big herds of longhorns, all the way from Texas to the Kansas yards.

It had been a fine life. He thought, as he had thought many times before, that the horse that had crippled him should have crushed his life out against the brutal hardness of the snubbing post. Then he wouldn't be condemned to live out his years as half a man.

He turned off the main road, braced himself as the wagon lurched down the steep side of a small washout, clung to the seat as the gray scrambled up the far side, the stones rolling under its hooves.

At last he came to the turnoff to the canyon. The last quarter mile was across the open prairie. The dry grasses rustled against the wheels. He reined in at the entrance to the canyon and sat for a time savoring the beauty of the night before climbing stiffly down. He had decided that a tangle of chokeberry bushes near the canyon entrance would be the best place to hide the things he had brought.

He tethered the gray, pulled down the tailgate and grabbed the T of scrap iron. He had it half out of the wagon when he heard the sound close behind him. He froze.

He heard a quiet sigh. "You made me wait a long time, Andres. Maybe you can tell me about the ghost."

Ike recognized the silky voice of Adams. He knew that Adams's eyes were as adjusted to the faint moonlight as his own. He stood motionless, still clutching the heavy T of scrap iron.

Suddenly, with a wild yell, he whirled, hurling the heavy device at the dim figure behind him. There was the sound of an impact, a hoarse exclamation, and the figure melted down against the ground.

Ike tried to move quickly, tried to force his broken body to carry him forward to where he could get his gnarled hands on the throat of Adams. He took two steps and the world exploded into fire, the heavens cracked open with a noise of thunder. He was on his back with something bubbling in his chest. The dry grass brushed his cheek. The stars swirled madly above. He couldn't take a deep breath. . . .

Dave jumped up quickly and hurried to the window. There was a hint of gray in the east. He had slept too long.

Ike should have been back long ago. He stepped quietly out the back door. The wagon wasn't back. Something had happened to Ike.

He dressed in haste, pulling on a dark shirt over the bright yellow one that he put on first. He had to make up time. The town would soon be stirring. He yanked his boots on, buckled on his belt and jammed the white hat on his head.

The door to the livery stable was unlatched. It creaked as he opened it. He stood still, heard the snores of the old man. The boards creaked as he walked back to the stalls. The old man snored on. He stepped into the stall, quieted the welcoming whinny with a hand over the tall black's muzzle.

He saddled up, led the horse out of the stall. He swung up, hinted with the hooks, and the black pounded across the boards. Dave ducked low as the black ran out the wide front door. Behind him he heard the yell of the old man. He lifted the black into a dead run.

He pulled in the black at the canyon and advanced cautiously. He was up to the wagon before he saw Ike's body.

He jumped up, his fingers tight on the gun grip, the muzzle swinging in slow horizontal arcs. Six feet beyond Ike the T of scrap iron bent the grass over. One end of the cross bar was stained dark. Near it was a dark spot in the grass.

At the crash of the shot, he dropped flat. The muzzle flash had come from a spot twenty feet away. He fired twice in the direction of the flash. The sky grew lighter. Flat on his belly, he wormed his way forward. At last he saw a dim shape in the grass. He aimed carefully, saw it jerk as the bullet hit.

Seconds later he rolled it over. Adams!

He touched the flesh of the man's hand. It was like ice. Adams had been dead for some time. Adams had his gun in his right hand. Burning grass glowed near the muzzle. Dave suddenly understood. Some reflex had caused it. Some tremor in the dead, stiffening body.

Adams's chin was smashed, and his throat was torn where the heavy strap iron had hit it. A trail of blood led back through the grass. The picture was clear. Ike had hurled the iron at Adams, tearing his throat. Adams had killed Ike and then bled to death as he tried to crawl back to his horse, his gun on cock.

Dave glanced at the east. The rim of the sun would soon show. There was no point in waiting until dusk. The death of Ike spoiled the entire plan. Everything was ruined. By the time he could construct the dummy of the sacking that Ike had hauled in the wagon, it would be broad day. Back in the town they would go into the back room and find him gone. Word would reach Hawson before noon. They would no longer think of ghosts. They would have guns ready for him.

He stood up, holstered his gun and looked down for several minutes at the dead face of Adams. He snapped his fingers suddenly. His mouth twisting with disgust, he squatted, unbuttoned Adams's sodden shirt and ripped it off.

He got rope out of the wagon, laid the T of strap iron on Adams's chest, and tied it there with knots that bit into the cold flesh. It took a long time to work Adams's limp arms into the sleeves of the yellow shirt. Dave got the roan, hobbled it and bound sacking over its eyes. It stood quivering.

He picked up Adams's body, hoisted it into the saddle. The roan smelled death and tried to shy away. The saddle horn had been reinforced and two holes bored through it which matched the holes in the base of the T. He fed the bolts he had taken tightly through the holes.

Adams sat upright in the saddle, his legs dangling limply. Dave tied his feet into the stirrups, tied his wrists loosely together in front of him, and fed the reins into the limp hands. He stepped back.

Since the first gray of dawn, Jud Hawson had stood on the flagstones of the *placita*, looking toward the east. During the night he had been tempted to go down to the bunkhouse, wake up the other five in his rough string and station them out in the flats to the east of the house. But he remembered how Quinn had reacted. And Adams.

The sun crept up until the great golden ball was above the horizon. Overhead the gray changed slowly to morning blue. Hawson felt a deep relief. The time was past. Pete Austin would not come again.

Hawson slowly relaxed. He sat down heavily in the chair behind his small breakfast table. He put the rifle on the flagstones at his feet.

He heard the distant thud of hoof, jingle of rowel hook, and suddenly he was standing, trembling.

His eyes widened and his breath stopped as he saw that the roan was headed directly for the *placita*. It came shouldering out of the mist, and on it was a silent man in a white hat, a yellow shirt.

He lifted the rifle, centered it.

Hawson smiled tightly and squeezed down on the trigger. He

cursed. A miss! He forced steadiness into his arms, fired again. The rider came on. The big white hat was pulled down low over his eyes, shadowing his face.

Hawson knew that he hadn't missed.

The roan was much closer. He saw the shattered chin, the blood on the shirt. The voice of Quinn sounded in his ears, . . . *and busted his chin all to hell on the way out the front.*

Hawson saw the dark holes appear in the yellow shirt. The roan was wide-eyed, foaming. Hawson knew that he was screaming, felt the muscles of his jaw crack as his mouth opened. He continued to yank on the trigger after the rifle was empty. He had no more breath for screaming. He threw the rifle full at the man fifteen feet away, and, as the horse thundered up to him, he dropped onto his face, covering his head.

The horse veered off across the flats, the hooves thudding ever more softly until at last Hawson could hear nothing but the excited servants around him.

He wanted the darkness. He didn't want eyes with which he could see a man in a yellow shirt riding a horse—a man long dead. A man whose head bobbed grotesquely.

He jumped up so quickly that those standing around him moved back in confusion. He saw the flat swarthy face of Miguel. He said softly, "Take your knife and take out my eyes, Miguel."

Miguel backed off, palms out in horror.

They looked at his face, heard his soft and wheedling voice, saw the clawing motions of his hands. They turned and fled.

When they were gone, Dave Austin slid off the black and came up the slope.

Hawson heard his step and turned. His face lighted up. In a voice like the voice of a child finding a delicious surprise, he said, "You have come to kill me!"

Dave stood for a moment and listened to the begging, the babbling. Dave holstered his gun and walked away.

It took him the best part of a half hour to ride slowly back to the canyon. By midmorning he had captured the badly spooked roan. Back at the mouth of the canyon he took the spade from the wagon and buried Adams, the T of iron and the doctored saddle. He replaced the turf and swept it clean of traces. He lifted Ike gently into the bed of the wagon, tied the black and the roan to the tailgate, and drove slowly back into Oracle.

He felt oddly light-headed. Once, as the wagon jolted along, he licked dry lips and said, "Ike, you understand, don't you? He'll be dead by nightfall."

But Dave found out later that he was wrong. Hawson didn't kill himself until a half hour before dawn the next day.

THE END

THE LONG ARM
OF THE LAW

Magurn came o
of his chair sho
ing.

CHAPTER ONE
Drygulch Suicide

Johnny Mason was surrounded by fried chicken. There was a big platterful of it on the bureau of Johnny's hotel room, and he was making mental bets with himself whether he could finish it all at one sitting.

He was picking a drumstick clean when the door opened and Dave Hollister came in. Dave was a bluff, hearty man. He was assistant manager of the Western Cattleman's Protective Association, with offices here in Cheyenne.

Stirring Novelette
of a
Powder-Keg Range

By

JAMES SHAFFER

 hell with being a range detective!" Johnny Mason roared. "With
000 of the green stuff in my pockets, I'm all set to retire!" But when
nny learned that a bushwhacked rancher had filed a claim the day
ɛr he was killed, he reached for his badge and his gun and started
making fast tracks for the frontier's deadliest hell-hole!

"Have some chicken," Johnny said, reaching for another drumstick. "I won three hundred dollars playing chuck-a-luck last night, so I ain't interested in going back to work."

Hollister fished around on the platter till he found a gizzard. He'd been keeping close tab on Johnny's fortunes at the gambling tables, and was well aware that his ace operator was still well heeled with money. Still—

"Bought that ranch yet?" he asked mildly.

"Uh, not yet," Johnny grunted through a mouthful of chicken, "but I'm still looking," he added quickly and almost defensively.

Hollister hid a grin behind a large chicken wing. About a month before, while awaiting another assignment, Johnny had won the tidy sum of eight thousand dollars. With this wealth bulging in his levis, he'd announced loudly that he was through working for the Association.

It wasn't no life for a man, he argued loudly, to be running all over the country, hunting down rustlers, horse thieves and the like. Never getting a good night's sleep and always guarding against some rustler's bullet. Always on the go and never knowing what part of the danged country you'd hit next. When a man reached his advanced age—twenty-seven—it was time for him to seek the quiet life.

A little ranch somewheres, with a bunch of white-faced cows; a pretty wife that could fry chicken; and hell—maybe even the patter of tiny feet later on.

"Life," Johnny had proclaimed, waxing eloquent, "is passing me by. I ain't gitting my share of it. I aim to start gitting, as of now."

Well, it looked like he meant it. He started riding all over the country, looking for a suitable ranch to buy. A week passed, and he was still looking 'em over. Another week and his trips to look at property became fewer. And finally, it had reached the point where he spent most of his time in the hotel eating chicken, or shooting pool around in the saloons. But there was still cash in his pocket, and he refused to work.

"That's right," Hollister agreed heartily. "Look 'em over carefully before you buy a place. After all, you're gonna spend the rest of your life on the ranch you buy."

"Yeah, that's right," Johnny grunted. But he was frowning slightly. He hadn't liked the sound of that phrase 'the rest of your life.' It sounded more like a judge pronouncing sentence than a man living a happy life.

"I wondered if you'd been looking at any places north of here," Hollister went on. "Say up around Big Lick Springs. In that part of the country."

"No," said Johnny warily. "I ain't. And I ain't gonna," he added defiantly, pulling the platter over closer.

"Got an awful funny case up there," Hollister went on mildly. He picked the last bit of meat off a wishbone and held it out for Johnny to pull. Johnny got the longest piece.

"Haw," he said triumphantly, and stuck the piece of wishbone in the band of his hat.

"Fellow named John Law from Big Lick Springs wrote us a while back to send a man up there. Said a neighbor—Duke Magurn—and some of his friends was robbing him blind."

"What's funny about that?" Johnny grunted. "Usual kind of case—that's the trouble working for the Association. Same old stuff, all the time."

"Little while later," Hollister said, "John Law writes us another letter saying not to send a man—he'd caught the gents that was robbing him."

"What the hell—ain't no case there," Johnny grunted.

" 'Course I don't wanna bore you—seeing as how you ain't interested in Association work any more," Hollister said apologetically, "but there's where the funny stuff comes in. An eastern insurance company wrote us then."

"What in thunder did—?" Johnny caught himself and lolled back in his chair with elaborate indifference. "No kidding?" he grunted. Hollister was busy with a chicken leg. Apparently, he hadn't noticed Johnny's quickly smothered interest.

"This John Law had a policy with this company. One of those policies that pays double if a man is killed accidentally. It seems that John Law had been killed when a horse threw him."

"That's an accident, pure and simple," Johnny said. "Did the insurance company think something was suspicious about it?"

"Don't know," Hollister said, "but the letter kinda upset us down at the office. We started comparing the letter we got from the insurance company with the last letter we got from John Law."

"Why?"

"According to the coroner's report that the insurance company had, John Law had mailed the last letter to us the day after he was killed."

Hollister stood up and wiped his hands on his pants. "But here I am boring you stiff, Johnny," he said, moving toward the door. "I plumb forgot that you weren't interested in Association work any more. The *real* reason for my visit was to tell you about a ranch I heard about over—"

"Phooey," said Johnny, "nothing funny about the case. The last letter you got from John Law was a forgery."

"This ranch has a stream running right through it," Hollister said. "Purtiest place you ever saw. And that letter wasn't a forgery. It was wrote by the same man, all right. This fellow's willing to sell that ranch dirt cheap. He inherited some money back east."

"But why did the insurance company write the Association in the first place?" Johnny asked impatiently. "Did they think something was phony about Law's death?"

"No," Hollister said. "It ain't Law's death that made 'em suspicious. It's the beneficiary of the policy—you know—the hombre that gets the money. This man ain't kin to John Law any way. His name is Ed French. It seems that Ed French and John Law both took out policies, each policy naming the other man as beneficiary."

Johnny had his curiosity under control again by now. He'd seen through Dave Hollister's slick scheme to get him all excited about this case so's he'd go back to work. Well, he'd made up his mind that he wasn't going back to work. Man couldn't spend his whole life chasing around straightening out other people's troubles.

"They musta been good friends," he said mildly, "making out their insurance to each other. What's the trouble? This here Ed French trying to make the insurance company pay more than's due?"

Hollister was almost through the door. He had it open and was edging through.

"Ed French don't want the company to pay him nothing. He wrote the company and asked 'em to please forget that John Law ever had a policy with them—and he sent the check back." Hollister then started out.

"Come back here—uh, that is—what's your hurry, Dave? Where'd you say this place was? Big Lick Springs? Hmm, I thought you said Big *Link* Springs—uh, matter of fact—there's a ranch I'd been planning to look at—near Big Lick Springs— funny—I thought you said Big Link Springs—say! Why the hell did Ed French send that insurance check back?"

Hollister came back in the room, keeping his face very straight and solemn. The chicken was about all gone, and he poked around through the bones a minute.

"Now, Johnny, I wouldn't want you to waste your time bothering with this case when you're up around Big Lick Springs. You'll be busy looking at ranches."

"It don't make sense, does it?" Johnny said, ignoring Hollister's remarks. "John Law writes you to send a man up."

"And we, being shorthanded, couldn't send one right away," Hollister said meaningly.

"Then before a man is sent you get another letter from Law saying *not* to send a man. Then you find out Law was killed and the letter mailed the day after he died, but the letter ain't forgery."

"That was damn good chicken," Hollister said. "Was it cooked at the hotel?"

"Then this Ed French, who stands to collect double on the insurance policy, don't want any of the money—in fact, he sounds like he don't want nobody 'round there to know anything about the policy."

"This ranch I heard about with the crick running through it is south of here," Dave Hollister said.

"The whole case sounds like it's a rustling easy, with maybe murder thrown in," Johnny said. "Yep, it sure does!"

"A day's ride to the south would get you to this ranch I'm telling you about," Dave said.

"I could catch the southbound train in the morning and be in Big Lick Springs by tomorrow night," Johnny was saying. "Not that I'm going back on the Association's payroll," he went on defiantly, "but since I'm going to be looking around and asking a few questions—maybe you better give me an Association badge and credential papers."

"Couldn't get 'em ready by then," Hollister said. "But if you're in such a hurry—I could mail 'em the next day."

"I better go tomorrow," Johnny said, "uh—that ranch— somebody might buy it right from under me."

Hollister got out of the room. Even then, he couldn't get out of earshot before he let loose a chuckle. Johnny Mason stuck his head out the door.

"Yah, don't think you're putting anything over on me, you horn-tailed old galoot!" he shouted. "I knowed what your game was, minute you came. If it wasn't for that ranch I wanta look at—'' His voice trailed off. He wasn't even convincing himself, so how could he be convincing Hollister?

The train ground to a halt. Johnny peered through the window into the darkness.

"This Big Lick Springs?" he asked the conductor.

"Nope, we're ten miles from Big Lick," the man said. "This is a cattle loading pen we're at. Every night a bunch of cowpunchers stop the train here and ride to Big Lick Springs. Don't know why, 'cause there's no train back. Just like to go for a train ride, I reckon."

Three men got on the train. Johnny was tired and drowsy from the long train ride and didn't pay much attention to them. The train started with a jerk, and people began to gather up their luggage and get ready to leave the train. He noticed that all three of them seemed to move around the coach some, and finally one of them sat down by him.

"Gittin' off at Big Lick Springs?" the man asked in the disinterested voice of a person who merely wants to make conversation.

"Uh-huh," Johnny grunted.

"Looking for a job?"

"Nope, not exactly," Johnny replied. As a matter of fact, he hadn't thought much about what he was going to do when he got there. Hollister was sending him his Association credentials and a full report of the case by mail. Until it arrived, he hadn't planned much of anything.

Still, he thought idly, drumming his fingers on the grimy train window, it might be just as well to ride out to John Law's ranch and make sure the rancher was dead—and maybe pick up a few facts.

"Know where a gent named John Law lives?" he asked the man, and if he'd been more wide awake, he would have noticed the man's sudden spurt of interest.

"Know where he used to live," the man said. "Used to own the Bearpaw spread—big place. Law let a horse throw 'im not long ago and got hisself killed. You got business with the Bearpaw?"

"Not exactly," Johnny muttered, slightly annoyed at the man's questions. "Just wanted to know where it was."

The man gave him directions as to how to find the Bearpaw

ranch, and then, as the train whistled shrilly, he got up and joined his two companions. Johnny noted idly that the three of them were the first off the train as it ground to a jerky stop at Big Lick Springs.

He stepped off the coach and stretched the kinks out of his legs. In the flicker of the streetlights, Big Lick Springs looked like all other cowtowns. Johnny left his bedroll and saddle with the station agent, and then started uptown to the hotel.

Most of the town was dark, the lights being concentrated around the saloons. He passed the brightly lighted section and kept going toward the hotel sign farther up the street. He was passing a darkened store when he heard a strange noise.

"That's him," a man whispered hoarsely.

There was a scuffling sound, and Johnny tried to dodge to one side. His hand streaked for his holstered gun, but he was too late on both counts. A million lights flashed before him, and a roaring pain shot through his head. He tried to keep his feet, but his knees were like water, then strong arms grabbed him.

Then later, he was fighting his way through the blackness and the waves of pain. There was something rough against his face. He tried to focus his eyes on it, but it was too close. Then he realized that he was lying face down and the rough thing was the floor. He tried to roll over, but didn't have the strength. There were voices.

"—searched everything he's got. He's no Association man."

"Then what the hell did he want to know about John Law for then?" another voiced growled.

"Look out. He's coming to! Let him have it again!"

There was a quick step, and Johnny heard the swish of a gun barrel in the air, and the world exploded again in a million brightly colored lights.

It was morning when he came to, and this time the awakening wasn't so bad. He must have dropped off into a deep sleep after the unconsciousness had worn off. He sat up and rubbed the two big lumps on his head. After a while, he got to his feet and took stock.

He was down near the freight station. He felt in his pockets, remembering the snatch of conversation he'd heard last night. There was nothing missing, although his belongings were in the wrong pockets, proving he'd been searched.

"Those hombres that got on the train last night," he muttered. "That's the reason they ride it every night—to spot an Association man before he gets to town. Now I gotta find out who don't want an Association man in town. Maybe that won't be so easy—but if I knew, things would be a lot clearer."

He picked up his hat and knocked the dust from it. Then he noticed something.

"That wishbone I stuck in the hatband," he muttered. "Gone."

He looked for it and couldn't find it. He went back uptown and looked in front of the store where he'd been slugged. He couldn't find it there.

"Well, it wasn't such good luck after all," he muttered.

CHAPTER TWO
Payable on Death

It was still early, and Johnny attracted little or no attention as he got his bedroll and saddle from the station and checked in at the hotel. He washed up with a great snorting and sloshing of water, then put cold wet rags on his head and stretched out across the bed.

While the rags soothed the bumps on his head, his mind was busy going over the case.

This John Law mentioned an hombre named Duke Magurn as the gent that was robbing him blind, he thought. Was John Law right? Or did he just suspect that Magurn was doing the robbing? If so, how did Law stop the robbing all of a sudden and write the Association not to send a man up?

And Ed French, he mused. How come he's refusing the insurance money? A man doesn't turn down money unless he's got a darn good reason; some reason like saving his neck, or something.

And the circumstances surrounding John Law's death, and the letter being mailed the day *after* his death. Johnny sat up straight in bed.

"That's the angle I better work on first," he thought, "Then I'll take up Mr. Magurn and Mr. French later." He flung the rags into the corner of the room.

Down on the street, he looked around at Big Lick Springs. Presently his eyes found the livery stable.

"That's the place," he thought, "where I start my investigation."

But first, he dropped into the saloon and bought a pint of whiskey. He shoved it in his hip pocket and made tracks for the livery stable.

"Want to rent a horse," Johnny told the liveryman. "But first, I'd like to get a little information." He dragged the whiskey out, pulled the cork and passed the bottle over.

The liveryman, a wizened oldster with scraggly whiskers and sharp, darting eyes, sniffed the bottle, then tilted it and let 'er pour down.

"Whatcha—ulp—wanna know?" he demanded.

"I'm buying broncs for a rodeo—killers to be used in bucking contests. Thought maybe you could give me a line on where I could find some." Johnny pulled out a blank piece of paper and looked at it gravely. "Got some notes here," he said, "of fellows that might own some. How about Ed French?"

The liveryman scratched his chin. "Ed might have some—though he believes more in gentling his mounts, 'stead of busting 'em."

Johnny studied his paper again. "What about Duke Magurn?"

The liveryman spat, then drank from the bottle like he was washing out a bad taste. "Anything he'd have would be plumb ornery—you can bank on that! Watch yourself when you're dealing with him; he's a—that is, Duke drives a hard bargain."

Johnny nodded gravely. Evidently there were other people in town who didn't think much of Duke Magurn. He played his trump card.

"Heard there was a fellow killed by a horse a while back. John Law, think his name was. Horse that killed him must be plumb mean. Like to buy that cayuse."

"Ornery!" the liveryman snorted in derision. "Why, the horse John was riding that day was as gentle as a lamb! That yarn about his horse throwing him and killing him is just the story the sheriff—"

He broke off suddenly and looked hard at Johnny. "You wanta rent a horse?"

"Yeah," John said. "You was saying that you didn't believe the story about John Law's horse killing him?"

"I wasn't saying nothing," the liveryman growled. In stony silence, he saddled a mount and led it out for Johnny. "I'm saying you're a durned liar about wanting to buy broncs for a rodeo. You ain't gitting nothing outta me—Mr. Whoever-you-are."

Johnny sighed and rode off, and as he followed the train to the Bearpaw, he pieced together the information he'd gathered. One thing was clear.

The folks around here didn't believe John Law had met an accidental death. And the liveryman didn't have much faith in the sheriff. Well, he was learning things.

The Bearpaw was a big spread and, as far as cow ranches go, was well kept. Johnny rode up to the corral and dismounted. There seemed to be no one about, so he walked up to the house. He heard pans rattling from the kitchen, so he ambled around to the back door. The person in the kitchen saw him and came out. Johnny gasped. A girl.

"How-do, ma'am," Johnny said awkwardly, not wholly recovering from his suprise. A place as big as the Bearpaw, he figured, would surely have a cook. "I was looking for the owner."

"I'm the owner," the girl answered, and Johnny noticed the tightness of her lips and the dark circles under her eyes. "My name is Virginia Law. What do you want?"

The question caught Johnny flat-footed. He'd been prepared to meet most anyone—except a girl, and a girl like this. Even the lines of grief around her mouth and the circles under her eyes couldn't hide the beauty of her face.

He realized that the silence was beginning to stretch out, and he blurted out the first thing that came in his head.

"I'm from the insurance company," he stammered. "Want to get a little more information as to the sad circumstances of your father's death," he finished lamely.

And the girl acted just like the liveryman had acted. She clamped her lips tight and stared at Johnny a moment. Then she whirled and hurried over to the big triangle hanging in the yard that was used to call the ranch hands to their meals. She banged the triangle loud and long, then waited, keeping her eyes averted from Johnny.

A moment later a man hurried around the house. He was a big, raw-boned gent, with cold black eyes and a jutting jaw covered with a week's stubble of beard. He was loosening the Colt from its holster as he walked up.

"You want me, Miss Jinny?" he asked, but his eyes were on Johnny.

"This man is from the insurance company," the girl said. "Will you talk to him—I've got to go somewhere. This is Pete Larew, my foreman," she told Johnny. "He can tell you anything you want to know." She hurried into the house, leaving Johnny with the big foreman.

"What's the matter with you people?" the foreman growled. "The insurance company was told that we wouldn't make no claim for John Law's death."

"You ain't Ed French, are you?" Johnny retorted. "He's the gent that gets the money. How come you're so all-fired anxious for him not to get it?"

The foreman looked Johnny over carefully. "You don't look like no insurance man to me," he grunted, ignoring Johnny's question. "You look more like a cowhand, or," his eyes narrowed, "a range detective."

"I want some information on John Law's death," Johnny said.

"You can go flat to hell," the foreman replied coldly.

Johnny sighed and rubbed his cheek. Somewhere, he heard a horse break into a gallop and the hoofbeats fade in the distance. That would be the girl, he thought to himself. He turned back to the foreman.

"Why did John Law suddenly change his mind about Duke Magurn?" he asked.

"So you are a range dick," the foreman grunted. "What d'ya mean, change his mind?"

"Law wrote the Association to send a man up—that Magurn was robbing him blind."

"That's right," the foreman nodded. "And he still is—he's trying to break the Bearpaw."

"Then why did Law later write the Association and tell them *not* to send a man up—that the case was settled?"

"That's a lie!" Pete Larew snapped. "John never wrote no such letter—that's some of Magurn's work—must have forged that second letter."

Johnny grinned inwardly. Those were the very same words he'd used, when Dave Hollister had told him of the letter. But he had confidence that if the letter had been a forgery, it wouldn't have convinced Hollister.

"Reckon maybe you're right," he muttered. "Guess I'll be riding along."

"If there's any way I can help you get the deadwood on Magurn," Larew said seriously, "just holler."

"What's the set-up with Magurn, anyhow?" Johnny asked.

Pete Larew studied Johnny for a long moment. Evidently, he decided to take a chance. "Magurn and his pals—which include Sheriff Honeywell—are out to run this whole county. The Bearpaw was the biggest and strongest outfit, and they had to bust it first. And they've dang nigh done it."

"Where does Ed French fit in?" Johnny asked.

"Ed was joining with John Law to buck Magurn and his crew."

"So Magurn's the curly wolf 'round here," Johnny mused.

"He is," Larew stated flatly. "You c'n take my word for it—or find out for yourself—if you stay 'round here a few days."

"And you think he killed John Law?"

Larew's brow wrinkled. "He did. I'd swear it—but nobody's been able to pin the deadwood on him. He's got a perfect alibi."

"And what's the alibi?" Johnny asked.

"About ten miles south of Big Lick Springs is some cattle loading pens—on the railroad."

Johnny nodded. "I remember the train stopping there," he said ruefully, remembering what had happened later.

"The night John Law was killed, the train stopped there, and Duke Magurn got on. John Law was there; he'd been trailing some stolen stuff. Law didn't get on the train, 'cause he was a-horseback. Law rode off before the train pulled out. The trail runs right along the railroad track, and that's where John was found the next morning, after the horse came home with an empty saddle.

"Horse throwed him, huh?"

Larew nodded. "The coroner's inquest opined that when the engine passed John's horse, it scared the animal, and he bolted, and John lost his seat, and the horse drug him to death."

"And Magurn's alibi is that he was on the train when all that happened."

"And you can't break his story," he said sourly. "The trainmen swear that John Law was alive when Magurn got on the train, and that Law rode off before the train pulled out."

"I'll be gitting along," Johnny said. "Thanks for the information."

"Remember, if you want any help, just holler," Pete Larew said as Johnny rode off.

Things, Johnny thought, were beginning to add up. But there were still a lot of gaps in the picture. The letter that was mailed the day after John Law's death, Ed French's refusal to accept the insurance money, and Duke Magurn's iron-clad alibi. Still, he thought cheerfully, things were beginning to break.

He was deep in thought and halfway back to town when a rider blocked the trail.

"Hold it," the man said, and emphasized his words with a cocked sixgun.

"Howdy," Johnny said laconically. "You sure you got the right man, mister?"

"Damn right," the man snapped. "You're from the insurance company. Ain't you?"

"Oh," said Johnny remembering the girl's sudden departure. "Then I must be talking to Ed French." He eyed the man with frank curiosity, wanting to see what kind of a man turned down money. Ed was young, about the same age as himself. He had a thatch of blond hair and a face that would be good looking, had it not been so grim.

"You're looking at Ed French, and I'm doing the talking," the man said coldly. "I notified your company I didn't want payment on John Law's policy. That still goes."

"Why?" Johnny asked innocently.

"None of your business!" Ed French snapped. "I'm giving you your orders—take the afternoon train outta here!"

"And if I don't—"

"Drop that gun, French!" A rider jumped his horse out of the brush bordering the trail. He was a big man, flashily dressed, and the fancy sixgun he carried was pointed at Ed French's stomach. "Drop it, French," he bellowed, "or by hell I'll let you have it!"

Ed French hesitated only a moment, then let his gun drop to the ground and slowly lifted his hands.

"So there was something to that tale about you having an insurance policy on John Law, huh?" Duke Magurn grinned evilly. "Trying to run the insurance man outta the country before anybody found out about it."

"This is none of your business, Magurn," Ed French snarled. "Stay out of it—ride on!"

"I'm making it some of my business," Magurn said. He laughed. "Looks like I finally got you—right where I want you. Let's go, stranger—we're taking this gent to the sheriff."

It was a rather quiet ride into town. The only sounds were the clop of the horses and the muttered profanity of Ed French.

But in town it was different. Magurn made quite a show of bringing Ed French in. They paraded down the main street with Magurn bellowing threats at French in case he tried to escape. Thus, they pulled up in front of the jail. The sheriff, a shifty-looking individual with tobacco-stained teeth and pale, nervous eyes, came out on the sidewalk.

"Caught this killer dead to rights, sheriff," Magurn bellowed loudly for the benefit of the small crowd that had gathered. "Got all the evidence we need now—and with Judge Hook in town, reckon we c'n have a quick trial tomorrow."

Sheriff Honeywell nodded quick agreement. He pulled his gun with a flourish and loudly ordered Ed French to dismount and precede him into the jail. Johnny Mason rubbed his cheek.

"Who is this gent French supposed to have killed?" he asked mildly.

"Why, John Låw!" Magurn said loudly. Johnny was watching the faces of the crowd around him. Most of them kept their faces expressionless, staring at Magurn with stolid indifference. But some in the crowd showed distaste and disgust at Magurn's declaration.

"I thought," Johnny said, "that John Law was killed by a horse—drug to death."

Magurn laughed, a nasty, rasping sound. "That's what Ed French *hoped* we'd believe," he said. "But that horse Law was riding that night was gentle as a lamb—and Law was a dang good horseman."

"I see," Johnny said, dismounting.

"I'll tell you the way it was," Magurn said, getting to the ground and handing Johnny a cigar. The crowd had not dispersed, but was still hanging around curiously, and Johnny realized that Magurn was actually building up the case against Ed French right here and now.

And this, he figured, would be the best time he'd have to find out just what Magurn's scheme was.

"When John Law was killed," Magurn said, "folks around here got suspicious that it wasn't an accident."

"I'll say they did," a man in the crowd muttered; and Magurn shot him a venomous glance.

"First everybody figured that rustlers had done it," Magurn went on, " 'cause Law had been losing a lot of cattle—but then things began to come to light. We found out that Ed French had loaned Law a lot of money—to keep the Bearpaw going. To play safe, we figure that French made Law take out insurance payable to Ed French.''

"And then when John Law couldn't pay back the loans,'' Johnny Mason broke in, "Ed French figured out a way to collect.''

"That's right,'' Magurn said loudly, and his tone indicated that he was well pleased with Johnny's remark. "He decided to kill John Law and make it look like an accident—collecting on the insurance then.''

"Why hadn't you arrested him before?'' Johnny asked innocently.

"We wasn't sure that there actually was an insurance policy on John Law,'' Magurn said. "But today—when I caught him trying to run you outta the country because you was here to pay the claim for the insurance company—well, that's all the evidence we needed. Ed French'll hang!'' Magurn concluded loudly.

The crowd began to break up after that, and there were angry mutters and dark glances thrown at Magurn as they drifted away. Magurn noticed it, but the grin on his face was a confident sneer. Johnny stepped into the jail and spoke to Honeywell.

"I'd like to talk to the prisoner,'' he said.

"What for?'' Honeywell asked nervously. "Hell, ain't you convinced—''

"It's my job to investigate this case thoroughly,'' Johnny said.

"Okay,'' Honeywell muttered, and Johnny passed down the corridor to Ed French's cell. French was seated on his bunk, rolling a smoke. He regarded Johnny sourly and went on fashioning his quirly.

"I wanta ask you some questions,'' Johnny said.

"I wish to hell you'd let me alone,'' French growled.

"How did Magurn find out John Law had an insurance policy, and that you were the beneficiary?''

French paused with the match halfway to his cigarette. "Sa-ay, I don't know!'' he ejaculated. "I never told anybody, and I'm sure John Law didn't, but Magurn knew about it and started spreading talk the day after Law was killed that I had killed him to collect on the policy. That's why I didn't want to accept payment.'' He frowned and looked hard at Johnny. "You know, you're a helluva tough-looking hombre to be an insurance man.''

Johnny grinned and told him that he worked for the Association.

"Why didn't you say so before?" French demanded. "It would have cleared this whole thing up. I'll git the sheriff and make him turn me loose!"

"Just a minute," cautioned Johnny. "You better let 'em try you. Magurn's building up his case tomorrow—figuring that I *am* an insurance man—and that I can *prove* in court that John Law did have such a policy. The case against you will fall to pieces when they can't prove that in court tomorrow."

"Yeah, that's right," French agreed, then frowned. "But suppose he *can* prove that there was such a policy. After all, he found out about it some way."

"That's what's got me worried," Johnny admitted. "Think hard now—how could Magurn have found out about that policy in the first place?"

Ed French scratched his head and thought. "No way that I can figure. Law and I bought the policies in Cheyenne—you see, I had one that named John Law beneficiary. We took 'em out for protection. We knew Magurn was trying to break us, and we figured he might resort to murder. If he did—well, we figured the policies would give the remaining man plenty of money to fight Magurn."

"Instead of that—Magurn turned the trick against you."

"If Law had been killed a couple of days after," French said, "this wouldn't have happened. The beneficiary of the policy would have been changed."

"Yeah?" Johnny said interestedly. "How's that?"

"Law told me a couple of days before he was killed that he'd found out something that would stop the rustling and hang Magurn. He said when he got the deadwood on Magurn, he was going to change the beneficiary of the policy over to Virginia."

"That's darned interesting," Johnny said.

French shrugged. "But he never did. When the insurance company found out about his death, they notified me as beneficiary—not Virginia."

"You and Virginia Law—you kinda—"

"Yeah," French said. "That's why John Law and I were fighting this thing together. To make this county a decent place to live and raise kids."

"Hmm," said Johnny. "I'll be seeing you."

He left Big Lick Springs and rode through the hot midafternoon sun to the Bearpaw ranch. He found Pete Larew repairing some harnesses, and together they went into the house.

Johnny told Virginia Law what had happened since he'd left the Bearpaw, and about Ed French being in jail. Then he turned to Pete.

"Get some horses ready tonight," Pete said. "We're going to get Ed out."

"That would spoil everything," Johnny argued. "They got nothing on French but circumstantial evidence—and we can rip that wide open at the trial tomorrow—maybe," he added thoughtfully, "pin the deadwood on Magurn."

"What have you found out about Magurn?" Pete Larew asked.

"Nothing," said Johnny disgustedly. "That's the trouble coming in on a case after the trails have gotten cold. All I've got on Magurn is suspicion and circumstantial evidence—but I'm hoping for some kind of break tomorrow at the trial."

Then he told her the real reason for the trip to the Bearpaw.

"I want to see that insurance policy."

"I'll get it for you," the girl said, leading the way into a small room that was fitted out as an office. "Dad always kept his papers in this safe."

It was a big iron safe, and the girl knelt before it and twisted the knob, then swung the door open. She rummaged around in the safe a moment, then whirled.

"It's—it's gone!"

Johnny rolled a cigarette. Hee wasn't much surprised. The policy *had* to be missing—because Duke Magurn had it.

"Could somebody have gotten into the safe?" he asked.

"No," the girl said positively. "There's always someone at the ranch, in the first place; and in the second, no one knew the combination but dad and me."

"And the safe hasn't been tampered with, that's certain," Johnny said. "Then the only person—besides yourself—that could have taken the policy out was John Law himself." He grinned. "I'll be seeing you at the trial tomorrow."

CHAPTER THREE
Sixgun Showdown

Back in town, Johnny returned his horse to the livery stable and was walking toward the hotel when he heard his name called. He glanced up and saw Duke Magurn leaning out of a second-story window.

"Come up here," Magurn called. Johnny climbed a rickety set of steps and through a door that Magurn held open for him. "This is where I do most of my business," Magurn said. "It's handy—right in town."

Johnny nodded and looked around. The place was supposed to be an office—a fact attested to by the presence of a roll-top desk and a few chairs. But riding gear and old clothes were strewn about the place, and it looked as if it had not been cleaned in a coon's age.

A man stood up as Johnny entered. A bluff, hearty man who'd had too much to drink.

"This is Judge Hook," Magurn said.

"Pleased t' meetcha," the judge said solemnly.

"Just wanted to tell you that the trial is for nine o'clock in the morning," Magurn said. "You seem to be running all over the country, so I thought I'd tell you so's you'd be sure to be there."

Johnny's eyes roamed around the office, missing no detail. "I'll be there," he said quietly. "Had to go out this afternoon and look over the place where John Law was killed."

"Huh?" Magurn grunted suddenly. "What the hell for?" he demanded.

"Gotta make a full report of this case to my company," Johnny said. He bent down and picked up something from the floor, and idly broke it between his fingers. "Don't worry; I'll be there in the morning."

Down on the street, Johnny looked at the object he'd picked up in Magurn's office.

It was the broken half of a wishbone of a chicken. He grinned, remembering that he'd had a wishbone stuck in his hat band the night he'd arrived in Big Lick Springs—and that he'd lost it when somebody slugged him.

Later that night, Johnny paid a return visit to Magurn's office—when he was sure he'd be alone. He took a good supply of matches and slipped up the back way.

He went straight to a pile of riding gear in one corner of the room. Saddles, bridles, chaps, ropes and other gear were piled helter-skelter in the corner. Johnny picked up a lasso rope and examined it carefully by the light of a match.

He carried the rope to the back of the building, where he could safely light a lantern, and studied the rope long and carefully.

Finally he put the rope back where he'd found it and slipped back to his hotel.

But he didn't go to sleep immediately.

He spent long, patient moments checking and oiling his gun. He fitted a spring clasp to his wrist and slipped a small derringer under the clasp.

This case, he knew, was drawing to a close. The time for asking questions, probing for information and gathering evidence was nearly over. It was time for the guns to start talking now. He grinned as he listened to the oily click of his sixgun coming to full cock.

"Time for gun talk is right," he muttered, "and I wouldn't want this gun of mine to come down with a case of laryngitis and not be able to say a word!"

The news that Ed French was to be tried for the murder of John Law spread like wildfire, and when Johnny awoke in the morning, he found Big Lick Springs abuzz with excitement. He pulled his clothes on hurriedly and went down into the street.

A group of men eyed him sourly, and he heard muttered comments on Duke Magurn's bald-faced attempt to railroad Ed French to a hangnoose.

And then there were other men in town; sharp-featured, hard-eyed men that just stood around and said nothing.

"Magurn's men," Johnny thought. "Spread out all over town to keep the lid clamped on and see that nothing goes wrong at the trial." He grinned and moved toward the post office.

When he was sure he was unobserved, he stepped inside and asked the postmaster for his mail.

"Big envelope for you," the postmaster said and shoved the big manila envelope through the window. Johnny tucked it under his vest and walked back to his hotel room. He was ready for the trial to begin.

Had it not been that a man's life hung in the balance, the trial of Ed French would have been one huge joke.

The lawyer Ed French had hired asked the court for more time to prepare his defense with, arguing that French had only been arrested the day before.

"Motion denied," Judge Hook grunted, and hid a hiccough behind his hand.

Johnny Mason let his eyes rove over the courtroom. He noticed grimly that Duke Magurn had placed his gun crew at strategic points throughout the room. Some were seated, but most of them stood in corners and near the doors, and, as before, their hands were near their guns.

Duke Magurn had a seat on the front row, the same as Johnny, and as Johnny watched him, Magurn grinned confidently at Judge Hook. For a moment, Johnny had a twinge of despair.

Magurn had this whole case sewed up, and his gunmen were ready at a second's notice to stop any trouble. And the trial was going just the way Duke Magurn planned it.

Ed French's lawyer argued heatedly about the choice of the jury, but gradually the jury box was filled with twelve tough-looking men. And Johnny knew from the muttered comments around him that the jury had been hand-picked by Magurn before the trial. He turned and grinned confidently at Virginia Law and Pete Larew.

Johnny only half-listened as the prosecuting attorney boldly accused Ed French of the murder of John Law. He watched Duke Magurn closely, while the lawyer brought out evidence that Ed French had loaned John Law money, and that Law hadn't paid the notes on the date they were due.

"John Law figured Ed French was his friend," the prosecuting attorney stated, "but he didn't reckon with the fact that Ed French was a cold and calculating person. Before French would loan John Law money, he insisted that Law take out an insurance policy— naming Ed French as the beneficiary."

The attorney paused, then thumped the table with his fist.

"When John Law couldn't pay up," he shouted, "Ed French coldly figured out a way he could get his money. He would collect on the insurance policy. But in killing John Law, he was not clever enough to make his murder look like an accident, as he had planned, and suspicion was aroused that Law's death had been murder.

"When this happened," the lawyer continued, "Ed French tried to shift the suspicion onto Duke Magurn, and very nearly succeeded in doing so!

"Had it not been for the fact that the insurance company sent a man up here to investigate, Ed French's evil scheme would have succeeded. But murder will out, and Ed French made his fatal mistake in trying to run this insurance man out of the country—and keep hidden the fact that he profited by John Law's death!"

It was a convincing speech, Johnny thought glumly, and it was building up a strong case against French. Duke Magurn was grinning confidently now, and the jury looked as if it could return a verdict of guilty without leaving the jury box.

"As a final piece of damning evidence against Ed French," the attorney went on dramatically, "I am going to bring to the witness stand the insurance man that Ed French tried to run out of the country. He will tell you in his own words how Ed French tried to run him out of the country, and how French refused to accept payment of the insurance—knowing that to accept that payment would put a hangnoose around his neck!"

"Mr. Johnny Mason—will you take the witness chair?"

Johnny's boots clumped loudly in the hushed courtroom as he walked over and took his seat. This is it, he thought. This is where this whole case blows up in gunsmoke—or where he would fail miserably. He had that hollow nervous feeling in the pit of his stomach that he got when he knew things were getting ready to flame into action.

"Now, Mason," the prosecuting attorney said, "tell the jury what insurance company you work for—and tell them the whole story about the insurance policy John Law had with your company—and how Ed French tried to run you out of the country."

Johnny didn't look at the jury, or the prosecutor. He kept his eyes on Duke Magurn. The big man was beaming at him as he opened his mouth.

"I don't work for any insurance company—and I don't know anything about any insurance policy that John Law had," he said, and he watched the smile wipe itself off Magurn's face, and the look of blank amazement and anger replace it. Ed French was leaning forward, listening intently to Johnny.

The prosecutor sputtered and stammered. "What're you doing as a witness in this case, then?" he demanded.

"Somebody got the wrong notion about me and ordered me to be a witness," Johnny said easily. "But since I'm here, I've gotten awful curious. You been making a lot of statements, and what I'd like to know—*just where is your proof that John Law did have such a policy?*"

The courtroom broke out in a loud babble of voices. Duke Magurn was cursing loudly, and Judge Hook was banging his gavel

for order. Sheriff Honeywell yelled for quiet, and the noise subsided, but the atmosphere in the courtroom had changed. Duke
Magurn was squirming nervously and casting quick glances around
at his men. The well-wishers of Ed French were sitting on the
edge of their seats—watching and waiting. Johnny noticed Magurn
make a motion to the prosecuting attorney.

"That's all, Mason—get out of the chair!" the prosecutor
bawled, but Ed French's lawyer jumped to his feet.

"Just a minute—I want to—"

"Sit down, you!" Judge Hook roared, but the damage had been
done. An angry mutter ran through the crowd and became louder
and more ominous. Sheriff Honeywell bellowed orders to quiet
down, but the crowd was getting ugly.

"This whole case is built on lies!" Pete Larew shouted. "You
ain't got a scrap of evidence against French!"

"Order in the court!" Judge Hook yelled.

"Show us some evidence or stop this trial right now!" Pete
Larew yelled back. "This is all a pack of lies by Magurn!"

Johnny kept watching Duke Magurn. He saw Magurn's face
register bafflement at the sudden turn of events, then slowly rising
rage at the frustration of his carefully laid plans. A couple of his
gunmen edged closer and looked questioningly at their boss, but he
waved them back. Finally, the roar of the crowd became too much.
Magurn leaped to his feet.

"Shut up!" he roared. "If it's proof you want—it's proof you'll
get!" He reached in his inside coat pocket and brought out an
envelope. Angrily, he flung it on Judge Hook's desk. "There's the
policy John Law had—naming Ed French beneficiary!"

Johnny breathed easier. The first part of his plan had worked.
He'd forced Magurn to bring out the hidden policy. He'd seen the
indecision on Magurn's face, then the sudden rage that had forced
him to bring the policy out.

"And that," Johnny thought, "is the blunder that's gonna cost
him—before it's all over."

The crowd calmed down quickly as Judge Hook opened the
envelope and studied the printed insurance policy.

"It's just what Magurn says," the judge said. "Reckon that's
proof enough," he added, looking significantly at the jury.

"All right, Mason, get outta that witness chair," Magurn said
nervously.

Johnny shook his head. "Nope, I ain't finished yet."

"Git outta that chair, you!" Judge Hook roared.

"Not till I finish the case I'm working on," Johnny said evenly. "It won't take long, now."

"What case?" Sheriff Honeywell demanded. "Who the devil are you, anyhow?"

Johnny was still watching Magurn, and he knew before he spoke that Magurn had already guessed it.

"I work for the Cattlemen's Association."

A dead silence fell over the courtroom. Judge Hook's mouth dropped open in astonishment. Sheriff Honeywell glanced uneasily at Duke Magurn, and Magurn's gunmen shuffled their feet nervously and watched Magurn for a sign. Magurn himself was sitting straight in his chair, his eyes narrowed and fastened on Johnny in a cold, piercing gaze.

"John Law wrote the Association to send a man up here. I'm him," he said.

"He also wrote 'em and told 'em he'd changed his mind—not to send a man," Magurn blurted out.

"That did it, Magurn," Johnny said quickly. "You killed John Law."

A gusty sigh swept the courtroom, and men braced themselves for the thunder of gunfire. Magurn came half out of his chair, his hand clawing over his sixgun. Johnny hadn't moved—noticeably—but he was tensing his wrist, preparatory to shaking the derringer into his hand.

Magurn suddenly relaxed, then laughed loudly.

"You're a fool, Mason," he said harshly. "And I'm going to let you prove to these people how big a fool you are." He paused. "Tell us what evidence you've got that I killed Law. And when you've finished, I'll make you eat your words—before I run you outta town!"

"First off," Johnny said, "you took that policy out of John Law's pocket the night you killed him. You see, he always kept his policy in his safe at home—but he took it out and had it in his pocket because he was planning to change the beneficiary to his daughter."

Magurn made no show of nervousness. He was still confident and cocky, Johnny noticed, and the fact made Johnny nervous. He twisted in the chair a little. Magurn laughed.

"Any more?" he sneered. "You don't think you're gonna pin that murder on me with *that*, do you?"

"Nope," said Johnny, "there's more. I said that Law wrote the Association for a man—and you said he wrote 'em back and told 'em not to send one."

Magurn nodded. "John Law suspected me of rustling his cattle. But the night he was killed, he met me and told me he'd been wrong." He cut his eyes around at Ed French. "He mentioned who he suspected of doing the rustling," he added meaningly.

Johnny laughed. "That's a good show, Magurn, but I'm not falling for your playacting. John Law *did* write another letter to the Association, telling them not to send a man. But the reason was that he had found enough evidence himself—to convict you, Magurn. He let that slip that night he met you down at the loading pens by the railroad. You knew then that you had to kill him."

"Go on," Magurn sneered. "You still ain't proved nothing."

"The man that killed Law took the insurance policy *and that letter* out of Law's pockets after he was killed. I know that—because, you see, the letter was mailed the day after John Law was killed!"

The first crack appeared in Magurn's iron nerve then. He wet his lips nervously, and Johnny saw perspiration break out on the man's forehead. His knuckles whitened as he gripped the arm of the chair. The whole courtroom was leaning forward now, intent to catch every word that Johnny said.

"Go on," Magurn said. "You still ain't proved nothing."

"That's right," Johnny grinned innocently. "An insurance policy and a letter ain't enough to convict a man of murder."

"This is all a lot of hot air," Sheriff Honeywell broke in nervously. "This is supposed to be a trial of Ed French. Git outta that chair, Mason!"

"This trial was called to convict the murderer of John Law," Johnny corrected patiently. "And that's what it's doing."

"When the train leaves the loading pens a few miles out of town," Johnny went on, "everybody gets up and stretches and starts to get their suitcases and get ready to get off the train."

"What the devil has that got to do with it?" Judge Hook broke in explosively. "I think you're drunk, Mason. Out of a clear blue sky, you accuse Magurn of killing Law—then you talk about insurance policies and letters—and now you're babbling about train rides."

"I was just showing you how easy it would be," Johnny went on, "during all that hubbub, for a man to slip out of the coach, climb on top of the train, *and rope a man riding along the railroad tracks!*"

"John Law was drug to death—supposedly by his horse—but he was drug to death by a rope. Then Magurn and one of his men hauled the body to the top of the train, took the policy and letter out of his pockets, then let John Law drop again—and the rope, with cinders and blood on it, is in Magurn's office—"

Magurn came out of his chair shooting. Johnny launched himself out of the chair and fell flat, and while he was falling, he was shaking his wrist, shaking the deadly little derringer down into his hand. The courtroom rocked with concussion as Magurn's Colt spewed flame. Then the spiteful frack of the derringer seemed to shut off the roar of the Colt like a faucet turns off water.

Magurn wavered; he fumbled and tried to get the Colt up and line it on Johnny, but he couldn't. Like a man living a bad dream, he stared at the widening red spot on his shirt front—then collapsed.

"I think," said Johnny, "I got splinters in my belly."

Johnny was in his hotel room eating chicken when Dave Hollister came in.

"I won eighty-five dollars in a poker game from the lawyer that defended Ed French," Johnny declared belligerently. "So I ain't interested in going to work."

"Naw, naw, Johnny," Dave protested. "I wouldn't think of nothing like that. I just heard of a ranch for sale up near Tumbleweed—ever looked at any property in that part of the country? Fine country. We got a letter from a rancher up that way. Kinda funny case . . ."

THE END

For a gent who had only known peace at the flaming end of a six-gun, Buck Reynolds had a strange ambition. He wanted to grow flowers—on a worse man's coffin!

"I hope you got so good rope handy," B said conversationally. I won't have to sh you. . . . "

BY TH

By
**MURRAY
LEINSTER**

GUNS FORGOT

CHAPTER ONE
Long Trail Prodigal

When Buck Reynolds got off the railroad train at Animas, he was fresh from the penitentiary. He was still a small bow-legged man with wispy, sandy hair and an expression of truculent stubbornness. He limped a little from an old bullet wound.

As the locomotive with its bell-shaped smokestack went puffing out of Animas, he glared defiantly about the station platform. Nobody noticed him. Time was, of course, when plenty would have recognized him, but now nobody thought to look at him twice. The town went placidly about its business. It hadn't changed much. There was the old familiar smell of horses at the hitching-racks, cattle in the shipping pens, and alkali dust everywhere. Buck went stamping off in search of somebody who might still be his friend.

He had two errands to attend to before his plans for the future could be realized. The first errand would be to see Joe Davis's widow. That was going to be tough. Selma Davis had never willingly been the wife of an outlaw. She'd stuck to him, but she'd spoken her mind about his goings-on, and she'd never had any use whatever for Buck. But he wasn't going to her for approval—she simply had his few legitimate possessions in her care, and she would turn them over to him. Almost certainly, though, with a pungent lecture on his misdoings in the past and his probable future. And Buck was going to have to take it.

The second errand would be to locate the Deacon. He had to see Joe's widow first, because she had his guns. But after he'd bowed under her wrath and gotten them, he meant to strap on those old, well-suppled hoglegs and hunt up the Deacon. It was not only that the Deacon had shot him from behind and so caused him to fall into the hands of the law. Buck would always believe that he'd killed Joe at the same time. He could never hope to prove it, but he'd always believe it. And he meant to discuss that old treachery with the Deacon, letting his sixguns do the talking.

After that he proposed to settle down peacefully in the hideout he and Joe had found up in the Abogados hills, and let the world find its way to wherever it was going without him. He was of an age, now, when peace appealed to him. More, up in the penitentiary he'd become a gardener, and he envisioned a ten-acre paradise where he and Joe Davis had hidden rustled stock and

stolen horses of yore. It would blossom like the rose for the satisfaction of his declining years. But naturally he intended to take care
of the Deacon first.

Perhaps, he reflected hopefully, the Deacon still made use of the
hideout and would be found there. In such a case, the Deacon
would become the occupant of a private, well-gardened cemetery,
and of evenings Buck could smoke his pipe in happy contemplation
of the Deacon's headstone. He would carve it lovingly, with a
strictly accurate description of the Deacon's antecedents, character, and undoubted home in the hereafter.

He had planned a contented old age for himself, but first he had
to see Selma Davis and get his guns.

He stamped truculently down the main street of Animas, passed
the Buzzard's Roost Saloon, and sternly repressed his thirst. He
passed a general store that he and Joe had held up once, when
retribution was close on their trail and they had to have supplies for
a six-months' hole-up. He passed a saloon that he, alone, had shot
up extensively in celebration of some event that now had slipped
his mind. He remembered that the proprietor of the saloon had
dived out a back window, borrowed a shotgun and buckshot shells,
and come back with aides, and that he would have been shot up as
thoroughly as the saloon but for Joe's timely assistance. He remembered . . . .

His progress down the dusty, sun-baked street was a parade of
triumphant memories. But he was merely a runty, dried-up little
man with a limp, just out of the state penitentiary after serving his
term. He had no regrets, though, save that his partner Joe was no
longer on top of the ground. Joe'd been a partner! There weren't
such partners nowadays. Buck sniffed scornfully at the sight of two
young cowpunchers grinning at each other as they shook hands,
obviously after not having seen each other for a long time.

He went up the street and saw no single familiar face. He trudged
back down the street again and saw none but strangers. There were
resemblances to be noted, to be sure. There was a right pretty girl
riding a Circle Bar horse, and on examination Buck became convinced that she was Sally Henderson.

She had been a skinny, freckled kid of thirteen when she'd found
him trying to run off a small clump of her father's cattle and had
tried—weeping with fury—to destroy him utterly with a twenty-

gauge shotgun, fired over her saddle from two hundred yards. Buck vexedly conceded that he'd been away for a long time.

He saw Hung Lo, who ran a restaurant, and was shocked at the formerly lean Celestial's elderly fatness. And there was an old man—a deplorably old man—smoking on the porch of the Commercial House, and Buck stared at him half a dozen times before he was willing to admit that it was no other than the former sheriff who'd sent him off to prison. But he felt no animus. Any revenge he might have wished to take had been already taken by time. Still, he felt a certain uneasiness that something might have changed in him, too.

Then he saw Miguel Guttierez and was cheered. Miguel was fatter and his moustache was more luxuriant, but in other essentials he was unchanged. In times past he had served enthusiastically as watchdog and informer for Buck and his partner in their careers. He'd passed on word when the sheriff was out of town, when a payroll was apt to be due, and when the local citizens were losing patience and talking about organizing a posse to hunt down the two local outlaws, with time and money no object.

Miguel dozed in the sun. Buck Reynolds stalked up to him and regarded him truculently. His shadow fell upon Miguel.

Miguel opened his eyes and blinked, and said plaintively, *"Perdoname, señor, pero el sol—"* Then his mouth dropped open. *"Dios mio! Señor R-r-reynolds! Dios mio!"*

"Yeah," said Buck. "How about gettin' a jug o' *vino* an' settlin' down somewheres to tell me what's happened while I been gone?"

Miguel beamed. Then he spread out his hands expressively. Buck scowled, but produced money. Miguel took it and shuffled away at what was for him practically breakneck speed. He came back five minutes later with a huge bottle of home-made sour wine.

"Eef you honor my humble 'ome, *señor*," he suggested, "we weel talk."

His home was reached through an alley between two saloons. It was the same tumbledown shack. His wife, also, was fatter, but the number of children had—this was truly remarkable—decreased.

"Mis niños," explained Miguel, "they grow up, they marry, they go away. Now I 'ave only seven!"

"Yeah," said Buck. "What's happened while I been gone?"

Miguel filled two glasses. Holding one in his hand, he began a recital of events. So-and-so was dead. So-and-so had been shot.

So-and-so had left town. The Buzzard's Roost had changed hands. The new proprietor of the Sidewinder was reported to cut his whiskey. The Elite Place Dance-hall—

"What's happened to the Deacon?" demanded Buck.

Miguel beamed.

"Ah, the Señor Deacon!" he said happily. "He ees smart man! You remember w'en he rode weeth you and the Señor Joe? *Seturo!* He laid low for a long time after Señor Joe ees keeled and you go away. He ees smart man, the Señor Deacon! He has a hideout that no one knows. Two—three of hees friends leeve there. And he ees most respectable! Oh, so respectable! No one theenks he would ever do anytheeng not mos' respectable! He ees smart! He ees my friend, Señor Buck. One dollar, two dollars, sometimes five dollars he geeves me for what news I can tell heem!"

Buck snorted.

"But who's he ridin' with?" he demanded. "What's he pullin' off? Rustlin'?"

Miguel beamed again.

"Ah! Señor Deacon is discreet! He plans! He contrives! Leetle tricks like small holdups—ah—he plans them, but he takes no reesks. He orders them. Hees men do them. But he remains at home. Only the very beegest, the most important jobs does he ride on. And then always he has a good excuse, told in advance, for being away. Oh, but he ees one smart man!"

Buck Reynolds's eyes narrowed very slightly. Miguel was now serving the Deacon as he had served Buck and Joe—as spy and lookout. If he felt any loyalty of any sort, now it was to the Deacon. But he would talk quite openly to Buck, because nothing he told Buck would be believed against the Deacon. And Miguel would tell nothing specific, anyhow. He would simply be amiable and ingratiating to Buck until the Deacon had decided what was to be done about him. Even then, Miguel would be blandly neutral—and he would cheerfully make himself useful to Buck if the Deacon was put out of the way, or the other way about.

"That's like 'im," snorted Buck. "Settin' back an' lettin' other fellas do his dirty work an' take all the risks! Huh! One thing more. The Señor Joe's widder, Señora Davis. Wheah's she at an' how's she makin' out?"

"Shee ees here," said Miguel. "She runs an eating-house, Señor Buck. She ees veree proud, an' her tongue eet ees sharp! She resolved that none should remember that her husban'—how you say—died with hees boots on. So she taught her son Sam to be a vairy nice leetle boy."

There was an overtone of spite, of malice, in the last. Buck waited.

"Too nice," said Miguel zestfully. "Thee boy, 'e grew weary of being nice. He ees een jail now—at Camino. Hees mother does not yet know, because he gave a false name. She theenks he ees in Tucson. But he ees in Camino, waiting trial for rustleeng."

Buck scowled. Then he turned away.

"Camino, eh? A'right, Miguel."

Miguel said blandly, "When he ees tried, he weel be set free. The Señor Deacon weel testify that they were together at the time of the rustleeng, so of course eet weel seem a mistake. No one believes evil of the Señor Deacon."

Buck stared, hard.

"Yeah? The kid was rustlin' under his orders? So the Deacon gets him outa trouble, an' the kid figures that's the way it'll always be? So he'll go on rustlin' under the Deacon's orders?"

Miguel grinned.

"The Señor Deacon ees smart, no?"

"No!" snapped Buck. "He ain't! You're goin' to tell him all about talkin' to me—hell, don't lie, Miguel! I know you. When you tell the Deacon about me, tell him I know he shot me from behind, an' that he shot my partner Joe that time we was standin' off the posse. You tell him I've been waitin' to come back an' kill him! An' you tell him I'm heah an' he can go heeled, because I'm sure goin' to let him have it on sight."

Miguel blinked. Buck knew what was in his mind. Miguel considered that Buck had just committed suicide. Because, of course, with men who committed crimes under his orders, a murder wouldn't be much anyhow. And the murder of Buck, a known outlaw just out of the penitentiary, wouldn't count, anyhow. Anybody could claim Buck had tried to hold him up or murder him, and anybody would be believed . . . .

Buck's stubborn, truculent countenance darkened.

"Yeah!" he said grimly. "You tell 'im that. He'll get a lotta fun outa it. But he oughta have what fun he can—while he can."

He turned and stalked away toward the main street of Animas. Behind him, Miguel shrugged. Knowing what he did, he had thought it quite likely that the Deacon would have Buck killed anyhow. Now it was quite certain.

Miguel poured himself another glass of wine.

CHAPTER TWO
No Fare to Hell

Buck went to see his partner's widow. It was easy to find the place, once the clue had been given. He found the eating-place, immaculately painted and aggressively neat. There was a sign on the door, PLEASE WIPE YOUR FEET. Buck wiped his feet. He went in. The interior was dauntingly tidy. There was another sign, GENTLEMEN WILL REMOVE THEIR HATS. Buck removed his hat. He stood uneasily. There was no one in sight, but he felt himself sweating a little. Therefore he scowled angrily and rapped sharply on the counter.

A voice from somewhere said with asperity, "We serve dinner from twelve to two only. Supper is from six to eight. Please close the door as you go out."

Buck did not stir. After a moment there was a rustling, and Selma Davis, relict of his late partner, came through dimity curtains from the kitchen, her eyes snapping. They fell upon Buck, and her mouth opened to repeat the statement that she did not serve meals at any and all hours. Then she recognized Buck. Her mouth stayed open without a word coming out of it.

"Yes, ma'am," said Buck, and despite himself his tone was apologetic. "It's me."

"Well, I never!" said Joe's widow acidly. "Just out of jail and already come to bother respectable people!"

She regarded him with marked disapproval. It had been a long time, of course, and she no longer wept for Joe. She had adjusted herself to widowhood. But her disapproval of Buck had not lessened with the years.

"I knew," she said with acerbity, "that you were due to get out of jail, Buck Reynolds, and I thought it a pity. And I did think you'd have the gumption not to come bothering me. You want the things I've been keeping for you, don't you?"

"Yes, ma'am," said Buck, twisting his hat. It enraged him that he felt humble before this woman—it was not his fault that Joe had been an outlaw. It was not his fault that Joe had been killed—or that he had married her. Buck felt a bitter rebellion that Joe's widow was a sharp-tongued pillar of respectability—with a son in jail in Camino that she didn't know about.

"You could've sent for your things," said Joe's widow, indignantly, "instead of coming brazen-like after them. You ought to be ashamed of yourself, Buck Reynolds."

"Yes, ma'am," said Buck.

"Leading poor Joe astray," she said, bitingly, "and maybe coming here in hopes of leading his poor son along the same bitter path! I got your things out and ready. You can have them. But for goodness' sake don't ever come here again."

"No, ma'am," said Buck.

"I'll get 'em," she told him coldly. "Stand right where you are!"

She marched out, back through the dimity curtains. Buck seethed to himself. She returned with a bundle tightly— vengefully—tied up in brown paper.

"My son Sam," she told Buck sternly, "ain't here, if you thought to tell him stories about what a wild life his father had. He's a nice boy, and sooner or later I expect he'll marry that Sally Henderson whose father owns the Circle Bar. My friend Mr. Hamby gave him a letter to the proprietor of a big store in Tucson, and Sam's up there now getting a respectable job—maybe so he can get married on it. But all the same, the sooner you make yourself scarce around here, Mr. Buck Reynolds, the better it will be for you!"

Buck swallowed. So the Deacon was her friend. The Deacon who'd shot Buck from behind, had murdered Joe and had young Sam rustling for him already. The devil take all good women, Buck thought bitterly.

"I—uh—don't expec' to stay around long, ma'am."

Joe's widow tapped on the counter of her eating-place. Her eyes snapped.

"I know what you intend to do," she said acidly. "You intend to go up to that hideout you and Joe had. You intend to start up again with that hiding-place to keep you safe. But I've fixed that."

Buck stared at her. Other men had been afraid of him in days gone by, but she scared him. He said uneasily, "You fixed it, ma'am? Nobody but me an' Joe an' the Deac—you never knew where 'twas, Joe told me!"

"And I didn't—but I've found out!" Her tone was bitter triumph itself. "Looking up your things, because I knew you'd want them, I came on a map poor Joe had made. It was for his son Sam, and it showed just how to get to the hideout. There was a note with it that said in case anything happened to him, Sam could go up there and he might find something he'd want to keep. Guns, probably, or something else equally bad for a young boy to have!"

Buck said thickly, thinking of his partner, "More likely, ma'am, Joe meant there might be a few head o' cattle theah, or some horses that could be sold to—uh—kinda help you out, ma'am. There's good grazin' theah, an' anything that was left would stay in good shape. But—uh—"

The Deacon had known about the hideout, and Miguel said he had a perfect place to lay low in. His men were using it. There'd be no stock there now. Of course.

"It doesn't matter!" snapped Selma Davis triumphantly. "I found the map yesterday. I thought it over all day. So today I sent it to the sheriff at Camino in a registered letter, telling him he'd better look into it. If you intended to start outlawin' again with that hideout as your headquarters, you'd better not. The sheriff over in Camino knows all about it and how to find it!"

Buck picked up his bundle and stumbled out of the place.

Outside, he swore passionately. He did not swear at Joe's widow, of course, because Buck Reynolds did not swear at a lady even in her absence. But this was disaster! That hideout was to have been the scene of his retirement! It was a sinkhole in the Abogados, a collapsed cavern above an ancient underground stream. It was two hundred feet straight down in the ground, with ten acres of green grass and fresh water at the bottom. There was but one way to get to it, and nobody had known about it but Buck and Joe—and, later, the Deacon. It was a perfect hideout. It was security and peace and isolation and comfort. In the last fews years in the penitentiary, Buck had laid it out mentally as a small-sized paradise of gardening, with everything from green peas to his own tobacco growing in neat rows, and the adobe lean-to against the sinkhole wall a riot of blooming flowers. It had been the mainstay of all his dreams. He had planned to live there in utter tranquillity, the world forgetting and by the world forgot. But if the sheriff at Camino knew about it, he'd drop in every time a few head of cattle or some fancy horse flesh turned up missing. And of course, if Buck found the Deacon and talked things over with him through gunsmoke . . . .

Buck stamped down the street in impassioned despair. Deeply and bitterly he regretted that Joe had ever married a woman like Selma Davis. It was the one flaw in an otherwise perfect partner. And he swore luridly.

Then he stopped short. Joe's son Sam was in the Deacon's gang! His mother thought he was in Tucson, but he'd been riding the hills under the Deacon's directions—and his mother had told the sheriff where to find the hideout of her son's outlaw gang!

That topped everything. Buck flung his hat on the ground and just stopped himself from dancing a war-dance around it in utterly uninhibited fury. Then he saw a small Mexican boy grinning at him and almost had apoplexy from added fury. But then he calmed to a deadliness of mood such as he'd never known when he and Joe were partners.

He went into the Buzzard's Roost Saloon and ordered a beer. He'd been given a railroad ticket back home and a five-dollar bill. He had a dollar and a quarter left.

He got his beer and said with elaborate unconcern, "Uh—I used to hang around this town, years back." The bartender was a total stranger who could not possibly know him. " 'Used to be a fella name of Hamby around. They called him the Deacon. Is he still on hand?"

The bartender said, "Deacon Hamby? Sure! He's around! 'Ain't in town right now, though. He's off buyin' cattle for somebody up Nogales way."

Buck drank his beer and went out. So he couldn't settle with the Deacon! Fate and chance had it in for him. But there was Joe's son over in the Camino jail. And there was something else. . . .

He stalked back to the alley between two saloons leading to Miguel's house. He stalked into that tumbledown edifice. Miguel's fat wife was visibly alarmed at his return. Miguel, she said apprehensively, had gone to visit a sick cousin. Buck knew better. Miguel had gone to pass on the word that he was back in town and was hunting the Deacon to kill him.

He snorted and opened up his package just enough to glimpse his guns, wrapped in their inside-out cartridge belt. What he was after was the original wrapper, covered over and reinforced by the strong brown paper Joe's widow had put about it the day before. He tore off a big piece of that, and then, in Miguel's house, painstakingly, with a stub of pencil, he drew a map. It was, on the face of it, a map of the way to his and Joe's hideout. But anybody who tried to find the hideout by its means would be disappointed. He folded it and put it in his pocket, his expression of truculence intensified. He tied up his parcel again. Just to be on the safe side, since the Deacon wasn't in town, it was best for him not to be wearing guns in case somebody did recognize him as an old law-breaker.

He took a drink of the wine he'd had Miguel buy and made a disgusted face. Then he sat in dour silence in Miguel's house until near sundown. Then he marched down to the railroad station and to the station agent's window.

The agent was pounding a brass telegraph key at the moment, but he looked up inquiringly.

"When's the next train to Camino?" Buck demanded.

"Six-forty," said the agent. "Mail train. Two trains a day."

Buck retired. The freight shed was open. It was now late dusk. He strode truculently into the shed. There was nobody there. He unwrapped his parcel. He unrolled his gunbelt and slung it about his waist, reveling in the feel of the heavy holsters again bumping against his thighs. Expansively, he ran his thumbs along the cartridge-loops—and froze, incredulously. They were empty! Joe's widow had given him back his guns, but she'd thrown out the shells from the belt. He snatched out his guns and examined them furiously. They were empty, too. He raged.

The train-whistle hooted in the distance. There was a clattering of hoofs. Buck, peering out, saw a wagon of unfamiliar type come up to the station with a shotgun messenger beside the driver. It did not ease his wrath. Obviously a shipment of bullion from the stamp-mills at Charleston, routed through Animas, away out of routine. It looked like somebody had been holding up bullion shipments a bit too regularly, or maybe a new route was being tried, or maybe this had become the regular route. In any case—

It was deepest dusk now. The freight shed was a place of cavern-ous, odorous darkness. Away and away through the hills, the rhythmic *chuff-chuffing* of the engine became audible. Its whistle hooted again—a long, sustained wailing which echoed and re-echoed among the hills. The engine headlight winked into view and out again. Buck almost burst with rage in the freight shed, surrounded by the smells of baled hay and barreled whiskey and soft pine shipping cases, with that other scent of engine oil which is inseparable from railroad stations.

Men gathered about the guarded wagon. Then one man strolled past the shed door. Buck Reynolds pounced. A gun jammed into the cowpuncher's ribs.

"Step thisaway," snarled Buck under his breath, "or you' goin' to talk to Saint Peter!"

The cowhand gulped. Buck's free hand found his shoulder, and he guided his victim into the darkness. His empty gun rose and fell with an infuriated precision. The cowboy crumpled.

The train *chuffed* more loudly, and then its noise dwindled as it passed between intervening hills. It was night. The noises of Animas were clear between the puffings of the engine. A piano in a dance-hall. Somebody whooping joyously as he rode into town for a night's festivity. The stamping of horses' hoofs. Now and again the squeaking of harness about the guarded wagon.

There were small clickings in the freight shed where Buck Reynolds swore balefully in a subdued voice over the obstacles to his planned future of peace and quiet. The distant headlight of the train winked on and off and suddenly appeared, seemingly very near, and shining as brightly as the brightest oil lamp before the most highly polished reflector could shine. The train itself appeared as a row of dimly lighted windows down the track.

Buck stalked out. His guns were slung at his side. The loops of his cartridge-belt were filled. He scowled at the train as it roared grandly into the station, its high-waisted cow-catcher the last word in locomotive grandeur, its funneled smokestack belching sparks, its polished brass-work and red and gilt nameplate impressive even by the feeble lamps of the station. It halted with a splendid outpouring of steam. There was a locomotive and a mail-and-express car, and no less than three palatial passenger coaches on behind.

Leaning dourly against the station wall, Buck looked into the plush and mahogany interiors of the coaches. He saw the elaborate swinging oil lamps with which the coaches were lighted. He even saw the rotund polished stove in each. He saw the passengers—cattlemen, miners, celluloid-collared travelers, screening their eyes with their fingers to gaze at the little cow-town through the darkness.

There was swift, orderly confusion up by the express car. Men loaded very heavy, very small, very strong boxes into the car. It was unquestionably a bullion shipment, and a big one. Then mail-bags went aboard. The clerk signed receipts while Buck glowered at the scene. He had exactly a dollar in his pocket. His old partner's son was in the Camino jail, and this train would carry a complete divulgement of the best hideout in the world to the sheriff in Camino. He had no horse. He had no friends. He had just committed assault and robbery, which could send him to jail for the rest of his life as an old offender. And presently he would be hunted by various gunmen, bent upon killing him before he could get at the Deacon. Perhaps his old partner's son would be assigned the job of killing him. . . .

The mail-coach door slid shut. The train bell clanged resonantly. The whistle howled. With a monstrous, deliberate *chuffing* the train rolled out of the station.

Buck waited until two coaches had passed him by. He stood by the bay window from which the station agent at the telegraph key could look up and down the line. There was a smoky oil lamp with a reflector casting a bright light on the telegraph table.

Buck poked the muzzle of one of his guns through the window. The sound of the train drowned out the tinkle of broken glass. He shot twice. The telegraph instrument was wreckage. Then he ran across the platform, swung on the steps of the very last car and put the palm of his hand in the face of the conductor, who, lantern swinging, essayed also to board the last coach in the time-honored fashion of train-conductors.

It all happened fast. The conductor went rolling over the cinders of the platform. His lantern bounced crazily. The train went roaring magnificently off into the night, its *chuffings* thunderous and its whistle hooting, so that the startled outcry from the men about the station went unheard.

Buck Reynolds opened the door of the last coach and stepped inside. His expression was defiant and challenging. The lights of Animas dwindled and went out, behind. The train traveled on, wheels clanking loudly over rail joints, the coaches swaying, the opal-globed lamps swinging dizzily, the air in its coaches filled with the mingled smells of engine smoke, oil lamp fumes, patchouli, bergamot, dusty plush and chewing tobacco.

The engine whistled valorously—*Whir-r-r-rooo-o-o-o!*

Buck, his hands on his gun butts, stalked down the aisle.

CHAPTER THREE
By the Guns Forgot

The point was, of course, that it was all completely unexpected. And Buck, truculent as he appeared, was no flamboyant figure with a bandana mask and bellowing voice, such as most people associate with violence. He went through the last coach. He grimly wrenched open its front door, and grimly closed it behind him, and marched across the bumping platforms between the cars, and wrenched open the door of the second coach. He looked like a passenger taken on board at Animas. He traversed the second coach, and automatically swerved to keep from brushing against the billowing ostrich plumes on the hat of a bedizened lady passenger. He went through the third coach and out its front door.

The train was not two minutes out of Animas when he banged on the door of the mail-and-express car, after trying its handle and finding it locked. As it is not normal for violence to be attempted within two minutes after a train leaves a station, the mail clerk naturally assumed that the knocking was the conductor with some last-minute information or an order picked up at the station left behind. He opened the door.

Buck pushed in, put a sixgun in the clerk's ribs. He closed the door behind him and locked it. There was not much light in the car—only a single tin-shaded lamp over the sorting rack where the clerk separated mail received en route. There was a desk, on which bills of lading and similar papers were spiked on a sharpened nail. There were boxes and bales and stacks of corrugated iron sheets and rolls of tarpaper. And half a dozen bags of mail.

The mail clerk gasped, "Hey! You—you don't know what you're doin'!"

Buck prodded him on.

"I got me an idea," said Buck. "Get up theah by the light!"

He backed his captive half the length of the swaying car. Here, so close to the engine, the swayings were wild and the puffings loud indeed, but even the engine's chuffings were minor sounds compared to the roaring noise of the wheels on the rails, the thunderous clanking of rail-joints, and the squeakings and bumpings of loose objects here and there.

"I hope you got some good rope handy," Buck said conversationally, "so's I can tie you up instead of havin' to shoot you."

"I—" The clerk stared at him, terrified. "I—hey! You're Buck Reynolds!"

Buck pressed the gun muzzle closer.

"You guessed right the first time," he said harshly. "So y'll know I ain't foolin'! Wheah's y'rope—"

The clerk suddenly grinned. He was ashen in the flickering light of the oil lamp, and his grin was distinctly shaky, but it was a grin.

"L-listen!" he said, and swallowed. "You used to ride with Deacon Hamby."

"He rid with me," said Buck, his face hard.

"Th-that's right," panted the clerk urgently. "Well—listen! He's going to hold up this train tonight!"

Buck almost rocked back on his heels—or maybe it was a lurching of the car. After an instant he licked his lips.

"Maybe. Interestin', if true. I'm goin' to tie you up first, an' then you can talk."

The clerk continued to grin, as shakily as before.

"You—you don't want to run up against the Deacon's gang! That's the bullion from the Blue Bird in those boxes. The Deacon and some of his gang are going to hold us up over by Yucca Pass. You—you're a friend of his. You'd better throw in with him instead of trying a lone holdup. The whole train crew's in on this!"

"I'll think it over," said Buck grimly. "Wheah's y'rope?"

The clerk trembled. Buck's face was not reassuring in the lamplight.

"L-listen! The Deacon's got everything fixed. You want to throw in with him—he's got the best hideout in the world—"

"Just for y'information," Buck said sardonically, "I only wanted to get a free ride to Camino, not havin' money to pay my fare."

He had left the clerk where he could not possibly see what went on at his desk and sat down comfortably to examine the mail. There was one parcel of registered mail from Animas, of three envelopes only. He slipped one out of the string around them. It was addressed to the sheriff at Camino.

"As far as the Deacon's concerned," he observed detachedly to the clerk who could not watch him, "I just got outa the penitentiary. I aim to have peace an' quiet. I'm goin' to raise flowers an' vegetables. I'm retired from outlawin'. Why should I get mixed up in a holdup? I aim to be law-abidin' from now on."

The envelope in his hand was the one Joe Davis's widow had mailed to the sheriff in Camino. Buck delicately licked the outside of the adhesive flap, held the wetted envelope above the lamp-chimney. The heat of the flame turned the moisture to steam. The flap peeled back. Buck carefully drew out the map his partner had made for his son and looked at it. It was close enough to the one he'd drawn.

He took out the map he'd made and slid it into the envelope. He pressed down the flap until it adhered. He slid the envelope back with the two other registered letters under their string. Then he touched a match to the original map and held it until it scorched his fingers. He stamped the ashes on the floor with a vast satisfaction.

He considered the possibility of throwing a monkey wrench into the Deacon's comprehensive plans. He could recruit a posse, perhaps, from the passengers—if they'd believe him. But the mail clerk, bound, would not be likely to inspire confidence. The rest of the crew would not cooperate. Even if he forced them to drive on through the block the Deacon would have ready, there'd be that affair at Animas to turn up afterward. A cowhand gun-whipped into unconsciousness and the telegraph instrument smashed, the forcible removal of the train-conductor from the schemes of things—no, an old-time outlaw could not turn into the hero of an attempted train-robbery in the space of hours. And there was Joe's son in the jail at Camino.

"It looks to me," Buck told the clerk acidly, "like I got to think about my skin. I think, fella, I'm goin' to get ready for company."

He set to work to shift freight. The train roared and rumbled on. It swayed and lurched and bounced and rattled. It squeaked and groaned and boomed and bumped. In the express car, Buck staggered as he shifted the express parcels and freight according to his notions of strategy.

The train went on through the night. Back in the passenger coaches, a gentleman dressed so elaborately that he must be a gambler made tentative advances to a lady so vividly tinted that her acceptance of his overtures was not surprising. A cowman slept heavily in his seat. A miner dozed. A woman with a small child in her arms seemed to be singing softly to it, though no sound could be heard. Only her lips moved, absorbedly. The train lamps swung and smoked and flickered, and the windows made shuddering noises, and outside there was only darkness. Only black night, with no lights of houses anywhere, and only the varying echoes of the train—now hollow and thunderous, now flat but still loud—to tell that sometimes it rolled over open range, and now and again through a more or less shallow cut.

At long last Buck mopped his forehead and sat down again. He saw the bound feet of the mail clerk beating a frantic tattoo on the floor. He'd paid no attention to his captive's voice over the noise of the train. He rolled the man over.

"What's on y'mind now?"

"We—we must be almost there!" gasped the clerk. "Buck—don't let the Deacon think I double-crossed him. He'll kill me—"

"Not much loss," grunted Buck, "but I'll set you up wheah you can explain things to him."

He hauled the clerk upright. He seated him in the anchored swinging chair at the desk. He tied him there. And then he pulled the cork from the clerk's ink-bottle and shoved it into the helpless man's mouth.

"Jest so you don't start too soon, I'm corkin' your mouth," he observed grimly. "If you spit out that cork, you get plugged!"

Then he sat at ease and rolled himself a smoke. The car was filled with smells and noises. The lamp smell mingled with the odor of dust, and all the present contents and many past cargoes contributed individual accents to the atmosphere. Buck smoked placidly, his eyes roving idly. Twice they went sharply to his captive as that individual made violent facial contortions around the ink-soaked cork. The movement of Buck's hand toward his gun butt seemed remarkably soothing.

The engine's whistle howled a banshee wail. There was a violent screaming of brakes and a monstrous series of crashes as the passenger coaches bumped and rebounded against their couplings, and the whole train screamed to a halt.

For perhaps a second after it was still, there was silence, then guns went off in rapid succession outside, on either side of the train. Men beside the track were shooting along the line of coaches to keep the passengers in. There were piercing yells.

Somebody swung up behind the express car. There was a rattling of the link-pin and coupling. A bellow announced achievement.

Buck turned baleful eyes upon his prisoner, who seemed about to strangle on the inky cork. He continued to sit at ease. Shouts and a shot came from the direction of the engine—for effect only, for there wasn't further commotion.

The train jerked into motion again. It picked up speed quickly. There were now only the locomotive and its tender and the mail-and-express car—the truncated train went racketing away through the darkness.

Buck listened carefully to the pounding on the door in the back, where the robbers wanted to be let in.

"Wheah'll the wagon be waitin' for the bullion?" he asked the clerk grimly. "No—keep that cork in y'mouth! How far? Ten miles? Twenty?"

He could almost guess the answer, knowing the location of the hideout to which the booty would be taken. The clerk nodded desperately at the word "twenty." Buck rose.

"You set quiet," he commanded. "An' you better still have that cork in y'mouth when I step back this way!"

He went to the front of the car. He had labored earnestly to pile as much as possible of the car's contents against the back door. Nobody could get in that way, but even with the engineer and fireman in the plot it was likely that at least one outlaw would be riding in the engine cab.

Buck opened the front door suddenly, gun ready, but the platform there was empty. He saw the blank wall of the tender before him and sparks shooting from the smokestack ahead. He heard the whistling of wind and the clanking of rail-joints and the monstrous puffings of the locomotive. The swayings here were wild and violent.

He climbed the short ladder to the back of the tender. The engineer and fireman were alone. They grinned excitedly to each other, shouting occasional exuberant comments above the train noise.

When Buck appeared suddenly behind them, they jumped. Then they grinned at him, thinking him one of the outlaw gang.

"How's it goin'?" bellowed the engineer. "Everything all right?"

Buck poked with his gun.

"Everything's all wrong," he said grimly. "Slow up—you're goin' to jump."

He meant it. They saw that he meant it. They looked sick with fear. Their logic would be that the Deacon would save money if they were killed. He wouldn't have to divide with them. . . .

The engineer jumped first. The fireman, with a gasp, jumped instantly thereafter. And Buck looked deliberately around the cab, found the throttle, and pulled it a little wider open.

For safety's sake he opened the furnace door and heaved in fuel. There was no point in watching out along the line. If anything went wrong there, there was nothing he could do about it. The train racketed on through the night. On the express car's back platform, men pounded at the door until fury overtook them. Buck kept an eye on the car roof, counting accurately on the sparks from the smokestacks to give him light to see by. Presently he saw a man crawling fearfully along the top. It was not a comfortable spot, with the car swaying crazily on badly laid rails and nothing to cling to.

Buck opened fire. What with the noise it took three shots to make that man realize that he was being shot at. The other turned around precariously and crawled back. Buck beamed. He opened the furnace door and heaved in more fuel. There was a cord hanging close by the engineer's seat. It ran forward over the boiler. He pulled it, and a satisfying, earth-shaking bellow came from the whistle.

Five minutes. Ten—fifteen. There would be argument behind the express car. On the narrow, rocking platform, those who had officially held up this train would be debating frenziedly what could be wrong—the door of the car barricaded, and someone shooting from the cab. Presently another man essayed to crawl forward. Buck drove him back, too, with bullets.

A fire appeared beside the track. The train roared toward it. The whistle bellowed in an exotic sequence of short and long hootings, suggesting derision. The locomotive thundered up to the welcoming figures by the fire, where a wagon waited hopefully for the train's cargo of treasure, its sides illuminated by the fire. The train hurtled on, its whistle howling in a humorous greeting and farewell. The fire was left behind. There was again only the night beneath the stars.

But as the miles sped by, the outlaws on the back platform grew desperate. They hadn't the least idea of the actual situation, beyond a profound conviction that they had been betrayed. But they knew they had either to get into a more favorable position than their present one, or jump from the racing train.

The roof of the express car wasn't practical with bullets sweeping it. They attacked the door. Bullets smashed its lock. Gun butts broke in its panels. Brute strength wrenched the frame loose, in fragments. And then they began to smash their way through the barricade Buck had piled against it.

When they crawled, sixguns in hand, through the last smashed box to bar their way, they saw the mail clerk sitting in his chair in the light of his desk-light, swathed in rope like a mummy. Like a mummy's, too, was his drawn, white, panic-filled face. Deacon Hamby advanced upon him while the other three savagely scouted the rest of the interior of the car. They saw the bullion boxes, but hardly noticed them. Their own getaway was the important thing now.

The mail clerk babbled unintelligibly. Buck had crawled to the back of the tender to watch. He let the Deacon shoot his confederate in cold blood. When he roared at his followers to storm the tender, Buck beat a retreat. The cab would permit him steadier aim, and he had no bullets to waste.

They swarmed over the back of the tender with their guns ready. A bullet knocked Buck's hat askew. Four men came plunging down the heaped-up fuel, and were partly blinded by the glare of the open furnace door. Buck shot very grimly and very savagely, making sure to wait that last fifth of a second before pulling the trigger, so that he wouldn't miss.

He didn't. Lead spattered all around him. Something burned his hip. But he got the first man almost at the back of the tender. He got a second a little nearer. The third man was halfway toward him, squinting agonizedly and spraying lead at random.

Buck's old sixgun almost touched the Deacon when he pulled the trigger.

When he looked up grimly from the carnage he had wrought, the lights of Camino were winking into view on the horizon. He threw in more fuel. He opened the throttle. He tied down the whistle-cord. He sent the locomotive hurtling into the town, bellowing as no train should bellow on any normal occasion. He flashed past the station, cut off steam so the train would come to a stop a quarter mile past

the signal lights, and slipped off and into the darkness before it had
ceased to roll.

Nobody ever understood it. Nobody ever figured it all out. The
train had obviously been held up. The passengers told about that
later, and there was plenty of evidence to boot. But it had arrived in
Camino with its bullion untouched, its mail clerk bound in his chair
and then shot dead, the car door smashed in—and four dead men in
the engine-cab and tender.

Three of them were well-known outlaws. The fourth was that
highly respectable citizen, Deacon Hambly. It looked like he'd
been with the outlaws, not against them. But nobody was ever
sure, because nobody ever really knew who'd done the shooting.
The engineer and fireman, picked up later, protested abysmal ignorance about everything. Suggestions that Buck Reynolds was
responsible were pooh-poohed. He was an outlaw himself, and had
been so broke that he'd had to rob a cowpuncher of shells for his
guns—he couldn't have had a gang working with him. It was
generally assumed that Buck slipped out of the passenger coaches
and skipped when they were detached from the engine. He'd
figured to run out, no matter what his share in the doings, and a
man who runs doesn't slaughter four hard-cases, provided Deacon
had dealt himself a hand with outlaws.

Half an hour after his arrival in Camino, Buck said peevishly to a
startled young man skulking beside him behind a closed-up general
store, "I got you outa jail, didn't I? You hush up—no, the Deacon
didn't send me. I stuck up the jailer an' gun-whipped 'im to sleep
on my own account. Your pa used to be my partner an' I done it for
him. Now you let me handle this! I'll get us a coupla horses in a
minute, but first I got to get in heah—"

He broke into the general store rather quietly, considering he
was a little out of practice and in a hurry, and fifteen minutes later
came out stuffing small envelopes in his pockets. He led Joe
Davis's son away from that neighborhood, expertly stole two saddled horses, and the two of them rode out of town within the hour.

Then, until dawn, Buck Reynolds spoke pungently to the son of
his partner. He pointed out the certainty that his mother would
learn of his evil-doing if he persisted in it, and he pointed to his own
term in the penitentiary as a further deterrent.

"Besides which," he said acidly, as the first rays of the sun appeared to eastward, "besides which, outa respect for your pa who was the best partner a man ever had, if I ever heah of you stealin' as much as a yellow dawg in the future, I'll come an' tend to you!"

Young Sam Davis was chastened by then. News that he had served his father's murderer and had depended on him for his own safety was humiliation past repair. With the Deacon dead, too, he could not even make a grand gesture of revenge. About all he could do was go to Tucson and try to get a job in a store there, or maybe—well—maybe he'd better go back to Animas and go to work on the Circle Bar. At least, if he did that, he'd see Sally Henderson sometimes. . . .

Buck saw that he was subdued when they parted. So subdued, in fact, that he felt it wise to give him sage advice about how to get rid of the stolen horse the boy was riding.

"Bury th' saddle," he advised, "an' turn th' critter loose. Walk a few miles home, thinkin' over what you're goin' to tell your ma, meanwhile. An' when she tells you I'm a scoundrel, you agree with her."

He waved his hand and rode away. He was out of sight in half a mile. And he was perfectly happy. He was out of the penitentiary, he had settled with the Deacon, and he was on his way to the hideout he and Joe Davis had known. His pockets were stuffed with assorted packets of seeds for gardening—taken from the general store in Camino—and he looked forward to long years of perfect peace, with ten acres to turn into a garden in his retirement, and with nobody to bother him.

Unless, of course, he had to kill one or two of the Deacon's gang who might have been let into the secret of the hideout's location.

THE END

DEADMAN'S
DERRINGERS

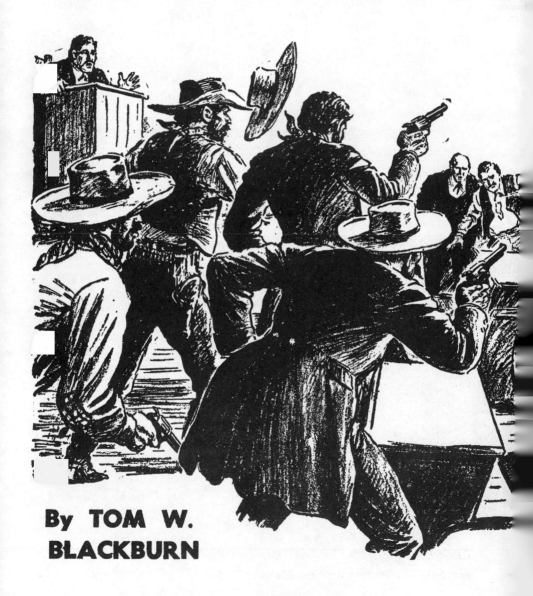

By TOM W.
BLACKBURN

A drum roll of
thunder echoed
in the hall.

Trigger-Fast
Chris Defever Novelette

Chris Defever, actor and derringer artist, played his greatest role — impersonating his own mourned and honored corpse.

CHAPTER ONE
Defever—Deceased

It had been a curious chain of circumstances. To the honorable Christian Defever—ex-actor, legislator extraordinary, and champion of the people—it made no sense. Crouched shivering in a culvert under the rails of the Julesburg-to-Grass City cut-off of the lusty young Union Pacific Railroad, with all of the cold wind in Wyoming howling down across the border of the Longbow State and through his threadbare and badly used coat, Defever stared at the crumpled newspaper in his hand. One outstanding fact had to be grasped first—accepted *prima facie* on the evidence of the *Grass City News*—Christian Defever was dead.

The newspaper said that Senator Christian Defever—long a colorful, familiar Capitol figure and affectionately known for his fearless attacks upon the vested interests which threatened the rights of the common man—had gone to his great reward. Chris Defever was taking a well-earned rest. He had expired. And a wide black border of mourning around the announcement gave it an exceptionally official appearance.

Having accepted this, there remained next to consider how this public tragedy had occurred. Chris was very hazy on this point. He had been on a fishing excursion with a judge, a saloonkeeper, a retired teamster, a mining magnate, and the editor of this very paper—all solid citizens and reputable men. As was usually true on such an excursion, fishing had been indifferent, but conviviality had been of the highest order. In fact, Chris suspected he had himself been rather generously inebriated, which perhaps now contributed to the haziness of his recollections.

They had driven down from the mountains in a buckboard on the homeward trip, intending to connect with the Grass City Express at Big Creek. However, certain delays had occurred, and the Express had gone on when they arrived. Chris recalled he had promised to find certain Union Pacific men in the Big Creek yards who would be most happy to make up a special train to carry so distinguished a party on to the Capitol. He recalled, also, that the Union Pacific men had been hard to find in the yard—and the night had been cold. An open box-car had offered a chance to briefly warm himself.

There were but three other recollections. He had carelessly dozed and awakened to find the car in which he lay was in motion.

He had found the car had another occupant—a large-bodied and truculent knight of the gleaming rails, who immediately developed a yen for Defever's sporting finery and a very forceful left hook which rapidly induced an exchange of clothing. The last recollection was of a sudden and terrible upheaval of noise and rolling stock which catapulted Chris through the open car door.

He had no more than a fleeting glimpse of the entire train writhing with the impact of derailment before he crashed heavily to earth in a roadside thicket with a force which completely blacked out his already uncertain consciousness.

This was all quite plain and substantiated by the newspaper account Chris now clutched. On the surface, it was all very simple. In this accident, the man wearing the Honorable Christian Defever's clothes had been killed in so thorough a fashion that his clothing was the sole means of identifying him. The assumption that Chris Defever was dead was therefore quite natural.

What plagued Chris was why he had hidden himself from those salvaging the wrecked train. Through much soul searching, he believed he had arrived at an answer. And that answer stunned him.

This was escape. This was freedom to rove. This was opportunity to again follow his large and inquisitive nose freely across the fair breadth of the land, looking to the welfare of none but Christian Defever. This was surcease from the burden of public weal heaped upon him by the constituency of Grass City, which had elected him to office in the Assembly. The gods who watched over men of the theatre, boomers, and like charlatans had at long last been kind.

Smiling, Chris crumpled the newspaper. Come night, he would move, by stealth and with care. There was a small cache of coin in his rooms at the Palace Hotel. He would return to Grass City and secure this. And then he would vanish. Chris Defever had long enough lived a life of political sainthood. He desired the lustier life he had once known—freedom to consort with the devil when a consorting mood was upon him. For once, death would have no sting.

The Palace Hotel in Grass City had an imposing facade and truly magnificent bronze doors, wholly befitting the most elegant hostelry west of the Missouri. Chris Defever had often passed through these portals on his way to his quarters, lordly in mein and well aware of the adulation of hired lackeys and idling populace alike. It now irked him considerably to slink up the alley behind the Palace like a hungry cur and stealthily try the narrow, unpainted service door. He was irked further to discover this was locked against night prowlers. Cursing irritably, he found the bottom of the fire-escape ladder and began a laborious climb.

Pausing for breath at the third-floor landing, Chris glanced above and saw that the windows of his quarters were ablaze with light. He ascended the last flight of the fire-escape with more caution and worked along the narrow iron grating of the landing until he could flatten himself against the wall beside the window which gave into his bed-chamber.

A number of men were idling in his room, coatless and sprawled on the furniture. Most noteworthy of them was a tall, gangling, impossibly assembled caricature of a man with long, weak, whiskey-debauched features. A veritable scarecrow of a fellow in build. It was with consternation that Chris presently noted that the man was wearing one of his own best suits and that the garment fitted him perfectly.

Knowing none of these characters and especially disliking the long-faced gutter-scum who had donned his apparel, Chris bent to lift the window and evict the lot of them. He but barely remembered his recent death in time. There was little he could do toward securing the supply of coin cached in an old shoe in his wardrobe until the room emptied.

He settled himself for a wait, only to have his attention drawn to voices coming from the open window of the adjoining sitting room of Chris's suite. This window was beyond reach of the fire-escape grid. Chris could not see into the sitting room, but he recognized the high-pitched voice of Angus McDowell, who had been politically Defever's staunchest friend, although there had been certain personal differences of opinion.

"But I tell you, we buried the Senator this afternoon with due respect and mourning. I, myself, viewed his shrouded body!" McDowell's bleat was patently a shocked protest.

"Mistaken identity," another voice answered. "Here's the facts. Senator Defever was set upon by thugs in the Big Creek railroad yards. He dressed well, if you remember. One of the thugs exchanged clothing with him. Unconscious and now dressed in the thug's rags, the Senator was tossed into a box-car. Later the thug in the Senator's clothing climbed a car in the same train. In the wreck, this thug was killed. His body was so disfigured identification was possible only by the clothes he wore. That's where the mistake was made. You buried a freight-car bum, McDowell!''

"But the Senator—where is the Senator, then?''

"I'm coming to that,'' the other man said easily. ''He escaped the wreck with severe facial wounds and in a dazed condition. He wandered to a farmer's house—we can produce the farmer. Not knowing the Senator's identity, the farmer called in a local doctor—we can produce the doctor.''

"But where is Defever now? If he's alive I've got to see him!''

"He's alive, all right,'' the other man answered. ''But this farmer and this doctor, now that they've learned who he is, expect a reward for treating his wounds and saving his life. The Senator has no money—''

"Wait a minute—'' McDowell's voice cannily dropped two octaves. ''This smells, Breen! The day before the Assembly recessed, Defever denounced you on the floor as a political blackleg, an organizer of unwanted elements in the city and the state. You haven't got Chris Defever; what you've got is an idea. This is a shakedown, and a clumsy one!''

Chris, listening on the fire-escape, grinned a grudging tribute to Angus McDowell's astuteness. So he was talking to Lefty Breen. Reviving a dead man was about Breen's calibre of a trick.

"The Senator's condition is still grave, McDowell,'' Breen said slowly, after a moment. ''Two doctors are in constant attendance on him. Moving him has exhausted him. But you've got me all wrong. The Senator maybe didn't understand me politically, but actually we've been on the same side of the fence all along. I've always admired him, and I've done everything I could for him since I discovered he survived that accident. You've got to believe me. I'm going to risk letting you see him, but you're not to talk to him now—not to ask him any questions. In a day or two, perhaps, but not now—''

There was a sound of assent. Chris turned and looked through the window of his bedroom. He saw the bedroom door open. Lefty Breen, done out in the vulgar finery of a riverfront saloonman, ducked into the room and closed the door behind him. He spoke tersely to the long man in Defever's clothes:

"The fool's got to be shown. Get out of that coat and those shoes, Louie, and flop on the bed. Ed, get into your white jacket—get the bandages on, quick. Put your glasses on your nose, Phil. You're another doctor. I've called you in from St. Louis. The rest of you edge out into the hall and beat it for a while."

The room was immediately plunged into action. The rotund man called Ed put on a white medical jacket which immediately transformed him into a fair example of a bumbling doctor. Using a length of muslin, he commenced winding a mummy wrapping onto the long face of Louie, the man in Chris Defever's clothes. The one called Phil clumsily clamped a pair of pince-nez glasses across his broken nose and assumed a stupidly thoughtful expression. The rest of those idling in the bedroom slid noiselessly out into the hall. Satisfied, Lefty Breen opened the door into the sitting room.

Angus McDowell appeared in the opening, a sickening look of concern on his face. He stared at the long figure in Chris Defever's breeches, lying on Chris Defever's bed. McDowell's eyes rounded incredulously. After a moment he backed out of sight into the sitting room. Breen followed him and closed the door. Their voices from the sitting room reached Chris easily.

"It is him!" McDowell breathed. "It's Defever, all right. Look, Breen, maybe we've all been a little rough on those saloon and dance-hall permits you wanted. Maybe you'd run the right kind of places, after all. You could have left Defever where he was. Maybe he really would have died. That would have suited you, after the treatment you got from the Assembly and from him."

"It might look that way," Breen agreed smoothly. "But before we brought him into town, the Senator was strong enough to trade notes back and forth with me a few times. He can't talk yet on account of the stitches in his face. We got the air *all* cleared. Glad to help him all I could. Sort of a public duty, you know—"

On the balcony, Chris retched at Breen's sugary saintliness.

Breen went on: "Wish I could carry the load of his expenses myself—"

"How much does Defever need?" McDowell asked cautiously.

"A thousand for care and fifteen hundred for the operations on his face—so far," Breen said.

"Twenty-five hundred!" McDowell choked. "Hell, his face never was worth half that—" He checked himself. "I'll see what I can do."

"In cash, here, before midnight," Breen urged smoothly. "The upstate doctor wants to hit for home tonight, and I've already got a better man out from St. Louis.''

"I'll try," McDowell repeated, anguish at the thought of the expenditure of that much money very evident in his voice.

Chris sat down on the fire-escape. He considered Breen's scheme from all sides. Rather neatly turned for a man not accustomed to the finer shades of skull-duggery. And fortunate from Defever's own standpoint. Chris had already discovered that the shoes which the bandaged imposter on his bed was wearing were those in which he had cached his gold. This small traveling fund was obviously already in alien hands and unavailable. It seemed likely wise to wait for Angus McDowell to deliver the twenty-five hundred dollars demanded by Lefty Breen. These were funds earmarked for the expenses of Senator Christian Defever. What could be more just than that Christian Defever, *Deceased,* should have them?

Despite the hunger in his belly and the discomfiture of sitting upon a slatted iron grating for some hours, Chris grinned contentedly.

CHAPTER TWO
Cavorting Cadavers

Shortly after Angus McDowell's departure, Lefty Breen's entire force returned to Defever's suite. Chris winced when he heard Breen order the elegant dinner and quantities of drink served to them charged to Defever's account at the hotel. Quite a big night seemed to be in the making—which in turn meant that Chris was in for a long wait before he could secure Angus McDowell's contribution to his welfare.

As the chilly hour of midnight approached, Chris was in increasing danger of sneezing explosively on the fire-escape. Lefty Breen and his companions made assorted wassail. Defever's impostor, in particular, turned out to be a notable bottle man whose courage and aggressiveness increased amazingly as he drank. He had knocked the bogus doctor from St. Louis into a corner and loosened three teeth in another companion's lip, as well as given Breen a deal of truculent talk—before a knock sounded on the door of the outer room.

Quieting his companions, pulling himself together, Breen left the bedroom and went into the sitting room to answer the summons. Chris then heard McDowell's voice coming from the sitting room, pleading for another look at Chris Defever before he parted with the money he had brought. Breen turned him away with the promise that the Senator would appear on the floor of the Assembly when it re-convened. The Senator would be in bandages, of course, and not speak—but he could write his messages to his fellow legislators and they could be read.

McDowell left the hotel.

Chris scowled at this information. He was beginning to see that Breen's hoax had been aimed not only at swindling Angus McDowell out of a sum of money, but also at securing Breen a voice in the Assembly. A scheme which might well besmirch the fine name Christian Defever had built for himself in this lusty new commonwealth. A pox upon the fellow!

With McDowell's money in his pocket, Breen's conviviality vanished. Abruptly he ushered the majority of his company from Defever's suite. When only the fake senator and himself remained, Breen jerked a rolled-up pallet out of a closet, kicked it flat on the floor, and ordered the imposter to sleep on it.

The fellow growled surlily. After all, he was impersonating this old goat Defever. He should sure as hell have the bed.

"Louis," Breen answered quietly, "you better not give me trouble. You got a lot of brave-maker in your belly. That's all. This is my party, and I'm steering it. If you want your cut, you be good!"

Breen snuffed the lamp and stretched on the thick bed. Louie folded up awkwardly on the pallet, cursing softly. Chris rose on the grating outside the window and flexed long-cramped muscles. Odds-blood, if he didn't soon get a meal into him!

Waiting grew intolerable. Chris could hear no sound from Louie. But Breen, after a few experimental turns on the bed, began to snore heavily. Chris placed long fingers against the sliding frame of the partially lifted window and slid it noiselessly on upward.

Breen had removed his boots and his coat. He slept, to the best of Defever's knowledge, in shirt and pants. And in the hip pocket of the pants, encased in a worn wallet, were the bills which McDowell had brought back to the hotel.

Chris slid his long frame carefully through the window and crossed the floor soundlessly. Breen lay on his back, fully upon the pocket Chris wanted. His stockinged feet offered a solution. Creeping around the foot of the bed, Chris touched the sole of one foot with a long finger, rasping gently along it. Breen stirred restlessly, drew the foot up, and finally turned a quarter over, in perfect position for Defever's purpose. Chris straightened and moved toward him. As he did so, Louie, his impalatable double, erupted from the floor in a reckless charge, at the same time raising his voice in a shrill yelp.

"Thieves!" Louie cried. And he struck at Chris. The weapon had weight and, but for the fact that the blow was glancing, almost felled Chris. Chris recognized the weapon as one of his own precious Allen and Thurber derringers, which he had often put to similar use himself, and which he had left reposing in the upper drawer of his bureau when he left for his fishing trip. This Louie was identifying altogether too far with Christian Defever. And this bleat he had let out made time an element upon which to reckon—to say nothing of Lefty Breen, now piling desperately off the bed.

Chris was driven to swift action. And he relished it. Louie had a stagnant breath and was in need of bathing. A revolting creature to pose for a minute as the Senator from Grass City. Before Louie could make a second swing with the derringer or bring it to cock, Chris seized his wrist and hauled powerfully, dragging the man toward him.

As Louie crashed into him, Chris shifted his grip, hooked the man's head in the crook of his arm, and bent, swinging Louie's heels into the air like the snapped end of a whip. With the fellow in this horizontal position, Chris pivoted toward Lefty Breen as Lefty bent beside the bed, leveling his own large pistol. Under the impetus of Defever's pivot, Louie's feet described an arc and crashed against the side of Breen's head just as Lefty fired his weapon. Chris felt the brush of the bullet.

Breen spilled across the bed. Chris, driven by the need for haste, took no chances. Jerking sharply up on Louie's head and then as sharply down, he slammed Louie's heels again into Breen's face. Releasing Louie, he rammed a hand into Breen's pocket and extracted the wallet. To Chris's surprise, Louie collapsed beside the bed. Chris bent momentarily above him. The man's neck had an unhealthy appearing kink in it, and it seemed doubtful that the man was breathing. Chris swore.

"When can a reed support a tempest as does a mighty pine?" he

murmured, finding the scorn of Shakespeare had a pleasant taste upon his tongue and full bearing upon this case. Flipping open Breen's wallet, Chris extracted McDowell's donation to him. The derringer Louie had swung at his head was on the floor. Chris retrieved it and found the other still in the bureau drawer. Since the Allen and Thurbers were uncommonly awkward belt weapons and required holstering of their own for proper handling, he paused long enough to rummage one of his vests with their especially made gun pockets.

Then, when feet were pounding down the hall outside the door, he slid himself out the window, lowered it again, and climbed swiftly on up the ladder toward the roof of the Palace, knowing that pursuit and search was like gravity—operating virtually always in a downward direction.

Presently, from behind the firewall on the roof of the building, he heard Breen, again conscious, luridly directing his own men in the investigation already commenced by hotel authorities and men from the office of the city marshal. Apparently an officer asked Breen a question.

Breen raged: "I know McDowell told you Defever was in that room with me! But McDowell's a fool and so are you. I use my head. I knew something like this would happen. Do you think I'd have brought the Senator back to the hotel until I knew it was safe for him? That dead man's a bum I hired to impersonate Defever in a try to trap those who are after him. Now, you boys find the killer. That's your job. When it's safe, I'll bring Senator Defever back to town," Breen assured him.

Chris chuckled and checked the loads in his derringers. He really felt sorry for Breen. The man had stretched himself to cook up this deal—and now Senator Defever was dead again. To keep digging up suitable doubles was apt to give Lefty Breen a lot of trouble.

Just short of dawn, when the searchers who had ransacked the Palace Hotel had withdrawn, Chris nimbly descended the fire-escape. His face begrimed carefully beyond recognition, Chris startled a sleepy clerk in an obscure apothecary shop by purchasing a small vial of spirit gum and a ragged toupee fashioned of coarse black hair which was on special sale as second-rate merchandise.

Retiring to the shelter of a bridge across Mud Creek, in the lower part of the city, Chris stripped the toupee and fastened it to his lank jowls with theatrical skill by means of the spirit gum. When he was finished, he had endowed himself with a magnificent black beard. Satisfied with this, he tried it upon a fat waitress in a teamsters' lunch-room above the freight corrals. The waitress seemed undisturbed by the contrast between the black beard and the silvering wealth of Defever's shoulder-length mane. What did disturb her was the prodigious breakfast he ordered.

"How many more in your party?" she inquired.

"Levity," Chris said severely, "is ill-advised before breakfast. Especially one as long-delayed as this. Bring on the snack instanter, Wench. I starve!"

The waitress eyed him with equal severity. "We don't feed bums," she said flatly. "That order'll cost you a dollar. I got to see the dollar first. Shell out or I'll call the cook."

Chris produced his roll beneath the counter and peeled a small bill from it with a reluctance indicating he might be excavating it from his shoe. The waitress took the bill, eyed it carefully, and reluctantly returned to the kitchen. Presently she brought the meal. Chris ate hugely and with enjoyment. He then returned to the streets.

East of Mud Creek in the draw of that unpredictable and soursmelling stream were a row of structures which had a bleak appearance by day, but which in lamp-light passed as varied palaces of pleasure. Here were the headquarters of the illegal and the unprincipled. Chris selected the sun-baked sidewall of a building he knew to be a low gambling den and settled himself against it.

Stretching his long legs out before him, clad in the dirt-encrusted pants he had inherited from the box-car bum who had stripped him, he composed himself in an attempt to create the illusion of a human derelict, sleeping untidily in the sun. The illusion was easy to create. He was sleepy and under the caress of the sun; he slid comfortably off into oblivion, well satisfied that he could set a trap and refresh himself at the same time.

CHAPTER THREE
Death's Double-Cross

Chris awoke to the prodding of a sharp toe. He opened his eyes. Lefty Breen and Doctor Phil were on the walk in front of him.

Breen's eyes were bright. It had been Doctor Phil's toe which had nudged Chris.

"Perfect," Breen said. "Anybody watching us?"

Phil shook his head. "All clear."

"This one's a natural. Better than that knot-head who got his neck broken last night."

"Somebody's onto us," Phil said uncertainly. "They'll be back. We're playing with something we don't know about, Lefty."

"Like hell!" Breen snapped. "Knowing McDowell, he cried all over town about that money he dug up before he brought it up to us. Some thief heard him and figured it was easy pickings. That's the story—and don't forget it."

Phil was eyeing Chris. "You ought to get this one cheap," he said dourly.

Breen said brusquely to Chris: "Want to earn yourself a week's good feed and a good bed and maybe a ten-spot on the side?"

Chris thought this a niggardly offer. He was about to raise his voice in protest against it, but remembered in time that while hair might disguise the Honorable Christian Defever's handsome features, nothing could disguise the flourishing oratory of his voice. Instead of speaking, he gave Breen a stupid look, then pointed to one large ear and then to his hirsute mouth.

Breen scowled. "A dummie!" he said disgustedly. "Can't hear and can't talk—" He broke off. "Phil! Do you get that? 'Can't hear and can't talk—' The devil, this is perfect! Here's one double that can't open his mouth and sink the whole deal. Here, give me a sheet out of that fake prescription book of yours."

Bending the tablet across his knee, Breen wrote hurriedly and handed the sheet to Chris.

How about a job—ten bucks, feed and a bed for a week? No work. Just loafing.

Chris read this, then rose to his feet with a distasteful show of eagerness.

Breen grinned widely and beckoned him to follow Phil and himself. Twice, when there was other traffic on the walks, Breen surreptitiously signalled Chris to fall back, so that idlers would not make a connection between them. In this way they circled back to the banks of Mud Creek and entered the creaky door of a villainous-appearing tavern.

Chris folded the message Breen had written and tucked it into a vest pocket, under one of the derringers. Buttoning his ragged coat, he followed Breen and the bogus Doctor Phil into one of the saloon's back rooms.

Finding a large sheet of paper, Breen went to work with his pencil.

Heard of Christian Defever? He's dead and you're him. Been in an accident. Face is all cut up and has to be bandaged. That's so nobody'll catch onto the fake. You're going to be a senator. Going to vote—the way I write it out for you. You got to be dignified. Do a good job and I'll make it ten bucks a day. Muff it and I'll see you really got to wear bandages.

Chris read this intelligence, nodded, and drew himself up in what appeared to be a passable, amateur rendition of personal dignity.

Breen seemed satisfied. He said to Doctor Phil, "Haul out another one of Defever's suits. And get another roll of bandages to cover that beard of his. Then find Angus McDowell. Tell him I've brought Defever into town and that he's in good enough shape to appear in the Assembly. It's supposed to convene tomorrow, and there's no use delaying."

One of Breen's men led Chris to a small, curtained alcove and tossed one of his own suits in to him. Chris changed, his spirits rising as he felt the familiar quality of a gentleman's tailoring again clothing his lank body. Issuing from the alcove, he found a basin and water and washed his face clean. Doc Phil did a passable, half-stifling job of swathing his face in bandage.

Then Chris and Doc Phil sat across the table from Lefty Breen. Chris thought of the two notes of instruction in the man's handwriting, already reposing snugly in his own pockets. Chris smiled beneath his bandages.

"It's got to go like this, Phil," Breen said thoughtfully. "First, we get Grass City changed from a town of its own to a state thing—like Washington, D.C. It's federal, and don't belong to any state. That kills the local marshal's job, see? Turns it over to the state. There ain't any state police, and we'll see that none are set up this session of the Assembly. So Grass City won't have any officers.

"Next, we get this business license thing repealed, so the public has got no squawk from a law standpoint at anything we set up.

Before the Assembly gets back in session, we'll have turned this town on its ear and emptied it of everything.''

Doc Phil shook his head lugubriously. ''Defever made a lot of noise in the Assembly,'' he agreed. ''But he wasn't quite the whole show. There's McDowell and Sam Thurston and a couple of others that counted, too. They voted with Defever before, but they think a sight of Grass City, and they've been clamping down for a couple of years on just the sort of thing you're figuring to operate. They won't vote with this Defever—even thinking he's real—against their own conscience.''

Breen nodded. ''Sure,'' he said. ''I figured McDowell and Thurston in. Our old boy is going to charge McDowell and Thurston with taking bribes—with planning to set up their own chain of gambling halls and saloons—with plotting to run the town themselves. Formal charges, Phil, right from the floor. It's going to raise a riot. It's going to make Thurston and McDowell look bad. Political careers blowing right up in their faces, exposed by the biggest man in the Assembly. When the public finds out the next morning that the two of them have *blown their brains out*—it's going to seem reasonable. Suicide instead of disgrace. Very simple.''

Phil said, ''I should have stuck to driving teams.''

''Stick to me and you'll be boss of every teamster in Grass City,'' Breen said. ''There's a cot in the storeroom across the hall. Lock the—er—Senator in that for tonight. See you later.''

By the time Chris had been loaded into a carriage the next day near noon, he had added quite a number of Lefty Breen's little slips of written instructions to those already reposing in his pocket.

He had taken considerable care with his toilet, so that in grooming, at least, he represented to the fullest degree the elegance Grass City had come to expect of Senator Defever. This extra attention had endeared him to Lefty Breen, who had dolled himself up considerably and could not refrain from delightedly chafing his hands together in satisfaction at frequent intervals.

Chris, behind his bandages, delighted with a satisfaction of his own—toyed with certain personal planning as they rode up the main street of Grass City to the accompaniment of cheers from the walks. Lefty Breen figured largely in Defever's planning. So, also, did a sizeable sum in green cash money which Breen carried in his pocket. Money which would sometime tonight—if Breen's plans were successful—be found as bribe money on the persons of Sam Thurston and Angus McDowell when their lifeless bodies were searched. An expensive but necessary piece of evidence to make the "suicides" appear justified. The money intrigued Chris.

As they drove up before the Capitol building, Chris noticed a structure of some sort apparently in the progress of construction in front of the main entrance. A spire-like affair draped in workmen's tarpaulins. He touched Breen's arm, beside him, and glanced curiously at the structure. Breen grinned widely. Reaching in his pocket for a pad and pencil, he wrote swiftly:

A monument to Defever. Today they'll want to tear it down. Tomorrow they'll want to blast it to dust—after we're through with them. Watch your step.

Chris nodded his bandaged head, carefully folded the note, and added it to the others in his pocket. The carriage halted. Assembly attendants forced the crowd back. Chris stepped from the carriage. A shout greeted him—the adulation of the multitude. He savored it. Solicitously, Breen took his arm and steered him up the steps. Quite close at hand, Chris heard one man in the crowd speak softly to another:

"The Senator's in bad company—"

The man's companion answered: "It's a good thing for us all that old Defever come out of that wreck all right. Breen could grab the whole works. But with Defever still on deck, Breen ain't got a chance. Old Chris could bait the devil right out of hell without him knowing it. This is going to be worth watching!"

The day was hot. Heat was amply present within the Capitol building. And the delay in the final recessing of the Assembly caused by the reported death and subsequent resurrection of Senator Defever had chafed his colleagues, most of whom were anxious to be gone from Grass City to the cooler slopes of the highlands. However, this special convention was well attended. Every seat in the assembly hall was filled. Chris proceeded to his own desk with dignity, followed by Lefty Breen and Doc Phil— both of them grinning widely at the fine and satisfactory figure their bogus senator was cutting.

Angus McDowell brought the session to order with a brief welcome to Chris, voicing sympathy for the injuries he had sustained and a hope that full recovery would soon follow. He then called for business. Prodded by Breen, Chris rose, taking a sheet from the brief-case with which he had been provided. A uniformed messenger boy took it forward to McDowell, who began to read.

The sheet stated that Christian Defever, on examination of facts and his conscience, was obligated to reverse his earlier stand concerning a certain sporting citizen of Grass City and the licensing regulations which had been enacted against him. In short, Chris Defever felt injustice had been done Mr. Lefty Breen and he demanded the Assembly consider steps to ease the discrimination against Breen.

Chris sat down. Talk rumbled up in the room. Some of it shocked, some of it angry. But all of it careful and considering. Breen sat hunched forward, watching the reaction. Chris chuckled at Breen's shrewdness. He had measured the Assembly well. Instead of landing with both feet and all of his demands in the middle of the lawmakers, Breen intended to let them adjust themselves slowly. Presently McDowell calmed enough to ask Senator Defever if he had concrete suggestions as to how any injustice to Breen he had mentioned could be rectified—the Assembly willing.

Breen handed Chris the second sheet from the brief-case, and Chris rose again. This was also carried forward. It was a terse request for the remission of the licensing regulations and the creation of the Longbow State Capital District to replace the present inefficient municipal government of Grass City.

McDowell launched an impassioned plea to his fellow senator to consider the inevitable result of such a motion.

Chris sat down in the midst of McDowell's speech, silencing him. McDowell was not an orator, and Chris did not want this to string out too long.

Discussion was heated. Chris bitterly regretted the bandaging across his lips. These fools were trying to voice protest, but little that they said made sense. All of it lacked conviction. If he could only send his voice out among them—but he dared not. He was dead. It was intention that he remain so—as far as Grass City was concerned. From the uproar which came from beyond the closed doors of the Assembly hall, it was apparent that the discussion had been taken up by the crowd outside, in addition.

Doc Phil looked worried. He leaned close to Breen. "Think we'll make it?" he asked nervously.

Breen grinned. "We can't miss. Watch—" Leaning forward, Breen prodded Chris and handed him another note. Chris read it.

Don't talk. Just stand up. Demand attention. Shut these fools up. You can do it. Defever bullied them all of the time.

Chris rose, sucking in a breath which made him seem to swell inches in height, and he lifted a hand high in the air. McDowell saw him and began to pound for order. As the din quieted, McDowell leaned across the rostrum with a truculent jut to his chin, carefully and grimly saying:

"Before I yield the floor to the Senator, I demand to know what proofs he has in his possession that his motion should even be considered. We have long voted together, but I can't vote for such a measure as this except in the face of iron-clad proof, and even then against my judgment and my conscience!"

Chris moved around his desk, slightly, so that he could not only see his fellow legislators, but also Breen and Doc Phil. In addition, from his new angle he could see the half-dozen well-instructed onlookers whom Breen had placed in the gallery. Breen, scowling a little, thrust the brief-case across the desk with a gesture that the further statements McDowell demanded were in it. Chris understood. He was to now send up to old Angus an indictment charging the speaker of the Assembly and Sam Thurston with a varied amount of deviltry on their own hook—accepting bribes, buying votes, selling the public short. The prelude to the later suicide of the two.

Chris also understood that this was his cue for what could well be his finest performance, and his skin roughened up in a thrill of anticipation. With one hand he parted the buttons of his coat, so that he could have free access to his vest. With his other hand, he swiftly loosened the fastenings of his head bandage. Pulling the sheaf of notes from Breen—his written instructions, damning and conclusive—from his vest pocket, he handed them to the messenger boy. And with a tug, he tore the loosened bandage from his black-whiskered face.

CHAPTER FOUR
Derringer Law

It was a tribute to Defever's skill at elocution that although he pitched his voice far above its usual basso to defeat identification, it lost nothing in window-rattling volume.

"Proof?" he roared. "There's your proof, Gentlemen! I, a hapless wanderer, have been victimized—hired like a mere chattel to impersonate your dead great, and upon pain of death. You, also, have been victimized. Read!"

A gasp went up from the crowd within the Assembly hall and ran swiftly through outer corridors to the street and the city beyond. Lefty Breen, who had a moment before been leaning back with smug satisfaction, now sat mouth agape. And Doc Phil, never too certain of the outcome of Breen's plan, had turned a wan green which Chris delightedly thought went admirably well with the shabby brown of his suit.

Breen's astonishment lasted only an instant. Then he piled up from his chair, an oath on his lips, and lunged out into the aisle toward the messenger boy bearing his notes of instructions up to Angus McDowell. Chris twisted around his desk and stepped into the aisle to confront the man. Breen, evidently hoping to salvage something from this debacle, did not reach for the heavy gun in his belt. Chris, for his own reasons, did not expose the two derringers waiting in the pockets of his vest.

Breen crashed into Chris, his fists clenched and cocked low. One of them lashed out. Chris pivoted a little, took the blow on the bone of his hip, rather than in his belly, as was intended, and wrapped long arms about Breen. A desk-leg fouled Breen's feet, and he went down on the floor of the aisle, Chris on top of him.

"You knot-headed old fool!" Breen gasped. "You stumble-witted idiot!" And he tried to drive one thumb into Defever's eye.

Chris banged the heel of one bony hand upward under Breen's chin and spoke chidingly, softly, into an ear before biting it.

"Peace, sirrah! Enough of your calumny. Where is the money?"

Breen writhed, attempting to use knees and elbows. Chris leaned forward, bearing down with all his weight on the forearm across Breen's gullet. With his free hand he reached within Breen's coat, and his fingers touched the wallet containing the tainted bribe money to have been planted on McDowell's and Thurston's lifeless bodies. Breen twisted frantically.

"You can't do it!" he choked hoarsely.

"I can try," Chris said, easing back as the wallet came free. With a swift sleight-of-hand, he dropped the wallet into his own pocket and rose to his feet. Breen scrambled to his knees and came up in a crouch. At the same time, somewhere back of them, Doc Phil sang out wildly:

"I've got him—"

A gun banged. Chris felt the wind of a passing bullet. He glanced at Doc Phil and the impact of his eyes had a strange effect. The man wheeled blindly and started running up the aisle. Somebody thrust out a foot, and Doc Phil went down onto the worn carpeting on his face. Cries rose from the gallery as four men piled over the railing, heading through startled Senators for Defever's desk. And in his crouch, Lefty Breen jerked his belt-gun free.

There was a certain reluctance in Chris—a feeling that this had been a fine, bloodless coup—that it was a great pity to break so fine a record. But the odds were piling up a little too fast. His shoulders squared, and the movement flicked the two heavy derringers from his pockets. Lefty fired once, scoring the desk beside him. The derringers thundered. Breen was batted half around by the impact and spilled across a neighboring desk. With the gunfire, the four men who had piled over the gallery railing, realizing they were far into hostile territory now, paused—loosening iron.

Chris sighted through them, shoulder high, so that the slugs would do a minimum of damage to his targets and, in case of a miss, would clear the heads of the Senators, now crouching defensively low.

A drum-roll of thunder echoed against the beamed ceiling of the hall, and as Chris fired, he started moving toward a wide side-window upon which he had already fastened his eye. As he passed the desk where Breen had fallen, the man rolled limply and glared up at him out of dulling eyes.

"You old goat—" Breen said with almost voiceless laborious-ness—"you—you ain't Defever—really—"

Chris bent close to him in passing. "No?" he said in the man's ear. "You'll never see a better imitation!"

Breen's eyes widened. He tried to force himself upright, to cry something out, but he failed in an effort and fell limply from the desk to the floor. Chris brandished the guns in his hands.

"Bury your dead; mourn your heroes. But I'm warning you all—let me get out of your town!"

Taking three long, running strides, Chris leaped upward and struck the window he had chosen with doubled-up knees. The glass shattered before him. He sailed from the hall and downward to the cobbled paving of an alley. Picking up his beaver hat, dislodged in the leap, he scuttled down this alley and emerged on a lower street. Several cabs were waiting on this, out of the press before the Capitol, around the next turn. Piling into one of these and permitting the driver a glimpse of one of the Allen and Thurbers, he barked an order:

"To the river, as fast as these wheels can roll. And keep your eyes ahead!"

Half a mile from the Capitol, as the driver of the cab rounded a corner at a reckless speed and with his full attention on his team, Chris left the carriage in an agile running-dismount. The back rooms of Breen's headquarters saloon were deserted. Chris ran a wash-basin of whiskey from a barrel in the storeroom, drank a considerable portion of it, and used the rest to cleanse the spirit-gum and unwelcome beard from his face. As an afterthought and further diversion, he started a bung in another barrel, tossed a match into the pool which formed before it, and quit the place.

Keeping to back yards and alleys and traveling with care, he reached the freight yards of the Union Pacific. The crew of this amiable carrier of the un-monied was engrossed by the fire and excitement uptown. Chris found himself a reasonably clean poor-man's parlor-car and closed the sliding doors.

Let them speculate as to when and how Defever had actually died and which of his incarnations had been his actual one. Let them raise their monument at the foot of the Capitol steps. He had done his duty for his fellow man. No longer would he be required to fashion the law—only his own pleasure. He fingered the sizeable wad of bills in his pockets. With these and the proper cards and a little liaison with Lady Luck, he'd have something he had always wanted—a million dollars.

Christian Defever, Millionaire, had a far better sound in his ears than the stuffy senatorial title he had borne so long with honor. From here on, he was a free man—the game no-limit and strictly his own. *"There is a tide in the affairs of men which, taken at the flood, leads on to fortune—"* he murmured to himself. "Well said, for a playwright" —he fingered the bills in his pocket again—"and this is a veritable deluge!"

THE END